Han's Cottage.

(Watchers in the light.)

Robin John Morgan.

First published (Paperback) in the UK in 2022 by Violet Circle Publishing.

Manchester, England, UK.

Print ISBN: 978-1-910299-36-4
Digital ISBN: 978-1-910299-37-1

British Library Cataloguing in Publication Data.
A catalogue record for this book is available from the British Library.

All paper used in the production of this book are sourced only from wood grown in sustainable forests.

www.violetcirclepublishing.co.uk

Also by Robin John Morgan.

Heirs to the Kingdom.

Book One, The Bowman of Loxley.
Book Two, The Lost Sword of Carnac.
Book Three, The Darkness of Dunnottar.
Book Four, Queen of the Violet Isle.
Book Five, Crystals of the Mirrored Waters.
Book Six, Last Arrow of the Woodland Realm.
Book Seven, Bridge Of Sequana.
Book Eight, The Circle of Darkness.

The Curio Chronicles.

Part One, Abigail's Summer.
Part Two, Curio's Summer.

Other works.

Rise of the Raven.
Han's Cottage.

Maybe we all have to walk through darkness, before we find our light, and then, we must not forget the light, for that is the gift of our darkness.

Cherishing those we miss the most.

For Memories of Pat.

best wishes.

Chapter One

Han

The wind had fallen, and the water on the lake, beneath the dark cloudless sky, had fallen still, and reflected the stars above from its mirror like surface. In the woodlands the owls, who had hooted for most of the night fell silent, and the mice and rodents scurried beneath the ground, almost as if they could sense the changes in the air. All was silent in the thick darkness, where one small light source, wove through the curtains, from the room at the front of house of Han. Randolph knelt by the bed, and bowed.

"Goodbye my trusted companion, my life has been enhanced by your presence, and I cannot imagine this world without you, it will feel less colourful, and less warm."

He swallowed hard, as he held her old wrinkled hand, she smiled, as she lay on the pillow, her dark sparkling eyes as shiny as they were when she was young.

"Lift your heart Randolph, I have lived such a wonderful life. In all the years of my life, from the moment we met, you have guided me through such wonder. I have no regrets, watch over the children, and when she comes, guide her as you have me. She has so much to offer, but she cannot see it, guide her onto the path, and show her the light, help her protect the children."

He smiled, and the tears filled his eyes, as he saw the light within her dimmish, she gave a smile, and the light flowed out of her soul, and he bowed his head and wept. Outside the cottage a stray dog howled into the black sky, and all around the woodland and lake, there was a sense of loss, almost as if the world felt her passing. Sadness stalked the shore of the lake, and under the trees, Hannah was no more, and it was marked with the rolling in of clouds. The sky filled and the stars were hidden, and darkness broke with the bright flash that shot through the sky, and danced across the lake. The boom of the rumble was deafening, and as it faded into the night, the heavens opened, and the rain pounded down. Two small lights on the bank of the island faded, and under the rumble, there were faints sobs.

I have never forgotten the day my Grandma Han died, the call came at two in the morning, it was from her friend, I had never met him, but I had heard so much about him in my life. I sat holding the phone as the tears streamed down my cheeks, as I heard the pain in his voice. My heart broke, as I realised my trip to see her in two weeks was gone with her, and never again would I sit in her garden, and listen to her wonderful stories of the magical people of the secret land. The call ended, and I broke down.

It was ten o'clock the following morning, when I called Shelly.

"Oh god, I hope you have a good reason for calling this early, my head is killing me?"

"Shell, my grandma died." She sat up in bed and closed her eyes, as her head thumped.

"Oh god, Emmy, I am so sorry, are you alright?" I gave a sniffle.

"No.... Shell, I don't know what to do, I am going to miss her so much."

"Alright Hun, I am on my way."

My Grandma Hannah, lived in a small cottage one mile outside the village of Hempsley. It was an old four bedroomed cottage with low ceilings, small windows, and surrounded by a low plant festooned, stone wall. It had a trellis porch round the door, filled with vibrant white roses, and a garden of gravel paths, where the flowers exploded out in a riot of colours, in a raggerty pattern, as they sprawled across the front garden, leaving just small areas you could step in.

It was a rich tapestry of colours and shapes, and as a young girl, I thought it was the most beautiful place on earth, as I spent my spring and summer holidays living with her. Grandma Hannah, was the most important person in my life, especially so, after my mother was killed in a car crash, when I was aged four, and due to my father's business, I ended up enrolled in at the Elizabeth Warner Residential School for Young Ladies, which I hated.

I hardly saw my father after that, it felt like I reminded him too much of my mother, and so I got the occasional weekend, or weeks holiday, but for the rest of the time I went home to see Grandma Hannah, or Han, as most people called her. She was my world, and the only real family I had, she was my mum's mum, and she would sit at night before I went to bed, and show me pictures, and tell me about her life. I think the only reason I have any memories of my mum today, is because through Han, I kept them alive, and through her stories, I knew who my mum was.

My father, John Stewart Duncan, was an architect, and owned his own firm, which was spread worldwide, and he spent most of his life in foreign lands designing and building. He liked the jet set life, was not short of money, and enjoyed life in first class.

He was always impeccably turned out, factual and precise in everything he did, he was not a bad man, he was a master communicator. Sadly, when you are six and wanted a hug, because you felt insecure, he was not the kind of father who would let you curl up on his knee and hold you. No, he would sit you down, point out the obvious, and talk you through it, showing as little warmth or emotion as possible.

Did he love me? I really did not know, I wanted for nothing, had more than an ample allowance, and nothing was out of reach if I needed it. His assistant Kate, would always arrive, and deliver whatever I needed, and I always got a card and cheque for my birthday. He never forgot me, it just felt like he avoided me. Han told me the day mum died, so did his light inside him, and in a way, I always felt he blamed me for it.

Grandma Hannah, was my world, and when I was sixteen, I left the private school, with my best friend, who I had grown up with through school, as she had the bed at the side of me, in the large dorm, Pamela Drewitt. We both went on to college to get our HNC in Ecology, and then went on to Uni to do our degree, and we had a wild time living in a house with a house mum. It was in my final year there, where I met Shelly Parkinson, doing her history degree, and specialising in folklore, and the three of us were inseparable.

When I qualified, Pam flew off to Florida, studying the flora and fauna, sponsored through Savannah State University, and I headed to Scotland to work on a woodland restoration project, with Shelly in tow. She wanted to study Scottish folklore and write a book. We were coming to the end of the project, two weeks before my twenty first birthday, when I got the call that Grandma Hannah had left me, and so I left early and travelled back to Exeter, then on to Hempsley in time for her funeral.

Shelly went back to her mums, and I got a flat, and as arrangements were made, I knew I could not walk in a cottage, which would be cold and empty, and devoid of her love, and so I attended her funeral at the old cemetery, from a hotel room in the village.

Mum's sister, my Aunt Jessica, handled all the arrangements, with her husband Peter, a very wealthy property developer. Han despised him, as all he talked about was the logging rights, and the potential of the property to be developed, and she had banned him from the land, which caused a huge rift between her and Jessica. Han was adamant, she would never sell it.

It appeared to me, with Han gone, Peter would finally have what he wanted, and I found it heart breaking to know, that my grandma's cottage, would soon be swept from the land and gone forever. That was probably another reason I did not want to visit, even though I knew eventually it would be gone forever, I did not want my last memory to be of me alone, in the cottage without her.

Pam flew back from the states, Shelly joined, and came with me, and we met at the hotel, and all in black we attended the funeral. A lot of the village turned out for her, as I stood at the side of her grave and looked at the casket, which had the same symbol as the pendant of my mother's, which I wore, burned into the wood.

It was hard to say goodbye, even though Jessica was here, Han really was the only family I knew and cared about. I felt alone and abandoned, and felt such a pain in my heart, and the strongest sense of loss and loneliness, as people hugged me and told me how sorry they were. I could feel it, they were, but the unbelievable pain I felt, was gut wrenching. I loved Pam and Shelly, they were my best friends, but even as they stood at my side and linked my arms, I felt I had lost my connection to everything.

Han was the only connection to my mum, and she was gone, and I felt like part of my soul had been ripped out, and I was cast adrift as I returned to the hotel, and sat on my bed. Pam sat down at my side, and handed me a drink, I had no idea what it was, I just stared into the liquid, as my life flashed through my mind, and I remembered her, with her long beautiful grey hair, pinned up in a large bun. Her loving and sparkling dark eyes, and that beautiful smile in her tanned wrinkled face, and her soft voice.

"Emmy my darling, there will be a day, when you are alone, and at that time you must look within, for there is more to you than you realise, and it will be then, you shall awaken, as you will see the world as it should be for the first time."

I looked up at her, as she sat on the bench in the sun, next to the white circular archway.

"I do not understand Grandma Han, I see the world, I am here sat with you, and I see it." She gave me that wonderful smile.

"Oh, my dearest child, this is just a small part of the world, and one day you will feel with your heart, and the world will open, and everything will show itself." I frowned at her, and she just patted my face.

"Oh, the light within you shines so bright, mark my words, you will see."

"Emmy... Emmy?" I blinked and gave a startled jerk.

"What... Yes... What is it?" Pam smiled at me.

"Phone, some guy called Higginson." I shrugged, I had no idea who that was, she handed me the phone.

"Hello."

"Miss Duncan, Emily Duncan?"

"Yes."

"Hello, my name is Matthew Higginson, I am your late grandmothers' solicitor, I have found it hard to track you down, are you in the village for long?"

I really was not sure, I booked in for three days, I have no plans after that, I have not really had time to figure out what I was going to do once I returned to the flat.

"Mr Higginson, was it? I am here for two more days, and then I will be heading back to Exeter."

"Good... Look, Miss Duncan, I really need to see you and talk, there is the matter of your grandmother's estate and affairs to discuss. I realise it is late, but could you visit my office in the village as soon as possible?" I was so confused, and finding it hard to think.

"I think my Aunt Jess is handling all her affairs, is it important?"

"Yes, I am aware, but I really need to see you as soon as possible, if you would like, I could come and see you today, it really is of the upmost importance?" I gave a long sigh.

"To be honest, I just left her funeral, and I am not sure I want to go out again into the village. If it would not be a bother, I am in room four, at the Milking Gate."

"Wonderful, give me an hour."

"Yeah, okay."

"Thank you, Miss Duncan, I will see you soon, goodbye." Pam was watching me as I put the hotel phone down.

"Is everything alright?" I drained my glass.

"Some solicitor, about my grandma's affairs, he is coming here, I really don't want to go out again today." She gave a smile and nodded at me.

"It has been a tough day, relax for a bit." I lay back on the bed and closed my eyes.

"I am so tired Pam, where is Shelly?" She gave a chuckle.

"Emmy, it's Shelly, she will be in the bar, questioning locals for stories of ghouls, ghosts, pixies and elves, you know what she is like?" I smiled.

"Yeah, her and her book research, poor sods will all have nightmares after talking to her." Pam gave a giggle.

"Relax, have a nap, I will wake you when this Higginson guy arrives."

I smiled, she was a good friend, she was everything young women espoused to be, young, pretty, slender, and had long blonde hair, and a kind happy face. She was a rock at Uni, so organised and efficient, and here she was taking care of me again.

I lay back and let my mind drift, as the day's events slipped through my thoughts, and pictures of her casket flowed through my mind. It was so hard to know she was gone, so painful, I could not imagine not heading back on a regular basis to be greeted at the door with her loving smile and soft embrace.

I drifted around in my thoughts, Aunt Jess and Uncle Pete, had hardly said a word to me, it was almost as if I was not really welcome. It is hard to think that she is my mum's sister, Han told me often they were like chalk and cheese, and my mum was the loving one. I cannot deny, watching today, she did not appear too emotional, some of the villagers looked more upset.

I could see their faces, filled with sadness in my thoughts, as the pictures again slid through my mind, all dressed in black, pale and in tears, stood on the opposite side of her grave, all watching draped in an air of sadness. Stood high on the hill in a bleak tree lined cemetery, next to the old church, surrounded by black railings, a place where one goes to add to the sadness of life.

It was a place to be alone, all of them gathered showing more love and more care than my aunt and uncle, and there in the trees, set back in the older graves, a lone man stood in a long brown cloak, a hood up over his head.

Who was that, my mind pondered, as the picture froze in my thoughts, why was he there, and so far away, who was that? He looked up.

I jerked and sat up with a gasp of air, and felt a mild shock to my heart, I looked round the room, not quite in the moment, and confused. I was in the hotel room sat on my bed, Pam was lay back on her bed, she looked at me.

"Are you alright?" I nodded trying to clear my thoughts.

"What... Yeah... Sorry, I must have been dreaming." I took a deep breath, and tried to compose myself, as I rubbed my face.

"It has been a shit day that's all, was I asleep long?"

"About an hour."

It had not felt that way, I had thought I had only been drifting in my thoughts for a few minutes. I turned and slid my feet off the bed, Pam sat up.

"Emmy, I have been thinking, what are you going to do, you

know, she was the only real family you have?"

I gave a long sigh, it was a good question, one I had yet to answer. I looked at her, she had always been so together, so organised, in a way I envied her, I was never that together, hell my whole life had felt like a shambles. She sat there with her bright blue eyes and sleek blonde hair completely organised, and efficient as always.

"Pam, I have not really thought about it, what can I do? I mean be honest, I have lost the only place I know as a home, and the only person who I ever really cared about in this family. Jess and Pete hardly spoke to me, I guess I will see this guy, and then head back to Exeter, and carry on consulting for Harry, until something better comes up." She gave a nod and leaned forward.

"Emmy, why not just leave everything behind, come join me in the states, you know you have all the qualifications, and let's be honest, me and you pissing about in the Savanna, it will be a lark?" The truth was I did not know, and at the moment I was too mixed up inside.

"Pam, you are my best friend and I love you; I just need some time, I need to get used to this, and just figure things out, hell I need to figure me out." She leaned forward and took my hands in hers.

"You know, I worry about you, have you heard from your dad, honestly, I would have thought he would be here?" I smiled.

"This place was never glamourous enough for dad, not enough glass and steel. To be honest, I did not expect him, I am beyond disappointment with him. He has never really shown much interest in this side of the family, hell, he hardly shows much in me." She patted my hand.

"Look the offer is there, no time limit, but I am serious, I have the house, and the grant money is good, and it is a good life. Sort yourself out and think about it. If things do not work out here, well you have a good back up." I gave a nod and smiled.

"Thanks Pam, I appreciate it."

There was a tap at the door, she got up and walked over towards it, and opened the door, I looked up to see a tall very well tailored older gent, he looked very official.

"Miss Duncan?" Pam stepped aside, and he could see me, he smiled. "Yes, I see it now, very like her."

He stepped into the room as I stood, and came over and offered his hand. He looked about late sixties, grey short very neatly combed hair, somewhat swept back behind his ears, and he had bright blue, kind eyes.

"I am so sorry for your loss; she was a most remarkable and kind woman." It hurt to hear it and I swallowed the wave of emotion.

"Thank you, won't you sit down, how can I help you Mr Higginson?" He sat in the one small chair available, Pam looked at me.

"I will go track down Shelly, and leave you two alone, okay?"

I nodded as I sat on the bed, and she slipped out through the door and closed it quietly. He lifted his brown leather case, placed it on his knees, and opened it, and slipped out some papers.

"Miss Duncan, I am here as I am charged with the affairs of your grandmother's estate, and I require of you, some signatures."

I gave a nod, I had not really thought about it, but I am sure she must have made some provision for me, after all, I almost lived with her for most of my youth. He looked at the papers.

"Let me see, oh yes, here we are. Right as sole heir to her full estate, I will need you to sign the transfer of everything into your name." I blinked.

"Excuse me?" He looked up at me.

"Is there a problem Miss Duncan?" I took a breath.

"Did you say sole heir, she has a daughter, Jessica. I just assumed she was the beneficiary of my grandmother's estate?" He shook his head.

"No, your grandmother was quite clear and precise, it is all yours, the cottage, the land, everything, even her mini bus, which by the way is currently in the garage, she had some concerns over it." He smiled. "You appear somewhat surprised?" I nodded.

"Yeah, I am, I just thought Jessica would get everything, I hoped for her picture albums, but nothing more." He smiled a kindly smile.

"Miss Duncan, she loved you deeply, you were her whole world, I know, I spoke to her often." I could not help the tears that filled my eyes, and gave a squeaky.

"She was mine too, I loved her so much."

He pulled his handkerchief out of his top pocket and handed it to me, I gratefully took it, his voice was so warm and kind.

"I am sorry to distress you, but she put a very precise time limit on my proceedings, and I must execute it to her wishes, otherwise I would have given you more time. I am so sorry Miss Duncan." I wiped my eyes and shook my head.

"It is fine Mr Higginson, really, it is fine." He smiled.

"There are just four documents, I have placed crosses on where you sign, all I need is your signatures and your current address, and I will take care of everything, and send all the paperwork on for you."

He slid his case forward and held out his pen, I took a deep breath feeling a little shell shocked, I was not expecting any of this. I looked at the paperwork, took the pen and signed where each cross was clearly marked, he gave an agreeable nod. He slipped a piece of blank paper onto the pile, and I wrote my full address in Exeter down for him. He smiled, took the papers and slipped them back into his case, and then lifted out a large padded brown envelope with my name on it.

"This contains everything you will need, the house keys, car keys, the boat and boat house keys, and a few assorted items she wanted me to personally deliver." He closed his case and stood up.

"I will leave you now and take care of everything for you." I stood up still wiping my eyes.

"Thank you, I appreciate it, I am feeling so lost at the moment, but really, I am very grateful to you." He lifted his arm and touched my shoulder.

"Take your time, but do not fear being lost, things have a funny way of turning around, life always reveals its purpose." I gave him a smile.

"She often told me the same." He gave a nod and walked towards the door, as I slowly followed him.

"She was right Miss Duncan; she was a very wise woman. I shall leave you to your grief, and hope next time we meet it will be under better circumstances." He pulled open the door, and looked back with a smile.

"I took the liberty of paying Tom at the garage, and transferring the insurance over to you. You will find all the bank details of the account she set up for you in the envelope along with the cards, as I said, she was very precise. Good day to you Miss Duncan, and take care." I gave a nod.

"Thank you again Mr Higginson, I appreciate everything you have done for me, and also for my grandmother." He smiled.

"It was entirely my pleasure Miss Duncan." I closed the door and wiped my eyes, oh bugger, I still had his hankie.

I walked back into the room and sat on the bed, and stared at the envelope. I lifted it and felt the keys inside, I tipped it up, and the contents fell onto the bed. There were keys, the bank cards, a piece of folded paper which had all the banking details on it and pass codes for internet banking.

The insurance certificates, the new vehicle registration, and a small pastel coloured envelope with her writing on it. I felt a surge run through me as I saw her neat careful writing, and read the word 'Emmy.' Oh god, I am so not ready for this, I opened it and slid out the neatly folded paper with the borders of printed wild flowers.

Dear Precious Emmy.

I did not want to leave so soon, but I am afraid the light has dimmed, and I feel I am to shortly return to the forest, to care for other children into eternity. I have not left you, I am still there, but now I will walk in the light at your side, whenever you go there.

You are not alone, you never were, the light within you always connected all three of us. I know you will not understand yet, but we were all born in the light, You, Your Mother, and I. There are many who will live in this world with closed eyes, and shut hearts, for they will never understand the wonders that lie beyond belief.

You are now the guardian and the watcher, one still walks in your shadow and he will come to you when you are ready to fully join with the light, I will stand in the light until your beautiful heart returns home to me, and my love will be with you, as is your mothers. Come to us Emmy and protect what we have guarded, and the light will show you the true wonder of this world.

I love you so deeply my sweet precious child, and I will be there when you need me.

My heart, love, and soul, is with you.

Han xx

I burst into tears, and shook, turned, and fell onto my pillow, and pushed my face deeply into it, and sobbed.
"I don't want you to leave me Han, I still need you."

Randolph stood before the mound of fresh earth covered in flowers, and gave a sigh.
"This will not be easy Han, she has had her heart closed for so long, I wish I shared your faith. I trust you, although I fear for the children, there is too much pain and darkness surrounding her heart, I fear the light will not get through."
He bowed, lifted his hood, turned, and walked into the darkness.

Chapter Two

The Decision

It had been almost a year since my grandma died, and I had not returned to the cottage. Mr Higginson as promised handled everything, and after several correspondence, because he does not use email, I had a courier deliver all the paperwork in a neatly bound red leather file.

I collected the car from the garage when we left the hotel and drove home, it was so much better than trains and buses. I had such fond memories of the mini bus, with all the back seats removed. I learned to drive in it, Han had me drive round all over the side roads, until she felt I was ready for lessons, so it did feel very familiar. It needed a bit of work, and I had a few things improved, such as a new radio CD player added, Han's radio, had never really worked well.

I left everything as it was, with its small hanging pendants of protection hanging from the mirror, and glass beads that sparkled in the sunlight. I returned to Exeter and worked for Harry Scott, a conservational small developer and landscaper, he was a hard man and I worked harder, but honestly, he drove me up the wall, with his nit picking, and endless complaints about the quality of the staff.

Pam flew back to the States, and Shelly came home with me, and eventually moved into the flat once her first book of Scottish Folklore was published. It did better than I thought, I cannot deny, she takes this stuff a little too literal for me, the idea of fairies, gnomes, and pixies is just a little too fanciful, but her illustrations were very beautiful. She was an amazing water colour artist, and even though I told her to focus on her art, she proved me wrong by publishing a book that had mass appeal. I mean, seriously, are there really that many people who believe this stuff? I slowly got back to normal and into the routine of life, and yet, there inside me just out of view, lay the pain and the bad dreams that came with it.

It had been another long hard day, and I staggered in through the door, dropped my bag, and walked through to the kitchen. Shelly was in the bathroom, I reached for the wine and unscrewed the cap, she poked her head out of the bathroom door, I poured the wine out.

"Bad day?" I looked up as I lifted the glass.

"Yep!" She walked out brushing her teeth, I took a large gulp.

"Oh god, you are cleaning your teeth, what is he called?"

She walked over in her knickers and t shirt, and sat down, the tooth brush still stuck in her mouth, she grabbed the bottle and poured another glass for herself. I shuddered.

"Please don't drink wine with a mouth full of tooth paste, it's gross." She gave a giggle, and sprayed white froth on the kitchen top.

"I promise, I will rinse first, although wine with a hint of mint is not that bad. He is called Craig; he is a poet."

"God you can be gross." I walked over to the sofa, and kicked my shoes off, and flopped back with my wine.

"Jesus a poet, called Craig, hell Shell, you know how to pick them." She headed for the bathroom.

"You know Emmy, it would not hurt you to actually slip under the sheets once in a while, how long has it been since Ken?" I lay back on the soft cushions, and closed my eyes.

"Please not again... It is two years and you know it, and I am perfectly fine as I am. I have no idea how you cope with all the bullshit, lies and games, I think you are secretly a masochist."

She came out of the bathroom wiping her mouth, grabbed her glass, and walked over to me, and slid on the sofa at my side.

"Come on Emmy, life is about living, there is someone for everyone, all you have to do is look." I gave a frustrated sigh, as I looked at her smiling with her short black sticky out hair, and her brown eyes, I shook my head.

"No thanks, watching you tick blokes off the list, is proof alone love sucks. You should write about that myth, love is bollocks, no one feels love any more, and if they do, well, it gets ripped out of them. No thanks Shell, I am done with it all." Shelly patted my leg.

"Emmy, you have to move on, how long are you going to mourn for her, it's been almost a year?" I gave a sigh.

"Please Shell, not tonight, I have had a day full of Harry and his shit, I cannot take much more, I need sleep." She lifted her glass.

"I take it the dreams are still as bad?" I pulled up my knees, and held my glass out in front of me.

"I have tried everything, nothing stops them. God, I would give anything for just one night of uninterrupted sleep."

"I take it, it is still the same, Han, the cloaked man and the bright light?" I rested my chin on my knees.

"Yeah... I don't get it, honestly, I have no idea why, but every time I close my eyes, he is there watching me, it freaks me the hell out." Shelly reached out, and rested her hand on my arm.

"Look Emmy, I know you think it is all bollocks, but trust me, you know where the answers are, you are just so stubbornly refusing to admit it. Emmy, you have over two thousand acres with a cottage, I have told you, it is time." I gave a frustrated sigh and drained my glass. I slid down my legs and stood up. Shelly watched as I headed back to the bottle, and refilled my glass.

"You will have to go back one day; she wanted you to have it. Emmy, it is the only home you know. It is almost a year."

My hand stopped as I reached the bottle, and felt the frustration and inner pain bubble over inside me, I didn't want this, but I could not help myself.

"CHRIST SHELL, DO YOU NOT THINK I DON'T KNOW THAT!?" She stood up, and I stared at her, and felt the tears rise into my eyes, she just stood looking at me.

"Shelly, I fucking miss her, okay, are you happy now? I know Shell, there has not been one second in the last year I have not thought of her. God Shell, I know, I know it's my home, and I want to, I really want to be there, but how can I without her?"

My tears dripped into my glass, and I looked down and bit my lip, I didn't want this, she came over and pulled me into a hug. I turned into her and tried so hard not to cry, she was as always, the beautiful human being who had been there for me, and I loved her for it.

"I am sorry Emmy, I really am, but you know I really care about you, and I hate watching you fade away, it is killing me. I just know, that whatever it is, the dreams, the grief, all the pain, I just know you will never solve it here. Emmy, you need to face this or you will never move on. It is almost a year and I think you should mark it; hell, remembrance is all you have left. Listen to me please Emmy, just go, put flowers on her grave and talk to her, I get you think it's weird, but if you do it, you will feel better. Trust me on that, you never said goodbye, and I think you need to."

I gave a snort, and wiped my eyes on my sleeve, as I pulled away from her.

"Shell, I know you are right, and yes, I need to do this, but crazy as it sounds, honestly, I am so frightened Shell. I am afraid I won't handle it being alone there without her." She smiled as she wiped a tear from my cheek.

"You won't be alone; I will be there right at your side."

I knew she would never quit; she had a faith in things I did not understand. She was right, all the dreams had only one thing in common, and it was Han. I had felt since the day I left, she was calling me back. I did not understand it, all I could say to myself was it is grief, and it will pass.

My last memory of Han was saying see you soon, I was going to go home for my twenty first, we had made such wonderful plans, and just two weeks before, I lost her. It still hurt and it tore at me, I felt I had turned my back on her like they all had, and it was wretched and painful. I had not done that at all; I could not bear the thought of not seeing her there.

Somehow it felt that going back would feel less like home, I had my room and my things there, but how could I sleep there, knowing she was not in the next room, or wake in a morning to not see her in the kitchen cooking breakfast?

The simple truth was, it would break my heart, and I was afraid of losing the love I held for the only real family member who cared for me. It sounds ridiculous, but to me, it felt like if I avoided returning to that empty house, then in many ways everything was still as it was, and I could pretend she was still there waiting for me.

I went to bed and slept late, Shelly went out with her poet, I vaguely remember the grunts, moans, and bumps in the night, so was aware the poet came home with her. I drifted into sleep again, and had weird dreams; I was a little girl again looking up at her kind face.

"Who is Randolph?" She smiled and patted my head.

"He is a special person; he is a friend who visits from time to time, and watches over me."

"I like that Grandma Han, it makes me happy, I always feel sad that when I go back to school, you are all alone." She gave a chuckle.

"My dear sweet child, I am never alone, you cannot be lonely when you walk in the light."

"Will I walk in the light with you one day?" She turned and smiled.

"You have such bright light inside you my child, and yes, one day you will walk into the light and find me." I gave her a frown.

"Will I lose you and have to come to the light?" She gave a chuckle.

"I think you will indeed, a day will come when you need me, and when it does, you will accept the light within you and come back to me, it is written in the tree stones."

I turned at her side, and a man in a long brown hooded cloak that hid his face stood beside us, his cloak parted and a large hand came out in a gesture of shaking it. I sat bolt upright in bed and gave a gasp.

"Oh shit!" I sat gasping in air as my heart pounded, I was clammy and felt the sweat run down my back.

"God will I never have peace?"

I slipped out of bed, and headed to the kettle to click it on, Shelly was lay on the sofa.

"I heard the poet, where is he?" She gave a frown.

"He is good with a pen and words, but honestly I was a tad let down, all talk and not much action, although the oral was good." I shuddered.

"Okay too much info, the less I know the better." She gave a chuckle.

"How are you this morning, did you sleep any better?" I poured out a coffee and yawned.

"Not really, different night, same dreams." I walked over to the sofa and sat down to sip my drink.

"I thought about what you said last night Shell, I won't deny, I am scared, but I would like to mark her grave, I owe her that much." I felt my stomach twist. "And if it stops Pete bloody emailing me, that would be a relief." She gave a nod.

"How much has he offered now?" I gave a long exasperated sigh.

"Two mil." She sat up.

"Bloody hell, seriously?" I gave a nod.

"Han always said she would never sell it to him, but I will not deny, there have been a few moments, when I thought just bloody sell it so he will leave me the hell alone. I wish he would just go to hell and leave me be." She leaned back on the arm, and watched me.

"What is it about the place that makes it so valuable, is it really that special?"

I smiled as I thought of the house and her garden, and the large lake with the huge island in the middle, I have so many happy memories of it.

"He only sees the price of the wood and the water rights, knowing him he would flatten the lot and build all over it. I get Han, I understand why she wants to keep it natural, in many ways I think it is why I went into ecology. She loved it so much Shell, to her it was a very magical and special place." She smiled.

"What do you think?" I glanced at her and giggled.

"You never quit, do you?" She gave a smirk.

"I like how you sound, and the look on your face when you talk about it, I would imagine I see you as you did Han."

I sipped my drink, and relaxed, I noticed her still watching me with a smile, I turned to her.

"WHAT!?" She laughed.

"Well... Are you going to go back or not?" I shook my head; I knew she would bang on and on until I did.

"I am considering it, I am still fearful, but I would like to mark her grave for her, I do think I owe it to her to be there." Shelly gave a nod.

"I do think that is a good first move, I mean, if you look at it, you are paying standing charges for power and gas, and have the housing tax to pay, you may as well, at least go there, and check it is fine and give the place an airing out, hell I would."

In a way she had a point, Han set me up an account which had seven hundred thousand in it, and all the bills had been paid by direct debit from it for just under a year, and I had not even been there. It was getting harder to face the inevitable, although, I was still not sure when I should go.

My phone started to ring, I got up and walked over to the kitchen unit and picked it up, I saw the name lit up and gave a sigh, I answered and put it on speaker.

"Emily, I thought I would ring to see how you are doing." Shelly frowned.

"I am fine Aunt Jess."

"Oh, that is so nice to hear that, listen, Peter is becoming concerned, because he tells me you have not replied to his emails, you know, it is more than a fair offer?" I carried the phone over to the sofa and sat down and lifted my coffee.

"Yes, it is a good price, the problem is as I have told him about fifty times now, I do not need the money or wish to sell it." I heard her sigh, and it sounded like someone else was there whispering in her ear.

"Emily, you know, you have not been there since she died, what is the point of keeping it, if you are not going to live there?"

"I am sorry Aunt Jess, but who said I am not going to live there, I may just not have gotten round to going yet, you know I have been working?"

"Emily, it has been almost a year for God's sake, honestly, if you were interested in living there, you would already be in there by now. Look, I understand you were close to her, I really do, but wouldn't it be better if you just let Peter and myself clear it out, and then use the land for the benefit of more?"

"No, it would not." She gave yet another sigh.

"I do think you are being as unreasonable as your mother was, you are just like her you know? Look, we know you are working with Harry; he was telling us just the other night, how busy things are, now be honest, you are too committed there. It is impossible for you to be in two places at once, now why don't you see sense and just talk with Peter, and just let go of the past?"

I was really starting to get pissed off, and could feel my anger rising.

"Aunt Jess, I am not selling, it is my home, and always will be, so please for the love of God, tell your husband to just back off and leave me alone. I am going back there; I have just not set date. It is my home; I will return at some point."

"Really, well no one in the village is aware of that?"

"Why would they be, it is also none of their business either. I am sorry Jess, I am in the middle of something, so I have to go, goodbye." I ended the call and looked at Shelly.

"Pack a bag, we are going today... We will probably need some food as well." She gave a screech, and jumped off the sofa.

"Finally, some sense, wow if I had known a year ago to really piss you off big time, I would have done it, and you would be there now."

Shelly had been right, I was delaying, and I was putting it off, I knew eventually I had to face up to the fact she was gone. In a way it was the same as with my mother, it took me a long time to overcome her death, and Han was the one that helped me come to terms with that, and I felt now was the time to end the pain, and do my best to face my future without her.

It was obvious Peter and Jessica were never going to leave me alone, and listening to her, and realising that they had even spoken to my boss and the villagers, that was the last straw. I had to grow up, face this, and move on, although I cannot deny, I was dreading it, and I felt the pressure inside me intensify.

I felt forced in a way to act, and it may sound insane, but my fear of my Uncle Pete was growing, I had been getting so many emails, he had swamped my inbox. This was from someone who before her death, had never even spoken to me. Come to think of it, the last time my Aunt Jessica had spoken to me, apart from a greeting at the funeral, which was cold, was on my ninth birthday, and I was almost twenty two.

I pondered if it was my intuition, because I was asking myself, why the pressure and why the rush, what was it about this land that made them so intense in their desire to have it? I had spent the better part of my youth there, I had boated on the lake, walked in the vast forests on the island, and fished off the jetty. I spent days out in the long back garden, with its terraces of cascading flowers and the path and steps that led down to a huge white stone circular arch, that led to the jetty. For me in my youth it was a magical place, made all the more special by Han and her wonderful stories.

I spent the afternoon packing a few things, and then headed out to the supermarket to pick up supplies. The great thing about the mini bus, was with the seats at the back removed, it was almost like a little van, and we had loads of room for storage. Shelly was very happy and lively, as normal, she packed pads for notes, and for artwork, as well as her laptop. I decided that I did not know how long I would stay. I would go and then see how I felt, Shelly agreed it was a good idea, I cannot deny, knowing she would be with me helped a lot.

I was nervous as I sat in bed, and built up the courage to leave in the morning. I did not want to drive down at night, I wanted to arrive in the light, after all, the power would have to be put back on, and after a year, the house would need to be aired out.

It was a strange night, maybe it was because I had finally decided to go, I lay back in my bed and dozed. I have no idea why it came to mind, but I drifted into dreams, I dreamt of the night I broke up with Ken. I had been with Ken for three years, and found out he had been fooling around with two other girls, one who was supposed to be a friend. I had a blazing row, and left his house, and went home to my flat, where I broke down. My mind drifted into that night, as I fell apart and called Han.

"Han, I cannot trust anyone, he told me he loved me, and like a fool I believed him, he is no better than dad." I wiped my face and sobbed into the phone.

"Emmy child, I know it feels like the worst pain ever, but trust me, not everyone is like that. Those who are blind to the truth of this life, will never understand, and you will meet many on your road to life."

"Han I am so tired, I hate this world, I hate this life, everyone deserts me in the end, and I am not sure I can take any more." I sniffled, and more tears ran down my face. "Han, I miss you so much, don't ever leave me, I am not sure I could live here in this world without you."

"Listen to me my sweet child, you too have no real understanding of this world and this life. I will never leave you; we are part of the light and we will always be connected. Come home, pack a bag and come home to me."

"Han I really want to, is it okay if I stay for a while, it is two months before I head to Scotland? Han, I really need to feel close to you."

"Then come home, Emmy my child, no matter what happens, this will always be your home, and I will always be here, so come back to me. Come back to me my child, and rest from the cruel world safe in my care." I gave a massive sob.

"Thanks Han, I will pack tonight and leave tomorrow, I want to be near you, you are the only living soul I trust."

"Good, I will make up your bed, and have it ready for you. I have missed you my child, I will be happy to have you close for a while."

"Okay, I am going to pack and sleep, I will see you soon."

"I will await you, and walk in your dreams to sooth you, feel my love reach out to keep you safe."

I jerked in my sleep, and felt her warmth surround me, the memory faded and I slipped into a deeper sleep. Through the night, the lights on the tree outside twinkled, and for the first time in a year, I felt safe and rested deeply. "I love you, Han."

I jerked awake, as Shelly sat on the bed. "Hey, I have coffee, we have a long drive today." I rubbed my eyes.

"What time is it?" She handed me the coffee as I sat up.

"It is seven." I lifted the cup to my lips.

"Christ, I think I am insane, why am I doing this Shell, I know this is going to kill me?" She smiled.

"Because it is time, I heard you calling her in your sleep, and I think she spoke to you, because after that, you settled and I think slept better than you have in months. It is time Emmy, and I will be there with you." I swallowed my coffee and gave a long sigh.

"Is it weird that some part of me feels I need to protect the place? Honestly, I cannot explain it, but I have this huge feeling deep down inside that it is in danger, it makes no sense at all to me." She gave me a shrug, and lifted her coffee.

"I think it makes loads of sense; your uncle is hell bent on taking that place away for his get rich quick development. If what I have heard about the place from you is true, then it should be saved, because it is a place of extreme natural beauty. I mean, let's be honest, your uncle does not give a shit about it, maybe you need to be there to stop him." I gave a nod.

"I think you are right, call it intuition, and as painful as it is to go back, something inside me is scared I will lose it, and I cannot let that happen, I cannot lose my only connection to her." She patted the bed, and got up.

"Have your coffee, get dressed, and then let's get going, the sooner we are there, the sooner we will know."

It took a while, but finally we packed the mini bus, and jumped in, Shelly was driving. I felt tense and nervous, and I had a strange feeling building in the pit of my stomach. It was to be well over an hour's drive, so I settled back, and drifted with the sun on my face, as we listened to the music, and I felt my eyes flutter. I closed them just for a second, as I felt warm and relaxed and peaceful.

I woke with a start, almost as if someone had shouted in my face, I looked round. The music was playing, Shelly was smiling and we were almost at the village, I saw the Milking Gate Hotel up ahead, I slid up in my seat, and yawned.

"I told you to wake me, and I would share the drive." Shelly gave a wink.

"That is the most peaceful I have seen you sleep, I figured after months of losing it, a deep sleep like that was a good thing, so I left you." I yawned.

"Go right through the main village, and when it forks, go to the right, take that road for a mile and we will be there."

I sat back and felt my stomach churn, I needed to prepare myself mentally, this was not going to be easy. Shell took the right hand road, and I watched as the trees began to thicken, the woodland round the property was dense, and rich with diversity. I think as a child, I had learned to identify every type of native tree just from walking around here. I pointed.

"Slow down, and take that road to the right, after that large pine." Shell smiled.

"Wow this place is really out in the sticks, it is really secluded and private."

It was, and that was part of the charm, Han liked a quiet life, she like to meditate and work on her garden, or weaving alone. She lived a simple life, she grew her own food, pickled most of it, made jam and wine, dried herbs for medicine or cooking. There was little she could not do, and everything she needed came from her garden, or the land around her.

Shelly slowed and turned, and I saw the long road between the trees. I remembered watching as the lorries tipped out the stone, and levelled it when I was ten, and then two days later, I watched from the gates, as the tar surface was laid down. Han had grown tired of pushing the wheel barrow down it, and filling in the mud holes with gravel, and so she finally admitted defeat and had it surfaced. As we drove up, Shelly leaned forward and gazed through the window.

"Is that a van?" I looked up, and stared through the window as we got closer, it was, and I knew the logo.

"That bloody snake, what the hell is he up to?" I felt my heart beat quicken.

Chapter Three

Home Again

For almost a year, I had felt harassed by my uncle. I was falling apart, trying to come to terms with the loss of Han, the only person who I feel has ever really truly loved me. Since age four, I had spent all my holidays with Han, and through her, I learned to leave my insecurity behind, and I was doing so well, I had qualified and was working out in nature, almost like living with Han.

Her cottage, just outside Hempsley, was the place I called home, and in my heart, the cottage and Han, were the place's I could run to when I was in need of being grounded. It was a base, a foundation, a source of stability, and somewhere to hole up to recover and recuperate. For a year, I had struggled with the pain of her loss, and as a result I had not gone home. I had moved from job to job, and bought a flat, as I hid away, racked with pain, and the fear of coming home to a cold empty house.

Uncle Peter was relentless, and I have no idea why, but he came across as obsessed, and because of it, I had finally decided to come home, and face everything. I think Shelly was right, it was time, and as much as I was afraid and my stomach was reeling, as I sat in the car, falling asleep, I knew it was the right time. I sensed a calling deep within me, to reconnect with this beautiful place, that held so many happy memories for me. To see the van with Uncle Pete's company logo on it, jolted me into reality, and as we approached, my temper and frustration from a years worth of harassment, began to bubble up in me.

We got closer to the old wooden gates, I saw the van and the black Mercedes, and it did not take too much to work out. Shelly drove in through the gates, and my blood started to boil.

"That shit, he has no right being here, what the hell does he think he is doing?"

Shell pulled up short of the house, and I saw him talking to a man in a yellow vest. He stood there with an arrogant smirk, and his short cropped slicked back greying hair, acting like he owned the place.

Shelly was a little hard on the brakes, and the bus slid a little, he turned saw the bus, and rolled his eyes, he knew what was coming, as I grabbed the door release.

The door flew open, and I exploded out of it, I felt so angry, as I marched along the low stone wall, not even noticing the house, my eyes locked on his, as he smirked at me. He was a sly piece of work; I could not hold myself in any longer.

"WHAT THE HELL DO YOU THINK YOU ARE DOING, UNCLE PETE!?"

It was actually pretty obvious, I saw the survey equipment, and knew it well, I had used it myself many times on a conservation project. He lifted his hands, as the man he was with looked surprised, I pointed back at the gates.

"GET THE HELL OFF MY LAND, HAN BANNED YOU ONCE, YOU SHOULD KNOW BETTER, I TOLD YOU, IT IS NOT FOR SALE!" The surveyor looked confused and stared at me.

"What the hell is going on?"

I marched right up to him, my insides on fire, and swirling within me. I came up close, Shell was out of the bus and right behind me, I looked right at my uncle.

"You are trespassing on private property, and I want you off it now." He looked at my uncle confused.

"Is that right Pete, you said this was family property?" My Uncle looked at me.

"I think you need to calm down Emily, I can explain." I shook my head.

"No, you thought you would sneak in because you thought I was not here, and survey the place for another of your grand schemes. This is my land, not yours, now get the hell off it, I will never sell it, not for as long as I live. This is Han's home, and it always will be. You have fifteen minutes, and if you are not gone, I am ringing the police."

He did not even seem to care, I literally had confronted his sly behaviour, and he did not even bat an eyelid, what the hell was his game? I turned and looked at the surveyor.

"I am Emily Duncan, daughter of John Stuart Duncan, I am quite sure you have heard of him? You are trespassing, and if you do not remove your equipment, I am calling my father, and he will have an army of solicitors up your ass before tea time, am I clear?" He nodded at me looking panicked, and stepped back with his hands up, and looked at my uncle.

"I hear you Miss Duncan, and yes, I know who your father is, and I have no wish to tangle with him." He turned and whistled, and his men looked at him.

"The job is off lads, pack it all up." I noticed four other men at the side of the house, I was so angry I looked at my uncle, I wanted to hit him.

"You are a piece of work, what were you going to do, demolish everything and then tell me?" He looked at me with hate in his eyes.

"You have no idea of the mistake you are making, that island alone is worth millions, you are a fool, and as blind as your grandmother." I had to hold myself in, or I swear to God, I wanted to punch him in the mouth.

"That island is a spawning ground for great crested newts, and it alone houses a small population of red squirrels, there is not a grey on that island." He laughed.

"So what?" I shook my head in disbelief, he was a developer, he should know what, but the surveyor spoke, before I could answer.

"Mr McDougal, they are protected habitats under law, you cannot develop them, that is what."

He shook his head, I think he was starting to realise the bind he was in, and needed to distance himself from my uncle. He gave a sigh and walked back towards the van; my uncle seethed at me; he was angry.

"You are an overindulged spoiled brat; do you know that; you are throwing away an opportunity of a life time?"

"Overindulged, what, like my aunt? Get the hell off my land, and never set foot on it again. I mean it Uncle Pete, I will drag you through every court in the land and destroy you, and I know my father will back me, now get off my land."

He was clearly pissed off, his eyes bulged, and he gritted his teeth, and clenched his fist, he lifted it, and shook it. "I will... I will..."

BOOM!

My head snapped round, and I felt my breath catch in my throat, across the large wild grass, at the end of the driveway, stood next to the treeline, was a man in a long brown cloak with his hood up. It had to be the same man from the funeral, he was holding up a rifle. He pulled back the bolt, and the case ejected, then he rammed the bolt back in, and reloaded the rifle. His voice was loud, and yet soft, but felt forceful, I could not really see his face.

"You heard the lady, get the hell off her land."

I turned to look back at my uncle, he was walking backwards towards his car, and was looking at me, with his furrowed brow, and narrowed eyes.

"We are done with you Emily, do not even come begging, as far as I am concerned, we are done forever." He grabbed his car door, I nodded.

"Suits me fine, you and my aunt have never been interested, my life will be pretty much as it always has been when I wake up tomorrow."

I watched as he got in his car, the engine started, and he raced off, his wheels spinning on the gravel. The sound of a gunshot, had increased the pace of the surveyors, as they loaded quickly, fumbling their stuff into the van, the guy in the yellow jacket walked over to me, and gave a nod, he had kind eyes.

"I am really very sorry Miss Duncan, I had no idea, Peter assured us it was a done deal. We will only be a few moments longer, and we will leave you in peace." I nodded at him.

"It was not your fault, you were lied to, I know you were just doing your job, although, I would say next time you work for my uncle, check the land deeds first, and the natural wildlife." He nodded and held out his hand.

"Again, I am sorry for any inconvenience." I took it and gave it a shake.

"Thank you, I hope your week is a better one." He smiled.

"I am sure it will not be as bad as this."

I watched as he walked back to the van, his men were inside strapped into their seats, he pulled the side door closed, walked round to the other side, and got into the driver's seat. Moments later, I watched as they drove onto the lane out, and I felt myself calming down, although I was trembling still with anger, and fear.

"Where did he go?" I looked at Shell.

"Who?" She pointed behind me.

"The guy from your dreams."

I suddenly realised and turned round, the tree line was empty, as quick as he had appeared, he had disappeared. I felt my stomach twist, Shell leaned into me.

"He was there right; I mean you did see him too?" I looked at her.

"Shell, he was real, we all saw him, he fired a gun... Seriously, are you freaked out?" She did look pale, as she stared at the empty tree line.

"What, are you telling me you are not?" I smiled.

"Some ghost hunter you turned out to be, Shell he was real." She nodded.

"So where is he, because tell me I am wrong, but that was the guy you dreamed about?" I shrugged.

"It could be, I did not really take a good look at him." She looked really pale, I shook my head, turned around, and suddenly I was confronted with reality, as I stood before my home, Han's home.

I looked at the gate with the small sign nailed to it, 'Han's Cottage' and gave a gasp, as I followed the path with my eyes, up to the porch of pink roses, and the dark green door. I felt the surge of emotion flood into me, and my voice fell softly off my lips.

"I am home Han." Shell came up to my side, and took my hand.

"This is good Emmy."

I felt the tears roll onto my cheeks, stood before the gate, just staring, it looked the same as it always had, and yet it felt different, less alive than it always had. I swallowed really hard and gave a gasp, Shelly handed me a tissue, I sniffled, and reached my hand out for the gate. I had to do this, I was finding it hard to move, but I had to, something inside me told me I have to protect this place, more so now than ever. I gave Shelly's hand a squeeze.

"Please don't leave Shelly, I cannot do this alone."

Across the wild grass, inside the treeline, hidden in the darkened shade, the cloaked stranger watched, as Emily faltered at the gate, he held his breath, feeling a little nervous, his voice was low.

"Come on, prove she was right to have faith in you, stop running, she needs you to do this, now open the gate and walk in, she is waiting."

I looked down at my hand on the gate.

"Shell, I am really scared, tell me honestly, do you think I can deal with this?" She leaned into my side and placed her hand on the gate catch.

"If you are asking me if you are going to be a blubbering, unstable mess for the next few days, the answer is yes, you are. Emmy, that is bloody normal, she was the mother figure in your life. If you are asking should you do it, I also say yes." I turned and looked at her.

"That did not help."

She smiled and the catch flicked, and I felt my hand move as the gate swung open, she gave me a nudge, and I stepped forward, I knew she was right. Shell pushed a little more, I was through the gate, and on the stepping stones through the gravel, I was terrified, but I knew there was no going back, I took another step, and then another, Shell held my hand tight.

I reached the door, and stared at it, with its dark green paint and the small circular brass plate of the lock. I took a breath, and pulled the key out of my pocket, my hand shook as I guided it to the slit, Shelly gave another squeeze of my hand, I think she was holding her breath.

The key wavered slightly, and found the slit, and I felt it slide slowly in, I looked at her, and she gave a smile and nodded at me. I felt the lock turn, and the catch gave, and silently the door moved back. I pulled out the key, the door was literally only inches out of the frame. I breathed slowly in, and then reached for the door still holding the key and pushed, the door swung back, and the room came into view. I felt my stomach twist, as I took my first step towards facing my life, the first I had taken in a year, I entered.

In the trees the cloaked figure gave out a long flowing breath and leaned back on the tree trunk.

"Finally, now you are here, claim it, your time is running out, claim what is yours, and bring peace back to this land. Han, I doubted you, and I am still not completely sure yet, but it is a start, and that is a good thing."

I stood in the middle of the room, and I felt a shiver run down my spine, nothing had changed, but that made it harder to see it. Her knitting was still in her basket at the side of her chair, the room was still clean and tidy, her shawl still hung on the back of her chair, it was almost as if I could call her, and she would appear from the kitchen and smile at me. I felt my legs shake slightly, Shelly was stood behind me, as my eyes wandered around the room, this was the only real home I knew, and then I spotted it, the large picture I had sent her the day after I last visited, it was the only new thing in the room.

She had printed it out and framed it, and as I reached out, and lifted it up from her side unit, and looked at her with her arm round me, and her wonderfully kind eyes as I smiled with joy, my eyes blurred and the tears flowed.

"Oh Han, I was so happy... Oh Han, I miss you so much, why did you leave me?"

The pain in my heart intensified and it broke. Shelly stood behind me as my shoulders shook, and with my head down, my tears rained onto the rug. I turned still holding the picture, and Shelly wrapped around me, and I buried my head in her shoulder and wailed, as a years worth of loss exploded within me, and it was the most painful thing I had ever felt, as it tore through me.

I am not sure how long I cried for, Shelly just held me and shouldered it all, my heart was broken and I felt devastated. When I finally took a breath and leaned back to wipe my eyes,

Shelly stood with her mascara streaked down her cheeks, where she had cried with me, it felt painful to see, I gave a sniffle as she relaxed her arms and I moved back.

"I am sorry Shell, you should not have to see this, it just came out. I am really sorry."

She lifted a tissue, and handed it to me, I took it as I sniffled, she pulled another out of the packet in her pocket and wiped her own eyes.

"You do not have to apologise to me Emmy, I hope one day someone shows me so much love. You needed to do that; you have for a year. This house by the way, is stunningly beautiful."

I wiped my face as I looked around, it was so familiar, I was glad to be back at the only place that I had ever known as a home, but as familiar as it was, it also felt strange. There was no rattle of pans, or her quiet muttering to herself, or that infectious laugh, the silence without her felt oppressive. I walked towards the kitchen door, which as always was ajar. Shelly watched.

"I am going to pull the van closer and unload. I think you need to take some time for you, just get yourself reacquainted, I will be right outside if you need me Hun." I looked back at her, and gave a nod, I felt weepy, and my insides were all over the place, maybe it was best I did this alone.

"Alright Shell... Thanks."

She smiled and headed for the door, I walked to the kitchen door, and pushed it open, the silence was killing me, there were no scents of cooking or baking, no sound of bubbling pans, or a knife on the cutting board. I walked round the kitchen, everything was as it had been, apart from a baking tin in the centre of the table, sat next to a pack of birthday cake candles, and a plastic number 21. I leaned forward and picked it up.

"Oh god, you were making me a cake."

I could not help it, my emotions were everywhere, and I had no idea what to do, I stood like an idiot bawling my brains out, holding it close to my heart, feeling utterly useless and alone.

Outside, Shelly walked to the bus, climbed in and started the engine, she reached for the gear stick, and her phone began to ring, she saw the name and lifted it off the dash and answered it, putting it on speaker phone.

"Shell, how is she?"

"What do you expect Pam, she is heartbroken and sobbing her heart out, the only person who was any sort of family has gone, and she is in a house full of memories?"

"Yeah sorry, that was a stupid question, it is good she is finally in the house though." Shell nodded at the dash.

"Yeah, I thought for a moment she would bolt, but she is over the first hurdle. It did not help we got here to find her slimy uncle surveying the place."

"You have got to be joking?"

"Nope, I am telling you Pam, I don't trust him, he is a sneaky bugger."

"Jesus, what did Emmy do, is she alright?"

"She was pretty emotional to start with, but it turned to anger, and she threw him off the property, she was pretty vocal, and a bit scary, but he left, which is a good thing. I was getting ready to jump on him, he was pretty pissed off, she showed him up in front of his crew, and he did not like it one bit."

"Do you think he will come back; you know, if you think it will get rough, I can take some time off and fly over, I have saved up my holiday time, you know just in case she needs me?"

"She is in the house Pam, it will be rough for a while, she has a lot of grieving to do, but for now she will be fine, I am not leaving her side."

"Thanks Shell, I am actually so relieved she has you, I really want to be with her, you know the three of us like old times? If it gets hard, call me, and I will be on the next flight over."

"Thanks Pam, you have been here before, haven't you?" She gave a slight chuckle.

"Yeah, it was our last term at Uni, you buggered off with that crazy Italian, so I joined her and hung out with her and Han. She was a pretty cool lady; I can really understand why this will be hard for her. Seriously Shell, I think she was the kindest lady I ever met, you would have loved her stories. Hell, you could have written a book about just what she talked about, she was very special, this will be really hard for Emmy."

"I am on it Pam, I am in the bus at the moment, I am unloading it, to give her a little space, and then I will feed her, and probably get her pissed, she will sleep better, so wish me luck, I am going to get back to her."

"Okay Shell, again, thanks for being with her, keep me posted. See you soon."

"Yeah, see you soon Hun."

Pam ended the call, and Shelly drove closer to the small gate, then parked up and jumped out. She walked round to the back doors and opened them, and leaned in for the bags. She grabbed them, pulled them forward to the back doors, and as she lifted them, she glanced over the seats, and saw two bright little flashes in the trees. She blinked, and put the bags down with a frown. Shelly walked round the back of the bus, and stood on the gravel drive, and stared at the trees.

"What was that, has our cloaked crusader not left yet?" In the trees the hooded figure moved fast.

"What the hell were you two thinking, have you any idea what would have happened if that girl had seen you? You know the rules, you must not leave the island, have you any idea what kind of trouble you could cause?" A quiet soft squeaky voice responded.

"Felix promised we would not be seen." The cloaked figure sighed, as he looked back from the water's edge through the trees.

"Esme, how many times have I told you, stop listening to him, his mischief one day will land both of you in big trouble, now go... Stay low, and get back across the lake."

"Is it true, has she come back, is that really her, she looked different, you know fatter, and I think she has shrunk?"

"Felix, that was not her, that is the other one, she was in the house. Now both of you go, before they find out you are here, go on, and for the love of the trees, stay over there."

He stood back, and watched as they sailed over the water, back towards the island, and gave a long sigh of relief.

"Those two will be the death of me one day."

It was hard to be back, nothing had changed at all, but really why would it? The last time anyone had been here, was a year ago, and it was her. I lifted the kettle, filled it, and clicked it on, and that was when I realised.

"Why is the water on, they told me it had been turned off?" I looked round as Shelly carried a box of food in, and put it down on the table.

"The water is on!" She shrugged.

"That is a good thing, isn't it?" I shook my head.

"I was told everything was switched off." I turned and clicked the wall switch, the kettle light turned red.

"The power is on too, Mr Higginson was adamant, he had shut off the water, gas, and electric, so who switched it on?" Shelly just stared at me.

"Honestly, I have no idea, while we are on the subject of strange, does this place have fireflies?" I looked at her unsure of where she was going.

"No... Shell, this is Britain, why do you ask?" She gave a sigh and shook her head.

"I didn't think so, but honestly, I am sure I just saw some in the trees out front. You know when you told me this place was magical, I thought you meant pretty, but honestly, something here is different from any place I have ever been, I cannot explain it, I just feel it, and it is weird." I smirked.

"Jesus Shell, you have not been here more than an hour, are you ghost hunting already?"

Having made coffee, and cried a lot, I felt a little calmer, seeing things that she loved, stirred up more emotions, but I tried to try at least to keep them under control. I saw her pen on the side, her flower covered mug on its hook, her cardigan hanging next to the back door. The calendar was a year out of date, and had a red circle round my birthday, the shopping list on the fridge door had 'icing sugar' on it, and each thing felt a little more painful. Memories flooded my mind, as I sat at the table and looked round, and I would swallow hard and try to hold back the tears, it was far harder than I had thought it would be.

I decided to help Shell put everything away, in truth I was avoiding upstairs, as I knew at some point I would have to walk past her bedroom. In Han's house, everything had its place, and without even thinking, I just automatically put things in the right cupboards. Shell grabbed some potatoes, and stopped, she gave me an odd look.

"This house has been locked for a year, right?" I gave her a

nod.

"Almost, why do you ask?" She looked towards the back door.

"Emmy, why are there fresh veg in the rack, it probably sounds daft, but wouldn't it have rotted, you know, it has been almost a year?" I walked round the table, and saw the cabbage and the carrots, Shell lifted a carrot and took a bite, she chewed.

"Yep, fresh as the day it was pulled." I shook my head.

"Shell that is not possible." She swallowed, and smiled.

"Emmy Hun, I know that and you know that, but honestly, I don't think this carrot knows it. Here, have a bite, it's fresh."

"No, I am not having that." I took the carrot out of her hand and took a bite, I chewed, it was fresh, earthy, and sweet.

"Shell, I am telling you, there is no way this carrot is a year old; it would have decayed." She smiled and took the carrot off me, and took another bite.

"So, you still think magic does not exist, because Hun, this carrot is lovely, and fresh, even if it is a year old?" I turned back for my coffee.

"Shell, there is a rational explanation, please, my emotions are already all over the place, do not go looking for the supernatural here. God, the last thing I need at the moment are ghouls and ghosts, just dealing with my uncle, is enough for one day."

We drank coffee, and put everything back, and I showed her where the pantry was, which was filled with glass jars of preserved food, I was not super hungry, but she insisted I eat. God she is a pain, so I made a cheese sandwich. It was enough, and it settled my stomach a little. I was trying to avoid the inevitable, when she asked.

"Let's get the bags upstairs and unpack, where is my room?" I felt my heart quicken. My stomach churned, as I lifted my bag and led the way up the stairs, at the top I turned to the right.

"There are two spare rooms there, the front is single, the back room double, pick one." I turned and saw the two doors.

"Mine is the back room." I pointed. "Shower, bathroom and toilet." She smiled and noted my face.

"It is going to be okay Emmy. Listen Hun, I realise that is her room, I will not be going anywhere near it, just relax, this is your home, put your stuff away, and I will open a bottle of wine." I nodded.

"Thanks Shell, I am not ready for her room yet, just this, has been a lot."

"It is fine, welcome home Hun, you have done good today." I gave a long sigh.

"I have bawled my brains out all over the place, how is that good?" She gave me a slight grin.

"Emmy, it is grief, crying is normal, and yet for a year you have not, well, not properly, you needed to, it is a part of healing, and if everything I have heard is true, she would want that."

I gave a nod, she was crazy at times, but she was a good friend. I turned and walked to my room and opened the door, and this time it felt familiar and unchanged. I walked in and looked round, now it felt like I was home again. I sat on the bed and dropped my bag on the floor, I looked at my small desk, my drawers and closet, and my dressing table, and hung on the mirror was her pendant.

I got up and crossed the room, and slid out my mum's pendant from my sweatshirt, Han's fitted into it, and made a complete circle, it was a tree of life. I sat down on my dressing table chair, and just looked at them joined together, and her voice sounded in my thoughts.

"Emmy child, she made you, and I raised you, and one day that pendant round your neck with be joined with mine, and in that time, the light will come, and you will be complete, just as the pendant will be." I stared at it in my hand.

"I do not feel very complete Han, I feel lost, afraid, and alone. I would be much happier if both of you were here wearing these. I never wanted to be alone in this world, I wish both of you had stayed with me. My dad has no idea how much I miss you both, he has no idea where I am or who I am. Oh god, this is so hard without you."

Chapter Four

Tears and Storms

I fell asleep slightly drunk, Shelly had sat in my room, which felt more comfortable for me. We drank wine and talked, as I told her of life here, swimming in the lake, helping Han in the garden, cooking and gardening. I wept a lot, and she asked me questions that distracted me, as she refilled my glass, and by ten I was out cold.

My sleep was strange, more restful and peaceful, almost like it had always been here, and my dreams were surreal, as I saw lights in the tree tops and circles of white light, and as strange as it sounds, I felt Han. I felt her holding my hand and stroking my hair, just like she had always done when I was a child missing my mum.

I woke with a start, the light was bright as it flowed in through the window, and I sat up, feeling groggy, my head felt cloudy and fuzzy. I slid off the bed and stood up, and walked to the window, the room smelt stuffy, and I thought I should air it through.

I reached for the latch, and as I opened the window, I saw it, the large tree filled island across the lake. I stood and stared out; it was as beautiful as it had always been. The lake was like glass, reflecting the banks of the trees in the water, as the sun shone down, glinting off its mirrored surface.

I had seen it millions of times, and yet today it looked more beautiful than it ever had before, and I felt a strangeness stirring in the pit of my stomach, almost like a pull towards it.

Across the island in the deep fern that grew along the water's edge, there was a shrill little giggle.

"Felix look, that is her, and she is watching... Felix she is watching us." A few leaves away, the fern moved.

"No, she is not, she cannot see that far yet, she needs to walk in the light before she will see all of it.

"I think she is beautiful."

"No offence Esme, but you think everything is beautiful, even the fat one." He sniggered. "Come on... Now we have seen her, we can tell the others."

I headed down stairs, and made a coffee, it felt strange being alone in the kitchen, Shelly was still in bed, she would sleep until at least ten. I decided to walk to my favourite spot, and holding my cup I walked outside, back towards the front gates, Shell had closed them.

I climbed up and sat on top of the gate, and lifted my cup, as I looked at the cottage. It had never really changed; I think I thought it might have. The cottage was beautiful, with its white walls, and dark windows, with lead strips creating small diamonds on the glass. The dark thatch on the roof, that curved above and over the upstairs windows. The arch of roses glowing pink and filling the air with scent, the garden that sprawled like a carpet of hundreds of baubles of thick tiny flowers, right down to the stone wall, which stood three feet high in front of it.

Shelly was right, it was a magical place, I think I looked at it today with fresh eyes, it was hard to believe it was mine now. It is insane, my dad is a billionaire, he has six houses across the globe, and I have never wanted to be a part of any of it, I have no room of my own in any of them. I have always worked hard for my money, and even though I have money in the bank, dad always ensures I get a cheque, I have never really used it, hell, I rode the bus up until a year ago.

I have always felt I do not belong to that life, I somehow thought I belonged to something more real, something that had a deeper value. On the few occasions I saw my father, which had got less as I had grown older, he had been frustrated with me, because I looked so plain and boring. I hardly wore makeup, my long brown wavy hair was always a mess, and he hated my tatty jeans and old knitted jumpers.

I find it strange he never really understood me, Han has told me so many times I was so like my mother, and he did after all marry her. I have often wondered why he cannot connect with me, why he is always so closed off. Did he ever really love my mother? It was hard to know why, but the simple truth was, we were like strangers, having an awkward conversation, fighting to find words that would resonate with each other, and neither of us understanding the other. I cannot deny, once I hit fourteen, I just stopped trying. My mind slipped into my memories from that time.

"There you are... I should have known, always on the gate." Han walked towards me her bright eyes with those lovely little smile lines on her dark round face.

"Thinking about him again, I ponder why you try to figure him out?" I gave a sigh.

"Did he love my mum, Han, I mean really love her, or was he just using her?" She leaned against the gate and gave a long sad sigh.

"Emmy my child, I can certainly tell you that Amelia loved him deeply, and to be honest, in a strange way I think he loved her just as deeply, I will not deny, they looked lovely together." I nodded as I glanced at her at my side.

"Why do I feel so unloved then, Han I am seventeen, and everyone tells me how like my mum I am, so why can he not see it?" She took my hand, and held it softly.

"Emmy, if you want my honest opinion, losing her killed all the joy in his heart, he was a mess for a long time, which is why you came to me. I will not deny, he changed after that, he was colder, more distant, and if you want my opinion, I honestly think, it hurt him deeply, and after that he was afraid to feel anything, let alone love."

"Han he is getting married again, he told me it was up to me whether or not I went. If he is afraid to love, then why is he marrying again?" She gave a long sigh.

"I have no idea Child, I really do not know, but if you honestly ask me does he love this woman, all I can say, is if he does, it is nowhere near as powerful as it was for your mother."

"I want him to love me, I want him to show it." I saw her glance at me.

"You cannot wish to be loved Emmy; it must flow like the light from your heart. I have always thought he did, but had become fearful of showing it, because he was afraid to lose it the way he did with Amelia." She lifted her pinny and wiped her hands.

"Come on, I made scones, and they are still hot, and I know how you like them hot."

I came out of my thoughts, Shelly was stood at the gates looking at me, I blinked. She walked over towards me.

"Sorry Shell, did you say something?" She walked up and looked at me.

"Am I fat?"

"What?" She grabbed at her stomach, and pulled out a lump.

"I said am I fat?" I shook my head.

"What the hell does it matter?" She gave me a strange look.

"Honestly, I think this place messes my head up. I got up and went for a pee, I mean, okay I was naked, it was hot in bed last night, and I could have sworn I heard a voice that laughed at me and called me fatty." I frowned.

"Yeah, you are right, you are messed up. I hate to say this Shell, but hearing voices in the toilet, is weird as hell." She looked down.

"I get it, I was a size ten at Uni, and maybe I have partied a bit, I mean, I am only a size twelve now... Okay, maybe on the cusp of fourteen, but by today's standards, this is not really fat, is it?" She looked up at me, I had no idea what to say, I shrugged.

"Does it really matter; you are happy enough aren't you?" She looked down at her stomach.

"I could use getting fitter again, maybe this is why I only seem to pull losers, at Uni I had a few pretty hot guys. Yeah, I think I will work out a bit and get more toned."

"Okay, do that then, honestly, if it bothers you that much, then fine, but Shell, hearing voices in your head telling you that you are big, that is not normal, I would worry more about your sanity." She looked behind her towards the trees, then turned, and leaned on the gates.

"So, what do you want to do today, to be honest I thought we would be doing a lot of cleaning up and sorting out, but the house is pristine, so there is little to do?" I slipped off the gate.

"I am not awake fully yet." I looked at the house. "Shell I am going to visit her today, I want to, I want to say goodbye." She gave a slight smile.

"I think that is a good thing, does this place have a florist?"

The village of Hempsley was small, although the area was quite large. It was a rural community, with a lot of farms and large houses scattered around the whole area. The actual heart, was the small one street village itself, it had a store, which was pretty much everything rolled into one, as it had all the papers, food, and general essentials. Next door was a small hardware come garden shop, which had a lot of the main essentials, it had been the one shop Han used the most, and she ordered her seeds there every year.

There were three buses a day, which went to the larger towns and train stations, it had a small butcher, a florist come plant shop, a clothes shop, and a bakery come café. To the side of the Milking Gate public house and hotel, which I stayed in a year ago. There was a large tarmac square, on which markets would be held on Tuesdays and Thursdays. On Monday and Wednesday, there was a mobile bank, library and fish monger. The landlord of the Milking Gate, rented a small side building of the inn, to Jean and Brian Coulson, who ran the Post Office from there, as the main village one had been shut down in a barrage of sweeping cuts to save money. They had managed to convince the post office to allow them to operate a small one, and so they opened from nine in the morning, until one in the afternoon every day.

The only other shops were an estate agent, a garage come petrol station, and a doctor's practice and Mr Higginson's legal practice. It felt strange parking up, I noticed the looks, after all, Han's mini bus had been a regular part of village life here for many years. I crossed the road towards the florist, people were watching, but also smiling, and faces I have known for years nodded at me, I had changed little since my last visit. Tom Bateson, smiled as I walked past the garage.

"It is nice to see her back in the village, I miss tinkering with her." I stopped and looked back.

"She has done well; I have used her every day." He gave a big smile.

"It is nice to have you back Miss Montgomery, I had wondered if I would see you again." I smiled.

"It is strange, but yes, it is nice to be back home for a while."

I moved on to the florist. Heidi Miller, looked a little surprised as I walked in, she had been a good friend of my mum growing up, and was a regular visitor to Han, and she gave me a huge smile as she came out from behind the counter.

"Oh Emily, you have no idea how nice it is to see you, how are you doing?" I swallowed hard; Shelly was behind me sniffing the carnations.

"I am holding it together, just, Heidi." She smiled and pulled me into a hug, it felt nice.

"Oh Sweetheart, I have thought of you so often, I knew it would take a long time to come to terms with things. It is nice to see you here." I felt a huge surge inside me.

"I want some flowers for her." I felt the tears again, but I did not want them. "I want to say goodbye." I gave a huge sob. "I am sorry, I am still not dealing with it very well."

"Oh Sweetheart, don't worry about it, you cry all you like, she was your everything, we all know that. I will not deny, I have shed many myself in the last year, I miss her like hell, but for you, oh god, this must be awful."

She let me go and looked at me with a sad smile, Shell handed me yet another tissue, and I wiped my eyes. Heidi, looked at me.

"I will make her up something special, I know all her favourite flowers." I gave a sniffle and nod.

"Thanks Heidi."

Shelly walked up to my side and slipped her arm round me, and I leaned onto her, as I watched Heidi, put together Lilies, Roses, and Chrysanthemums in white, Han always loved white flowers. I dried my eyes, and tried to calm down, Heidi looked up at me.

"I know you do not see much of your dad, but you know, he took care of her, he had her a stone done to match your mum's." I felt a jolt of surprise.

"He did, when, because he has said nothing to me?"

"I went up to put flowers on your mum's grave, and that woman... I think she is called Kate; she was there supervising. A week later, I saw him drive through the village, and when I went up, there were red roses on Amelia's grave, and white on Han's."

It did not really surprise me that he had said nothing, that would mean showing feelings, and I had learned at age four, that was not appreciated. I watched as she wrapped the flowers.

"He said nothing to me, but as you know, that is not unusual." She gave a nod.

"I take it there has been no thaw between you two then?" I shook my head.

"I am not sure there ever will be." She gave a sigh and handed me the flowers.

"Honestly, if he would just stop in the village, I would kick his ass, you know I always thought that losing her killed his heart. He really loved her Emily, he adored her, I know, I was there. I think you are too big a reminder, you know I have to tell you, it makes my heart flutter when I see you, God, you are her double. When you walked in, I almost fainted, you look more like her every day, that cannot be easy for him." I understood that, Han told me that a million times.

"I am her daughter Heidi, I am a part of her, and it should count for something, sadly though, it doesn't." She handed me the flowers.

"Those are on me, tell her I said hi, and I miss her." I smiled.

"Thanks, and I will... I will see you again before I go back." She looked disappointed.

"So, this is only a visit, I am sorry to hear that, it would have been nice to come round and see the old place again."

"I will be around for a few days, you still have my number, call round."

"Yeah, I will, I would love that, Emily."

I walked back to the car holding the flowers, and took long deep breaths. I did not want to be stopped again, I had been fine, I just wished my mums best friend was not the florist. I placed the flowers on the seat behind me, and Shelly jumped in, and started the engine.

Driving out of the village, it was obvious where I was going, as people watched me turn onto the steep rise to the church and old cemetery. Shelly sat back in her seat; her head turned to me.

"I have to say Emmy, I find it odd that your dad would do that and not say anything, don't you think it is a bit weird?" I watched the road, as the bus roared up it in second gear.

"It would be weird for you to do that, but in all honesty, not him, he is like that, he shows no emotion, and never gives you the chance to provoke him into one, that is who he is now." She gave a nod as she thought about it.

"Why did that bloke in the overalls call you Montgomery?" I saw the church, and headed for the wall and gate at the side of it.

"It is because of Han, I think they saw me more like her daughter, and it was her name, so they use it for me as well. To be honest Shell, I prefer it to Duncan." I pulled up and pulled on the hand break.

"We are here, Shelly, I know it sounds strange, but could I do this alone, I know this is going to be hard? Would you mind staying here, I don't want to do it in front of you?" She looked at me, and then reached across and put her hand on my shoulder.

"I can do that if you want, but if it gets too bad, text me, and I will come to you." I leaned over the seat, and lifted the flowers off the back seat, and tried to smile.

"I know it sounds mad, but this is between Han and me."

"Okay Hun, I will be here if you need me."

Walking from the car, up the long path, and across the neatly cut lawn to her grave, felt like the hardest walk of my life. I saw the white stones that sat three feet apart, as I turned from the path. Deep down inside, I felt the pangs of emotion, and tried to focus, I had to do this, hell, I needed to do this, I had been away too long.

I walked up to both stones and stood between them, and looked down, the graves were identical, both white, with a white raised surround that came down the full length of their plots, and were filled with white stone chippings. I felt the emotion surge, as I saw my mother's grave, clean and neat, with her name carved precisely out of it. 'Amelia Montgomery Duncan, beloved mother and wife. I felt the tears building, as I turned my head, and read. 'Hannah Montgomery, beloved Wife, Mother, Grandmother.'

I knelt down and unrolled the paper, and placed the white flowers on her grave next to a bunch of white roses, the card was from my father. 'Thank you for saving her.' I pulled a single white rose out of the bunch, and turned, and laid it on my mother's, grave next to my father's huge bunch of red roses. His card read,

'I will love you always, I miss you, John xx.' It just felt like too much for me, my shoulders shook, as my eyes blurred.

"Mum, Han, you are together again, and I miss you so much, I wish I was with you."

I placed a hand on each grave, and I shook as my tears filled my eyes, and deep bitter sobs flowed out of me. It was hard and painful, and tore at my heart, as I grieved for a mother I did not really know, apart from a few precious memories as a small child, and I grieved for Han, who was my world, and the most precious person in my life.

She had been more than a grandmother, she was a mother, a friend, a shelter from the pain of the world, she was my rock, and the only reason I had made it this far. Losing her, felt the like hugest pain I had ever known and felt, it tore at me, in ways even I did not expect. I felt so lost and so utterly alone without her, I had no idea how I would continue, I just sat on the grass rocking slightly between the two graves, with a hand on each of them, my face down, as the tears dripped off my nose.

I cried until I could not cry anymore, and I quietened down, as I looked at the white stone, with her name, and the tree of life symbol sunk deep into the stone.

"Han I am so lost, and I have been for a year. I wanted to come sooner, but it hurts so badly, I really need you, but the house is empty. Han, I need you so badly, I wish I had gone with you, so I could be with you and mum again. You always knew what to say, you knew the right words to lift me up and keep me going, what will I do now without you?"

I have no idea how long I was there; my tissues were useless; I had soaked them all. I stood up, and looked down on the flowers, in a strange way, I was glad to see my father had been. I was glad to see he missed my mum, it proved in some strange way he was human, I wiped my eyes on my sleeve, and took a deep breath.

"I cannot stay Han, not without you, I will come back for visits, but I cannot stay. It is too hard here without you at my side. I needed one of you, and both of you have left me. Forgive me, both of you." I stepped back from both of the graves.

"Goodbye Han, thank you for everything you did for me, I love you dearly and I will miss you so much."

I turned, wiped my eyes again and walked back towards the path, I saw the old figure of Mr Higginson stood watching, he gave a kindly smile.

"Miss Duncan, I am sorry to impose on your grief, I just wanted to say how nice it is to see you in the village. I saw your grief, are you alright, can I be of service?" I shook my head.

"I am fine Mr Higginson, my visit was long overdue, but thank you for such kindness." I wiped my eyes, the thunder rumbled in the distance, he gave a nod.

"May I walk back to the gates with you, I feel a storm is brewing?" I walked slowly along the path heading back towards the gates, the clouds in the sky were blowing in fast and darkening.

"If I may be so bold Miss Duncan, I could not help but overhear some of your words. Some in the village have commented how nice it was to see you again, are you really determined to leave again?" I gave a sigh.

"I am sure no one really understands, but without Han, I feel lost and adrift, my life in Exeter is not wonderful, but I know and understand the life there, there is nothing here for me now." He nodded and he watched the gates up ahead.

"I can full well understand how you would think that, but if I may, your grandmother had a full and active life here, I feel you are not fully aware of her life here. I may be wrong, but I feel there is more here than you realise, possibly things of far greater value than the life you live in Exeter."

He stopped and took my arm softly, I halted and looked at him, he had such a kind face and smile, and his eyes appeared filled with life.

"May I ask of you one thing, for as far as I am aware, you are still twenty one years old, and will turn twenty two shortly?" I gave him a nod.

"My birthday is in just over two weeks time." He smiled.

"Then there is still time. Miss Duncan, I ask of you one thing, and it would please me a great deal, if you would consider it, especially knowing of your uncles' intentions." If he wanted my attention, he had it, just the mention of my Uncle Pete, angered me.

"What do you ask of me, Mr Higginson?" His eyes met mine.

"Do not rush, you are still grieving, think carefully about the house and the land, and watch over it. All is never as it seems, and there are some who would bring chaos to this village and the land. I know of your studies, you know more than most, the importance of the land you own. Just promise me, you will consider everything fully?" It felt a little strange, did he know something I didn't? I felt a cold shiver run down my spine.

"I am here for a little longer, but I have a job and a flat in Exeter, I will have to leave at some point. Mr Higginson, you must understand the importance of Han, the cottage was her home, and I will never sell it, but my home was Han. She meant everything to me, and yes, I talked often with her of living here one day, but those plans always involved both of us sharing the cottage, it was never meant to be alone." He looked like he understood. I looked out over the landscape.

"I will never forget this place, how could I? Every memory of here, this village, these beautiful hills and the lake, they will always be with me, because here I was always beside Han, and I will never forget her, she was my whole world."

The clouds were rolling in, and large droplets fell from the sky, and hit the path, we turned and hurried to the gates, as the rain began to fall, I reached the mini bus, and he turned.

"Just think carefully Miss Duncan, it is all I ask, there is still time."

I gave him a nod as I opened the door, Shell gave a jump, she had been dozing. The sky filled with light, and then the thunder rumbled, and the rain intensified, and bounced down onto the roof of the bus. I clicked my seat belt, and started the engine, it was getting really dark, I switched on the headlights.

"Christ Shell, I think we need to get home fast."

I reversed, and spun the bus round, and headed back to the road that led down to the village, the wipers were going on their fastest setting, as the rain smashed into the glass. Shell leaned over and turned the blowers on, as the windscreen started to mist over.

"Jesus Emmy, does it always rain like this around here?"

I pressed the brakes; this hill was steep, and I had no intention of driving off the road. I was a little freaked out, never in all the years of being here, had I known the weather turn so fast, and driving in it, was frightening me, and by the look of it, it was the same for Shelly.

"Go slow Emmy, I want to make sure we stop at the bottom."

We reached the bottom of the hill, and turned left towards home, people were running around, pulling in their stands from the shops and taking shelter, the rain was bouncing up off the road, and I stared forward, as the wipers raced across the screen, to give limited visibility. It was so loud with the rain pounding on the roof, I had to almost shout.

"Shell, crack your window, I need to get the fog off the window!" I saw the fork in the road and headed right, the good thing was, this road was not travelled much, and so at least there was not heavy traffic.

The wind was rising, it was like a tornado the way it shook the tops of the trees and the bus. I drove along with my lights on full beam, it was so dark as the clouds thickened, and the lightening striking made us both jump in our seats. The crack of thunder was deafening, the wind howled through the gap in the windows, and blobs of rain would shoot through and hit my cheek, startling me. The bus wobbled on the wet road, and Shell grabbed the wheel to help steady us.

"Hell Emmy, I am frightened, I have never known weather like this." I saw the turning up ahead.

"Not long and we will be home, hang in there."

I was trembling, this was scary, and knowing my mum died in an accident in a storm, was in the back of my mind. I turned off the main road on to our long driveway, the leaves were blowing off the trees, and landing on the windscreen as they hurtled through the air. The wipers cleared most of them, but there were so many, and I couldn't see properly, I stamped on the brakes, and looked at Shell, as she sprang forward in her seat and then got pulled back sharply. The bus slid to a halt.

"This is insane, they are sticking to the window too fast, Shell I am driving blind."

The engine was running and the wipers slid over the leaves that were pressed flat against the glass, she looked at me, she was very pale.

"What do you want to do, we can try and make a dash for it,

but Emmy, that wind is insane, it is not going to be easy?"

I was not sure, the lightening flashed, and I could just make out the cottage. I leaned forward, almost onto the steering wheel, and slipped into first gear.

"Shell I will crawl in this if I have too, I am not sure I could stand up out there, look how the trees are bending, oh god, I hope the cottage is fine, it would break my heart if it got damaged."

I started to crawl forward in the bus, peering through the glass windshield, twigs and leaves smashed into it, making me jump, as the wind whistled down the side of the bus. I knew the engine was running, but the hammering of the rain was so loud, I could not hear it. The bus crept forward at a slow pace, my heart was pounding in my ears, Shelly was almost on the dash board, as she leaned forward to peer through the small gap in the leaves.

"We are almost there, the gates are open, and swinging, I hope you don't mind a few dints in the van?" I could just make them out.

"Better the bus than us Shell, those things are heavy, we rolled near them, as they came thundering round and swung out, I took a deep breath, and pushed on the accelerator, and floored it. The wheels spun, and we shot through, I saw the stone wall, swung the wheel and stamped on the brakes. Shelly bumped into the glass, as the gates behind us swung round. I sat back feeling panicked, my heart was thumping, and slipped my hand in my jacket pocket for the house keys.

"Okay, I think we go out through your door, and make a run for the cottage, here grab the keys."

I turned off the engine and lights, locked my door, and then slid back up the seat and pulled up my legs, Shell watched ready. She gave a nod, pulled on the release, and was suddenly dragged out of the bus and tossed through the garden gate, she landed with a crash and squealed in shock. The wind was so strong, I had no idea it could be like this, I watched as she staggered up to her feet, and half crawled, half ran for the front door.

I took a huge breath, and slipped out of the bus over Shelly's seat, the wind gripped my legs and almost dragged me to the floor, I clung to the top of the door and worked my way along it. I tried to pull it shut, but I was just not strong enough, I swung round the end, and pushed with all my might against the wind, my feet slipped as I pushed the bus door closed, and I hung onto the roof, then turned. My jeans were flapping round my legs, Shelly was struggling to put in the key, and stay stood up. I let go of the bus with one hand, and reached for the gate post, and the wind battered my body, I clenched my teeth, I honestly thought I was not going to make it.

I was terrified of being blown away, I could hardly see as the rain pelted into my face, and it stung my already red eyes. I felt desperate, and so frightened, I let go of the bus and grabbed the post with both hands, I could feel the wind on my legs, and my feet were slipping on the gravel. I closed my eyes, oh god, was this it, was this weather intent on killing me? I have no idea why, but I closed my eyes, and screamed out at the top of my voice.

"TAKE ME, I DON'T CARE, TAKE ME, TAKE MY LIFE, AND LET ME BE WITH HAN!"

The wind stopped, and suddenly there was silence. I opened my eyes; my hair was stuck to my face. I let go of the post, and wiped it off my cheeks, and out of my eyes. The clouds rolled back and the sun came through, I stood dripping, not really sure what had happened. My head turned, and I saw Shelly staring at me, her face was as white as snow.

"What the hell did you do?" She was shivering, I shook my head.

"Shell, I have no idea."

I looked around as the sun shone and the dark clouds drifted away, Shelly turned the key in the door and it opened, she stood just inside dripping and staring at me in fear, she took a deep breath.

"Emmy, you yelled at the storm and it stopped, what the hell are you?" I looked at her, not quite understanding.

"Shell, don't be stupid, no one can do that, it was just a coincidence." She shook her head, and I could see her shivering, as she dripped on the mat.

"Not from where I am standing, you bloody glowed white, and then it stopped." I frowned.

"Shelly, that is not even possible, don't be ridiculous."

Chapter Five

Lights

In the trees, on the edge of the island, the hooded figure sat low in the bracken, and smiled, as the rain dripped off his hood.

"Oh Han, you may have been right all along, her grief today has taken some of the darkness off her, and a little of her light escaped. I feel the time for our meeting is close, all she needs now, is to decide to stay, and show that to the light."

"But surely the light knows that?"

"No Esme, she told the old man she was leaving, and the light reacted, and yet, when she asked it to take her, and reunite her with Han, her light connected and everything balanced. I find myself fascinated by her."

"Everyone felt it, Felix ran away and hid, but I thought it was beautiful, all the others know she is here now."

"They do my little friend, they do indeed, and I think that could be a good thing."

I came downstairs rubbing my hair, having had a shower, Shelly stood in front of the fire, as it crackled and snapped, wrapped in a towel, she was sipping a whiskey. She had found a bottle in the kitchen, and was still shaking, she looked at me as I walked into the room.

"How are you, are you normal now?" I stopped rubbing and gave a sigh.

"Shell, chill out, I am just normal boring me, please don't go putting all your weird voodoo theories on me. I can assure you; I have never glowed in the dark." She took a sip of her drink, and blew out a long stream of air.

"Emmy, I know what I saw, maybe you are not aware of it, but

I did see it, honestly, I wish I hadn't."

I plopped down in my chair, it is funny really, I have always sat here by the window, I held the towel from my hair in my hand.

"Shell, I need everything to be normal, today was really tough for me, and as much as I resisted it, I finally did it. It was exhausting for me, then all the rain bullshit has just about maxed me out. Please, just drop it and stop walking on egg shells around me, you are acting like you are afraid of me, and it's freaking me out." She nodded, and looked down.

"Yeah, I am sorry, the rain freaked me out too, although you know, you are a great driver, I would have abandoned the car a lot sooner, and probably got swept away." I leaned back in the chair, and rested my head, and closed my eyes.

"I am glad you know how to make the fire up; I am so tired; I wouldn't have bothered."

"I didn't make it up, it was ready, so I lit it, didn't you make it up this morning while I was in bed?" I opened my eyes and stared at her.

"No... I thought you did it while I was in the shower?" Shelly looked back at the flames in the hearth.

"Oh crap, you see, I am telling you, there is some freaky shit going on round here, first food that does not decay, then fireflies in the woods, disappearing cloaked men, you glowing white, and now fires that make themselves. I am really going to hate myself Emmy." She looked nervously round the room and lowered her voice.

"Are you sure Han left?" I felt the cold prickles run down my spine, and the hairs on my arms lifted.

"Okay, shut up, I mean it Shell, just shut up. I am already way passed my freaked out level, just stop, I seriously do not want to hear this." I gave a violent shudder, and rubbed the hair on my arms back down.

"I am going to dry my hair, and open a bottle of wine, and forget today happened." Shell looked as freaked out as I felt, she sipped from her glass.

"Yeah, the only spirits I am interested in tonight, are going in this glass, I need to slip from reality for a while, it is way too messed up for me at the moment."

I sat and dried my hair, Shell was hungry, and headed into the kitchen she took the meat out of the fridge and started to prepare it. I finished my hair, and felt a little more relaxed. I headed upstairs to my room, found some clean jeans, and slipped on a t shirt, and walked to the window, and reached for the curtain, it was warming up again after the rain, and I could see the mists forming in the trees of the island.

I stood and watched for a while, I always felt so relaxed and calm looking at it, Han had always told me, it was where all her children lived. I never really understood what she meant, in all the years we walked over there, I never saw a living soul, were the trees her children? I suppose they were, had I not called the trees I planted in Scotland my babies as I patted the soil around them? My mind drifted to Han, as I remembered walking on the island, and listening to her talk.

"Oh, my Child, the land is sacred, that is the problem with today, people see the land only as a resource, which when managed properly it can be, but sadly they do not, they cut and burn everything, and they destroy and hurt the heart of the earth." I looked up at her.

"How does it hurt the heart Grandma Han?" She glanced down and smiled.

"Emmy my child, every plant, every tree, and every animal or insect is a life, and all life is sacred. See look at that huge Oak, it has thousands of other life forms that depend on it. If you cut that down or burn it, then all those other lives are affected, and many lose an important habitat."

"What is a habitat?" She gave a happy chuckle.

"For us Emmy, it is the cottage, that is the centre of our world, it is the centre of who we are, and we need it to thrive. Trust me, one day you will leave here, and go into the big world, and then and only then, will you realise how important it is. You cannot see it, but that cottage is your paradise, only when you have to leave it for good, will you fully understand that. When you kill the Oak, all the others who depend on it lose their paradise, and their centre."

"Why is it my paradise, Grandma Han?"

She stopped and crouched down, and her bright eyes came close, and she smiled as she placed her hand on my heart.

"Emmy, here is your centre, here deep inside you, there shines a light so white, it will wipe out the sun, and here in this place, is the centre of who you are. One day you will leave it, and your life will be fine, but deep inside something will always feel like it is missing. You will lose your sense of belonging, your mother did, and it was on her return that she had her accident, and she never made it home. Remember this Emmy, when you feel like you are alone and you do not belong, come home, for this will always be the place you truly belong." I smiled.

"So, I can come home and live with you?" Her eyes twinkled.

"This is your real home; this is the house you were born in. Emmy my Child, this is your centre, and you will always be welcome to live with me forever." I blinked, and was stood by the window lost in thought, my hand on my heart.

"Forever!" I turned from the window.

"Forever is not real Han, no matter what you thought, forever is a pipe dream." I left the room, and glanced at her door for a moment, then walked past it and headed downstairs.

I mucked in with Shelly, and together we cooked a really good meal, I had not eaten a huge amount recently, as Shell often reminded me, so with a steaming plate of beef, potatoes, carrots and cabbage, I feasted. Shell opened the wine, and we sat side by side talking quietly.

"You know Emmy, I like the silence here, I could really gather my thoughts and write here, is it weird that this place makes me really at ease?"

"I thought, it freaked you out, what with this year old veg, and strange lights in the forest, and my obvious bioluminescence in rain storms?" She gave a chuckle.

"I still say, I saw what I saw, but to be honest, I get why this place means so much to you. I could see myself living in a place like this and being really content." I lifted my glass, and took a sip of my wine.

"You know Shell, I am going to be leaving soon, I have work to get back to, I only have a week off work, but honestly, if you want to stay, you can." She put her fork down, and looked at me in a strange way, I glanced at her.

"What?" She sat back and lifted her glass of wine.

"You baffle me, Emmy." I stabbed a potato and slipped it in my mouth, and chewed.

"Why?" She looked at me, almost as if not believing me, she took another drink of her wine.

"You hate your job, you especially hate Harry, and you are always complaining how the flat is cramped, and yet you have all this, and you walk away from it. Seriously, how can you just up and go, and make out like you don't care. Emmy, this is your real home, it has been the centre of your life for years?"

I nodded in agreement, she was right, it was my home, and had been for years, but she missed the obvious.

"Shelly, Han was my home, she was the centre of my universe, and she is no longer here." Shelly got up and lifted her empty plate, she walked round the table to the sink and placed it in the bottom, and then turned round and looked right at me.

"Emmy, that is such utter bullshit, she may not be here physically, but she is here, her knitting, her pictures, her garden, everywhere you look has her stamp on it. Talk about a cop out, I have watched you for four years, and how your eyes just zone out, and you smiled to yourself, as you thought of her. That is the bloody point of this place, here you are still connected to her, you know you make a big deal about how important she is, and yet you are going to turn your back on her and walk away, how the hell can you do that Emmy, she left all this for you, to ensure she never left you?"

I felt shocked and swallowed hard, as the tears welled in my eyes. Wow, I had never heard her so forceful with me, was she angry, had I done something wrong? It hurt to hear her say it, I was not abandoning Han, she had left me, could she not see that? She gave a sigh and walked out, I heard the door to the stairs go, and then her footsteps as she walked up to her room, and I was suddenly left feeling very alone.

I gave a long sigh, God, today felt rough, I lifted the bottle, and refilled my glass, and then stood up. The sun was still shining, as I walked to the back door and unlocked it, I had not been out here yet. I stepped out, and it looked exactly as it always had.

The path led across the top terrace to the first three steps, either side, the wide flower beds were filled with lush green vegetable plants. Tall canes were covered in the green vines and bright orange flowers of the dwarf beans. Carrots were tall and fluffy, cabbages with thick with dark green, grey leaves, and chard grew in thick lush lines of yellows and greens, with thick red veins, that ran into the thick deep oval leaves of the spinach.

I had loved this garden so much as a child, I noticed the thin canes of the peas, I had spent hours at her side popping the pods and filling a bowl with fresh green peas. The smell of the damp earth surrounded me and filled my nostrils, it was such a deeply ingrained memory for me, of times filled with love and happiness.

I walked down the steps to the next terrace, with lines of raspberry, and strawberry, which were covered in small white flowers. I crossed to the next steps as I walked down the garden, heading down towards the lake, and the large circle of white brick, that led onto the long jetty.

I reached the steps and walked down, onto the wide thick stone paved area before the jetty, and the small wooden bench that looked out across the lake. I sat down and lifted my legs up, turning and pulling them up, so my knees came close to my chest, as I held my wine glass, and rested my wrists on my kneecaps. The sun from behind the house glinted off the water, which was a still as glass, and it was so beautiful. I stared out across the water.

"No one understands me Han, they have no idea how hard it is to be here. I wish you had waited a little longer, I did not want to say goodbye, not yet, it was not the right time." I felt so emotional, so conflicted as my insides swirled, and I felt a huge unrest boiling within me, it had been there for a year.

"I don't want to leave Han, I really don't, but how can I stay, how can I live here without you? They do not understand, they do not understand the joy, the love, the happiness I felt here at your side. Han, I want so badly to be like you, but I do not think I am strong enough. I love this place, it is my home, it is my heart, but I feel such a hole inside me where you used to be, and I do not know how to heal it."

I put my head down and the tears came, as I quietly sobbed alone at the bottom of my garden.

A cabbage leaf lifted up and Felix lifted a long thin finger to his lips.

"Shush!" Esme looked out with large bright blue eyes, and gazed in wonder, her voice was soft and very quiet.

"Felix... She is beautiful." He watched, holding up the leaf, he had tiny tears in his eyes.

"She is sad Esme, she misses Han like we do, and it makes me sad too." Esme gave a sniffle.

"I know, I feel it and it makes me dull with sadness, my shine is going." She pulled at a small dandelion leaf, and wiped her eyes, and gave a quiet sniffle.

"Emmy?" Felix gasped and dropped the leaf.

"Quick, hide, it's the fat one."

Shelly came down the garden towards me, I did not really notice until she sat down at my side, and put her arm round me.

"I am sorry Emmy, I was horrible, I should not have said that. I guess I am still freaked out after earlier, but it is no excuse, I should not have taken it out on you." I sat up, and she handed me a tissue, I took it and wiped my eyes.

"It is not you Shelly, it is me. I wish I could find the words to explain what being with her was like. Honestly, I want to, I really do, but all I can say is I feel this huge part of me that is missing, and I really miss it, I guess I am not dealing with it very well." She rubbed my back.

"It is early days Hun, hell, you have been here just a day, and be honest, your uncle did not make things easy on arrival, it is a lot to handle? Give yourself a day off Hun, and take it as it comes." I gave a sniffle, and took a drink of my wine.

"God Shell, I am so tired of crying, it is all I have done for a year. You were right by the way, I feel her presence all around me, but that is the problem, everywhere I look I see her things, it is like she is still here, just in another room." Shell gave a shrug.

"To be honest she is." I slipped my feet off the bench and swung round to her, and looked at her.

"How do you mean?" She looked at me, and her eyes looked so bright.

"If you think about it Emmy, her whole life is here laid out right in front of you, just she is in another place. You can call it a room, another plane or dimension, but her presence is still here. Do you not feel it, because I feel something all around you, maybe she is in a parallel dimension, but sat right at your side? I know you don't believe things the way I do, but if you ask me, she is right there with you, I feel it."

In a strange way she made complete sense, I could feel her, I had since arriving, and yet not being able to hold her and touch her, made it even harder to bear. I wanted to hold her once more in my arms, I wanted to look her in the eyes and tell her how much I love her, but she went before I could, and it hurt so badly, it was unbearable. Shelly made some sense to me, and in a very odd sort of way, it gave me comfort. I lifted a hand to her cheek.

"Thanks Shell, that helps, it really does." She smiled.

"I am pretty messed up in the head, but occasionally I make sense, I am glad Hun."

She looked round, and checked out the jetty and the steps, she frowned and turned back to me.

"I probably have had too much wine, but earlier, when you were out here, did you hear a quiet little voice, and it called me fat?"

She looked really weirded out, and I have no idea why, but I felt a quiver in my stomach, and suddenly I gave a gasp of a giggle, and I smiled. Then felt another giggle bubbled up with me, and I started to laugh, she looked so freaked out and funny. I laughed for the first time in weeks and it felt infectious, and felt nice. Shell smirked.

"It's not bloody funny, I know I heard it, honestly Emmy, I heard a squeaky voice calling me fat." I just laughed louder and pulled her into a hug, and laughed so hard. I did love her; she was a great and true friend. Shell gave a gasp.

"Honestly, I am still a twelve... Well just... Oh god, I have some sizest spook following me round, I need to diet, just to get rid of the bugger."

I sat with Shelly, as the sun fell slowly in the sky, and we both looked out across the lake, and I talked of my childhood, and the boat trips, and how Han taught me how to swim in the lake. I smiled, as I remembered all the problems, I had at boarding school, trying to swim properly, and how after a summer here, being instructed by Han, I went back to school, and in the first term back, I got a prize for being the second faster swimmer in the year.

Oh god, I had forgotten so much, as I tied myself to the loss I felt, but sitting there quietly in the back garden of Han's Cottage, leaning on Shelly with a wine glass in my hand, all of it came flooding back, and spilled out of my lips, as I told her of my life here, and the wonder that was my Grandma Hannah.

It probably sounds silly, but just remembering and talking, gave me a warmth inside, that seemed to radiate through me. Shelly sat smiling and listening attentively, and I could see how much she enjoyed hearing about Han. In a strange way, I wondered if this is what it had been like for Han, as she told me as that tiny young girl about her life? I too had sat like Shelly, watching, listening and smiling.

For me as a young girl, it had been one of the joys of my life, and even now, I remember everything she told me. In times of need, all I had to do was close my eyes and drift, and she was there, talking and giving me the sound advice I needed. Shelly was to a degree right, she was with me, she was inside me, and I wondered if that is what she had meant that day we walked in the woods when I was only eleven?

Was that what she meant about here being my centre? Did Han tell me all of this, just so one day when I was alone and she was gone, I would be able to return and use the memory of her to find myself again? Was that what she meant when she touched my heart and told me, it was all inside, was Han my light?

It was getting dark, and starting to get chilly when I picked up my empty glass, and side by side we walked back up the steps, towards the cottage door. Shell stopped as we approached it and took my hand, I turned and looked at her, she looked serious.

"Emmy, thanks for tonight, I loved hearing stories about her. I felt like you sharing these deeply important memories was a real privilege for me, and you know what? I found it touching and inspiring, and I think I understand you better now. I really am sorry for earlier, I was out of line, Han was pretty amazing."

I smiled, I felt better for it, I think it actually did me good, I felt a little less of the burden. I pulled her hand.

"I am glad you enjoyed it Shell, it was nice to talk about her, I think it did me good to remember her, and you are right, I felt her with me tonight." She smiled, and we stepped in through the door and I locked it behind us.

The cabbage leaf lifted up.

"Felix! I cannot believe you fell asleep, wake up, you really missed something beautiful."

"What... hmm... I am tired Esme." She gave a sigh, and dropped the leaf.

The lights were out, the house was locked, and I felt safe and warm in bed, it had been a really long day, and very emotional. I pulled my pillow close and hugged it, and felt my eyes flicker.

"Night Han."

"Goodnight, my sweet child."

Outside across the lake, the trees filled with tiny lights, the word was out, and all the Nairn had gathered on the banks, hidden under the ferns, and surrounded the cloaked figure, as they listened to Emily talk to her friend who Felix had told them was the 'Fat One,'

They sat silently, attentively listening to the stories of Han, and all of them remembered the long summer nights, when Han had told similar stories to the young Emily. For the first time in a long while, it felt like balance had been returned to the lake and the forest island, as families of Nairn sat close and quietly listened to the wisdom contained in the memories told by Emily of Han.

As the two girls walked to the house and entered to sleep for the night, Barrack turned to the cloaked figure.

"She has much light, and yet she wants to leave, I find this hard to understand. Can you explain to me, why one so powerful would not stay?"

The hood moved as he lifted a long stemmed pipe to his lips and lit it, for a brief moment, his long locks of grey were highlighted, and then disappeared as he drew a long draw on the pipe, and the bowl flared in red. He blew out a long stream of grey smoke.

"Barrack you are right, she does have as much light as Han, the problem is my good friend, she is not aware of it, and time is ticking. In fifteen suns, the time will expire, and if she has not claimed her birth right by then, we will have to move on, for we will not be safe here." Barrack looked out across the lake at the dark house.

"Her land is threatened, the light knows this, you must show her Master Sage Feather, open her eyes and make her see, for if she leaves, we shall lose everything. Our numbers have lessened, the Nairn will die out if we have no safe haven, the tall ones will take everything before they understand their folly." He pulled on his pipe and thought for a moment.

"Our time to cross paths is close, but I have to walk carefully. Han knew it would not be easy, it is my task to finish what she started, and I have my work cut out for me. I am aware Barrack, I am a watcher, I know the risks involved, and I will not risk the Nairn. I promised Han I would save her children, and I will not break my vow to her."

Shelly yawned and stretched on her bed, she lifted her laptop and slipped off the bed, and walked to the small unit next to the window. She put it down, and a twinkle caught her eye, she turned and looked out across the lake.

"Holy shit, there are thousands of them."

She turned, and hurried to her bag, she pulled out her camera, and then flicked off the bedroom light as it powered up. Carefully, she snuck back to the window, and from the side by the curtain, she leaned round with the camera and hit zoom. She stared at the picture on the digital screen on the back of the camera, not really sure what she was seeing.

She pushed the button, and the camera clicked, she pressed it again, and there was another click. She slipped back from the window, and sat back on the edge of the bed, turned the camera up, and flicked the settings button to view pictures. Clicking the menu and the side buttons, she enhanced the picture and increased the size, of what looked like a shimmering light. Her thumb clicked the small side button, the image grew on the back screen of her camera, she stared at the image and gave a gasp.

"Bloody hell, I finally got one."

As Shelly looked at the image on the back of her camera, she could not believe her eyes, the image clearly showed a picture of a figure, it was bathed all in white light, but had wings, and it was tiny, and there was no mistaking it. She could not believe her luck. After years of study and ridicule, she had the proof she had so badly sort, and smiled with utter joy.

"Oh my god, I did it, bloody hell, fairies are really real, I am not mad like everyone tells me, they are bloody real." She gave a little giggle, and fell back on her bed looking at the picture.

"They are not fireflies, they are bloody fairies, and there are thousands of them." Shelly had a thought and sat bolt upright on the bed.

"Oh my god, Emmy does not know… Han did, and she told her, but she did not realise, oh crap, the children Emmy never saw were actually fairies, she did not see them because she does not believe in them."

She stood up and walked back to the window and looked out, everything was darkness and the lights had gone.

"Oh crap, the light, the bloody light is inside her, but she is too hurt to realise, I have to find a way to get her to find her light. I bet Han was their guardian… Holy shit, Han is gone, it's Emmy, she is their guardian, and she does not know it." She turned round and grabbed her laptop.

"I have to find a way."

She sat down on the bed, and typed into her search engine, 'How to convince someone fairies exist?' A long list of articles came up, and she opened one up in a new window, and began to read.

"Please let there be some other lunatic like me out there who can help me, Emmy needs my help."

Her eyes, moved as she started to read, her mind was swirling as she began to understand the bigger picture, and things started to make sense to her. Her eyes followed the lines of text down, and suddenly she had a thought.

"Hang on… Do they think I am fat?"

Chapter Six

Confusion

For the first time in a year, I slept without dreaming, and I slept deep and long, and when I woke up, it was just gone noon. Shelly was up, and was sat in the garden with a coffee and her pad, painting with her watercolours. I stood back a little way behind her, and looked at her picture, she was painting the island, and to be honest, it was beautiful.

I took my coffee down the steps, and sat on the bench in the warm sunshine and sipped my coffee, I felt really good, more rested and stronger than I had for a while. I gave last night a lot of thought, Shelly's outburst, and then our long time sat on this bench, as I talked of Han.

It was strange, but telling her the stories of my life with Han, made me feel happy, and I felt some of the sadness and weight on me lift. Maybe saying goodbye at the graveside had given me some closure, I really was not sure, but today I felt so much better. I drifted in thought, holding my coffee in both hands, just staring at the island, behind me Shelly looked down at me.

"Emmy, if I ask you something, will you not think I am totally bonkers?" I blinked and came out of my thoughts.

"Too late for that Shell, I have always thought you were totally bonkers, what is on your mind?" Her voice was a little hesitant, and lower than normal.

"Emmy have you ever seen anything sort of strange round here?" I turned and looked up at her, she looked a little puzzled, as she stared at me.

"Like what?" She looked awkward.

"Okay promise you will not think I need committing, but last night I saw thousands of lights over there on the island, so I got my camera, and zoomed in, and took a couple of shots." That did not sound so strange, she took more photo's than a Japanese tourist, so that was not at all odd for her.

"Why is that strange, you take loads of photos?"

She put her pad down, got up, and walked quickly down to me, and sat just in front of me on the bench. She leaned in and lowered her voice.

"Emmy, when I looked at the pictures last night, I saw the shape of people in bright white light, and yet this morning when I checked the camera, the pictures were just black, with nothing on them. I know it sounds mental, honestly, I swear they were fairy like people, but this morning... Gone, no proof at all, I am not lying Emmy, I had them, and now they have just gone completely, and I am a little freaked out."

I did not know how to respond to that, I loved her to bits, she was an amazing friend, but she was also sounding like a nut job.

"Shell, you sound mental and messed up, seriously, if you had taken the shots, they would still be there, are you sure you actually had them, and it was not just wishful thinking? I hate to point this out, we had a lot to drink last night."

She sat back and gave a long sigh; she appeared really down about it. I watched her as she put her head down, and stared at the floor, I reached over and put my arm on her shoulder.

"Shell, don't take it to heart, look you thought it was something, that is all, why is it so important?" She shook her head.

"Emmy, I love you, it is why I am here trying to be supportive, but honestly, neither you or Pam have ever really understood the work I am trying to do. I don't think what I do is nonsense, and there are a lot of people out there like me, sadly you and Pam are not one of those. I know this seems silly and irrelevant to you, but honestly, listening to you talk about Han last night, I knew, she would understand a part of me no one else did." That caught me a little off guard, I really did not expect that, I struggled to find the right words.

"Shell, it's not that I don't believe you, honestly, I think you really do believe all of this. It is, I just find it hard to see how in this world, no credible evidence has ever been found to support it. Honestly, Han told me a lot of fairy stories and I loved them, but Shell they were just stories." She stood up and gave another long sigh, and shook her head.

"Forget it Emmy, I should not have said anything, just forget my utter stupidity and ignore me, I am obviously an idiot."

I watched as she walked off up the steps, and snatched her pad off the floor, then lifted her paints and walked inside. I felt guilty, but what else could I say to a theory that fairies lived on an island I had walked on thousands of times in my life? The facts were, I had never seen any evidence, how could she possibly believe anyone who would be sold by a photo taken whilst drunk?

There really was nothing I could do, and my mind was already filled with the millions of feelings I had felt by simply coming home, to a home without Han in it. I got up and walked slowly up the garden, there was so much I had to do, so many feelings I had to confront, and in the back of my mind, two places were playing on me. I still had to confront her study, and her bedroom, so far, I had been afraid to go in them.

There was no sign of Shelly when I arrived back in the house, I wandered into the living room, and just looked around. The disturbing thing for me, and was actually the hardest thing, was nothing had changed. The house looked and felt exactly as it always had, and yet the lack of Han, changed nothing. It has to be the most unsettling thing of all.

I am not sure, is it me? Maybe in the back of my mind I had expected something different, but the fact remained, that her passage away from this world, had changed nothing. Everything was exactly as it had always been, and in some weird way, I think I wanted there to be something different, some huge change that actually showed that she was no more. Yet here I was, surrounded by memories of her, and the only problem was, that even with so many reminders, she was gone forever.

In a way it really opens your mind, and makes you stop and think. This cottage, the flowers in the garden, her knitting, her pictures, those little pot statues that meant so much to her, none of it mattered anymore. Han had lived a life, and gathered around her a life's worth of small things, insignificant to others, but they had meaning to her, and so she treasured them. Now she was gone, they just felt like objects, unimportant to anyone else, and only relevant to a life that was no more.

I have to ask, is that what it all comes down to, a house filled with things that no longer mattered, because the owner had passed on? We spend our lives obsessed with the gathering of things around us, but to me, stood here in the remnants of Han's life, it all felt pointless. None of these things that meant so much to her, could hold her here, all of it was now just the clutter of what was. Their only relevance now, was I knew how Han felt about them, I was the only living soul who could lift them up, and equate them to their original meaning, and if I left, they would no longer serve any value at all.

It was a startling thought, I was the only thing left, that made them worthwhile, without me, they were useless, is that why she left them to me, was that her idea? I had always thought this place would go to her daughter Jessica, I knew it was once all promised to my mum, but she had died. I never thought for one moment she would leave all this to me, and I was struggling as I tried to do what was right for Han, but also right for me.

The truth was, I did not want to go back to Exeter, but I did not want to live here without Han, and I was caught in the middle looking for a reason to do one or the other. For almost a year, I had stayed away and avoided coming back, my life in Exeter was not great, but there were moments of joy and happiness, especially living with Shelly. This was my home, or at least the only real home I had known, but it had always been Han's. I never really owned it, I just lived here because it was convenient for my dad, as he jetted off to build his metal and glass monstrosities across the planet, so could I really call this a home at all?

I gave a small sigh of conflict, I suppose it was mine now, I really had to accept the fact that all of this belonged to me. I had to do something with it, but I was so unsure about everything, and my feelings were not really being that helpful at the moment, as they swirled around in mixed emotions that would peak and bring me into a crash of tears and pain. The one thing I really needed, was the one thing that was gone, Han was the person I went to for advice, her wisdom had always guided me, so who do I ask now about how to deal with her death?

I noticed Shelly outside, she was sat on the wall painting, and

I thought I was best leaving her for a while, I walked towards the doorway, and saw the door to Han's study, for a moment I paused, was I really ready to do this?

I took a breath, yes, I had to, it was why I was here, and a small part of me hoped there would be some sort of answers to help me understand me, my situation, and how to deal with all of this. The one thing I had always known about Han, was she prepared for everything, and I had to wonder if there was something important to guide me behind the door.

I lifted my hand to the latch, it gave a soft click as I pressed down, why was I being so hesitant? I had always just breezed into the room with a huge smile, to greet her sat behind her desk. Somehow today, I was not sure breezing in was possible, I felt nervous about it and my stomach felt off. The door swung open, and I stepped in.

In many ways, growing up, this had always felt like her room, she had a lot of book cases, her work table, where she would do crafts, or sew, and at the other end was a large oak desk. I have sat at the side of the desk all my life, in the small soft chair, as Han showed me her picture albums and talked of my mother. I felt the tug at my heart as I walked round, everything was so familiar, but it hurt to see it now.

It occurred to me, that I was not unsimilar to my thoughts, had I not grown up like an empty room? Han filled it with the only memories I have of my mother, which was the memory of sitting here, listening to her talk of her daughter, Amelia, my mother.

I stopped at the bookcase that held the large brown photo albums, there were so many, I think she recorded all her life, her daughters, and mine. I stood staring at them, wanting to lift them out, but afraid to do so, I had seen the ones with my mum a hundred times, and yet for some strange reason, today I was afraid of them.

I took a deep breath as I looked at all the shelves, stacked with books, on herblore, crafting, plants, gardening, and wine making. I smiled, it was like a library for off gridders, any one into self sufficiency would thrive with this room filled with knowledge. I saw the long line of picture albums, all brown and thick, my stomach twisted just looking at them, as I understood, she would never look at them and read them out to me again. I swallowed hard, trying to keep the swirling emotions that were coursing around inside my stomach from bubbling up.

I turned and faced her desk, her chair looked worn, and faded, it stirred me deeply as I remembered the day. I sat next to the work table and watched as she stitched the fabric squares together to make the new seat cover. It had looked so bright and vibrant, and yet now it looked dull, worn from years of sitting and talking to me sat on it. I walked to the chair I had always sat on, and sat down, my mind was swirling with thoughts and memories, this was harder than I had thought, as I sat staring at the empty the seat, which had once contained Han.

It was like I could almost see her, just sat there, her eyes so bright, her worn kind face, and that wonderful smile, as she spoke softly to me, about my life and my mother. The pictures flowed into my mind, as I remembered.

"Oh Emmy, Child, you are so like her, you have her eyes and her face, and many of her qualities. She had such a big heart, and an infectious smile. It was impossible to be around her and not smile, she was a joy to raise, I see her every day in you."

"I do not feel much joy in me at the moment, my life feels like such a mess. I have so many doubts and no direction, and I am obviously lousy at picking men." She gave a little chuckle.

"Emmy, you dwell too much on the negatives, life was never meant to be easy, in many ways it can be very cruel, and you probably understand that better than most. Look it is the small things that bring the joy, life does not have to be perfect, to be honest, I have always felt that it is within all the imperfections that you see the wonder of everything. You are so busy looking at all the pain and misery, you miss the real wonder of everything. There is so much magic in this world, and yet people are blind to it, not everything is black and white, there are many shades of colour in between, you just need to open your eyes and see them, because that is where the light lives."

"I don't understand Han, what magic? Han, I hate my job, my flat is a mess, everything keeps breaking down, and Ken turned out to be arse. I just feel so lost and alone, all I have is you, I am not sure what I would do if I lost you too." Han smiled and took my hand, and gave it a squeeze, and it felt so warm and filled with life.

"Emmy, do you remember the story of Master Sage Feather, and how he walked in two worlds, and led the Nairn with Barrack out of the forest that burned?" I gave a sigh.

"Of course I do, you have told it me all my life. He met with Barrack when the developers moved in to cut down the trees and plough it all up to build a town. They started a journey to their sacred lands, and faced many dangers before they finally found a safe haven in the land of the light." She gave a happy smile and her eyes twinkled.

"Their life was harder, because few could see and understand them, and along the way, many were lost. Their journey was a harsh one filled with pain and fear, and yet, they walked into the light and found sanctuary and protection. Emmy we all have a journey to make into the place we belong, and yet it is only when we embrace the light, we find our true place in life. It appears to me that you spend too much time looking into the darkness, look for the light, and find your joy." I gave a sigh.

"That is not that simple, it is hard to keep going at times." She gave a nod.

"Yes, and the journey of the Nairn was the same, but they looked for the light in everything, and it was that, which guided them onto the right path. There is light in all darkness, you just have to seek it out, not everything is as it looks." She smiled and squeezed my hand.

I gave a jerk and opened my eyes, and just for a moment, I felt her hand on mine. I blinked and looked round the room, it was getting dark outside, I felt confused and disorientated. I sat forward and rubbed my eyes. I got up out of the chair, and made my way slowly towards the door, I was so tired, exhausted, and yet all I had done for weeks was keep drifting off and napping. I pulled the door and walked into the living room, and Shell gave a terrifying scream and dropped her plate, I jumped out of my skin.

"WHAT THE HELL SHELL!" She stood looking white in the face, shaking and holding her heart.

"JESUS EMMY, YOU SCARED THE LIVING SHIT OUT OF ME. I THOUGHT YOU HAD GONE OUT FOR WALK."

Her eyes were huge in her face, as she stared from her very

pale face, and I could not help it, I smirked.

"Some bloody ghost hunter you turned out to be, God Shell, if you are going to be this jumpy all the time, maybe you need a calmer line of work." She took a deep breath and smiled.

"Yeah, I get it, I am just a basket case." I gave a long sigh.

"Shell, look, I am sorry, it is just me at the moment, this is so hard for me, honestly I am starting to wish I had never come back here, nothing at the moment makes any sense to me."

She knelt down and picked up her plate and her half eaten sandwich, and looked up as she lifted it back onto her plate.

"Yeah, I get it, honestly, I do, just ignore me, and sort yourself out. If you want my advice, you need to just sit and chill out a little, and stop putting even more pressure on yourself." She stood up with the plate and looked at me.

"Emmy, do not be in such a rush, take your time and think things through. I know I never met Han, but if you ask me, I think she would have sat you down, and had a long talk with you about why she thought it was important to leave all of this to you, and not her eldest daughter. Emmy if everything you have ever talked to me about her is true, then she had a bloody good reason for giving all this to you, and honestly, walking away from all this without thinking about a why, to me appears foolish."

I nodded and gave a smile, she made a really good point, after all my aunt Jessica was actually her daughter, my mum had died, and actually Shell made a lot of sense, why did she cut her out of the will and leave me all this? I had a thought as Shell turned to the kitchen.

"You know I never thought about that Shell. I must admit when Mr Higginson came to see me that day at the hotel, I just assumed Jess had got everything, and I was so shocked when he handed me all the papers. Why did she leave all this to me?" Shell shrugged and she stood in the kitchen door.

"You got to admit it is strange, although considering who she married, that had to be one of her reasons, but honestly, I think there is a lot more to all of this than you realise, the problem is, who can we ask? I am going to make a coffee... Do you want one?" I followed her through to the kitchen and sat down at the table, Shell filled the kettle and clicked it on, she turned and gave me a smile.

"I know I come across as flaky Emmy, honestly, everyone I have ever met has pretty much told me, but you know what, I may appear bonkers at times, but I really do believe that not everything at times is how it appears." She turned to spoon coffee into the cups.

"I wish I had met Han; I am sad in a way because I think she had a handle on things, and understood a lot more than she let on. I really think I could have learned a lot from her."

I had to smile, she would have loved Han, and in a way, I think that is probably why we became such great friends, in a strange sort of way, she reminded me of her at times, I watched as the kettle boiled and she poured it out.

"You would have loved her fairy stories, she had so many, I grew up listening to her telling me such wonderful stories, I remember telling her that she should write them all down and put them in a book." Shell turned to me with the coffees.

"Why didn't she?" I gave a chuckle.

"She told me her stories were only meant for the ears of few, and she would never put them at risk by writing about them. She really believed in them Shell, to her they were not folklore, they were real. Like you, she believed with all her heart in them, they were not the tales from a book, they existed and lived amongst us." Shell sat down and shrugged.

"Stranger things have been known Emmy, you know the world today is so quick to dismiss this stuff, I mean, look at you, what was it you said, no credible evidence? Think about it, if you were a mystical being, honestly, would you put your home and life at risk by giving evidence to people who would exploit you?" I smiled at her as I lifted my cup.

"I love your total belief, I really do, you remind me of her at times, but look at the facts Shell, everyone slips up and makes mistakes. No matter how much you would want to hide, someone would discover you eventually." She nodded.

"And yet today, people still argue about the Bermuda Triangle, hunt the Yeti, investigate ghosts, Loch Ness, even Roswell, and although there are small amounts of evidence to suggest these things are real, everyone shakes their head and denies them. Think about it, what if the masses have been conditioned to be blind, what if science knows, but those who did the research realise the danger they put all these things in and covered it up to protect them? You know, I think Han was right, maybe she too felt like she had to protect them, maybe she saw them as innocent like children, and decided the world was too cruel for them, so hid them." I felt a cold shiver run down my spine, and I shuddered and felt the goosebumps rise on my arms.

"Children, why would you say that?" She shrugged.

"Innocence is always portrayed as childlike, I love kids, they do not cloud everything with the bullshit of life, they look at things honestly, and they are open minded enough to just accept the facts. I think kids are lucky, the cruelty of life has not broken their spirits, and so they are open to everything. Look at it for what it is Emmy, even you once believed in them." I sat back in my chair.

"Shell they were just stories written by people like J M Barrie and Lewis Carol, they were made up for entertainment. Han did the same, she used them to help me get over my mother's death." She sipped her drink.

"Barrie wrote Peter Pan after seeing the magic and purity of children, and seeing the magic in them. Maybe he knew of things, and this was his way of sharing the tales, without revealing them, he was after all Scottish, and that land as you know has many tales from the past. I mean, look at Robert Kirk?" I frowned.

"Who the hell was he?" She gave a snigger.

"He wrote probably the greatest book on fairies and fauns, and other so called mystical creatures, called the Secret Commonwealth. He was a clergy man in the seventeenth century who travelled all over Scotland documenting the stories and experiences of people who had encountered them. It is regarded as a bible for those who believe."

Wow she really did know a lot about this stuff, I was actually a little bit interested, she had never really spoken about it in depth, and shamefully, even though I have a signed copy at home, I have to confess, I have not read her book. Shelly stared at me from over her cup, I looked at her.

"What?" She moved on her seat and looked a little uncomfortable.

"I have no wish to piss you off, but can you answer me one question honestly?" Okay, so that bothered me, I looked at her trying to work her out, but failed.

"What do you want to know?" She put her cup down.

"Did Han ever lie to you... You know, about anything at all?" So, that bothered me, why did I feel she was about to spring a trap? I shook my head.

"Never, she answered every question I ever asked her honestly, even when she knew I would not like the truth. No, Han never lied to me." Shell nodded and sat back in her seat.

"So why don't you believe her stories?" I felt shocked as I looked at her lost for words. I had no idea at all how to answer that, Shell shrugged and lifted her cup up.

"You know Emmy, you didn't believe in ecology until you studied it. Before that you did not understand the truth of how everything is connected, but that did not make it a fairy story. Once you opened your mind to ecology, it was like opening a doorway to the truth, what if Han opened a door few know about, and discovered a greater truth?"

I cannot deny, she had me, I bloody knew it was trap, she had me cornered and she knew it, no matter what I said, I was caught. She knew how complete my belief in Han was, she knew I could never think ill of her, and in knowing, she hit me with the one question I could never answer. She smiled.

"It is okay, you do not have to answer, but you know what, just think about it, sometimes we are so stuck in the darkness, we fail to see the light. That is why the world lives in denial, because no matter how you live, we live in a world of blindness and we are conditioned to write off the unknown as superstition or myth. I like to look for the light, but because of that I am seen as a fool, I would imagine, Jessica saw Han the same way you and Pam see me, but it is okay, I am used to it." I was lost for words, I simply did not know what to say, she winked.

"I love you still though." She smiled and I nodded at her.

"I love you too, you are all I have left now Shell, and it does mean something you know?"

Chapter Seven

Cold Reality

As the darkness fell, across the water at the heart of the large island, set within a rough built room of stone, with an open doorway, within a circle of large stones, Barrack sat on his stone seat. In front of him was a stone table filled with offerings of food, and small bowls of oil with lit wicks, that illuminated the gathering. Around the tables edges sat a further twelve members of the Nairn. He looked round at them.

"She has the light, and it is strong, but time is running out, we have decisions to make." The others all considered the point, a woman of extreme elegance and beauty looked at him across the table.

"I realise the time is limited, but it has not run out yet, we still have time." Barrack gave a nod.

"I am aware Aubrianna, Han always assured us that she would embrace the light, but her life has worn on her, and she has walked into darkness. I fear that she may come to the light too late to save us." A sturdy looking Nairn in green who was sat crossed legged on his seat looked at them both.

"What does Master Sage Feather think, after all, he walks in both worlds, and he was the one who last spoke with Han, he must have more understanding of this creature than we do?" Barrack gave a sigh.

"I will not deny, he has doubts, but like us he saw the light within her and he understood it's full potential. He agrees Han was not wrong, but with the loss of her mother and then Han, her light has been buried deep. It concerned him, she wanted to give up her life so freely, and asked the light to take her." Chandak understood.

"Then it is time to prepare, we must wait as long as possible, but when the day of renewal ends, we will have to move. If she does not embrace the light, our time here is over, for we all know the peril that awaits us if she leaves."

"The fat one knows and understands us." All of them looked to the doorway, Barrack gave a sigh.

"Felix Dillberry, this is not a meeting for the young, and I may add, for the ears of those who cannot control their tongue." Esme peeped round the corner of the doorway, and Aubrianne gave a long sigh.

"Esme, you know of the importance of this meeting, why are you here?" She stepped out with her head down, and her voice was low.

"I am sorry Mother, I did tell him, but he would not listen and I was trying to stop him." She looked up with large sad eyes. "Honestly, I was trying." Barrack gave a smirk.

"Esme, I have warned you many times of the perils of my grandson, I have told you, leave him, if he wants to endanger his life, then that is his folly." She nodded, as Felix frowned.

"I am sorry My Lord, but please, he is right, we heard her talk, and she does understand us." Chandak appeared interested.

"Just how exactly is he right?" Esme turned to Felix who shook his head looking worried, she turned back to the members of Nairn Council. Felix looked panicked.

"We heard her." Felix gave a gasp and looked even more worried; Barrack stared at Felix.

"Tell me Felix, just how exactly did you hear her from all the way across here?" He swallowed hard and his legs started to tremble.

"Does that really matter? She understands like Han did, and Emily trusts her, but does not understand her. Grandfather, the fat one can help us." Barrack sat back in his seat and gave a gasp of exasperation.

"Felix, what have you been told about crossing the water?" He put his head down and Esme gave a little squeak and started to tremble.

"Not to." Barrack nodded.

"And yet once again, you ignore sound advice and have gone over there. Felix, Han is no longer there to protect you, as she once did. Until Emily decides, you cannot leave the island." He nodded and looked at the floor.

"I miss her, I stayed hidden, but being there is comforting, and Emily is so beautiful and filled with such light, she reminds me of Han." Aubrianne smiled a soft smile.

"We all miss her Felix, but you have to understand, it is no longer safe there." He nodded and two tiny tears hit the floor.

"I just wanted to help, I don't want us all to leave here, I love our home, and I don't want to leave the memory of Han behind, I loved her so much."

Esme swallowed hard and nodded. Barrack looked round at the others, it was clear they all felt the same way, the thought of leaving here would be painful for everyone. He looked at Felix.

"We all miss her Felix, and she was loved dearly by all of us, for she was a very caring watcher of our people, but you cannot disobey us, because we have to remain hidden to survive. As the sun rises, you will report to Marmaduke, and serve duty on the walnuts." Esme gasped and Felix looked up.

"But that will take forever, they are so hard to crack." Barrack looked at him sternly.

"That is the price of disobeying the family, go, work, and learn your lesson." Esme looked terrified as she looked at Felix, she reached out and took hold of his arm.

"Felix be careful, Zakary got flattened by one falling, and I don't want that to happen to you." Aubrianne smirked, and put her head down, Barrack tried to hide his smile.

"Go... Sleep, and report at dawn."

Felix nodded and turned with his head down, as Esme took his hand and they walked away into the ferns. Veda chuckled as she looked at Barrack, she was probably the oldest member of the family.

"He shows some wisdom for his younger years, and be honest, he is not unsimilar to a certain leader of the council was when he was that age?" Barrack gave a frown.

"I was a little wild, but never that irresponsible." Veda chuckled as she looked at him and he smirked. "Well maybe... Just a little." She looked round the table at all of them.

"The other one is close to Emily, you know, Felix may have a point?" Barrack sat back in his seat to consider it.

"We have never involved outsiders, I am uncertain as to if we can trust her. I think I will need to speak with Master Sage Feather, I cannot risk our survival."

Sleeping did not come to easily, maybe it was because I had dozed off earlier, or maybe it was Shelly and the things she mentioned. It bothered me that she mentioned children, and it bothered me even more that she had asked me if Han had ever lied.

I had always had such an open and honest relationship with Han, I had never once lied to her about anything. Every time I had asked her something, she had always sat with me and carefully talked to me, telling me the truth of my mother and father. She was even really honest about her dislike of my Uncle Pete, her voice sounded in my head.

"He is a snake, never trust him, that man lives for wealth and has no insight into the wonder and value of those who live around these parts. I banned him, because he would not give a moment of thought to the lives of value we have here with us. If he thought he could hoodwink me, he would pull the house down whilst I slept in my bed to build something he could make a profit on. I still find it difficult to come terms with the fact that your mother was safe once she left here, and yet the moment she announced to the family she wanted to come back and live here, whilst your father worked in Africa, she met her end."

I was only around eight at the time, but I remember asking her what she meant, and she looked at me with sad eyes, and tried to smile, as she reached out and cupped my cheek.

"Ignore me, it is just the ramblings of an old woman. I see things others do not see, and I know far more than people realise, he cannot be trusted, and that is all you ever need to know my sweet child."

I lay in the darkness as my mind swirled, what was she trying to say to me, was she trying to tell me something that would really devastate me and was trying to soften the blow? I had dismissed it at the time, but actually as I think about it, I was never going to understand back then, and yet now, suddenly her words have become relevant. Was that her plan all along, did she somehow know that as I sat in bed in the middle of a dark night in my early twenties, having endured the pain of losing her, I would awaken?

"Oh god, I am going to drive myself madder than Shelly." I sat up in bed and rubbed my face, and took a long intake of breath.

"I think I am slowly losing my mind... Yep, I am talking to myself, oh hell, what am I going to do, this feels like it is just too much to handle?"

I slipped out of bed, and grabbed my cup off the side, and headed for the stairs, it was pointless even considering sleep, my mind was now wide awake. I walked slowly and the stairs creaked, I did not want to disturb Shell. I reached the bottom of the stairs and turned into the living room, Shell was sat by the fire, staring into the flames, she turned, saw me, and lifted a finger to her lips.

"Shush!" Okay, so I panicked a little, as I stared at her. I walked over and looked down at her, and I have no idea why really, but I whispered.

"Shell, what the hell are you doing sat in the dark?" She stood up and leaned in close keeping her voice down.

"Emmy, I am not sure about you, but honestly, there is a whole lot of weird around us at the moment." I frowned.

"What do you mean, I am not weird, I am just sad, and actually, considering things, I think that is pretty normal." Shelly shook her head.

"Think about it, the gas, power, and water on, fresh veg in the rack, a fire that made itself up, strangers with guns and lights in the trees, it is freaky. You know I was thinking, who replanted the garden, it makes no sense? Well, not to me, and to use your own words against you, it is not credible. So, I was turning it over in my mind, and I figured it was one of two things, either, someone has been coming in the house without us knowing..."

"Shell, let me just warn you, if you say Han, I will push your head on the fire." She smirked.

"I was going to say magic, Emmy ghosts do not make fires or pick and wash veg and then put it neatly in the rack." I nodded.

"Okay, I can live with that, because honestly, the last thing I need is Han's ghost." She shrugged.

"Well at least you would be able to see her and talk to her, I mean, someone coming in to stock veg and make the fire up freaks the shit out of me. Think about it, I sleep naked." I gave a shudder.

"Oh, please just don't, my mind is already so full, I cannot handle your weird shit as well." I took a deep breath, and tried to calm down, my heart rate had just increased, and I did not want to encounter anything unnatural.

"Okay, I get it, but why sit by the fire alone?"

"I was sat listening out, to see if I could hear anything."

"Like what?"

"You know, footsteps, doors opening on their own, that kind of stuff."

"Oh shit, I really do regret talking to you now, I should have stayed in bed, you are freaking me the hell out." She giggled.

"Look on the bright side, down here you know what is going on, up there, alone in your bed, you would have no idea if I was murdered, and then dragged to lake." I felt a jolt run through my system, and my voice got a little squeaky.

"Why the hell would you be murdered? Shut the hell up Shell, you are freaking me out." She shrugged.

"Emmy, we are in the middle of nowhere, be honest, your uncle could have us wacked, and that lake out there is deep, with the right weights, we would never be found." I stepped back.

"Okay I am not talking to you now, I came down to sit calmly with a coffee, and enjoy the peace, and now I am a bag of nerves. Shell, I have always felt safe here, and so thanks, now I am filled with terror, I am not sure I will ever sleep again." She giggled.

"It is okay, all the doors are locked, I checked, if anything gets in, it will not be of this world." I looked at the kitchen door.

"Shell, I love you, but I do wish you would shut the hell up, because there is a part of me that trusts you, and now there is a shadow at the back door." She spun round fast.

"WHAT!" I giggled.

"That is what you are doing to me, welcome to the freaked out club." I sniggered. She gave a sigh and turned back to me.

"Don't bloody do that, I am already scared shitless." I shook my head.

"Are you like this on your ghost stakeouts?" She nodded.

"Yeah, pretty much, it is a fine line, I want proof, but I am terrified to prove I was right. It fascinates me, and I know they are just residue energy, but honestly, I am not sure how I will handle seeing one."

I had no doubts in my mind at all, I never wanted to see one full stop, and I was never even going to remotely place myself in a situation where I would. Honestly do they exist, I have no idea, and I also never want to find out? My life was hard enough as it was at the moment, and I had no intention of making it harder. I walked towards the kitchen door, the moon was bright, and the whole of the kitchen was bathed in light, so I left the lights off, and walked to the kettle and lifted it to shake it.

With the kettle filled, and the red light on it illuminating the work top, I spooned out the coffee and sugar, as the water rumbled within the kettle. I was focused on the task and not really paying attention, and so missed Shelly as she walked backwards into the kitchen. The Kettle clicked and I turned for the fridge, and noticed her, she was stood still, staring at the front room windows. I swallowed hard.

"What's up?" She glanced at me.

"Something out front is crunching; I think someone is coming up the drive." I felt the goose bumps run up my arms.

"Shell, if this is a piss take, just stop it." She shook her head and looked at me.

"It is not, Emmy listen."

I left the fridge and walked slowly down the kitchen to her side, I stood frozen at her side, it was slow, but yep, that was a footstep there was no doubt. I gripped Shell by the arm.

"Oh shit, what do we do?" She took a deep breath; her face was white.

"The door is locked, so we are safe, but honestly Emmy, I am shitting myself, it is three in the morning, who the hell would that be?" I could feel my legs trembling, and had to take a deep breath.

"I have no idea, but whatever it is, I am not sure it is a good thing for us." Shell nodded. Both of us jumped as we heard the creak of the gate, I gripped Shell tighter.

"Oh shit, Shell, they are coming in." I felt her hand on mine, as she reached across her stomach to me.

"Emmy, the door is locked, unless they have a key, we are safe."

Both of us stood in the doorway to the kitchen frozen with fear, as we heard the gate open and then quietly close, someone was in the garden. Shell was trembling as my ears sharpened try to pick up any kind of sound at all, there was a quiet thud near the door, I breathed in and swallowed, they were right outside. My ears strained as I heard a weird noise, almost like something unscrewing, I mean, that could not be right, there were no bolts and screws outside to undo.

Shelly tightened her grip on my hand, she was holding her breath as both of us just stared, unable to understand what was happening. My heart almost stopped, as a black shadow suddenly shot past the window and Shell jumped.

There was a squeal, a thud, and then whimpers and thumps, and I could hear the sound of running water, this was driving me insane, I have no idea why, but I had just about had enough, I pulled my hand out of Shelly's.

"Oh, screw this, I have bloody well had enough."

I walked across the living room towards the door and reached for the key. Shelly panicked and ran across to me and grabbed my hand as it closed round the key.

"Jesus Emmy, what the hell are you doing?" A muffled grunt came from the other side of the door. I pulled back on the key.

"Shell, that out there is not a spook, it's bloody human, and I want to know what the hell is going on. I am done with this shit; this is my only safe place and no bugger is going to ruin that for me." I shoved the key hard into the door and turned it, then yanked on the handle and it swung inside. I stopped feeling confused.

"What the hell?"

Outside the door was a large white can, lay on its side and the contents were spilling out onto the path and flowing down to the gate, Shelly wrinkled her nose.

"Holy shit, is that petrol?"

I leaned out of the door, stepped into the porch, and looked round, and my heart gave a thump. I stepped out onto one of the paving stones.

At the bottom of the drive, the man in the long hooded cloak held a guy against the fence, and was binding him with rope to it, he turned back and looked at me, I could not really see his face as it was shaded by his hood.

"STAY INSIDE, AND LOCK THE DOOR, THERE ARE MORE." I panicked, what the hell was going on. Shelly grabbed my arm.

"You know what, freaky as all of this, listen to him. He backed you up last time, and honestly, if he says get inside, yeah, I am going to listen to him." She pulled hard and I staggered back, I felt angry.

"Shell, who the hell is that against the fence, and why was he pouring petrol outside the house?" Shelly closed the door and locked it, and then leaned back against it breathing hard. She was as white as ghost and trembling.

"You know what, I don't want to know, because honestly, what I am thinking at the moment is too scary to contemplate."

I nodded, and leaned over and clicked the light on, I was done with darkness, I wanted light. Both of us stood shaking just staring at each other, my heart was pounding, as I began to understand some of it, and I really did not want those thoughts in my head.

"Shell, it was petrol, and this is a thatched cottage?" She nodded looking terrified.

"Trust me, I was there five minutes ago, and honestly, I am freaking the hell out, Emmy, someone wants us out of here." I felt the chills run down my spine, and I shuddered.

"Shell, if we were in bed, the house would have burned down before we could get out." She nodded.

"I know Hun, I just do not want to contemplate that, because honestly, that frightens me in so many ways."

The gravel crunched and the gate swung back, both of us tensed up, and then the same rough voice of the guy in the hood came through the door.

"Are you still there?" I nodded, and Shell smirked, my voice was a little strained.

"Yes, I am here."

"Emily... I am a friend of Han's; you are safe now." Shelly watched me carefully; I was shaking like a leaf.

"How do you know my name, and who are you?"

"I told you, a friend, no harm will come to you here, I will not allow it. I promised her I would look out for you." I gave a gasp.

"I know your voice, are you the man who phoned me about her?" It was quiet for a long moment.

"Yes." I gave a huge sigh of relief, and felt tears rush into my eyes.

"Can I talk to you; I really need to know she did not suffer?" I gave a huge sob.

"Not yet Emily, not tonight, but that time is coming, I promised her I would. Do not upset yourself, Emily not everything is as you think, and we will talk." I took a huge breath.

"Thank you... Thanks for being here and helping us, we were so scared, so thanks." The tears ran down my face with sheer relief, as Shelly watched me. Just knowing Han had prepared in advance, helped.

"It was my pleasure, Emily, do not give up, she loved you so deeply, think of everything she ever told you, all of your answers lie there. Try and sleep, I will take care of this for you, goodnight." I felt a huge sob come up in my throat, and my voice went really high.

"Thank you."

Shelly moved forward and pulled me into her arms, and I felt the huge surge inside rush up, and I broke down, as Shelly pulled me into her arms and just held me as I shook and wept into her shoulder. Everything felt out of control, and I was struggling to understand any of it, and all I needed was someone to sit and talk to, knowing they understood all of it.

"Let it all out Hun, you need to."

It took a while to calm down, and Shelly made the coffee, both of us were unsettled, and even though tired, neither of us wanted to go to sleep, so we settled down on the sofa facing each other and quietly talked.

It felt strange to know that someone had tried to pour petrol over our door. It was pretty frightening to think someone would actually do that, and even though I did not want to admit it,

Shelly clearly had no problem.

"Emmy, do you think it was arranged by your uncle, you know he has hounded you for a year to get this house, I don't know him, but you do, tell me, is he capable? From where I am sat, he is the only person I know of that would want to hurt you."

In truth I felt he was capable, but I really did not want to admit that, I mean, how could anyone admit that their own relative would want them dead? What bothered me most, was Han, she had mentioned she felt he had something to do with my mum's death. Was that what she was trying to tell me, would my uncle really consider taking a life to get his hands on this property? The thought terrified me, and I really did not want to think about it, I looked at Shell.

"Honestly, I don't know, and in a way, I never want to. Shell, that is just too scary to contemplate, I mean there is no love lost, but killing someone, that is pretty bloody extreme." She shrugged.

"This land is worth mega millions once developed, I reckon that is worth killing for, especially if you are cold as him." I shuddered.

"Okay let's talk about something else, I am nowhere near calm enough to even consider that." Her eyes sparkled, as she leaned forward.

"So, at least our mysterious hooded man is not a ghost, that is sort of comforting, at least we know he is real, and he may have the answers you seek." I nodded.

"I hope so, I am certain that this is the guy she called Randolph, and if he is, Han knew him for a very long time, so maybe he does have the answers. The problem is, how do we find him?" She sipped her drink, as she watched me.

"If you ask me, I don't think we will have to, I actually think he will find us. I am not sure this is a guy who advertises his whereabouts, especially considering he dragged off an arsonist. It is probably better you never ask him about what he has done. Although, I won't deny, I am pretty interested in meeting and talking to him, I think many answers lie with him, and I for one, would like a few of my own solving." I gave her a nod.

"Yeah, my list is growing, I hope he can help, I have so many doubts, some advice would be really useful about now, especially in regard to Han's wishes." She smiled.

"I won't deny, it's creepy, but I am glad he is watching out for us, well we know he is definitely watching out for you, so I am staying right at your side. It looks to me like Han expected this, and she prepared, although, I wonder what he meant by all is not as it seems?"

Yeah, I was wondering about that too, I cannot deny, it bothered me, just what exactly did he mean, we were alone in a cottage in the middle of nowhere, and Han was definitely gone. I was there at her funeral, so what was he referring to? The questions in my brain were growing, and I honestly was starting to think it was going to overload.

Shell gave a long sigh and closed her eyes and leaned back on the cushion, she was tired, it had been one hell of a night. I felt weary, but I cannot deny, I am so glad she came with me, I do not think I would have made it without her.

Chapter Eight

Randolph

It was late morning when I woke up feeling stiff, Shell was still flat out. We had the blanket off the sofa back over us, I assumed she had pulled it on to us in the night. I slid out slowly so as not to disturb her, and lifted our cups off the floor.

I walked into the kitchen stretching the aches out of my back, I still felt really tired, but I ached so much, I needed to move and loosen my stiff limbs. I stood by the kettle and gave a sigh, what an awful night. I still felt shaken, in a way not really knowing or understanding what was going on was getting to me, and as much as I did not really want to know to truth, I think just to stay sane, I needed to know.

I made a coffee and walked to the back door and unlocked it, I stepped out into the sun, it was a little breezy, but it felt nice, as I sat on the step and looked out over the water towards the large island. It is strange really, because I have sat here a thousand times, and yet sat here today as I sipped my coffee, I thought it looked richer, even denser with trees, than it had ever been.

My mind was once again full, as I sat staring at the sunlight glinting off the water, in all truth, it felt so surreal that someone would actually try and burn down Han's home. As much as I did not want to admit it, Shell had pretty much vocalised my thoughts of last night, it was clear, the most obvious candidate was my Uncle Pete. I gave a sigh and looked down at the floor, where a lady bird was running across the paving to the flower bed, and I had to ask the only question I could think of. It came out of me in a soft voice.

"Why is he so damned obsessed with this place, I have told him, why has he been so bloody persistent, when I have constantly told him no?"

"Emily?" I looked up and turned to the side of the house near the old woodshed, Heidi smiled.

"Sorry, I looked through the window and saw your friend asleep, and the back door open, so I came round. It is alright, isn't it? When I heard about last night, I thought I would just check to see if you are alright." I frowned at her, and then shook my head as I stood up.

"Yeah, it is fine Heidi, what do you mean when you heard about last night?" She walked down the side of the house towards me.

"Well, you know, the young man who tried to set fire to your house, he was found tied to the garage door this morning with a note? Tom called his brother in law, who is the local police officer round here. Have they not been to see you yet?" I shook my head.

"No, not yet." She looked very concerned, and gave a sad smile.

"It is terrible, nothing like that has ever happened round here, how are you two, it must have been terrifying for you both?" I nodded and stepped back into the kitchen.

"I am making another coffee; do you want one?" She followed me in as I returned to the kettle, filled it and sat down at the table, I clicked it on and turned to her.

"To be honest, we stayed indoors, I have no idea who it was who came to our help, they spoke through the door to make sure we were fine. We were both pretty shaken, and if I am honest, I was too afraid to go out, so I was not aware they had taken the person who did it to town." She gave a nod.

"You poor girls, you have enough on your plate with coming back after the loss of Han, and now this, have you any idea of who would want to do such a dreadful thing?" I gave a long sigh and the kettle clicked, I turned round to spoon out the coffee and grabbed a second mug.

"I have my thoughts, but honestly, I hate thinking them." I poured the water into the cups.

"I will not deny Emily, you may not say it, but be honest, both of us have a good idea who has moved heaven and earth to get this place. I mean honestly, he pestered Han so much she banned him, and even then, he still tried. Emily he was seen in the village a few days ago." I grabbed the milk from the fridge, and wanted not to think about him. I poured it into the cups of coffee, and grabbed the sugar bowl, and turned.

"I cannot believe he would burn the house down, just to get rid of me." I slid her coffee towards her, and sat down, and watched as she spooned out the sugar into her cup and stirred it, she looked up at me.

"Really, I would not put it past him, he can be ruthless you know Emily? You have been off the scene for a long time, but I can tell, you, after the Jenkins farm incident, no one here likes or trusts him." I sat back.

"I have not heard about that, what happened?" She lifted her cup.

"Your uncle was working on the property at the side of old Mr Jenkins farm, it was well known he had offered Jenkins a lot of money, but he had turned down the offer, and would not sell. Your uncle put a lot of pressure on him, and you know he was not a young man, apparently, the brakes on the brick truck failed, and when the driver climbed out, it rolled off through the fence, down the hill and went crashing through Jenkins farm house, it ruptured the gas main, and up it all went. Mr Jenkins only just got out alive, he was quite badly hurt." I swallowed hard.

"Holy shit." She nodded.

"Indeed, Tom used his big tow truck to pull the brick truck out, and according to him, he felt the brakes had been tampered with, he swore blacks white the airlines had been spiked. Han at the time was convinced, she actually told me, it was just like Amelia all over again." I felt a jolt to my system.

"My Mum... You know Han warned me about him, I always thought she suspected my mum's death was not an accident. I never really got her to talk about it, she always brushed over it and just warned me about Pete." She put her cup down on the table.

"Emily, you suffered enough, she always wanted to protect you from the cruel aspects of life, she never forgave Jessica for marrying him. She warned her again and again not to marry him, and so did your mum, but by then it was pointless. She was too in love with the glamour of his lifestyle, and to be honest, she still is. She hardly spoke to any of us at the funeral, and just looked down her nose at us all." I really did not know what to think.

"I am sure Heidi, this is all fiction crime, and the sort of things you read in books, but Pete, the guy is a fop. I mean yes, he is arrogant and conceited, but risking people's lives, I really am not sure. Heidi we are talking about his wife's sister, I am no fan of Jess, but honestly, her sister, it sounds way to farfetched." Heidi smiled.

"You are so like her, always looking for the good, but listen to me Emily, never let this place go, especially to him." I lifted my cup and took a swig.

"I have told him already, I will never sell this house, it is Han's."

"Emily, it is yours." I gave a sigh and sat back.

"It will always be hers to me, I know I have the title deed and everything, but to me, this will always be her home, the place I came to feel safe." She smiled at me.

"You know I remember the day Han told your mum she was leaving the house to her and not Jess. That was when the little tea shop was open, we used to meet for coffee every few days when she was home. She was preparing for her wedding, and she told me when Han mentioned it to her, she told Han not to, but to pass it on to any children she had. Emily you were born two years later, it is like she knew she would have you. The first time I saw you, I mentioned it, and she told me Han agreed, and the paperwork was to be done. That was the last time I saw her, she went home to John, and sadly when he got all those big contracts from abroad, she decided to come home for a while. I was really looking forward to it, she was my best friend, sadly, she had the accident on the way here, and, well, you know the rest."

I took a huge breath, I felt yet more emotions rise up within me, and tried to swallow them back down.

"I have never understood why she married my dad, all I have ever heard is how caring and loving she was, and honestly, he is cold. I have never really understood that." She shook her head.

"Emily, he was not cold then, oh, he was lovely, we were all jealous of her getting him. John was quiet, thoughtful and so caring, he doted on her. Emily, trust me, he loved her so deeply, they really were a perfect couple."

"You see this is what makes no sense to me at all. I have spent my whole life being avoided and dismissed, it is like he does not care one bit about me. I mean, he fobbed me off on Han to raise, he has taken no responsibility for me at all." She gave a soft nod at me.

"Emily, don't blame him, losing Amelia broke him completely, he was such an organised man filled with life and laughter, and yet when I saw him after her death, it was like all the joy and happiness had been sucked out of him. I can tell you now, he came here for a few months and Han helped a lot, Emily, he was not capable of raising a child back then, he was utterly broken. Han was the one who offered to look out for you when he finally went back to work, and if you ask me, he booked so many foreign jobs, simply to hide away and grieve. I am not sure really, but maybe it was easier on him to avoid coming back, you know, you are her double, it cannot be easy for him." I put my cup down.

"Probably not, but has he ever thought about how easy this has been on me?" She clearly understood.

"Yes, I do understand, and on the few occasions we speak, such as their anniversary or birthday, I always tell him he should spend some time and talk. I really think it would do both of you good, but not yell and scream at each other, actually talk. You know, in a strange sort of way, he might actually listen to you now." I frowned at her.

"How so?" She gave a chuckle.

"Emily, you are so like her. You look, sound, and think exactly like her, honestly, it is a little unnerving. I am sat here talking to you, and I cannot deny, it has pulled at my heart, because I have missed her so much, and just sitting like this, it is quite a challenge for me. Hell, you even stand and make coffee like her, it may be a long shot, but you know, he may listen to you now, what is there to lose?" I smirked.

"Yeah, I can see that, but how the hell do I pin him down long enough to talk?"

"That is easy enough, it is her birthday soon, and be honest, you know where he will be."

Shell woke up and staggered into the kitchen, as I sat talking to Heidi, she rubbed her eyes and made a coffee, as Heidi looked at me.

"So, when will you be leaving?" I gave a sigh and stared into my cup.

"I am not sure, I have a lot more to do here first, and after last night, I am a little rattled about things." She gave a nod of understanding.

"Emily, I hope you don't mind me asking, but why, why leave all of this, you know she told me often that it gave her a sense of security knowing you would be here?"

Shell flopped down in a chair, and sipped her drink as she looked at me over her cup. I could almost read her thoughts, I looked at Heidi.

"Everything is up in the air at the moment and I really need to get my head straight. I know people do not get it, but being here without her is not that easy for me, and I have a lot of soul searching to do, because let's be honest, I am truly alone now." Shell frowned.

"No you are not, you have me, and I am not going anywhere." I smiled at her.

"I know Shell, but all of this, and how I feel about it, is a decision only I can make, and at the moment, things are kind of crazy. I need some space to come to terms with everything, and once I do, I will decide." She gave a nod and sipped her coffee.

"I don't get it, you love this place, I have seen it, and you hate your flat and hate Harry even more, especially now that weasel is talking to Peter and Jessica. I do not see your issue, you have cash, and this amazing place, and yeah, I get it, you have a lot of memories here, but in time they will mean everything to you. I may be wrong, but I think your heart is here, and you can hide it all you like, but eventually, you will have to admit it." I gave a slight smile, as Heidi smirked.

"Shell, I will do this my way in my time." She shrugged.

"Fine by me, I love it here... By the way, we have no bread, will we be shopping any time soon?"

Heidi had walked here along the side of the road, she told me it helped her stay fit, but I had to shop, and offered her a lift back. I asked Shell to stay back at the cottage, I was nervous about leaving it unattended. It was a nice day and she was happy to stay, drink coffee and do more sketching out front, so she would have a good view of the road.

I made a list and jumped into the mini bus, and Heid climbed in at my side and we set off back. I had the window down slightly, as it was getting quite hot, as I drove along slowly chatting about the town, shops, and how much it had changed since I was a child. We arrived in the village and I parked up near the garage, and Heid gave me a huge hug.

"I have really enjoyed today, Emily, you have reminded me of a lot of happy times, thanks." I smiled as I gave her a squeeze.

"Yeah, it has been nice, thanks for coming, you are always welcome when I am down here." She gave a sigh and smiled.

"I am here if you need me, you know that don't you?" I nodded.

"Yeah, thanks." Heidi headed back to her shop, and I walked past the garage, Tom came out wiping his hands.

"How are you, nasty business last night?"

"I am okay, it was pretty scary, but we are fine." He gave a nod.

"Our Bob has him now, although he was being pretty tight lipped, Bob will more than likely pop round at some point for a chat." I gave a nod to him.

"I am around a little longer, so the next few days should be alright, I have to get on, I need supplies." He smiled.

"Aye, Han did a regular trip, well as long as you are alright, that is all that matters. See you around." I gave him a smile.

"Yeah, see you."

I walked along the street, it does not change that much, to the far end where there is the only store for miles. The doorbell pinged as I walked in, and lifted a basket, and walked onto the aisle to find the few things we needed.

I liked the village store, I always had, it was like half supermarket, and half locals supplied, there were shelves of pickles, chutney and jams, and a small cake counter of freshly baked cakes, all done by Mrs Rachel Hannity, the store owner. It was quite a big place, it looked like three shops had been converted into one, and it had newspapers, magazines, some kid's toys and bit of hardware, as well as all the aisles of tinned and packet foods.

Han did most of her own preserving, and we had a pantry stocked to the brim at home, but I grabbed some tinned baked beans, fresh eggs, milk, and headed for the baked goods counter, Rachel looked up and gave me a big smile.

"Emily, what a lovely surprise, oh, it is so nice to see you. I was sorry to hear about Han. How are you, it cannot be easy for you?" I gave a smile.

"I am doing alright, I am managing, it is not easy at the moment." She looked at me all sympathetically and sad.

"Oh, bless you, it is nice to see you, it has been too long." I nodded.

"I know, it was not easy to come back, too many memories." I could feel the emotion building inside. "Have you got two farm house loaves left?" She turned to the shelf behind her where there was a row of loaves, and grabbed two and wrapped them in paper.

"She is really missed, she was so important to village life, will we be seeing more of you?"

You see this is the problem with small towns and villages, they never ask one question at a time, they layer them, and slip them into four or five comments as they dig for the gossip.

"I am not sure yet Mrs Hannity, I still have a lot to sort out. I have not really decided what my future holds, I just want to get everything sorted out first." She handed me the loaves and put them in my basket.

"Yes, I would imagine it is not easy for you, bless you, but you know, you will always be welcome here, it is after all your home and where you belong." I smiled.

"It is nice being back for a visit, and to see everyone again, thanks Mrs Hannity."

I walked towards the checkout counter, where a young man tilled in my goods with a smile, I am not sure why, maybe it was the tight jeans and the jumper. I slipped off my back pack and put my stuff in, I carried the loaves in my hand. I paid and he watched me walk towards the door, he had hope in his eyes, but yeah, he could hope, I was not walking into that nightmare again, I was done with relationships.

I sauntered back to the mini bus, and gave a sigh as I looked around. I used to think this was the most perfect place, and yet as I looked around, I was no longer sure. Was it simply the lack of Han that dimmed my view, just knowing she was no longer a part of this? I did not know, although, my mind had so many questions and riddles in it, I was not sure I really understood anything about me anymore.

Shelly sat on the wall in front of the garden, as she sketched the trees in the woodland in front of the fence. There was a tall larch separate from the pack, and she loved the way the branches swept down towards the floor, almost like weeping hands of green fir. She looked up, to look at the tree, and then down at her picture, as her hand moved with skill, sketching the lines of the branch.

It was really warm, and she was enjoying herself, at her side was a glass of white wine, and a packet of chocolate chip cookies. She got the angle of the sweep of the branch right and glanced up at the tree, and there stood in front of her, was the tall cloaked figure.

"You are good." Her heart jerked as she shot to her feet, dropping her pencil, as she gave a squeal of alarm.

"JESUS BLOODY CHRIST, YOU SCARED THE LIVING SHIT OUT OF ME!"

She felt her heart beating inside her chest, and she caught her breath, and took a few good inhales of air to calm herself.

"Sorry." He bent down and lifted her pencil, and handed it back to her. Shelly gasped for air.

"You know, for a paranormal investigator, you are a little bit skittish?" She took the pencil off him, as her breathing started to regulate, she looked at him.

"Are you bloody well surprised? Have you ever heard of footsteps, you know it helps announce your arrival, you should try them?" He smiled, and held out his hand.

"I am Randolph." She looked at his rough hand with tanned skin and dirty finger nails, it was obvious he worked on the land.

"You know, I hate to be impolite, but if I shake your hand, it will be solid won't it?" He gave a chuckle.

"I can assure you; I am very solid; I am Han's game keeper." Shelly took his hand carefully and gave it a squeeze, it was quite solid.

"Nice to me you, I am Shelly." He smiled again.

"I know, I have read your book, it was quite illuminating." She frowned.

"You have read my book?" He nodded.

"You are Shelly Parkinson, author of 'Folklore and Mysteries of the Scots,' are you not?" She looked surprised.

"Yeah, that is me alright, I hate to be impolite, but you do not strike me as a book reader of my sort of genre. I would imagine, off grid living, building log cabins, and hunting your own dinner would be more yours." He gave a chuckle.

"I could probably write them, so you are not completely wrong."

His eyes were dark, and his face lined and tanned. His long grey hair rested on his shoulders under his hood, and yet his smile was kind and sincere. Shelly looked him up and down.

"You are the guy from last night aren't you, you have quite a distinct voice, very deep, and yet warm and friendly?" He gave a nod.

"Yes, that was me, as I said, I promised Han I would watch over Emily, and by the look of things, she was right, and it was required."

Shelly sat back down on the wall, she felt no fear of threat, well not now her heart rate was calming down, and he did sound very sincere.

"Did Han think Emmy would be in danger?" He gave a nod.

"Miss Parkinson, this is a very special and precious land, which holds many secrets, and it was her wish to protect it always. She dedicated her whole life to watching over it, and she knew of the threats, and whom it would come from. Emily is not really aware of the full story, she thinks this is just an ordinary place, for it was here that she was raised, but she was unaware of many things here. Han wanted more time, so that as Emily approached her twenty first birthday, she could open up all of the real truth and secrets of this place, for there is a very important role for her here, which is the legacy she inherited from her mother." Shelly nodded.

"I won't deny, there are unexplained things here, and I have seen things here that make little sense, so I suppose in a way, I can believe that." He smiled at her.

"I know you have seen them; you have no need to hide from me, you are the reason I am here now. I know you believe, although I would like to point out, fairy is a loose definition, and you were wrong about them being in Scotland, they were forced to leave." She gave a gasp and her eyes opened wide.

"Oh my God, they are here, this is where they came, I always thought that was an old wife's tale to throw people off the scent. They really were guided away from that land because man was building everywhere." He gave a sincere nod.

"They were indeed." Shelly breathed in and wafted her pad in front of her.

"Wow... You have no idea how happy that makes me, just knowing they are safe gives me joy." Randolph gave a nod.

"Miss Parkinson, you cannot write about this, it is my job to protect them, as it was Han's. If the truth gets out, they will scatter to the winds, and it would place them in great danger, no one must ever discover their whereabouts, the trust I am placing in you is great." She nodded.

"Yeah, I get that, I really do, you have no fear, most people think I am a basket case anyhow, but I will never speak about their location. You know I hate to point it out, but my book is sold in the myths and mysteries section, not many think they are accurate." He suddenly looked serious.

"Miss Parkinson, have you ever heard of the watchers of the light?" She frowned.

"It rings a bell, I did hear something a while ago, aren't they a people who walk in two realms, one the living world, and the other the light realm, or secret commonwealth? If I am right, and I am a bit sketchy on this subject, but their job is to keep the balance and protect the unknown from discovery, or something like that?" He gave a broad smile.

"You are actually almost correct. Walkers of the light come to power in their twenty first year, where they are offered a role watching one of the many unseen lines. They are humans of great ability, who have had bestowed upon them at birth the gift of light. Han was one of them, and one of her daughters was set to inherit a role to maintain the balance. With her demise, Han kept the balance in hold, but sadly, that came at a high price, and the strain it placed on her, brought forth, her early demise." Shelly took a deep breath.

"Emmy's mum." He gave a sad smile.

"It is such a shame; she truly was a beautiful soul." Shelly understood.

"You say the balance was kept in hold, does that mean without Han, that everything is out of balance?" He took a deep breath, as he watched her.

"It is, like all things, just as there is day, there is night, and where there is light, there is darkness, and those that prey on the light, do so, because those they watch over hold many gifts that man desires. Miss Parkinson, one such child that was taken from the light was Emily's aunt Jessica, but a fatal mistake was made, because the power within her was limited, as Amelia was the one destined for the light. The man who prayed on Jessica, and tried to discover the truth of her light, miscalculated, by assuming it was the first born child, he assumed wrong."

Shelly was starting to get the picture, and understand more than she thought she would.

"Peter is the one of the darkness preying on the light, and once Emmy's mum died, he thought he was home free, but Han fought him, and made sure he never got onto the land, which actually, explains why he was so persistent with Emmy this last year."

Randolph gave a nod, he was pleased she understood, surprisingly, Felix was right about her. Shelly looked into his dark eyes, as if trying to read them.

"Okay, that makes sense to a degree, so these gifts man desires, what are they that makes them so important?"

"Think about it, what does man take from the land that can cause a rush of greed and desire, to enhance the life of the greedy?" She shrugged.

"Well, many things, jewels, metals, and even the timber, all of them create wealth and value to the lives of the greedy." He smiled.

"Those are some, but there are many things in the realms of light of great value for those who would count the paper money. They are rare in this world, but they hold great power in the light, which is why those of the light are drawn to them and keep them hidden, for within the light, is also the force of many lives. Miss

Parkinson, over the span of man, these places which are sacred, have grown fewer in number, and as man discovered them, great numbers of those in the light were wiped away, the few that remain have great power, but if they fall to the greed of man, many will die, and the hidden lines could be wiped out forever, they must be protected."

"Yeah, I have read some things around this concept, so what is it you want, is that why you are here?" He shook his head from side to side.

"I have time, but even my days are numbered, I need to restore the balance, that will make up for the loss of Han, and then find a replacement for me, the only problem is, a walker of the light must choose their role before knowing of it. It must be a decision made freely in their own heart, so that their light will be tied to the land they walk on, and time is running out here." Shelly suddenly understood.

"Oh Christ, you are talking about Emmy, but she has lost her faith, she does not believe in any of this, and her birthday is a couple of weeks away." He smiled.

"Which is why I am here talking to you. She cannot know of her task, but she must choose to remain here of her own accord, and then claim the realm and her task here to protect the land she owns. Miss Parkinson, once she chooses, she cannot leave this house." Shelly understood.

"Okay so that bothers me, because this place is so important to her and she loves it deeply, but without Han here, I am not sure she will stay, it is very painful being here with all her memories and Han's things. I am not sure she will choose to be here."

"That is my problem, and why I am talking to you, Miss Parkinson, I know from your book, you understand the worlds I walk in, and so you know what is at stake. Before her twenty first year ends, she must choose to remain, and then walk in the light, if not, many souls will be lost, and the number is dwindling with each passing year."

Shelly understood, she really did understand this more than most normal people ever would, her problem was Emmy had lost all faith in her beliefs and herself. She had lost everything of value to her in her life, and at the moment, Shelly could see the impossible odds that Randolph faced. She took a huge breath.

"I will do what I can, but at the moment, the odds of her staying, especially after last night, I would say are pretty slim." He gave a nod and stepped back, and looked to the road.

"The people of this land will be forever in your gratitude if you can aide them, I feel her approaching, we will speak again, say nothing of our meeting." Shelly gave a nod and turned to the road where she heard the mini bus coming, she turned back to Randolph.

"You better dissap... Where the hell did he go? Oh hell, this place is just getting weirder." There was no sight anywhere of him, the mini bus came in through the gates, and Shelly smiled as Emmy drove up.

"Great, after that, I really need a sandwich."

Chapter Nine

Home?

It was nice to be home, and I felt settled a little as I packed away the shopping, Shell helped and made us both a cool drink. It was getting hot, and I pulled off my jumper. I could feel Shell watching me as I opened cupboards and put tins away, I turned and looked at her.

"What?" She gave a shrug and smiled at me.

"Nothing much, I just like how you know where everything goes, I can see how used you are to all this, it really is your home." I closed the door.

"It's Han's home." She leaned against the table.

"Yeah, keep believing that, you may convince yourself one day." I lifted my glass.

"What is that supposed to mean?" Shelly looked me right in the eyes.

"Emmy, who are you trying to fool? Hun, I get it, she has gone, but you know what, you have talked for years about how much you love her, and how important she was to you, and yet look at you. Emmy, she wanted you to have this, it was her dying wish, do not tell me that means nothing to you because I don't believe it."

Wow, talk about out of nowhere. I took a deep breath, as she watched me, I felt so mixed up, so confused, and so God damned lost, I really had no idea of what to do. I gave a sigh.

"Shell, do you think I do not know that? Christ Shell, I have spent a year agonising over it. I love this place, and yes, for me this has always been home, but Shell, she was always here, she made this more of a home, hell, she was home."

Shell pulled out a chair and sat down at the table, she lifted her drink and sipped at it, as she considered it. She looked at me, and honestly, I really did not want to hear her words, because as flaky as she could be, ever since I had known her, she always had those moments of sanity that cut through me and dragged me back to reality, and I somehow felt that was about to happen again.

"Emmy, stop pissing about and make a choice. Look, the way I see it, you hate your job, you hate Exeter, and you need time. Emmy this is a massive thing, did you honestly think you could just run down here and deal with everything in a few days? No matter how many shades of Han you paint this, it is still the place you have seen as a haven, a sanctuary, and the place you have called home for as long as I have known you, and you know what, it still is. Losing Han is terrible and painful, honestly, I get it, I do, and if you want my advice, I would say the only way you can deal with that properly, is by being here. I mean, hell Emmy, you have spent a year in the flat torturing yourself about her death, and it has solved nothing."

Yep, I knew it, she was hitting me with facts, and I hated it. I leaned back on the cupboard and looked down, I was tired, and weary, and felt the emotions bubbling up inside me, my voice lowered.

"Shell, she was all I had, I don't want to live here without her." Shell stood up.

"Okay, so the jetty and lake are there, walk off it and kill yourself and be with her, you might as well be, and let Peter bulldoze the place and kill everything here, because that is what is going to happen, unless you deal with your shit and stop him."

I felt my breath catch in my throat and looked up, as the tears rushed to my eyes.

"How could you say that Shell?" She shrugged.

"Why not, you have thought it? Emmy, you have always run back to Han, well you know what, there is nowhere to run now, and whether you like it or not, this time you have to stand and face your life. I am staying here, I have cash, I will pay rent, but if you are going back to Exeter, you will be going alone. I am going to stay and make sure Peter stays the hell off this property, this place for me is magical, and I aim to write here. I fancy a walk, Pam told me the pathways are beautiful, and I want to photograph them. Join me if you want."

She walked out of the kitchen and headed up to her room, and just left me, and I had no idea what to do. I stood staring at the table unsure of everything, and that was the problem, I had always thought I would have more time with Han. I just assumed she would always be here, we never expect someone to leave us, we go through life with that security that if all else fails, they will always be there for us, but it is a lie we tell ourselves.

My mum was married at eighteen, had me at twenty two, and was heading home three weeks after her twenty sixth birthday when she was killed. She planned to live here for five years, with trips out to see my dad, and Han like me, naturally expected her daughter to come home, but she never made it. It must have felt the same for her going through the hell of losing her child having all of my mums' things there in her room as a constant reminder, which could not have been easy.

I suppose in a way I filled the void, she had me to raise, which she did until I was six, and then I went to private school, and lived here at term breaks. Shelly was right, this really was my only home, well, I had the flat, but for me that had always just been a temporary thing, I had always intended to sell it when I moved on. I snapped out of my thoughts as Shelly appeared with her camera bag, I looked up at her.

"I am sorry Shell, this cannot be easy for you, I hated what you said, but you are a good friend." She nodded, and gave a sigh as she looked at me.

"I hated saying it, but honestly, I think Han would say the same thing... Do you want to join me? I think both of us need to just get out in the air and take a pause, and clear our heads, last night was pretty scary, and I am still a little freaked out."

It was a good idea, I grabbed my travel mug, and filled it with cold juice, and then locked up and joined her. Up the side of the woodshed, there was a small gate in the fence that led onto the path, and skirted the edge of the lake. I had walked it a thousand times, as it rose and fell, winding through the trees and undergrowth. It felt nice to just walk, as Shell stopped and took pictures.

I breathed in deeply, the only sound was of the lapping water from the edge of the lake, and it felt soothing. It reminded me so much of my young teenage days, where I would explore the woodlands and run wild as Han walked along the path. Shell was right, I really did love this place, it was a part of me, a huge part of me. Shell stopped and turned, her camera gave a soft click, she smiled at me.

"That was a nice shot, you looked so lost in thought, you had a serenity to you." I gave a soft smile.

"Well, I have never been called serene before, but you are right, I really love this place Shell, it is very special to me." She smiled, and gave a soft nod.

"It shows. You know Emmy, you are an ecologist and this place is filled with diversity, why have you never got a grant and studied it?" It was an interesting point.

"I suppose I have never thought to." She looked round and across the lake.

"You should, you know you hate working for Harry, why settle for that when you have all of this? I can tell you, if I had your qualifications, this is where I would be. I bet there are thousands of things lying undiscovered in an area this big, and you know what, with a full scientific appraisal, that would make this a place of scientific interest, and protected. Peter would never have a chance to get anywhere near it." I gave a soft giggle; she never gave up.

"Shell, why does it matter to you so much what I do, you have a life away from here too?" She shrugged.

"Emmy, I meant what I said, I want to stay here and write, let's be honest, it is perfect for researching, miles away from all the noise of Exeter. I could really focus my thoughts better here and have the peace to just stop for a while and unwind a bit."

"But what about all your stuff, and not to mention the poet and his friends, there is not a lot of social life round here you know?" She looked out across the water towards the large island in it centre.

"I do not really need much Emmy, I have always travelled light, gone from flat to flat, Mike was a disaster, Doug was a prick, I think the only settled time I have had has been sharing with you. Is it wrong to want more, you know, to crave meaning, and something of substance?"

"Hell Shell, welcome to my life, and my head. I had that with

Han, which is why it has felt so hard coming back. Look at it from my side, my dad is not exactly there for me, my mum is gone and Pete and Jess only want to know me, so they can take this place away. I thought I had roots here, but now it feels like they have been torn away." She shook her head.

"They have not been torn away; they are still here. If you ask me, very deeply planted, but you hurt too much to notice." She turned to look at me, her dark eyes filled with life, and her short hair slightly moving in the breeze.

"Emmy you and this place are one, I see it, and have since we got back here. Han knew that, which is why she left it you. If you want my advice, don't be in a rush, take your time, and really think things over, I do not think a few days is enough. There is a strong magic here, and I really do think you will regret turning your back on it. This place is very special." I understood all that, but there were other things I had to deal with.

"Shell, I have to get back to work, I only have a week off, and Harry was not happy with me for that, it is a busy time for him. No matter what you think, we do have another life, and it is not here, and at some point, we will have to go back to it." She shook her head.

"Not me... Emmy, they tried to burn the place down, and when we got here surveyors were crawling all over the place, honestly, I don't want to leave. Let's be honest, we know Harry is talking to him, the moment you leave he will be back. Ask yourself this, what if you go back to Exeter, and a few weeks later return to find all of this cut down and rubble, because you know that is what he has in mind? As I said, you have a lot to think about and just a few days, but you really need to think deep."

Esme came belting through the fern and skidded to a halt, she peered out and looked round, Felix was alone, so she snuck quietly out and lowered her voice.

"Felix, you have to come, come on, she is walking the paths like she used to." He looked at her looking worn and tired, stood next to a large walnut.

"Esme, I have to break this, I have done five, and Chandak said I had to do at least six, I am exhausted and my arms hurt." He chipped at the seam with a sharp piece of stone, she watched confused.

"Use the light." He shook his head.

"He won't let me, he said it had to be hand done to teach me a lesson, but I am so tired, I don't think I have the strength."

Esme gave a frustrated sigh, she looked round, and then scurried over to Felix. He had done over half. She lifted her finger and ran it down the seam, and it glowed bright white, there was a loud crack, and the nut fell into two parts.

"Right, it is done and you didn't use the light, come on." She grabbed his hand and dragged him into the fern.

"Esme, he will know it was broken with the light." She gave a snigger, as she ran along the thin path.

"So, it was, he said you could not use the light, he said nothing about me."

She gave a little high pitched giggle, and Felix smiled a big smile as he ran at her side, she was his best friend in the light, and he loved her for it.

On the edge of the eastern side of the large island, an old tree had fallen, and lay on the bank over a rut. The floor was covered in a soft moss, and the gap was large enough for Felix and Esme to crawl under and lie down to watch. Esme gave a huge smile.

"Good they are still there, look, they are talking... She is so beautiful, but so sad, I wish I could talk to her and make her happy." Felix shook his head.

"She does not know about the light; it would scare her to see us." Esme stared across the water with large wide bright blue eyes, and shook her head.

"No Felix, she is like Han, she would love us, and be gentle."

"Yeah, but the fat one is clumsy, she would probably step on you, and, SQUISH! No more Esme." Esme jumped and gave a shudder.

"You are mean, I think the other one is nice, she must be, because she takes care of Emily." Felix shook his head.

"She smells funny, like Randolph after he has been chopping wood in the sun. I like Emily's smell; I want to just sit in her lap and smell her." Esme turned and looked at him.

"You are being strange again, smelling the big people is not normal." He watched Emily far away across the water.

"She smells of flowers, I like it, it reminds me of Han's garden." Esme turned back to watch, as Emily talked with Shelly near the water's edge.

"She is troubled I feel it, she is missing Han, and her heart is full of pain, I do not like her sad, I want her to be happy. Do you remember when she would swim in the water and laugh and scream with happiness?" Felix nodded.

"She will again Esme, Randolph and the fat one will help her, and then she will be happy again. She has Han in her heart, she cannot see it at the moment, but she will."

Esme gave a soft sigh as she watched across the water with her head resting on her hands. She watched Emily carefully.

"Felix, we do not have much time, my mother talked to Barrack alone last night, they are sending others out to the other places to see if they are safe. Felix, I do not want to leave her, she will be all alone then, what will she do?" He turned and looked at her as her eyes filled with tears, and she gave a sniffle, he stretched out his arm and rested his hand on hers.

"I won't let that happen Esme, if I have to, I will break the laws and show myself, and then tell her what Han did, and how much we need her. Emily cannot leave us, and I will not let that happen, I promise."

I turned and looked back across the lake towards the house, it looked so small in the distance, we had walked further than I had wanted to.

"I want to head back, you carry on if you want, I don't like being too far away after last night." She gave a nod.

"Yeah, okay, I just want some shots of the rocks in the trees, and then I will catch you up."

I left her to it, and walked slowly back towards the house, I had so much to think about, too much, and my mind wrestled with everything going on. Shelly was right, Harry was an arse, who was talking to my uncle, which to be honest, when Jess had mentioned that, it had bothered me. I suppose the question I had to answer was could I live here? Three and a half days was not exactly the longest time to make a decision, and I did have until the weekend here, although Harry had been really pissed off when I had rung him at home.

I have no idea why I was surprised, to be honest; he was never the kind of man that would understand grief, all he cared about was getting the surveys done, and getting paid for the work. Shell was right, all he cared about was me earning for him, he even sulked when I came here almost a year ago to attend the funeral. I walked up to the small gate and saw the white car, I walked slowly round the woodshed and looked round.

There was a man at the door, he was tall, wearing a suit, and looked official. He looked about mid forties, and knocked, then just stood there looking at the floor. I stepped out into view.

"Hello... Can I help you?" He turned and looked at me and smiled.

"Miss Montgomery?" I walked towards him.

"It is actually Duncan; my grandmother's name was Montgomery." He gave a slight nod of understanding, and walked down the path towards the gate.

"Miss Duncan I am Robert Bateson, I am the local police presence here. After last night, I wanted to talk to you and get your side of things." I had wondered when he would arrive.

"Sorry I went for a short walk, I only have the key to the back door on me, would you like to come round, and we can talk, although I would wipe your shoes, I have not cleaned the petrol off the step yet." He gave a smile as he walked towards me.

"You have a beautiful property; I would imagine it is quite a lot to deal with?"

He joined me as we walked round towards the back door, he was polite and appeared to be quite a cheerful man, although thinking about it, this place was so quiet, his job was probably not that hectic.

"The place pretty much runs itself, my grandmother had everything running pretty smoothly when she was here, so I am just following her lead, as she taught me when I was a girl." I slipped the key in the lock, and opened the door and stepped in, he smiled again.

"Yes, I forgot, you were raised here, I went to London to train, and have only been back for four years. I worked in London to begin with." I walked towards the kettle, as he wiped his feet on the mat outside.

"Can I get you a coffee, or tea, possibly a cool drink, it is very warm?" He entered and pulled out a chair at the table.

"Tea, two would be nice." I clicked on the kettle and reached for a clean mug, and turned to him, he lifted out a pad and looked up at me.

"Miss Duncan, as I know you are aware, a youth was detained here last night and then taken to my brother's garage and tied to the door. He is in the main station over in the town now, so firstly, you can relax, you are safe." He opened the pad, and read his notes.

"He has admitted to the offence, and we found five hundred pounds cash on him, which he claims he was paid to burn the house. Unfortunately, he will not say who by. Although, he did mention, he was told the house was unoccupied, so thought no one was here. He will be held and then taken to court for trial, I have made it clear that he is a danger to yourself, so he will remain in custody."

I nodded and was a little relieved, although it bothered me that someone had paid him to do that. Robert looked up from his pad.

"Miss Duncan, he claims he was attacked and assaulted by a man, but he could not provide a description. He says the man attacked him from behind and hit him, and threatened to set him on fire with his own petrol. To be honest, he is very afraid and glad to be held in custody, as he claims the man threatened him that if he came back here, he would drown him in the lake. He says the man told him to admit to his crime, as it would be safer for him." The kettle clicked, and I took a deep breath, as I made the drinks.

"Officer Bateson, we did not see who did it, he spoke through the door and asked if we were alright, and he told us to stay inside it was not safe. Honestly, we were terrified, we could smell the petrol, but we were frozen with fear and afraid to move. We both slept downstairs last night, as we were afraid to go upstairs just in case they came back."

"So, you did not see the man at all?" I shook my head, as I placed his tea down.

"No, I was terrified, it probably sounds wrong, but if whoever it was that came to our aide had not shown up, we may have been burned alive. This is a thatched cottage, and if that had caught fire, the whole place would have gone up. I am not sure I will sleep much tonight to be honest." He lifted his tea.

"You will be safe from him, but I am concerned that he says someone paid him. Miss Duncan, is there anyone at all you can think of who would want to burn this house down, you know, people who have something against you?" I shook my head, although, I pretty much had a very good idea of who it was who wanted me out.

"I have not been home for a year, and when I was here before, I only came home at term breaks, I was educated at a private boarding school and then went to Uni. I know Heidi, your brother and the Hannity's, from when I lived here, but I really do not know that many people from the village, I have only been back three days."

He sipped his tea, and watched me, I sat back and lifted my cup, and he smiled.

"What about your friend, I believe you are here with a young woman?" I nodded.

"Shelly, Shelly Parkinson, she is my flat mate from Exeter, I was nervous coming back alone, so she came for moral support. She is a writer, she is out taking pictures, she will be back shortly, I think."

He wrote it down, and gave a nod, then reached down into his pocket, and pulled out a small card, and placed it on the table.

"You say that both of you were together the whole time?" I nodded.

"Yeah, it sounds sad, but we huddled together, and then heard the commotion and then a man's voice spoke through the door and asked if we were alright. As I said, we slept downstairs we were so freaked out by it." He lifted his cup and drained it.

"Are you here for good, or just visiting?" I gave a sigh.

"I am not sure at the moment, this is not easy for me, Han raised me, and it is hard to be here without her, I am still getting used to not having her here for me. It has taken me a year to pluck up the courage to come back, but I won't deny, it is hard here without her, I miss her terribly." I felt the tears in my eyes and wiped them on my sleeve. "I am sorry, I am very emotional at the moment, I am not normally like this." He stood up with a sad smile.

"She was a very special person, I am sorry for your loss, my condolences and I am sorry if I upset you. I have what I need, but I will leave you my card, if you have any other problems, please call me straight away, I live just outside the village and can be here very quickly." I stood up and gave a sniffle.

"Thank you, that is really kind of you, and thanks for coming to check on us." He gave a nod and walked to the back door.

"Just for now, keep everything locked up when you are in bed or out walking." I nodded.

"Yes, I am." He gave a smile.

"Good afternoon to you Miss Duncan, and I hope your visit here is more of a pleasant one, you are the owner of a wonderful piece of land, enjoy it while you are here." I tried to smile.

"I intend to, thank you."

He left and I sat back in my chair and finished my drink, and once again, I had yet more on my mind, honestly, this was harder than I ever thought it would be.

Shelly slipped her backpack off her shoulder and crouched down, she unzipped it, revealing all her different lenses, and unscrewed the lens on her camera, which she slotted into a square foam padded hole. She lifted out her long lens, and attached it, twisting until it clicked.

She stood up and changed the settings on the top of her camera, and pulled it up, looking at the screen as she panned round, following the large rocks within the trees, and caught a glimpse of a waterfall, from the rocks that rose up above the trees. She zoomed in, and could make out the water flowing over the edge and falling, and so followed the line of rocks to where it came spilling into the lake.

"Wow, that looks so beautiful, this place is unbelievable."

She moved forward watching the path, it bent and wove as it made its way along the side of the lake, scanning the lake further and further along the path beyond the waterfall. As she looked the whole length of the lake, quietly talking to herself.

"I am going to spend days walking this, actually I think I need to get a bike, it will take hours to walk that far, but I am definitely going to travel this whole path, I love this place."

With Shelly still out taking pictures, I decided to cook, the day was moving on and it was already early evening. I opened the fridge and took out the beef steaks I had placed in their earlier, and opened the oven to get a baking sheet, slipped one out and lay the steaks down on it, and rubbed some oil on them. I lit the oven and set them to cook on low, whilst I washed and prepped the veg, and grabbed two saucepans off the rack.

With everything prepared and on to boil, I pulled out a bottle of wine, grabbed a glass off the draining board, opened the bottle, and poured. I needed to clean the path, and grabbed the washing up liquid and ran the tap whilst I got the bucket, just letting my mind wander around, as the bucket filled with hot water.

Grabbing a stiff brush from outside the backdoor, I headed through the house and opened the front door, it smelt horrible, even now the fumes were strong. I gave a sigh and squirted the washing up liquid onto the step and then dipped the brush in the hot water, and started to scrub the paving stones. There were lines of gravel between the stones, but nobody ever really walked on it, and I figured, a good swill would take care of it. I then swilled the path down, and prayed I never had to do it again.

It was hard work, but in a way, I felt happy, I was taking care of the house, just like I used to at the side of Han. My mind flooded with the endless tasks we had done together, gardening, her teaching me to cook and bake, preserving food, making jam, even making wine, she taught me everything I needed to know about country living.

I learned to sew age seven and made my own quilt cover, I learned to type on an old battered type writer, learned how to grow food, how to maintain the boat, and repair the fence, I even spent a summer chopping logs for the wood pile. I stopped and leaned on the brush near the gate.

"Was she teaching me how to live here... Alone?"

It is crazy in a way, I had never really thought about it, but I stood there lost in my thoughts, I realised, every holiday and visit, she had taught me something. As I looked back on those fond and wonderful memories, I realised, Han had taught me everything I would need to know to live here in the cottage. It was like she knew one day I would have to make it alone here, and survive without her. I was more than capable of maintaining her lifestyle, and taking care of myself, if anything, I was completely self sufficient. Having lived here for every term break of my school life, I could slip right into Hempsley life without a hitch, even if it was remote and secluded.

Mind you, looking at life in the city, I had not done that well in the last couple of years. Finishing Uni and going straight to Scotland on a tree planting management grant was pretty good, but that was only for three months, and for the rest of the time I had worked for Harry, in Exeter, and been pretty much reclusive in my flat. Well apart from Shell, and the odd visit of Pam, but for most of the time I had been alone, which was not unsimilar to life here with Han.

I came out of my thoughts and lifted the empty bucket, the smell was not as bad, so I walked into the house and closed the door. When I reached the kitchen, Shell was turning the steaks on the tray, she looked up and smiled.

"I saw you day dreaming and thought I would leave you, although, it was a good job I got back, you would have burned the meal." I smiled at her as she closed the oven.

"Yeah sorry, I have a lot to think about, I drifted a little." I lifted my wine and took a sip. "How was the walk?" She poured herself a glass and turned round.

"Honestly, it was mind blowing, I love this place, it is beyond beautiful, I took loads of pictures, it gets my creative juices going... By the way, your phone pinged." I looked at it on the table and lifted it up, then swiped the screen, it was a text from Heidi.

'He ordered a dozen white lilies; he will be there at eleven on Friday to wish her happy birthday. Good Luck."

I closed the screen and took another swig of the wine, Shell looked at me, and frowned.

"Good news I hope?" I glanced at her.

"My dad will visit my mums grave on Friday. He ordered flowers, I have to decide if I will be there to try and get him to talk to me."

"Ouch!" I smirked.

"Yep... I need to get some answers, although I am not living in hope."

Chapter Ten

Remembrance

Thursday was spent mainly worrying and plucking up the courage to meet my father. I did not sleep well and was up early, Shell was flat out in bed, I had awoken in the night and heard her typing. At nine thirty, Friday morning, I set off walking down the road towards the village. I left Shell a note telling her this was something I had to do alone, but would call if I needed her, and I headed towards Heidi's shop to collect the white roses I had ordered yesterday.

I planned to arrive before him, and sit further down the path on the benches, out of sight. I suppose in a way I was intrigued, as he had married again and yet he was still a frequent visitor to my mother's grave. I was interested in knowing why, especially considering he had done everything he could to avoid me for most of my life.

I collected the flowers and Heidi promised she would say nothing, then I walked slowly up the steep hill, towards the cemetery at the top. My stomach was uneasy and filled with nerves, meeting him would be hard, and I still had no idea what I was going to say. Yesterday, Shelly had suggested I play it by ear, and that felt like the best idea.

I arrived at ten twenty six, and walked down the long wide path, and passed the path to my mother and Han's grave, to a seat a few yards down. I sat with my back to the path, and held up my phone, and flicked on the front facing camera so that I could see behind me, and get the angle right. I had full view of the path as I looked at my screen, and watched the time tick past on my phone. It seemed to drag, which did not do my insides any good at all, I felt queasy and very nervous, which was stupid, he was my dad, I should not have to feel this way.

Although thinking back, the last time we had talked, was when he phoned and asked if I was going to his wedding, and the conversation had been filled with awkward pauses. It was strange really, because he wanted me there, and yet I think deep down, I felt pissed off, and decided not to go, simply as an act of revenge for ignoring me all these years. Movement caught my eye, and I came out of my thoughts and looked at the camera, he was there walking slowly up the path. He had not changed much, a little older, a bit greyer, but he was as always immaculately dressed, and groomed to perfection.

He walked slowly onto the path holding the flowers, and I let him walk further up, and then stood up. I suppose I was not that well turned out, in faded jeans and a red woollen sweater under my black canvass coat, with boots. I walked across the path and onto the grass under the trees, between the grave stones of others, until I was almost right behind him a good five hundred feet away. My heart was pounding, why the hell was I so nervous, he was my father after all?

Is it crazy, as I thought about it, that I felt a sudden terror course through me, and felt my heart rate increase a little more? It is stupid, he is my father, and yet as I walked very slowly, watching him, I became terrified. He knelt down, unwrapped the flowers, and placed them carefully in the stone pot next to the other pot filled with his red.

I was too far away, but I thought he was talking, I saw him lift my single white rose, and say something, he placed it with care in the central empty pot, and pulled a bottle of water from his side coat pocket and watered it. I have no idea why, but it surprised me, I walked slowly closer as he knelt there talking to her, feeling my heartbeat increase. I reached the path, it was just six feet of cracked tarmac, then four feet of grass, he had his back to me and his head down, and I stood there watching him, somehow feeling I was invading something I shouldn't. He lifted a handkerchief out and wiped his eyes, holy shit, was he crying?

I took a huge breath, and stepped onto the path, and walked quietly, is it silly that I tip toed? I reached the grass and stood there staring at my mother's grave, just like I had every birthday she had for all my life with Han, watching him with his back to me weep. I took a deep breath; it was now or never. My mouth was dry, and my voice a little strained, but low.

"Dad?"

He stood up and wiped his eyes and turned, I felt my leg tremble, and swallowed hard. He looked at me and gave a gasp, his eyes filled with tears. I have no idea why, but that hurt me so deeply, and I swallowed again trying to hold back my own tears. He looked down and wiped his eyes again.

"Emily, how are you?" I gave a sniffle, and tried to speak.

"I am okay considering, I miss her, Han told me so much about her, it was like I knew her better than I did." He bit his lip and nodded.

"You gave me a fright, Emily, you are her double, I found it shocking to look at you."

Okay, so I was not expecting that. I guess I was used to being told that by those who knew her, it had never really registered on me. Hearing him say it shocked him, rattled me a little, but I suppose he of all people knew her best, after all, he married her.

"It's her birthday, I brought her more flowers." He gave a nod, he looked awkward.

"Yes, I miss her too, it is a nice thing to do for her, she loved white roses." I nodded at him, and shuffled my feet, I felt so awkward and not certain of what to do.

"Yeah, Han told me, I am normally here earlier." He took a deep breath, and looked at me.

"I know, I have always seen the flowers you left for her, I have always appreciated it. I have always been sorry you lost her so young, I wish things could have been different." I gave a nod, unsure of what to do or say.

"Yeah, me too." He looked at me.

"She truly was a wonderful woman; I loved her a great deal." I smiled, and my eyes filled with tears.

"I know that Dad, I have seen it. I just wish..."

I stopped myself, and I think he understood, it was clear I was going to say you loved me too, and yet I didn't say it. I couldn't, I felt it, but looking at him stood awkward and grief stricken, as crazy as it sounds, I did not want to hurt him. He nodded; I suppose I had no need to say it.

He just stared at me, finding it hard to form the right words, I could see his pain, so I unwrapped the flowers, and walked round the other side, knelt down, and placed them in the pot with my single white rose.

"Happy birthday mum."

I rolled up the paper and slipped it in my pocket, stood up and wiped my eyes, and then looked at him watching me. It felt really strange, this was a man who gave multi million pound presentations to buyers, a man filled with confidence. Yet here at the side of my mother's grave, he looked lost, and like he could not find the courage to talk. I looked at him, and he swallowed hard, and spoke quietly.

"Are you here for good now, or will you be going back to your flat?" I shook my head.

"I am not sure yet, I have a lot going on inside me at the moment, I have to think it all out and decide what to do. Being there without Han is not easy for me, it is still very painful." He appeared to understand.

"Emily, never sell it, never sell the house Amelia grew up in, hold on to it." That surprised me a great deal.

"I am not going to, Pete is on my back day and night, he has hassled me for a year to sell it to him, and I have told him a million times I am not, but he just won't quit." He appeared to understand that, I suppose he knows Pete better than any.

"Would you like me to get him to back off?" He looked at me and gave a sigh. "Emily I can help, I want to help, I know him, one word from me and he will. I am happy to do it if it will help."

I gave him a nod; I think that is the first time he has ever actually offered to do anything to improve my life. Honestly, I could use the help.

"Yeah, I would appreciate that, because honestly, he scares me." He frowned at me, and his voice appeared concerned.

"Nothing has happened, has it?" I shrugged.

"Nothing I can prove was him, but honestly, I do not trust him, and would put nothing past him, he is obsessed with getting that land." He nodded.

"You have your mother's instincts, trust them. I will make it known to leave you alone, it is not much but I am happy to help..." He took a tiny step, and leaned in slightly, I thought he wanted to say something important, but paused. I just watched him, hoping he would, he took a deep breath.

"Emily, never think I don't care, I do, I know you don't see it, but I am here for you if you need me."

Oh god, I felt a huge lump in my throat, and hit me so hard, he had no idea how much I had yearned to hear that. The emotion that was deep inside, it just flowed up into me as my eyes again filled with tears, my voice gave a squeak as my words came bubbling out.

"Then why can't you show it, because I am so alone now, I have no one?"

My shoulders shook, and my sobs came out bitter and painful, as I stood, looking down, dripping tears on my mother's grave, and a pain I had carried for most of my life surged up into me. I just stood there shaking, feeling utterly heart broken and lost, as I wept. Suddenly, I felt his arms come round me and pull me close, and I pressed my face into his shoulder and wept. His voice was soft and caring, not at all like the man I had spoken to in the past.

"I am sorry Emily, I know, I should have been there more, but you have to understand, losing her destroyed me, and I was not brave enough to face you. I ran away and it was wrong, Han promised she would care for you, and I agreed because I was utterly broken. It is wrong, but by the time I came to terms with it, I was too ashamed to face you. I know I have been a lousy parent, I never intended to be, I do love you a great deal, you are so like her it is hard for me to cope with. It is no excuse, and it is wrong of me."

I sniffled into his shoulder, is it crazy this was the first time in my life, my father had hugged me, and much to my surprise, it made me really happy?

"Just talk to me Dad, don't ignore me, you know we both miss her, we both feel it. It is probably the only thing we have in common, don't shut me out, because honestly, I really need a parent at the moment. I am so lost and afraid." I slipped back, and looked up at him, his bright blue watery eyes glistened. He gave a nod.

"I am sorry, I don't want to be like this. I will try harder." I took a huge breath.

"It may not show it, but I do need you." He smiled.

"I am glad to hear that, because I thought you didn't." I shook my head.

"You are all I have, and yet I feel so alone." He gave a smile.

"Walk back to the car with me, where are you parked?" I sniffled and wiped my eyes on my sleeve.

"I walked here." He gave me a nod.

"Come on, I will drive you home."

We turned from the graves, and made our way off the grass, as he walked at my side, and we walked along the road back towards the gates, slowly, he glanced at me.

"How is the cottage, it has been a long time since I was there, you know, if it needs work, I can arrange all that for you?"

It felt strange to be walking and talking, and yet it also felt good, although it was not the free flowing feeling at ease sort of conversation I would have with Han. I suppose we hardly know each other, he is my dad, and yet in many ways, we are strangers to each other.

"The cottage is fine, Han took great care of it, for me the hard part is being there without her, seeing all her things and knowing she is gone is difficult for me." He gave a nod.

"I really understand that, but it will get easier, you know you never forget, none of it leaves you. I suppose over time, you simply manage better, but it is always there inside you, all the love and all the care. I owe her a great deal, she was there for me at a very bad time, so I understand." I nodded, I suppose he did understand, after all, he has had to live without my mother.

"Yes, I suppose we also have that in common, we have both lost someone who meant everything to us." He gave a long sigh.

"What are you going to do Emily, you need to have a focus, what would you really like to do?"

I really was not sure. I stared ahead, seeing the green lawns and the white stones, my mind in utter chaos, trying to come to terms with everything, and more uncertain of my future than I had ever been. He walked along slowly at my side, as awkward and as unsure as I was.

"Shelly wants me to stay here and do research on all the flora and fauna of the place, she wants to stay here too and write, so

I suppose she wants us to live together and house share. To be honest I am caught, because I would love that, but I have a job in Exeter, and a flat." He gave an agreeable nod.

"Your mother loved this place, I always felt guilty I took her away from here, you know, I would say, follow your heart. Emily, you know what life is like here, you grew up here, to be honest, this is your home. I can see the appeal of Exeter, but to be honest, you can do better than Harry, he always was a grumpy old sod. You know if you need work, I use a lot of firms, a good ecologist is not that easily found." I smiled; I suppose in a way he was trying to help.

"I will not sell the cottage, it means too much to me, and I never want that land developed, if anything I want to protect and preserve it. Han loved it so much, and she worked hard to keep it safe, I want to continue that." He gave a nod.

"I am pleased to hear that; your mother felt the same way. When she was heading back, that was why she was returning. I was offered a good job overseas, and we were building the firm, it was a large scale project, and Han was having trouble, she was returning to help protect it when her accident happened." I looked at him.

"Really, I did not know that?" He took a deep breath.

"It is strange, she was not that much older than you are now, she was twenty six when it happened, she was so young, so full of life and so happy to have you. Emily, she loved you so much, all through her pregnancy she was so excited, we had talked of another child, we really wanted a little sibling for you. Life is so cruel that it robbed both of you from each other, and yet, I look at you, and she is stood there right in front of me. You gave me quite a shock earlier, you really are her double, it is uncanny." We came through the iron gates, and stopped at the car, and he looked at me.

"You have two thousand acres of some very special property, if you want my advice, treasure it." The car bleeped and the doors unlocked. I opened the door and slid in; it was pretty plush.

He turned the key and the engine started, although it was so quiet it was hard to detect, I pulled the seat belt across me, and clipped it in place.

"Would you come in for a coffee with me, I would really like that?"

He took a deep breath, I felt like it was sort of an olive branch between us. It is strange, because he is my father, and yet in many ways, he feels like a complete stranger to me. I probably have more knowledge, of the guy who lives in the flat next door to me in Exeter, and I only see him about twice a year. I sat back and turned to look at him, he was watching me.

"It has been a long time since I have been inside, lots of memories, some very happy, and some not so much." I understood that.

"I have enjoyed this, I feel it is the first real conversation we have ever had, I guess I don't want it to end yet."

He smiled, pulled out his phone and placed it in the holder, the dash gave a beep, and the blue tooth connected. He pressed the screen and hit speed dial, a woman's voice answered, I recognised it.

"Yes Mr Duncan."

"Kate, can you clear the deck for a couple of hours, I have been delayed?"

"Is everything alright?"

"Yes, there are no problems, I am having coffee with Emily." She sounded surprised.

"Really...? No problems, I will clear the rest of the day and reschedule, take your time."

"Thanks Kate, I will see you later."

He gave me a smile and moved off, and we headed down the hill, and headed back towards Han's. At the bottom of the hill, he turned and I saw Heidi outside her shop watching, she gave a smile as she saw me in the car. I would have to thank her before I left, she had done me a huge favour. We drove out of the village heading towards the lake and Han's. he turned his head slightly to glance at me.

"Would you mind if we stopped off, there is something I always do on her birthday, and I would like to show you, if that would be alright?" I nodded at him.

"Yes, that would be fine." He gave a smile, as he watched through the windscreen.

It is strange really, because I have not been this close to him for a long time. I glanced to the side and watched him, and could see how his hair had lost some of its colour, grey lines seemed to weave into his dark brown, above his ears. His skin was tanned, and yet his face appeared worn with creases. I mean, for forty six he looked pretty good, and he was in good shape, he clearly took care of himself.

"How are you for money?" We took an early turning, he was heading onto the main road that skirted Han's property, he clearly knew his way around the area.

"I am doing alright, I don't exactly live in the fast lane, so I spend little, and Han left me quite a bit, so I am more than comfy."

"Good, if you need anything at all, just let me know. I am there you know, I understand your independence, your mother was the same, but if things get rough, you know, you can always reach out to me?"

It felt strange, I had seen many pictures of him, and we had a life of brief meetings, where he was always aloof and uneasy, and yet here in his car, he was more relaxed, well more than normal. It still felt like there was a huge wall between us, but whereas before it had always felt impenetrable, this felt like there was a small a window through which we could communicate with a slightly less awkward ease.

He turned off the main road onto the old woodland track heading towards the lake, the road was rough, but had been repaired in parts, I looked through the window seeing the trees and noting how dense they had become over the years.

"Are we heading to the falls?" He gave a smile.

"Yes, I come here every year on her birthday, for me it is a very special place, it was for her too." I could understand that, I came here many times growing up.

We arrived at the end of the road and there was a wide area that had been cleared and gravel scattered. It was a bit weed ridden, but he pulled up and applied the hand break. I unclipped my belt, and he reached for his door. I pulled on mine and got out, and closed the door behind me and looked at him, he really did have the most intense blue eyes. He smiled at me, and I felt he was a little more relaxed, a little more casual than he had been in the cemetery.

He held up his hand to show me the path, and I followed him, as we walked towards the falls. I have never walked this path; I always came to them from the water's edge. We walked slowly; it was a little uneven.

"When I first met Amelia, I had been out fishing, and was sat at the top of the falls, I was fifteen. I had caught a really good trout and was making a fire to cook it, and she just appeared. She had been swimming naked in the deep pool below, and she saw the smoke from the fire. I suppose she thought I had been watching her, but to be honest, I had not even noticed I was so busy with the fire."

His voice was soft and caring, and I could hear the affection in his words, it was strange, I had never seen this side of him.

"She just appeared and asked me what I was doing, and told me it was private land." He gave a slight chuckle.

"She was quite forceful. I apologised and told her I did not know, and then asked if she would like some. Her hair was wet, so I asked if she had been swimming, I think it surprised her, and she asked if I had seen her, so I told her no. She was beautiful, she looked exactly the same as you do, with her long hair and intense hazel eyes, I think that was the moment I fell in love with her. She agreed to share the fish with me, and we sat and talked, she knew who I was, but I was clueless about the cottage or her life here, as I look back, it was one of the most magical days in my life. We met every day that summer, and just became friends. It was about a week later she asked if I wanted to meet Han."

We arrived at the falls, and the wide flat plane of stone, through which the water ran down from the hills behind us, and then fell twenty feet into a large wide pool, he stood looking round, and took a deep breath.

"She was a wonderful person Emily, so happy and filled with life, and tough, she was strong and very independent. We started to date, I took her out to the pictures and we explored all around the village, it was the happiest time of my life. At Uni we wrote to each other and met up at weekends, and when I qualified, I asked her to marry me, right here, in this spot on her birthday. It is why I come here every year, this place is so special to me, I stand here and I remember her, and think of that day as I knelt down and held up the ring."

He took a breath and swallowed hard, I could feel his emotion, and I took a breath myself, this was blowing my mind. I had always seen him as cool and aloof, and in a way, I could see some of the aspects of him Heidi had told me about. This made more sense to me, after all I had heard about my mother, the one thing I had never understood was why she had married him, and yet standing here listening to his soft caring voice, I could really understand why. Was this more of the man she fell for, was this a part of him that was just hers? It was difficult to comprehend, and yet standing there listening, I thought it was. He pulled a ribbon from his pocket and pointed behind him, I turned and saw a single hawthorn, with red ribbons tied to it. Many of which were weathered and thread bare.

"I tied her first birthday present up with red ribbon, I was so nervous she would laugh at me. Once she had unwrapped it, she took the ribbon and tied it to that tree, she told me, she did it so the memory of that moment would be forever marked, and every year since I have added a ribbon. Every year on her birthday, I place flowers on her grave and then drive here, and add one, so she will never be forgotten."

I stood staring at them all, gently moving in the breeze, and I felt the tears in my eyes again, I could not believe this, I stood there frozen, looking at the tree. He had been doing this for over twenty years. It was startling, heart-breaking, and nothing at all like the man I thought he was, he walked over to my side and held up the ribbon.

"You do it, tie one on for her." I looked at him and wiped my eyes, he gave a gentle nod.

"She would love the idea of this, both of us together, honouring her." I took a huge breath, and swallowed as my emotions ran wild. I lifted my hand and took it from him as he smiled, and gave his head a nod.

My father stood back and watched me as I nervously approached the tree, and slid the ribbon round just above the one he had placed last year and tied it on. I suppose in his mind, watching me was like watching her do it that day all those years ago. I knotted it well so it never came off and turned, he had his handkerchief to his eyes and was wiping them. I felt lost completely, this was all so new, so different, so unexpected, and I felt so unbelievably overwhelmed by it all.

I had been told all my life about his love for her by Han, and had never really seen it, but this, all this precious and caring side of him, I had not seen any of this growing up, and I had to ask myself, why had he never been like this with me? Why had I never seen this side of him, every thought I had about him growing up was wrong, he was nothing like the man I thought he was, and it just blew me away. I stood looking at him, struggling for words.

"It is beautiful what you have done for her here, I am struggling for words and feeling overwhelmed. I am sorry to ask, but why now, why after all these years, why could I not see this part of you sooner?" He gave a nod as he wiped his eyes.

"To be completely honest Emily, it was fear." I frowned not understanding.

"Fear, I am sorry Dad but that makes no sense at all." He gave a long sigh as he tried to control his emotions.

"Emily, I loved her so much, and I do love you, I remember the night you came into our life, and I see those pictures in my dreams all the time. She was so happy, so filled with love for you, it was the happiest time of my life. Emily, I loved her deeply, and I lost her, she was taken so young, and you will never understand the pain I suffered because of it. I guess I locked myself away and lived in fear you would be taken from me too. I know this makes little sense, but holding back and trying to stop myself from caring as much, I thought it would keep you safe. There is too much to tell you at the moment, and I know you do not understand, but I just wanted you safe and protected, and I knew that Han could, and so I let her. Silly as it sounds, I wanted the best part of your mother to remain in this world, in this land, and Han could ensure that, I couldn't, and because of that she was taken from us." He took a breath, and turned to look out over the falls towards the island.

"I never should have taken her away from here, she belonged here, her and this place were one." He turned and walked back towards the car.

"Come on, I will take you back."

I will not deny, some of what he said made no sense to me, how could he think I would be in danger, I was nobody, and only important to Han? I sat in the car and my mind was a blur, as I tried to process and understand everything, although today had been nice, painful, and yet I had liked seeing this side of him, seeing the love and care within him. I had felt some sort of connection with him for the first time in my whole life, and I was glad he had done this. The car motored along under the tree lined road, and I turned to him.

"Thanks for this Dad, I am glad you showed me it." He nodded.

"I want things better between us, trust me, Kate and Heidi have lectured me a great many times over the years. I am glad I did this too; I was ready to, and I do want things better between us, I have lived in fear for too long."

We turned onto the long drive and headed up it towards the house, and I felt a sense of relief. I had spent most of last night dreading today, and yet it had gone nothing like I had thought it would, and I felt a little relieved, as I had not wanted more chaos. We pulled up and I jumped out, I opened the large gate so he could drive through. I clipped it back as I closed it and turned, he was stood by the car door looking at the house, it clearly brought back a great deal of memories.

"How long is it since you were last here?" He walked towards the gate.

"About fifteen years I think, the last time I was here you were in bed sick, I came over, but there really was no need, Han had already taken care of everything. I sat with her for a long time talking, and she filled me in on all your progress."

I walked to the door and unlocked it, and stepped inside holding the door.

"SHELL I AM BACK!" She popped her head round the kitchen door and gave a squeak.

"Yikes, visitors." She disappeared as my dad looked round the room.

"Wow it has not changed a bit." Shell came through with a towel wrapped round her waist and smiled.

"Sorry, ignore me, I need pants." She hurried through the room, and I turned to the kitchen.

"Tea or coffee?" He smiled.

"Coffee, black, one sugar."

Is it strange, that I do not even know what he drinks? I walked through to the kitchen as he took off his coat, and simply stood looking round, he spotted the picture of Amelia on the wall and gave a smile. He walked through the kitchen door as I made the coffee, I was surprised when I turned round and saw him touching the table. I carried the cups and placed one down for him, and then sat down, he gave a soft chuckle, as he looked at me.

"She always sat in that seat, I always sat here, she would reach out across the table and hold my hand." He sat down at the end of the table, and gave a long drawn in breath.

"It is hard being here, we spent a third of our time sat here talking."

"I understand that, I have lived most of my life sat here talking or helping Han, I really miss her, it feels strange here without her." He gave a soft smile.

"I owe her so much, you have done really well, everyone I have spoken to has always told me what a lovely young woman you had become, and how like Amelia you were. It made it even harder for me, because I still miss her Emily, some days I yearn to be with her again, I have so many regrets, they haunt my dreams."

It was surreal to see this side of him, he clearly loved my mum as much as everyone had told me, and maybe I needed to see it first hand to understand it, but I cannot deny, there was one question I really wanted him to answer. I sat back and looked at him.

"You know, the thing I don't get, because after today especially, and seeing how upset you were, and hearing you talk of mum, why get married again, do you love her as much?" He gave a smirk.

"The simple truth is loneliness. Jane is a nice woman; she is caring and compassionate, and a very good companion. I enjoy her company a great deal, and she has helped me at those times where I felt shrouded in darkness. We were good friends for a long time before we got together." I could understand that.

"But you do not love her like you did mum?" He shook his head.

"Emily what I had with your mum, went beyond all definitions, her love was so pure, no one will ever come close to matching it. I do care about Jane, I am not using her, but in my heart, deep inside, she could never replace her, and she does understand that. We talked about it for a very long time before we moved into a relationship." He reached across the table and took my hand.

"Emily, what are you going to do, I am worried about you, you have had to endure so much alone, you need some sort of direction, and again, today I have seen you flounder around like your compass is spinning?" I shrugged.

"I am torn between two lives, one here without Han which is painful, and one in Exeter that I hate. I am trying to work it all out, but I am so confused about everything." He gave a nod.

"Do you want my advice; I am aware I have no right to give you any?"

I looked deeply into his bright blue eyes, I could really see why mum fell so deeply in love with him, he had such love and compassion in them, and yet I had never noticed it before.

"Tell me, what would you do?" He squeezed my hand softly.

"Stay here where you are safe, take care of this land for your mother and Han. fulfil your mother's wishes, because that is all she ever wanted, to keep this place safe. She told me many times, the importance of this place was beyond anything people realised, and she would say it with such sincerity I believed her. Emily let me help you, I want her dream fulfilled."

Wow, talk about pressure. It was true, just like her this place was a part of me, and I loved it, and with Pete threatening it as he was at the moment, there was a huge part of me deep down that did not want to leave, but it was a big piece of property and there would be costs, it was not that easy to just say yes.

"Dad, it is a huge task, and the costs of conservation are high, I am not sure I am the one to do it." He gave a nod and looked at me.

"My company invest in a lot of ecology projects, let me set up a trust to help out with that. Emily, I have piles of money doing nothing, I will certainly never spend it all, give me this, let me back my daughter in something I know will lead her to happiness. Study this place, log everything, detail every aspect of all the things living here and their connection to each other, and live here safe under my protection." BOOM! My mind was blown.

"Dad, that will cost millions." He gave a shrug.

"If that is the price of your mother's dream, I will pay it happily to see it come to fruition. Emily, I have it, let me use it to protect it, this place has so much more than you realise."

Shelly walked in wearing pants and smiled, as she walked towards the kettle carrying her cup. I looked up and smiled, she was a little red round the cheeks.

"Shell, this is my dad, John Duncan."

She stopped, turned, and looked at me and then my dad, as he stood up and smiled and held out his hand.

"Nice to meet you Shelly, I loved your book." She stood frozen with her jaw open and then realised and blinked.

"Hi, Emily's dad, wow!" She frowned. "You read my book, seriously?" He nodded.

"Yes... It was a good piece of work, Amelia, you know Emily's mum, she read every book written on folklore, she was very into it, I guess it sort of rubbed off on me. Anyway, I really enjoyed it." He shook her hand and she looked stunned, I had to smile. he looked down at me.

"I will have to go, but thanks for today, it felt very special, I loved it."

I got up out of my seat, as Shelly stood looking dumbfounded, and followed him through to the living room. He lifted his coat, and walked to the door, I stepped out, and he followed me through. I looked up at him and smiled.

"Today was special, I was missing them both and it helped me a lot, thanks, it means more than you realise." He gave a soft smile; his eyes were so alive and loving.

"Look Emily, you now have two good options, and both will give you an income and a life. Think very carefully and choose, and then let me know. Can I call again next time I am down here?" I smiled.

"You have always been welcome, wherever I am." He leaned in and hugged me again, and I pushed into him, and lifted my arms round him.

"Thanks Dad, thanks for being there when I needed you."

"We were there for each other, you made such a huge

difference for me today, I am glad you walked up when I was with her, she would have loved it." He kissed the side of my head and I wanted to cry.

I stood at the gate and watched as he got in the car, and turned it on, he smiled and waved, and I waved back, as he turned and drove out through the gates. Today was so different from every other meeting I had with him in my life, and even though I was close to tears and felt my insides swirling, I felt a glow of happiness in me for the first time in over a year, and it was nice.

Chapter eleven

The Paradox

Watching my father leave, was bitter sweet, in all honesty I had not wanted him to leave, I actually wanted him to stay longer and continue as he was. I had to ask the question, was it just today, and when I saw him again, would things be as they were. I wanted him to stay as he was, and I really hoped he would. Shelly was a little thrown, probably as thrown as I was in the grave yard, as she also felt my dad was avoiding me, and as I told her about the day, she was staggered.

She actually pulled me close and gave me a huge hug, telling me how happy she was to see us together, and I was actually very happy about it. So, as we sat and ate our evening meal, I talked happily and honestly, as Shelly smiled. I think she was just glad to see me more uplifted than I had been, although, I made no mention of my dad offering me a research grant. It was an intriguing idea, and when Shelly had first mentioned it, I have to admit, I did like the idea, but I was not about to rush into things.

You see the problem with living in Hempsley, is that there are no short cuts. Take out is not an option, and neither is convenience shopping, eating and shopping are a big endeavour. Han went into the large town once a month and did a mammoth shop, and she had to prepare every meal, which okay, I loved growing up, because that meant I learned preserving, bread making, and a million other home based craft skills. My concern, was my own self doubt, admittedly, for the last year I had lived in the negative, and doubted every decision I had made. Thinking back, picking Ken as a boyfriend and Harry as an employer had not exactly worked out well for me.

Taking this place on as a study ground, would involve a huge amount of work to set up, because as well as all the science work I would do, I would also be running a business, because people like the inland revenue will need to be kept in the loop. It is a giant leap for me, I have always worked for others, and never worked for myself, and I am lacking in confidence when it comes to getting everything sorted and organised, as well as adding a huge lifestyle change, like I will have to in order to live here.

Shell set up her laptop on the table, so she could go through all her pictures, and I lifted my glass of wine and headed out of the back door. It was a warm evening, and the lake was as still as glass. I walked down the garden through the round white archway of brick, and onto the long Jetty.

This was my thinking spot; I had sat here a million times in life as I puzzled things out. I sat on the end of the jetty and dangled my legs over the edge. I sat back lost in thought, just staring into space across the water towards the island, I lifted my glass and took a sip, as I gave a sigh, my head was spinning, and I still had no idea what I was going to do. At some point, I still had Han's bedroom and workroom to sort out, which although I tried to deny it, I was avoiding it.

It was Friday, and I had to be back in work on Monday, so if I was going to go back, I had to make up my mind before Sunday. I closed my eyes, put down my glass, and leaned back on my arms, and let my mind wander, why was everyone convinced this place was special or magical? Even my dad today, mentioned how special this place was, do they not think I feel the same way, do I come across as hating it?

I love this place, it is the biggest and happiest part of my life, why could no one see that? I wish I could just sit up and say, hey, I am staying, like Shell did. It is alright for her, she is a writer, her life is simple, she does what needs to be done, and then sits and writes in her free time, life for me will not be that simple. Research is pretty in depth stuff, and it is not just a case of saying I have newts and red squirrels here, because both of those are on the island. I would have to find a valuable research topic, and currently, I was not sure what was here, it would have to be surveyed first, and that takes time, certainly a lot more than two days. I lay back on the jetty, my legs still hanging over the edge and breathed in.

"Han, why did you stay, what had mum and you so captivated that you felt so strongly about this place, it has to be more than just trees, water, and squirrels?"

My mind drifted as I softly breathed the warm evening air, and in the back of my mind I heard her voice.

"Emmy dear child, there is a lot of magic here, and many things that should be cherished, life is not just about money, it is about everything, and should be cherished with great care."

"Like what Grandma Han?" She gave me a soft smile, as she sat on the end of the jetty with me.

"Every tree is a life, every shrub, fern and flower, and all the insects and animals. All of them have a role to play in this life, all of them have great value, whether you see it or not, and to be honest my child, here there is a lot that is not seen, and it is in that, the greatest value lies. Your mother understood that, which is why she was returning here."

I gave a jerk as my mind jolted, hadn't my dad said something today? I played the day back through my thoughts, as I focused, and remembered.

"I am pleased to hear that; your mother felt the same way. When she was heading back, that was why she was returning. I was offered a good job overseas, and we were building the firm, it was a large scale project, and Han was having trouble, she was returning to help protect it when her accident happened." I sat up and opened my eyes.

"Protect what?"

"No idea, what are you thinking about?" I turned and glanced back; Shell was sat with her wine.

"Shell, why does everyone keep telling me this place is special, and magical? Today my dad told me my mum was coming back when she had her accident, because Han was struggling, and she wanted to help her protect it. He did not say this place, or the region of the lake, he said it. What does everyone know that I don't?"

She shuffled on the deck, and crossed her legs, and lifted her wine to drink, took a sip and lowered her glass.

"Most people never ask me that out of fear of my weirdness, but I cannot say. I have not spoken to any of them, apart from a few brief lines with your dad who has read my book. Emmy,

Han, your mum and dad, all believed in this place. If what you have said is true, this place was more than a green oasis teaming with life to them, it was their heart, their soul, and their source of life and joy. Maybe they saw something here you haven't, let's be honest, when you were a kid, even you saw the magic here, maybe you are far too jaded now to see it, I do not know?" I lifted my glass.

"It was magical for me, but that was Han and her stories, she made them so real, believe it or not, I believed all of them."

"So why did you stop? Han, and as I found out today, your mum and dad believed in them. I mean, Han was in her eighties, your dad is what, mid forties? Your mum would be early forties if she was still here, they would all be sat here still believing in the magic. I suppose the real question is, why did you stop?" I pulled my feet up onto the jetty and turned round to face her.

"Shell, you are almost twenty two, are you seriously telling me you believe in all those fairy stories, and all the other mystical and mythological stuff you wrote about in your book?" She stared at me, and I could see her complete belief. She nodded her head.

"Yes... Yes, I do, I have seen things no one can explain, not even me, but I still saw them Emmy, and I was not drunk. I know what people say about me, you know, like what you and Pam think? I am telling you straight, ridicule, call me stupid all you like, they exist, and I know that for a fact." I gave a sigh and looked down at the wooden planks of the deck.

"I admire you, in a way, I wish I could be so sure." She lifted her drink.

"You cannot see, touch, smell or taste the conscious mind, and yet everyone knows it exists. The same goes for the air we breathe, it does not taste of anything and can only be seen as vapour on cold days when it is mixed with carbon, and yet every scientist alive will swear it is there. Is it so hard to believe, that not everything has a cold rationale trail of evidence Emmy, is it so utterly ridiculous it must be ridiculed by everyone out of fear of being laughed at?" I looked up, and saw her staring at me.

"Shell, I study living environments, my research is based on known facts, there are no facts that science can prove to show any of the creatures you write about exist." She smirked.

"Really... Okay, let's talk about a small cellular organism that is dependent on light, that somehow and magically, turned into a water breathing fish. Once it had done that, it decided it wanted more, so crawled out of the water onto the mud and learned to breathe air. Then it could not make its mind up, so decided to change through strange magical processes into lizards and birds, and monkeys. And one of those monkeys lost all its hair and decided not to swing through the trees, but grow a bigger brain and adapt to walk upright on the land. Slowly over time with extra magic applied, it built bridges, aeroplanes and cars, and littered the earth with its brick dwellings and turned its back on nature. That creature once filtered air out of the sea to survive, and now it breathes air, eats other animals and wears clothing because it felt superior to all the animals and needed to show it. Holy shit Emmy, what an utterly ridiculous story, who the hell would believe that, we all know it was really God?"

"You are being stupid." She shrugged.

"Okay, show me your soul... Go on get it out, I want to have a look at it, and feel its texture. I mean, I know there is no credible evidence for it, but hey I am open minded and let's be honest, we all know they exist, right? You and Pam laugh at me... Really, because from where I am sat, you two are the ones who look ridiculous, I mean, honestly, a soul, you must be having a laugh, if that was true and they got trapped here, that could actually mean ghosts are real." She stared at me.

"See, is it so far fetched to think that somewhere on this earth something exists that we do not know about yet? Emmy everyday as you well know, new species of insect are being discovered in the Amazon, and in the deepest parts of the oceans, new creatures are still being found. What if, there are other intelligent forms of life that have seen the wicked and cruel way we have treated this earth, and have decided to stay the hell out of our way?" She took a sip of her wine.

"We are so preoccupied with our arrogance, we think we are the smartest, and yet we kill and maim each other in wars for money and gain, hunt our fellow creatures for sport, and farm animals we consider too dumb to realise for food. It is utter arrogance to think nothing could exist that may be as intelligent as us, and as an ecologist you should know better."

Wow, she schooled me completely, I was actually quite

impressed, but I had no idea why, I had seen her many times assassinate people with her theories. I gave a long sigh, how the hell do I answer that?

"Okay I get your point, and yes, we have discovered many new life forms as technology has advanced, but Shell, we are talking fairies, gnomes, sprites and things, and magical beings. You have to admit, there is a massive lack of proof to even give a substantive case." She smiled and gave a small chuckle.

"You just cannot admit it can you, it is so extreme to believe that maybe magic exists, and yet you are surrounded by it? Emmy, life in itself is magic, if we are lucky, one day, we may have the privilege, of creating a new life, and growing it inside ourselves like our mothers did, and then give it a free life with birth. No matter which way you look at it, that is pure magic." I shook my head.

"Well, Biology actually." She shrugged.

"Biology is the study of life's organisms, not life itself. The life is the magic bit, I mean hell, a fish evolved into a man, how fucked up is that, and yet it still happened?"

I gave a smirk as she reached round and dragged the bottle towards her. She leaned forward and refilled my glass, then filled hers. I lifted it up and took a drink.

"Alright Shell, I will humour you for now and go with your train of thought. If they really were such things as fairies, explain the combination of a human form, and the wings of a dragon fly like creature together." She shrugged.

"Okay, you explain to me first, dwarfism, conjoined twins, the world's tallest man, mixed gendered humans, who have both female and male qualities, I mean let's be honest, it looks like a young girl, has boobs, but down there, man tackle. Two hundred years ago no one thought that was possible." I frowned at her.

"Those were all aspects of nature, it tried male and female, and between the spectrum there were variations on a genetic and molecular level." She gave a giggle at me and lifted her eyebrows.

"Oh really, so this nature, which created this molecular level, which blue printed every design, could not, oh, I don't know, it turned a fish into a bird, and a fish eventually into a man. So you tell me Miss Scientist, could it have along the way not took the wings of a dragon fly, and matched them with a man on a molecular level, and genetically created a tiny person that could fly?" She gave a laugh. "You answered your own question before I even began, evolution creates everything."

She did make me laugh at times, I actually admired the way she thought up her arguments, they were all plausible, but not at all provable.

"Shell, there is absolutely no evidence in the evolutionary history to even show that man evolved any form of bone structure to fly." She gave another happy shrug, I somehow thought she was really enjoying this.

"Really, so the skeleton of a bird's wing does not look like a long arm with a big hand then? Hell Emmy, bats, flying squirrels, flying fish, and all the others, be honest, nature has tried every aspect of various developments. If my books are right Dragonflies used to be huge, they could have a wing span of up to three feet millions of years ago, then they shrunk down to as we know them today. That suggests to me they were man sized at one time, so why could they not evolve on a human like creature? The way I see it, if a fish can become a bird, and the same fish became a person, we cannot rule out the theory of tiny flying human like creatures, and if it is human like, you cannot rule out intelligence. I mean, who would have thought that proportionally an ant is stronger than everything else, and yet it is?" I giggled, she was fun, of that there was no doubt.

"Okay, in theory, it is possible, in a really weird way, but for arguments sake, let's say I accept your theory, it is still disproven, there is no credible evidence to even back up your theory, that is the point of science."

She gave a smile, and pointed with her finger as she took a swig of her wine.

"Good point, but science is only ever right, until someone proves it wrong, and until that happens, everyone believes what is current. Most of this planet thought the earth was flat until it was proven beyond doubt it was a sphere. Flat earth theory was credible evidence for a very long time, and yet it was wrong. Emmy that is my point, we just do not know, because we have never found the proof. Look at this month, a whole new dinosaur was found that no one had ever known about, until they dug it up." I shook my head.

"There would still be some evidence Shell, some aspect of them would be found."

"So, why is that cemetery on the hill not absolutely packed and hundreds of times bigger, because people have been dying for hundreds of years, and yet the number of graves up there does not match the amount of people who have died round here in the last two hundred years?" I frowned at her.

"Are you pissed? That makes no sense at all, firstly only a few can afford a burial plot these days, and secondly, most people get cremated and scattered." She raised her glass in salute at me.

"So intelligent life forms have found a way to dispose of their dead without leaving full corpses to be discovered, wow, clever little buggers." I gave a chuckle.

"God you are impossible, I am not going to win, am I?" She took a swig of her wine, and smiled.

"Emmy, I know what I have seen in this life, and I really wish I could show you and prove to you that I am not wrong. Look, I cannot prove it, but by the same chalk you cannot disprove them, so it is like Schrodinger's cat theory, they are neither alive or dead, and no one will know until they open the box. So, in theory, which is what science is, they exist, and don't exist at the same time, which is why you cannot say with any credibility that they are not real." She made a good point, and I had to concede.

"Okay, good point, it is a paradox, but I will let you have that." She smiled.

"They do though, I have seen inside the box, and they are there."

She made me laugh, and I loved her for that, I had suffered so many days of sadness in the last year, and she had always been there for me, and I loved her for it. The sky was darkening and I got up and stretched, and turned towards the lake and looked across at the island.

"This is a beautiful place at this time of day, I love it here, you know you were right Shell, no matter how I may look at things, this is the only home I have ever known, and it is a part of me. I can understand why my mum wanted to come back, she must have missed it so much, I know I have. I just wish Han had not had to leave so soon; I was not ready to say goodbye just yet. I wanted more time with her."

She came up to my side and put her arm round my waist, and stood looking out across the water with me.

"I have no proof, but if you ask me, her spirit is still here, you cannot love a place that much and completely leave it behind, I think some of it lingers on always in the place we hold in our heart. I think your mum's spirit is here too, this truly is a magical place, there is so much to marvel at, I saw that yesterday out walking. Emmy, I meant what I said, I do not want to leave here, I want to stay on. I have cash, I will remain here and protect it, and keep the likes of Pete from destroying it."

I put my head down and gave a sigh, I understood her, but the thought of going back alone without her, felt hard, she had been such a strength for me in the last year, I am not sure I would have made it without her.

"I need to call Harry and try and get a few more days, I still have so much to do, although, I am not looking forward to it, he will be an utter shit as usual."

"What if he refuses to give you the time off. Emmy, you know what he is like?"

I nodded as I turned, and saw her watching me.

"I will deal with that if it happens, honestly, at the moment I do not want to think about it, my life has too many questions at the moment, please do not add to the pile." She smiled at me.

"Yeah, I get you, call him tomorrow and take it from there Hun." I gave a sigh, I felt tired.

"I am off to bed, it has felt like another long day, and it was pretty emotional with my dad. I need to process everything, and try to get my head round it all."

"Night Hun, try and sleep, so don't think too much." Now there was a thought.

"Night Shell, thanks, I really enjoyed tonight." She gave a soft smile.

"Any time, go sleep."

I walked slowly back towards the house, my thoughts swirling with pictures of my dad, his tears, his eyes, his soft voice as he spoke about my mother. It was nothing like I had expected it would be, and it was always as I had dreamed it should be. Once again Han was right, she had told me often that he was once a deeply caring and loving man. I cannot count the times she had talked of his love for my mother, and today seeing the tree covered in red ribbons, and knowing he had been there every year to mark her birthday, was yet another reminder of her deep wisdom.

I undressed and sat on my bed, and slipped the letter off my bedside table and opened it. I had read it a thousand times in the last year and knew every word written, and yet I still continued to read it. I looked down at her neat hand writing.

'You are not alone, you never were, the light within you always connected all three of us. I know you will not understand yet, but we were all born in the light, you, your mother, and I. There are many who will live in this world with closed eyes, and shut hearts, for they will never understand the wonders that lie beyond belief.'

"Oh Han, are my eyes closed, have I shut my heart off, I just don't know. If we are connected, why can I not feel it?"

I gave a gasp and lay on the bed, and closed my eyes, I was so weary, so tired, when would all this pain trapped inside me end?

Shelly stood alone at the end of the jetty, watching as the sun set, and the water at the far end of the lake glittered in an orange red. She looked down at the bottle, and there was about half a glass left, she smiled and poured it into her glass.

"I wish she would believe, she must not leave here, she needs to protect you, and I have done all I can to try and make her stay without knowing what was meant for her. I believe in all of you, I know you are all out there, but what can I do to help her, I am trying so hard?"

"Don't give up on her, tonight, you made a good case for the need to trust her instincts."

She turned to see Randolph at the end of the jetty, sat on the low stone wall. She walked slowly towards him, swinging the empty bottle.

"She is hurting too much, she is blinded by the pain, and I do not blame her, she has gone through a lot. If you ask me, she has always been too trusting, and because of that, others have hurt her, and at those times, all she had was Han. It was good her father was nice to her, but it is her mum's birthday, will he be that nice again, or does she have to wait another year?" Randolph gave a nod at her, and peered out from under his hood.

"A lot of good was done this day, what happened was also

his wish. Maybe he needed her to grow into the likeness of her mother before he saw the truth of her, for she is very much the double of her mother. Another shadow was lifted from her heart today, and the light will flow more readily within her because of it." Shell sat on the wall at his side and sipped her drink.

"Time is not on her side, she has never gotten over losing her mother, and Han died only a year ago. Since then, I have seen how she closed down and lost all her faith, and I really do think without it, she will never fully open up again." He gave a nod.

"The path of a watcher has never been an easy one, even Han had moments where her faith was shaken badly. Losing Amelia was a severe blow to her, and she had her fair share of dark times. I would often sit and talk to her when young Emily went back to school, she put on a brave face for her, but when she went back, she would grieve, it took her many years, but she never truly got over it. It gives me comfort knowing they walk in the light together again here in this land, I have felt them together again, and it has been nice."

Shelly leaned forward and held her glass in front of her, as she thought about everything.

"If Emily refuses, can she be replaced, you know, can another take her place and watch over everything?" His hood twitched and he turned.

"What are you suggesting?" She lifted her glass and took a swig.

"I am still twenty one, and my birthday is not for another month, is there a way to take in this light, because I would stay here forever and watch over everything, as you know, my belief is total?" Under his hood he gave a smirk.

"That is a noble gesture, but until her time passes, we will not know if she has a successor, only then will the light reveal them, for the light protects all that walk in it." Shell gave a giggle.

"Not Amelia, why did it not protect her, Emmy would have been grateful for the help?"

"It chose to save Emily." Shelly felt the shock ripple through her, and sat up quickly.

"Emily was in the car?" The hood moved.

"Yes, she survived the accident, she was strapped into the front, and as the car spun out of control, Amelia dived over her to shield her." Shelly swallowed hard.

"Holy shit... Does Emily know?" Randolph's hood shook.

"Only Han and John know, no one else, well now you do. Han felt it better she never found out, she thought the guilt would be too much for her to handle." Shelly closed her eyes and took in a deep breath.

"Me and my big mouth, honestly, I wish I had never asked. Is that why her father has avoided her, did he resent her for living?"

"No, he is not that sort of man, I think in a way, he wanted to protect Emily, he blamed himself for a long time over Amelia's death. He too has suffered, and in many ways, both Han and I felt he avoided her because he did not have the heart to hurt her by telling her. It has taken him almost twenty years to face her, but when he did, he listened to Han and said nothing. I still feel she is better off not knowing the truth, I am not sure considering everything, she would be able to cope with such news." Shelly shook her head.

"Who would, that is a hell of a thing to have hung over you, Christ will it ever get any easier for her?"

"If she makes the choice to embrace the light, then she will feel her pain lessen as wisdom engulfs her. Nothing can hide from the light, and so she will learn everything, but the light will help her heal fully, we must wait, and see what the outcome will be."

Shelly drained her glass, she stood up and faced Randolph, she gave a smile, but wavered slightly as she looked down at him.

"I'm glad you are here, until I met you, I thought I was going mad, but actually, compared to what you know, I feel saner. Thanks for looking over her and protecting her, she is a very special person who I love dearly, she is my greatest friend, so I am happy to know there are others who see her as I do, so, you know, thanks." The hood moved.

"I have always watched over her, and trust me when I say, I see her light, and she cares for you deeply, you have been a very good friend and companion to her, and all of us appreciate that too." Shell smiled and patted his shoulder.

"Night Hun." She swayed as she staggered up the steps, and Randolph gave a little chuckle, as he watched her make it to the door.

"Sleep well children, Han is with you."

Chapter Twelve

Awakening

When Shell checked in on me, yeah, she does that, I was
fast asleep, lay across the bed in my underwear, she pulled the
bedding over me, and left me to sleep. She returned to her room,
a little bit tipsy, and settled down with her laptop, intending to
write.

In my dreams, my father talked and hugged me, and I felt
a strange warmth all around me, as I slept deeply filled with
happiness. As I lay curled up, snug and warm, across the lake in
the darkened woodland, there was movement.

Randolph walked through the thick trees, on the northern part
of the island and came to a dense row of holly, filled with hanging
ivy. He stood on the path and closed his eyes, and there was the
faintest of white glowing light all around him.

Before him on the path, the ivy swung back from the holly,
revealing a doorway, made of thick heavy ancient stone, not
unsimilar to those made in many of the large stone circles around
the country. He walked through the heavy doorway, which was a
good three feet thick, into a huge circle, walled in by huge thick
grey stone, similar to those that made up the doorway.

In the centre of the circular compound was a dais, made of a
circular set of three steps, and in the centre, on the top, was a
tall standing stone. Other doorways led into the large circular
area, some leading to stone built cells in which to meet, or lay
offerings, others into smaller circles of stone. The whole place
was a complex that was older than the memory of men, all grey
and weathered, marked with large pale growths of lichen, larger
than ever seen in the world of men.

He walked to the tall central standing stone, and knelt at the base of the steps, his hood and his long cloak spread on the floor behind him, as he worked with purpose. From his pocket, he produced a folded piece of thin green leather, and laid it down, and smoothed it out flat with his hands. He reached into his under jacket, and pulled a long clear wand of crystal out, and lay it with reverence onto the green leather, on the bottom step of the dais.

He sat back on his haunches, and lifted his hands under his hood, and reached for the chain around his neck, and unclipped the clasp, drew out his hands and pulled on the chain, and it came up from within his tunic, revealing the round circular disk which contained a tree of life, laden with fruit. He placed it carefully down, so that the chain ran parallel to the long crystal wand, and then lay the tree of life pendant, so that it connected the two touching the end of the wand tip.

He sat back and bowed his head, as he silently said the words of the watcher in his mind, and then gave a small bow to the standing stone. Slipping his hand down to his pocket, he dropped it in, and pulled out a small bottle and a chunk of bread and cheese, wrapped in brown paper. He laid them out on the second step, and then gave another bow to the stone, took a deep breath, leaned forward on his knees, outstretched his arms, and lowered his head to touch the bottom step, just in front of the leather containing the wand.

"Gather to me."

The wand flickered, and then glowed a bright intense white, as above the woodland the clouds separated revealing the bright stars in the sky, and a breeze blew around the inside of the stones.

Esme sat up in the grass and turned to Felix, she felt the power, she turned quickly and grabbed at Felix's arm, and shook it hard. He moaned and smacked his lips.

"I am tired Esme, watch the fat one alone, let me sleep." She shook him harder and his head rolled from side to side.

"Felix wake up, we are being summoned, come on, we are needed." He stretched out his arms and gave a long yawn.

"I did six, I am tired." Esme shook even harder.

"Felix, Randolph has summoned the clan, and actually, it was five and a half." His eyes snapped open.

"Why, it is not time, what is he playing at?" She looked at him, looking worried.

"I don't know, but he has summoned all of us to the temple, we have to go, now hurry." He sat up fast, and looked round at her, she smiled and nodded.

"Felix, it is happening, Randolph needs us, we must hurry." He gave a nod and jumped to his feet and his wings unfolded behind him, as he took her hand.

"Come on, we must hurry." She gave a big smile as they both glowed white and lifted into the air.

Lights streamed across the woodland above the ferns, coming from every part of the island, like millions of darting fireflies, and all heading to the islands centre, and the stone circle hidden within a ring of thick dense holly trees, covered with ivy.

Emily groaned in her sleep, and spoke, from her dreams. "Han... Han, I need you, where are you, I really need you." The bedroom door opened a little space, and Shelly leaned her head through the gap and swallowed hard.

"Oh shit!"

Emily was glowing with white light and floating a foot above the bed, her hair hanging down touching the sheets. She took a huge breath, and tried to calm herself. Her voice was a quiet whisper, more to herself than Emily.

"I knew it, I knew this place was bloody full of weird. Living humans are not supposed to float, or glow for that fact, what the hell are you Emmy?"

Her hand came through the gap below her head, and lifted up her phone, she hit the button on the screen, and held it still, as it filmed.

"I really hope this does not erase; she needs to see this."

Within the circle, Randolph lay flat chanting to himself, as balls of light flowed in through the doorway and lined the walls of the large inner circle. Every so many feet there was a flat raised stone, and the brightest lights hovered above them, as all the others formed in the spaces between. The lights expanded, and white intensely bright human like forms grew up, and then settled, and all around the circle, was masses of elegant faintly glowing people. Below the largest stone, Barrack stood the size of a fully grown human man, he looked around the circle as others appeared, and waited.

Two high speed balls of light came hurtling into the circle and hovered as if looking for a place, and then shot into a free gap, and then elongated into the forms of youngish teenage children, Barrack gave a nod as he looked round, and then looked to Randolph.

"We are gathered Master Sage Feather." Randolph sat back on his haunches, and pulled his arms to his side, Barrack gave a respectful nod to him.

"Name the reason to gather."

Randolph bowed to him, and rose to his feet, and turned slowly looking at everyone who had gathered around him, he nodded his head to each of the elders.

"Greetings and well met my friends." All round the circle, all of the Nairn gave a respectful bow of their head and spoke.

"Greetings and well met, Master Sage Feather."

Randolph slid back his hood, and his long grey hair fell to his shoulders, and he looked round the circle and then faced Barrack, he pointed to the stone dais.

"I seek your aid, Emily has but two days, before she must leave and time is slipping through the hour glass. This day I have seen the love in her heart for this place, and it is stronger than it has ever been, yet a veil of darkness clouds her thoughts, and is holding back the light." Barrack gave a nod, and looked to the other council, they too gave a nod, he looked at Randolph.

"This is news we have already greeted Master Sage Feather, all of us see the love within her, but it does not warrant a gathering of the clan." Randolph gave a respectful nod.

"Before you with my offering is the wand I made to hold Han's light, and I have travelled here to ask your favour, and help me to remove the veil that clouds Emily's mind." Veda White Shell spoke, from behind him, and he turned to face her.

"Master Sage Feather, what purpose would require the light of Han, for I see no use of it at this stage in the process?" He gave a bow.

"My Lady Veda, Han left whilst Emily was away, part of the cloud that surrounds her, is that she was not present to say the things she had always wanted to say, and the pain of that guilt is what veils her mind. This day with her father, I had hoped the veil would thin enough to allow her light to pass, as she learned of her mother, but it was not enough. I beg this council to aid me, and allow me to send Han's light to her, and let them walk in the light, even if only for a small time, I know it will aid the cause of all of us." Veda gave a nod, Barrack watched on with interest, as he understood Randolph's intent.

Chandak watched the events, and understood what the intention of Randolph was, but he was unsure. His face looked grim as he considered all that was said.

"Master Sage Feather, this cloud of darkness has been with her for many years, why do you not offer her the light of her mother?" Randolph turned to face him and gave a respectful bow.

"My Lord Chandak, your words hold truth, and I have on my being, her wand also, but I feel the time yet is not upon us, for the purity within the wand of her mother, is the purest I have encountered, and is too strong for her at the moment."

He slipped his hand into his inner pocket, and drew out a long roll of pure white silk. All the Nairn felt its power and leaned in with a gasp, as Randolph gently unrolled the fabric, he held it up, his hand still covered by the silk so as not to touch it. Felix gave a gasp.

"Oh, leaves of the land, that is beautiful." Randolph smiled.

"Amelia was indeed a beautiful force within the light, and for her, I crafted the purest crystal I could find from below the falls, and yet I feel, that Emily could be so much more powerful, for like her mother, she is filled with love for all living things."

He turned slowly holding the wand, as all the Nairn marvelled at the wonder of what looked like the most perfect and clearest crystal they had ever seen. Barrack watched on, taking note of all his people gathered within the circle. Chandak leaned over and whispered to Barrack, he nodded.

"How do you know Master Sage Feather that this will work, this is not the way things have been done in the past?" Randolph turned and smiled.

"Lord Barrack, can you not feel her already responding to the wand of light on the sacred stones. Feel her as we speak, her yearning to connect is strong, her light is trying to reach here." Barrack gave a nod and smiled.

"I feel her Master Sage Feather, and also the struggle within her, but it is not the way things are done, we have customs and traditions that have always applied."

He looked round the circle of his people, he knew they felt the desperation of their plight and needed hope.

"I say this, considering things, I shall decree that it is for all gathered to judge, and the outcome will be in their hands." He looked to the circle, and his voice rose loud and deep.

"WHAT SAY YE!?"

Felix and Esme closed their eyes, and held their breath as they squeezed out with all their tiny might to glow bright. All around them, those in favour did the same, and all the light that flowed out from them, spun round the circle, Chandak disapproved and did nothing, and a few of the council followed his lead. Randolph fell to his knees and hoped, as the light spun faster, and the wand on the step began to vibrate and glow brighter. He held his breath in hope as a long thin beam of light appeared and stretched up from the wand.

Felix gave a mighty squeeze and grew brighter than he ever had, as he yearned for the power to help Randolph, and slowly a figure of white started to form. Randolph's eyes filled with tears as he smiled, and looked up at the glowing white image of Han, she smiled, as she looked down.

"Hello old friend, I see you listened. I shall go to her." He gave a gasp seeing her again, but smiled more.

"I have missed you, and she needs you more now than ever." She gave a nod and turned to Barrack.

"My Lord, with your grace, I will go to her." He smiled and gave a nod.

"Take the love you hold for her with our blessing." Esme and Felix fell to their knees and wept, as did many others to see her again.

Shelly shook as she stood at the door glued to the scene, and the solid form of Emily separated from the light, and slowly descended to the bed, leaving a white glowing shape of Emily floating in the air. She gave a gasp and her hand trembled.

"Okay, so I am now completely freaked out, when I said show me your soul, I was just debating, I did not mean it literally. Please go back in so she does not die, I do not want to be alone in the middle of nowhere with the body of my friend."

She leaned on the wall as her legs shook hard, and she felt giddy and weak. She took deep breaths and tried to calm her inner panic as she watched the white glowing soul of Emily hover above the bed. Outside the wind appeared to rise, and Shelly breathed harder as she tried to suck more air into her lungs.

Outside the window, the whole back of the house lit up, and Shelly's eyes opened even wider, as she saw a white orb pulsate outside in the darkness, she gave a nervous squeak, as it floated through the glass window, and then hovered in the room, and began to form into the shape of an old woman.

"Oh Shit, I hate it when I am right, Han really did not leave."

Her legs grew weak, and folded under her, and she slid down to the floor, and flopped onto the carpet out cold, in her faint. Han reached out her arm, and touched Emily's white glowing soul.

I felt restless and could hear her, and shouted out as I could not see her. "Han... Han where are you, Han, I need you?"

I felt the warmth around me and I turned, and everywhere lit up around me in the brightest of white, I blinked and she was there, she smiled as she lifted her hand to my face.

"I am here child." I felt the tears, and threw my arms around her.

"Han... Han, I miss you so much, why did you leave me?"

I snuggled into her and felt that warmth of her love radiate around me, as she slid her hand to my hair and stroked it back as she always had.

"Emmy, my dear child, I am in your heart, I never left you, can you not feel me, I am there next to your mother?" I held her tightly.

"I miss you so much, and I feel so utterly alone, I did not want you to go, I wanted you to stay longer."

"Emmy, you are never alone here. I told you, we are connected by the light, as is your mother, you can never be without us, but you have to open your heart to us, you have forgotten my most important teaching. Emmy, it is the love, that is the only thing in this world that will connect you always to everything, for it is your love that controls the light."

"Han I am struggling to remember, I dream, but they frighten me, and when I wake up, they haunt my thoughts. Everything feels so dark in my life since you left me, and I am finding it so hard, no one understands what it was like to be with you."

I leaned back and she smiled that wonderful soft loving smile, and her eyes were so bright and filled with life. She slipped her hands down, and took both my hands in hers.

"Emmy my child, remember your tenth birthday, remember the night of the lights. I sat you on the end of the jetty, and told you to close your eyes and open your heart. You have to leave your mind and your thoughts behind, in this land, you have to feel your way, feel everything. Emmy focus on your heart and your gut instincts, for it is there that the answers lie. Your tenth birthday, remember the lights, always remember the lights."

I sat bolt upright in bed and took a huge breath of air, and held it in for a second, and then gasped it out. I was sat on my bed in my knickers, tangled in the sheets, as I gasped in more air and my mind cleared. I felt my breathing start to regulate, as I just sat there, trying to puzzle out the dream that had felt so real to me.

I looked round in the dark, and saw the light on the floor, and frowned. I leaned over to see Shelly lay down, her phone camera app was open, as it faced the ceiling. I gave a shudder, and slid my legs up to untangle them from the sheets.

"Shell... Shell, what the hell are you doing sleeping in the doorway?"

I slipped off the bed, my legs felt weak and shaky. I was really hot and sweating, as I staggered towards her and crouched down, and gave her a shake.

"Shell... Shell, wake up, what the hell are you doing?"

She moaned, and disturbed, and then suddenly her eyes snapped open, and she sat up quickly, and looked at me, she gave a loud gasp.

"Thank God for that, you are not dead and your back."

"Huh?" I stared at her.

"What do you mean I am back; I was in bed?" She shook her head and her eyes looked huge.

"Oh, bloody no you weren't... Well not in it anyways... Emmy you were in the bloody air floating above it... Oh shit, I fainted again." I stood up and stared at her.

"Ha bloody ha... Just how pissed were you?" She swallowed hard and took a deep breath.

"Not pissed enough if you ask me, holy shit, when Han appeared, I was completely freaked out." I frowned at her.

"Okay Shell, that is not funny, I can handle your strange humour, but keep Han out of it." She looked at me and shook her head, actually she looked a little pale, as she lifted her hand and held it out, she was trembling.

"Humour, oh Hun, I was not joking, you were calling out to her in your sleep, and oh shit, she floated right in, straight through the bloody window." She swallowed hard. "Christ that freaked me out." I stepped over her and gave a sigh.

"I am going to go down and make a drink, I had strange dreams, and I am not in the mood for your weird theories right now."

I headed over to the stairs and left her sat on the floor, my head felt groggy, and I needed to clear it, I looked back at her and shook my head. I had no problems with her delusions of spooks, but I did not want Han a part of them. Although, I was dreaming of her, which was strange, how did Shell know?

Shelly sat on the floor and breathed in again, as she leaned back on the wall and closed her eyes for a second, she still felt slightly dizzy.

"Dreams, oh hell, I wish it was, dreams I can handle, but souls leaving bodies and floating round the room, that is really going to take some getting used to. Maybe I should tie her to the bed at night, just in case."

I stood in the kitchen and waited for the kettle, outside it was pitch black, there were no stars tonight, clouds had rolled in. The kettle clicked and I turned to my cup, and poured in the hot water. Shelly came into the kitchen almost running, as I put down the kettle, and turned to the fridge for the milk, I noticed her stood at the end of the table, and looked at her.

"What now?" She swallowed hard.

She looked really freaked out, and was as white as a ghost and trembling. I stopped, something felt off, my eyes fixed on hers.

"Shell is everything alright, you look really pale?" She swallowed again, and took a huge breath.

"Emmy, it was real, I was not making it up, see!" She held up her phone. I frowned at her.

"It is kind of a small screen, and I am all the way over here, so it's a little difficult, what is it?" Her voice trembled as she spoke, still holding up the phone.

"You... Emmy, it is you, floating." I looked at her and sighed.

"Shell, a joke is a joke, but pack it in, it is not funny. I have to deal with too much, I had a really weird dream tonight." She shook her head.

"Yeah, I get it, Han came to you tonight, didn't she?" I felt a cold shiver run down my back.

"How do you know that?" She took another huge breath.

"Emmy, it was not a dream, it happened, I filmed it... Then fainted... Sorry, but it was my first real ghost." I could feel the goose bumps lifting on my arms.

"Shell it is not funny, please don't make fun like that." She shook her head and walked down the kitchen towards me.

"Emmy, honestly I am not, I filmed it, she was here, see for yourself."

I looked down at the frozen picture on her phone, I was floating and shimmering white. I felt my legs go weak, and leaned back against the kitchen work top, not quite understanding what I was seeing. Shell leaned over and hit the play button, and I could hear me calling Han's name as I floated. So, okay, I was starting to freak out as I watched. Shelly was breathing really fast, as she watched it again, but this time with me. I just stared at the tiny screen, my body lowered to the bed, leaving a floating mass above me, and then the whole room turned white, dazzling the screen, which was pretty freaky. What came next left me ice cold, it was Han's voice, of that there was no mistake.

"I am here child."

I felt the air run out of me. The camera crashed to the floor and filmed the ceiling, and the audio went on the fritz. Shelly looked at me as I looked at her.

"Emmy, she is here, she is with you, the camera did not get her, I think it was too bright for the camera, but I am not lying. I saw her clear as day touch you and talk... Then I completely lost it, pissed my knickers and fainted, sorry."

My mind was a whirl, and I suddenly felt weak, I leaned forward and grabbed the chair, Shelly snatched at me to steady me, as I collapsed into the chair, I felt giddy and unstable, my heart was racing and I felt really hot, as I shook.

She put the phone on the table, and crouched down at my side, and took my hand in hers and gave it a squeeze. I turned to her, feeling completely mind blown and overwhelmed, my throat had gone dry, as I tried to speak.

"Shell, that was her voice, it is not possible, but it was definitely her voice." She smiled and her eyes filled with tears, as she squeezed my hand.

"She kept her word, Emmy; she never left you."

I felt a huge surge inside me, as I swallowed hard, I was shaking as I looked at her with tears rolling down her cheeks.

"Shell it is not possible, she died." She wiped her eyes and smiled.

"Looks like you got to see inside the box Emmy, and she was there inside waiting for you to look."

Randolph walked through the woodland, cradling Esme and Felix in his arms. They were utterly wiped out and exhausted, they had given their all to create a strong enough light to pull Han's light out of the wand. He gave a sigh as he looked down at them.

"I know you love her, but it is not worth expending all your strength, we had enough between all of us." Esme opened her weary eyes.

"It was not everyone, some did not join in. We had to make sure Randolph; Emily needs us." He smiled and gave a nod.

"Felix was already tired from his labour, it was a big risk you took, it could have really done a lot of damage to you both, and I for one, think both of you are too precious to risk yourselves so easily." She gave a sleepy smile.

"She is so beautiful Randolph, and she needed us, we believe in her." He gave a little chuckle.

"I feel that is very evident, and I am sure she will one day thank you. Esme, listen to me, make him rest, you know what he is like. He needs a lot more sleep, staying up late every night is not helping him. I am watching over her and her friend, he needs to sleep more and worry less."

He reached the place he wanted and crouched down. Carefully he lowered them to the floor, and then grabbed two large dock leaves. He reached over for some pine sticks, pushed one into the floor and then slipped one end of the large leaf over it, so the stick came through. Randolph lifted the other stick, and pushed it through the other end of the leaf, wedging it into the floor, creating a small hammock.

He lifted Felix carefully up, and laid him on the leaf, where he curled up in his sleep. He then made another, and gently placed Esme in it, she smiled as she looked at him.

"We love you too Randolph, thank you for taking care of us." He gave a wide smile.

"I love you too, as I do all your people, but you two are special." She gave a big smile and yawned. He gave a sigh.

"Esme, I have made these here so you can see her house, so do me a favour, just lie back here and watch whilst you both rest and get strong again. Tell him, in the days to come, Emily will need us, so he must rest properly, and no trips across the lake, save your strength for when we need it." She gave a nod and closed her eyes and snuggled down on the leaf.

Randolph stood up and looked out across the lake, the kitchen light was on, and he smiled, he knew that she was up with Shell, and they were talking.

"Good, she has started to awaken, Han has such powerful light, she was right, she knew her way straight through all of Emily's defences. She will be missed, although it was nice to see her again, even if only for a short time." He turned, and walked back into the woodland, and his raft on the other side, where it waited to take him back across the lake to his cabin.

We talked as we sipped our coffee, for a little while, and then

I felt exhausted, my whole world had tipped upside down again, and I needed to rest quietly. We turned off the light and headed back to bed, it was three in the morning, and I felt weary. I made my bed back up and slipped in, clicked off my bedside lamp and lay back in the dark and closed my eyes, and drifted in my thoughts.

"Remember my tenth birthday."

I relaxed and breathed out, and felt my whole body go limp, I felt so incredibly tired, and turned and curled up, and pushed my face into the pillow, and felt a small twinge of happiness.

"She was here, she still is, I knew it, I knew she would never leave me." I looked through the darkness to where I know on my mirror hung mum and Han's pendants.

"Night Han, night Mum."

I gave a sigh of happiness, and felt my body slip into peace. My tenth birthday... That was the night Han showed me how to close my mind, and feel the world around me. I have never forgotten it, I have never forgotten opening my eyes to see all the lights in the sky, and Hans soft voice.

"Look at them my child, Emmy, all of those are the souls of those who love you, and that biggest and brightest one there, well that is your mother showing you all her love as she looks upon you. See they are all there, living in the light and watching over you, because that is what they are, they are watchers of everything, and all of those up there, well my child, one day, you will guide and protect them too. Never forget, the watchers in the light."

Chapter Thirteen

Facing Facts

The sun was up and the sky looked clear and blue, as I opened my eyes. I sat up and rubbed them, my life felt surreal, last night my world turned upside down. The film of me floating was just too weird for me, and then hearing Han's voice as clear as day, had left me lay in bed questioning everything.

Is it weird, that today it feels like Shell is the more stable of the two of us? I am not sure what I would have done, if I walked into her room and found her floating. Actually, I probably would have screamed, lost it, and fled. I know for a fact, I would not have my shit together enough to open my phone, swipe up, open the camera app, and film it. Oh God, my life is getting so bloody weird, I have no idea what to make of it.

Han had always delighted me with her stories of hidden magic, fairies, and the strange forces of people, and as I slowly started to come to life sat in my bed this morning, I am starting to wonder if they were actually made up stories, or reality. Well, to be honest, her reality, not mine, I mean, my life has never been easy or simple, but planting trees, loving the outdoors and working for a tyrant surveying outdoor sites to be destroyed by builders, has been my life of late, and all of it has been pretty grounded in reality, but last night, hell, how do I come to terms with that?

I had a headache, it cannot have been the wine, I only had two glasses, maybe it was the stress and shock, because watching that video shocked the shit out of me, and the fallout in my mind has felt pretty bloody stressful. I slipped out of bed and felt the soft carpet below my feet, I looked out of the window and down to the jetty, and the memory of that night. I gave a sigh; I was not awake yet.

"I hope they were stars, not glowing figures in the sky."

I grabbed my phone off the bedside unit and headed down to the kitchen in search of coffee, and sanity. It was still early, well, too early for Shell, it was only nine thirty, she would not surface for a while. To be honest the thought of going back to bed suited me fine, sadly, I had things to do, and one of those was having to deal with Harry. I closed my eyes.

"Oh God, do I have to?"

I put my phone down on the table, and headed for the sink, then reached for the kettle to fill it, I grabbed it and frowned, it was full... And warm. I looked out of the window, and down the garden, Shell was sat with a coffee on the low wall with her feet up on the seat. Wow, she was up, although, thinking about it, she was probably as freaked out as I was, I mean, after all, how many times do you walk into a room to see your friend floating above the bed glowing?

I clicked the kettle back on, and it started to heat up with a soft rumble, as I spooned out the coffee and sugar, and headed for the fridge for the milk. With my drink made, I grabbed my phone and headed for the garden, I was just in my knickers, but hey, I live in the middle of nowhere, who is going to see, right? It was warm, as the sun heated up for the day, it felt like it was going to be a roaster.

I walked down the steps yawning, and sipped my coffee. I reached the bottom and Shell turned with bleary eyes, she looked knackered. She smiled and moved her feet off the bench.

"Hey Hun, you okay?" I sat down and looked along the jetty.

"Honestly, I am not awake, so feel little, and actually, I am happy about that." She gave a quiet chuckle, then yawned.

"I didn't sleep very well, I tossed and turned all night, you know that saying, be careful what you wish for? Well, honestly, this morning I am debating it all in my head, and I do not have enough headspace for the conversation going on." I nodded.

"Yeah, I get that, I am trying to avoid any thought of it until I am awake, the problem is I do not really want to wake up at the moment." She nodded and sipped her drink.

I stared out across the island as I sipped the coffee, trying to focus my head on the job at hand, which was Harry, but kept seeing the jetty and drifting back to the memory of that night, and Han's soft voice telling me to remember it. Something came to mind and I turned to Shell.

"Shell, do you think it is possible to shut off your mind, and just feel with your heart and instincts?" She gave a shrug.

"I have never tried it, but I suppose people who meditate do something like that, I am not sure, I have never done it myself. You know if you think about it, we all probably do it at some point." I frowned.

"Do you think so?" I lifted my cup to drink; she looked over her mug at me.

"Think about it, how many times do we do something, and just get carried away in its beauty, that cannot really be the mind can it? We simply just feel, almost like it is a natural process, you know, like just knowing you like or love someone, you just feel it, then say to yourself, yeah, I like them."

I suppose that made sense, yesterday, as I looked at my dad, I wanted to be angry with him, but I couldn't, I looked at him, and felt his pain and sadness, and so held back. I did not think of it, I just naturally did it, was that me feeling with my heart and instincts? It was an interesting point, come to think of it, I was dreading phoning Harry, so I was feeling that without even thinking, I just knew without any thought, he would not be happy with me. Shelly smiled as she watched me.

"So, when are you going to ring him?" I blinked and came out of my thoughts.

"When I have had enough coffee to be fully awake, so I can hold my shit together."

"Why put yourself through it, just tell him to sling his hook, there are better jobs with better bosses out there Emmy. You know I have never understood why you put up with him." I took another sip of my coffee.

"He is an ass, but I really like the work, I really like driving out to sites to explore them, and look at what wild life it has. I love the freedom to just roam around looking for the signs of life, and logging all the flora, it gives me a lot of pleasure." She nodded.

"But you have that here, Emmy you now own two thousand acres, how much of it have you actually explored? Seriously, have you ever wandered off the paths and just gone rogue in the undergrowth, and really looked at what is here?" I gave a smile.

"You never give up, do you? Shell, I grew up here, I do actually know quite a lot of what is out there." She shrugged.

"Yeah, as a kid, but what would you discover now, with your training? I bet there is a huge list of things out there to pique your interest and set your spirit free, and be honest, not having to answer to the likes of Harry would be a bonus."

She was right, this would be a perfect place to work, and I had already spotted two orchids that were considered rare. I know there are parts I had never explored and it would be fun, but she was forgetting one thing.

"Shell, I get paid to do what I do for Harry, who would pay me to work here? You know, it is alright owning all this, but I still have to earn a living to pay my way. Han spent eighty percent of her inheritance to live here, and she was not skint when she started." Shell shrugged.

"Life here is simple, it cannot be anywhere near as expensive as living in Exeter. Han was pretty self sufficient, and be honest, there would be no rush to get the work done. Hell, we are young, this place could be a life's work, and it would be a hell of a lot less stressful than Harry." I smiled, and drained my cup.

"I need more coffee before the stress of him, you want another?" I held out my hand, and she passed me her cup with a smile. I headed back to the house for more.

There was no putting off the inevitable, and after two more coffees, and armed with a new cup, as the day warmed, I sat on the bench at the bottom of the garden, with Shell on the wall at my side and lifted my phone with a sigh. Shell gave a titter, as I pressed dial and put it on speaker phone. It rang twice, and then he answered.

"Well, it is about bloody time." I sat back and looked at the phone.

"What do you mean Harry, I booked the week off?" There was a sound like the flicking of pages.

"Well, I don't see it in my diary, I had you off for one day." I frowned at my phone, how could he say that, I had been quite clear about what time I needed.

"Harry, I told you, I had to sort out things at my gran's cottage, driving there and back alone would swallow a day."

"Well a day should have been plenty, you know I do have costs, and covering for your lazy ass, has a price." Shell raised her eye brows as she stared at me, I looked at the phone.

"Hold on, my lazy ass, no disrespect, but there are few with my qualifications that would tolerate your abuse or lousy pay, I work my ass off for you."

"Well not according to my diary, I have had to cover for you all week with a temp, so I hope you will be in Monday at seven am?" I frowned.

"Why so early, I don't start until nine?"

"Someone has to make up for my losses, two extra hours each day will cover your absence costs." Shelly looked at me, and I knew what she was thinking.

"Do I get paid for an extra two hours?"

"Hell no, I am not running a charity here, this is a company with overheads."

Shell sat back, and I could see she was pissed off, I looked at the phone and could feel my anger growing.

"I am not working for nothing Harry, if you covered me then you got paid for that work, I am not subsidising your business, and you have always made a good return on charging extra because of my qualifications. You can sod off, if you think I will let you bill those companies and not pay me for those hours." I heard him give a sigh.

"Well then, I think we have reached a stalemate then, Pete said you would be like this." Shell sat up as I stared at the phone.

"What the hell has Pete got to do with it?"

"Nothing, we were merely talking."

"Yeah, I can see that, well keep me out of any bloody conversation with him."

"So will you be in tomorrow?"

"What? I never work Sundays." I could feel my blood starting to boil.

"Well then, I know where I stand don't I?" I could not believe what I was hearing.

"Oh yeah, and where is that exactly, in Pete's pocket?"

"Emily, I feel I have been very fair, but if you are not here at seven tomorrow morning, I will have to consider our working arrangement." God I was getting so angry.

"Really, well you know what, start considering them now, because there is no bloody way I will be there tomorrow at any time. My gran died, and I have had to sort out her affairs, and if you cannot understand that, then bugger you."

"Emily, I took just one day when my father died, you get over things, and come on, isn't it just another excuse, after all she died a year ago?"

Shelly took a huge breath and breathed out slowly, I could see she was getting as angry as me, I looked at my phone as it lay on the bench, and I felt like smashing it.

"I am sorry, but I am not as cold as you, Han actually meant something to me, and I cannot just get over her in a day, I am not you." He gave a laugh.

"Well obviously, if you were, you would have been here."

"You know Harry, this is the first holiday time I have used in over a year, and I am entitled to at least another twelve days, there are rules and laws you know, and you are not above them, no matter what your ego says?"

"Emily, be here at seven tomorrow, or don't come back at all." I felt my breath catch in my throat.

"Fine, I will send you my address, send my p45 and reference here, and good luck finding someone else who will tolerate all your bullshit... Bye Harry."

I hit the phone screen to end the call a little harder than I meant to, and it slid towards the edge of the bench. I panicked and snatched it just in time, and then gave a little scream and stamped my foot on the floor.

"GOD, I HATE THAT MAN!" I took a huge breath, and Shell smiled.

"Feel better?" I took another long breath, and held it in a moment, and then let it go as I tried to calm down. She giggled and I looked at her.

"I hate him, I bloody hate him... Oh God, Shell, I think I just lost my job." She slipped off the wall and pulled me into a hug.

"You know what, good, there has to be better ways to earn money than working for him, he is an utter shit."

I breathed out slowly, as I tried to calm my anger, and the

reality of my situation kicked in, I was about to be unemployed. Shell appeared quite happy about it, and just smiled at me as she slipped back across the bench.

"Be honest Emmy, that job was pure stress, you have to be a little bit relieved... I mean just a little bit?"

In a weird way I was, I did feel a lot of pressure lift off me, I cannot deny, I hated the idea of going back, even though the last few days had been hard to deal with, it had been nice not having to put up with Harry's outbursts and insults. I looked at her and her eyes twinkled as she looked at me, and I gave a small smile.

"I am a little bit, I hate working for him, but Shell, I will need to find another job pretty quick." She shrugged.

"Why, take some time out, sort out this place and really come to terms with things, you know, somewhere in all this you have lost touch with who you really are. Emmy, take a little time for yourself, and get used to things, we have plenty of time, as I said, I have cash, I am happy to chip in. Relax and enjoy being home for a little while, you need to focus on sorting out Han's stuff, and be honest, that was never going to be easy whilst working for Harry, which is why it has taken a year to get here? Emmy, this here, is what you need to be doing, get that office sorted out, and get your desktop computer from the flat, and set it up here, be honest, it will be better looking for a job from here than Exeter?" I gave a slight nod.

"I get it, honestly I do, you will never quit, will you?" She shook her head.

"Not after last night, no. Emmy, I am still not sure what happened, I just know it was meant to be, and Han came to you, face it, you belong here close to her?"

Once again, I had a lot to think about, in a way I was relieved to not have to go back to Harry and his awful manner, maybe Shell was right. There have been so many days in my life where I would come home angry because of something he had done, and so many weekends living in dread because I had to go back to work on Monday. Maybe it was time for a change, I had felt for a long time like I was treading water and not moving forward. Perhaps now was that time, as I started to move again, and actually aspire to the dreams I had dreamed of, lay on my bed in

Uni planning my future.

To be honest, I had become a bit of a disappointment to myself, I did feel I had let myself down many times in the flat in Exeter. My dad was so driven, and from what I had heard from Han, so was my mum, I had started to wonder if I had some sort of recessive gene that gave me a lazy edge? Although, I had really worked hard for Harry, maybe the change of pace for a while would do me some good? The problem was I simply did not know, I had pretty much lost all my self confidence, and had doubted every decision I had made in the last two years.

I felt tired, so grabbed some blankets and pillows, and laid them out on the jetty in the sun, I grabbed a book, and my sunglasses, and lay out to think. I lay on my stomach reading, not really seeing the words as my thoughts drifted.

How could Han come to me, how was that possible, and why did my dream have to be filled with so much light? It got me thinking, there has been so many times in my life, when Han talked of walking in the light, but what did she really mean? I had always thought that she meant the love that surrounded us, but I could not help but feel her words had a much deeper meaning. After last night, I cannot deny, I was really starting to wonder.

I was not brave enough to see that video again, it had freaked me completely out, and challenged every perception of my world. But as I remembered the images on Shell's phone, the one thing that stuck with me, was the bright white light around me, and even brighter light when Han came into the room. I wanted to make sense of it, but I couldn't. Was Han a ghost, bound to this place, destined to stalk these paths forever? If she was, why did I see her at the very same moment in my dream, surely if she was a ghost, or at least my perception of a ghost, then she would not have come to me, because I was asleep? Oh God, this is all so confusing, but the way I saw it, in order to see a ghost, I would have to be awake and looking at her, and yet I wasn't, I was definitely asleep, so how did she walk into my dreams?

I think I am turning into a basket case, but I was starting to wonder if the light was some sort of spiritual plane? Yep, I am losing my mind and turning into Shell, but I had to wonder, was the light some sort of spiritual energy? I rolled over and looked back at Shell, who was sat painting near the large round painted circle of bricks, that formed the arch at the bottom of the garden.

"Shell, what do you know about living energy?" She looked up holding her brush.

"What, you mean like the energy that powers the mind?" I sat up.

"Sort of. You once talked about us all being a form of living energy, that moved into different states, or at least something like that." She put her brush down, and gave a nod.

"Yeah... Okay so my physics is not a strong point, but the way I read it, our brain and nervous system, run on electrical energy within the body, and when Derek, do you remember him, sort of chubby, with tatty black hair, and squinty eyes, but a big smile? Anyhow, when he wrote his book, it was his theory, that it sort of changed, and remained, when the body died." That made a little sense.

"So, we are basically battery powered... Sort of?" She nodded.

"Emmy, science says energy cannot be destroyed, it can only change or transform, so if that is true, the conscious mind, which is not just our thoughts, but also our feelings, our sense of self, are one form of energy contained, for want of a better term, in a body, which is flesh and bones. We are sort of a meat and water battery, and the body is sort of the vehicle to carry our electrical selves in." I could accept that to a degree.

"So, if you cannot destroy energy, what happens when the body dies, that would be like pulling the plug out of a toaster, it would lose power and stop?" She nodded.

"The theory is, that the energy changes form, and leaves the dead body, and is released into the universe. I kind of think that is cool."

She smiled, she must be loving this, a chance to convert a sceptic, I somehow felt that after last night I could possibly be eating humble pie soon.

"Okay, so, what about light energy?" She gave a big smile.

"You know what, I am glad you are trying to puzzle it all out, I have been trying to all day." I nodded.

"I just hate not being able to explain things." She gave a nod and put her pad down.

"Okay Hun, light energy is a form of electromagnetic radiation.

It is built up of photons, which get produced when an object heats up, which is about the extent of my knowledge. Although, if I am right about that, and I almost think I am, then what if the energy in the body somehow heats up, could that illuminate an effect of a solid white image? You know, that could to a degree also explain ghosts?"

This is the problem with Shell, she uses science to explain the unexplainable. Her theory, and it is a theory, sort of makes sense. I certainly know how energy can brighten a bioluminescent algae, and in some weird strange way, that leads me to think that Han's energy, was sort of heated up, when she came to me. The truth is, as good as it sounds, it is hard to prove, most ghosts do not want to sit in a lab and have tests done. I rolled back over and lifted my book, none of this was making enough sense to prove, and I hated that.

As I lounged on the jetty in the sun, and tried to do the mental gymnastics to try and explain exactly what happened to me, back in Exeter, Harry sat in his local pub with Peter and sipped from his larger, as Pete enjoyed a scotch. Pete had smirked when Harry told him of our conversation, and appeared pleased.

"Good, I know her, and the thought of being fired will shake her up, and bring her to her senses. Trust me, she will be back on the phone before you know it, and high tail it back here. There is no way she will find work out there, well, not until the resort is built, and then people will flock there." Harry put down his glass and relaxed a little.

"She is a good worker, I have never had anyone who can get the jobs done as efficiently, and her detailing is impressive, I hope you are right, because I will not replace her easily." Pete flicked his hand in a dismissive way as he spoke.

"You worry too much, she is so like her mother, she was highly strung and sought constant validation as well. No, you mark my words, just the thought of a blemish on her CV, and she will melt down and return in tears begging forgiveness, and we will have that property vacant once again." He gave a nod.

"I hope you are right; she has been a good earner for us, her credentials brought in a lot of extra work for us. As you say, you are family, and you know her well, and I trust you Peter." A shadow appeared on the table top, as the light from the window was blocked out.

"Gentlemen, may I join you?" Peter turned and looked up, his face changed, and he stood up quickly, his voice sounded a lot less confident.

"John!" John Duncan smiled; Peter looked nervous as Harry smiled.

"Long time no see John; you are looking good." John eyed Peter closely.

"Yes, life is good, or at least it is since I spent an afternoon at the cottage with Emily." Harry gave a sigh, and lifted his half drunk pint. Peter tried to feign a smile.

"You and Emily are talking, I was not aware of that, good, she needs someone now?"

John offered his hand to request Peter sit, and he pulled out the chair in front of him, and sat down. Peter nervously sat back down and lifted his scotch.

"So how long have you two been talking, Jessica will be happy to hear that?" John leaned back, and eyed Peter carefully.

"We have never stopped talking, I admit, it has not been as often as it should be, but with the loss of Han, I think she needs a guide to help her with her loss. Someone to keep a watchful eye over her, after all, she is too trusting like her mother, and I would hate someone to exploit her, or take advantage of her good nature." Peter nodded.

"Yes, very wise, she needs a strong example, to show her the way." John smiled.

"She is all I have left, and so like Amelia, I feel very protective towards her, so felt I should be more active in her life. You know, there are some who would exploit her?" He turned to look at Harry, who had shrunk back in his seat. Harry gave a nod.

"Yes, she is a lovely girl, a father should be there for her... She is wonderful at her job, very skilled, and a real asset to the company." John gave a nod of agreement.

"I am happy to hear you think that Harry, but I cannot deny, her level of pay concerns me, I have juniors working for more." Harry gave a sigh.

"You know how things are John, the whole industry has been on its knees, times are tough and not as stable as they were ten years ago. We have all had to make cut backs?"

John Duncan sat back with a smirk, as he eyed the two men carefully, he had been around people like this all his working life and was no fool.

"That is strange, Kate seems to think both of you are doing very well and on the up, she has actually commented how well you two are doing, and as you know, nothing can be hidden from her?" Harry gave a smile, Peter chipped in.

"We are doing well enough, I would say your dominance is a big hurdle, your company appears to have been expanding again, you know John there is only so much property, and enough to share." John gave a nod as he lifted his glass.

"There is plenty out there, we only take what we need, and have our hands full, and you seem to be doing alright Pete. I was talking to Tom Clements the other day, he appeared very happy that you may be looking to build some sort of high end country resort, he was quite excited at the prospect of his teams building it." Peter looked panicked.

"Well, you know the trade, nothing is set in stone, you know what land deals are like, you make an offer and they hold out thinking it is worth much more." John smirked.

"Emily did mention you were persistent, she will never sell that land Pete, you should back off a little, she is still grieving. I am actually interested in the place myself." Harry's eyes opened wide.

"You are?" John gave a nod, as he turned to him.

"Oh yes, it was Amelia's home, I am trying to convince Emily to survey it, and preserve it under some sort of trust, you know the game boys, there is always someone looking to apply the heat for land of that size. No, I want Amelia's birthplace saving and preserving. I would move heaven and earth to stop it being developed, it means a great deal to me, I want it to stay the natural beauty it is." Harry shook his head as he looked at Pete, with annoyance in his eyes.

"The problem with that John, is what would Emily do, she says she wants to live there one day?" John put his drink down and sat back.

"I want her to live there full time. Sorry Harry, I hope to steal her from you, I want her as the project manager, she is the only one I trust, to oversee her mother's memory." Peter looked at him.

"Aren't you missing one minor fact John, she is the land owner, she wants the place leaving alone?" He lifted his pint and took another drink.

"I miss the ale here, that is the only problem with being global, the ale is never as good as home. I am aware of how Emily feels, which is why she will be in charge, she will have a free hand, and run her own ship with my funding, I am happy to give her whatever she needs. I would spend billions to hear her laugh like she did as a small girl. When it comes to her, money is no object, and neither is my protection of her."

Harry lifted his glass, he was looking very unhappy, he finished his pint, and put the empty glass down, then stood up and reached for his coat, he looked down at the two men.

"I have things to do, so if you don't mind, I must press on. Nice to see you again John, it has been too long." John looked up and smiled.

"You know Harry, if things are slow, I have a few things I could pitch at you, I don't want to see an old Uni pal struggle having to do bad deals. Call Kate on Monday, and we will sort a few good paying jobs that your guys can handle your way." He gave a nod and smiled.

"Thanks John, a few deals I was doing look like they may fall through, I would really appreciate that, thanks pal." John smiled.

"Any time, what are pals for, tell Kate to book us a lunch meet, we can do a little catching up, I will be around for quite some time, as I want to stay close to Emily for a while, I have some making up to do." Harry smiled.

"Yeah, she misses you more than you realise, it is good you two are working hard to help each other." Peter looked upset, as Harry gave a nod and left, and John turned back to Peter.

"I won't keep you long Peter, so let me just say this, stay clear of that cottage, or I will swallow all your contacts, and put you out of the trade. Destroy wherever you want, but step on that land again, and I will destroy you, and trust me, it is in your best interests that Emily stays healthy and active. I know where that young man came from, and who paid him. One scratch on my daughter, and you will wish you had never been born. The only reason you are still sat there, is because you are married to Amelia's sister, and so therefore family, leave Emily alone."

He stood up and looked down at the pale faced Peter, as he sat in his chair looking frightened.

"I still have the car, it is locked away nice and safe, and I have a lot of circumstantial proof, and one day I will find the part I need. You know as well as I why that place is special, and I know what you seek. Trust me, stay away from there and forget what you know, you will live longer, Randolph has not forgotten you."

He turned and walked towards the door, and Peter pulled his hankie out of his pocket and wiped his face with a long sigh. He reached for his scotch, and his hand was shaking, he looked down and closed his eyes, lifted his other hand and wiped his mouth.

Chapter Fourteen

First Step Forward

Esme sat on her hammock made of leaf, her large eyes watching as she leaned her elbows on her knees, and rested her face on her hands. She wore a huge happy smile, as she stared across the water towards the jetty, where Emily lay out in the bright sun. She gave a long happy sigh, and her quiet voice was soft and dreamy.

"She is so beautiful, so delicate, and fragile, and yet so strong inside."

She sighed with happiness again. Felix sat up and blinked his eyes, he gave a wide yawn, and lifted his hands to his face and rubbed it hard to wake up. Esme turned with a smile.

"Look Felix, she is so pretty and elegant."

Felix sat on his leaf, as he blinked again, and looked out across the water. He did not see Emily at first, as she had plumped up her pillow, and was lay back.

"I hope you don't mean the fat one?" Esme frowned at him.

"Felix, that is not nice, you know, some days you think like that old ugly slug on the small beach?" He gave a yawn again, and Esme turned to look back across the water.

"I was talking about Emily, but you know, the other one is pretty, she has beautiful eyes, and she is very clever, she understands our world very well. You should be nicer to her, my mother says she is called Shelly, and I think it sounds pretty." Felix gave a shrug.

"It sounds like a fat name, I bet that old slug has a granddaughter called Shelly, slithering around somewhere." Esme gave a frown, at him and shuddered.

"You are mean, that is such a horrible thing to say. I was going to get you some pollen balls to give you more strength, but you can go and get them yourself now." He gave another shrug and leaned forward on his leaf.

"I will... So, what are they doing?" Esme turned back to watch and smiled a large happy smile.

"She is resting in the sun, and I can feel all the calmness washing out of her and floating across to us. Oh, Felix, she is so beautiful, and so full of light, my mother says she has the same beauty and power of her mother." Felix gave a little nod as he watched.

"I feel her power, and it is stronger since Han went to her, there is no power in the fat one, well it is hard to feel it through all her skin." Esme gave a tut.

"I am not going to talk to you if you are going to be mean, Shelly is pretty too." Felix gave a chuckle.

"Yeah, pretty big in the middle. I am hungry, are you coming to get pollen balls?" Esme shook her head, and gave him a scowl.

"No... You are too rude today. I hope you get fat like Mugwump, and cannot fly, that way you will be kinder to others."

Felix gave a chuckle as he swung his legs round, and slipped off the leaf. He dropped to the ground with a soft plop. He looked up at Esme, who was now watching the girls again with a smile, Felix sniggered.

"Well if I do get fat, at least that fat one will see me, and not step on me, although looking at the way her middle has grown, if she sees me, she might eat me with the cabbage." Esme turned and scowled down at him.

"You would deserve it for being so mean."

Felix headed off through the fern, and gave a giggle as he went in search of pollen balls, Esme turned back to her watch, and gave another long happy sigh.

"I think they are both beautiful." She rested her head on her hands, and just stared across the lake feeling happy.

We had loved the afternoon, it was really hot and I was feeling sticky, Shell had finished her picture, and her pad of thick paper was lay on the jetty floor drying, she really was good at water colours. She leaned back and gave a pant.

"I am hot and I am sticky, I need a shower." I rolled over and looked at her.

"Yeah, I am sticky, it is almost time to eat, so I think I will freshen up Han style."

I stood up on the blanket, and slipped my knickers down. Shell looked at me like I was mad.

"What the hell Emmy?" I gave a chuckle.

"I swam in here every day when it was hot as a kid, are you coming?"

I turned and ran to the end of the jetty and launched myself into the air, and dived into the cool Lake. Shell stood up and ran along the jetty and dived in, I surfaced and gave a gasp, it was cold, but it felt so wonderful. Shelly bobbed up and gave a huge gasp.

"Jesus Emmy it's freezing, you could have warned me." I chuckled as I kicked my legs.

"Not hot and sticky though, are you?"

Felix came running back through the ferns, looking panicked.

"ESME, ARE YOU ALRIGHT?" He slid to a halt, and she looked down at him confused.

"I am fine, what is all the noise about?" He swallowed hard and pointed out across the lake.

"Did you see the size of the wave that fat one caused, it was bigger than ten Nairn?" Esme gave a huff and narrowed her eyes at him, stood holding his pollen balls with a smirk.

"Felix Dillberry, you are horrible at times, if you choke on a pollen ball, it will be justice served." He sniggered and held one up.

"You want one?" She turned back to watch the lake, and folded her arms with a scowl.

"NO!"

I turned in the water, and swam back towards the jetty, I heard her splash behind me, as she followed to the ladder. I climbed up and out of the water and shook my head. As the water splashed everywhere, I felt alive and tingling all over. It felt good, and I could hear Han in my thoughts as she laughed at me with happiness, from those times when we swam together.

I grabbed one of the blankets and pulled it round me, I felt amazingly good. Shelly came shivering down the jetty and grabbed the second blanket, I noticed her soaking wet knickers, as I picked mine up.

"Wuss... What are you worried about, I have always skinny dipped here?" She wrapped the blanket round her and shivered.

"I do not know what lives in there." I gave a giggle.

"Please tell me you do not want fish looking at your lady parts?" She gave a small laugh.

"Not so much looking as nibbling." I shook my head.

"I am quite sure fish are not into that, and after some of the weird shit I have walked into at the flat with your poet friends, I always thought you liked the idea of being nibbled there." She looked down, at her wet knickers.

"Ryan was so good at that, oh God, I wish he was here now. I guess I was unsure as to what lives in there, I was just being careful." I laughed at her.

"Come on, we need food, and take out round here is not an option."

I pulled the blanket tighter as my hair dripped on the floor and walked back towards the steps of the garden back up to the cottage.

We were not that hungry, it felt too hot to eat, and we had a little salad left, so while Shell boiled some eggs, I opened a wine, and we sat at the table eating a good salad with bread. We talked as we ate, and I told her of what it was like growing up here with Han, and the long hot summers of swimming and walking in the wilderness that surrounded the house.

She leaned on her arm, as she forked the food into her mouth as she quietly listened to me, and smiled.

"Your life here sounds idyllic, I was actually quite surprised to see you strip and just dive in, I have never seen that side of you. I like your free spirited side, I think it is more of the real you." I sipped my wine as I wiped the inside of my mouth with my tongue.

"Shell, we were at Uni together, and you live with me, you have seen all my sides." She gave a nod.

"I am not so sure; this place brings out other aspects of you." I frowned at her.

"Like what?" She smirked.

"Wow, suspicious much? I like the way you talk about Han; I like the love you feel for her and this place, and how it just radiates out of you. You use a tone when you speak, I have not heard before." I shook my head.

"You are just bonkers." She chuckled.

"I love living with you Emmy, I love our friendship, it means the world to me. You know at Uni I found it hard to fit in, and yet you and Pam just accepted me as I was, you know that really counts, and I will always be here for you. Emmy you are not alone, and whatever you do, I will back you up." I smiled at her.

"I know that, and as you know, I have your back too." She nodded and stabbed at her lettuce.

"So, after Harry's little revelation, have you considered your options?" I wiped my mouth and sat back.

"I think for now, I will take a little time out. I am tired Shell, this has taken a lot out of me, and I want to get this place sorted and safe, so we can stay put for a while. Then I have to decide my next step, I do have other options." She looked surprised as she refilled her glass, and passed me the bottle.

"Do you, what exactly?" It was pointless to hide what he had said, although I edited it a little.

"Like you, my dad thinks I should stay here, and work around this area, and to be honest, I am tired of the city. I grew up here in the peace and quiet, it suits me, and I have cash, so it will not be that big a struggle to survive here. In a way, Han taught me everything I need to know to live here, and I think in a strange way, last night made me realise how special this place was. I cannot say I understood what happened last night, but let's just say she was reaching out. Well, after a lot of thought today, I feel I should listen to her, she has never given me bad advice, and if she thinks for now, I should stay here, I think I will." Shelly gave a big smile.

"I hope I am included in the deal; I would hate to go back to the flat alone?" I gave a little chuckle.

"You are like a barnacle, I am not sure I could shake you off if I tried, but I like that, our friendship means something to me too, so I think we should relax and chill, and I will sort this place out slowly instead of rushing." She lifted her glass.

"Here is to life at Han's cottage." I raised my glass with smile. "Us, and life in the unknown."

That was exactly it, my life now was unknown, I really had no idea of what I would do, and I still had to come to terms with the cottage. I had been putting it off, as I really did not want the hurt. I knew I would feel some pain, especially sorting out her bedroom. I had settled in a little, I think just coming back was in itself a huge step, but it was time to organise, and I looked up the table.

"When I have eaten, I think I will arrange the office area of the workroom, I want to move the desk, I am not a fan of working in the middle of a room, I think I will put it in the far corner against the wall. At some point, we will have to head back to Exeter and grab our stuff." Shelly gave a nod, as she chewed on her salad.

"I have been thinking that. Emmy will this place be safe whilst we are gone?" I gave a long sigh.

"My dad said he would warn Pete off, although, I am not convinced he will listen, he wants this place badly. We will have to risk it, and set off early and drive back later. Shell, I don't have much, and I can leave some things behind if I have to."

"Or we could hire a van, leave the mini bus in Exeter, unload, and then I will drive back and get the mini bus, leaving you to watch things here. It will let us bring all of it back here and clear the flat." It made sense.

"Will you be okay with that, it's a long drive Shell?"

"Yeah, I can always crash at Steve's for a night."

She gave a big smile, I should have known, being out here is pretty solitary, and men are scarce, she would hook up with Steve for the night, sate her libido, and then return.

With the meal over, and the washing done, I walked back into what would become my office space, which was Han's old work room. It still felt hard to be in here, the whole place was filled with happy memories from my childhood. Today they felt lesser than they had, not because they were not happy, because they were, put simply because Han had made them that way for me. I have found it hard to explain to Shelly what it feels like for me. I am not really certain I can fully explain it to myself, except to say, that to touch something, or see a specific special thing, or open up a drawer and see things exactly as they always have been, which to be honest, back then was just a normal everyday experience, suddenly feels different and loaded with emotion.

Her knitting bag has a half finished jumper. It has one sleeve missing and the reality that it will never be finished, hurts. Yes, I could finish it, the pattern is there, and Han taught me to knit, but if I finished it, then every time I look at it, I would know she left me before it was complete. Had she finished it, I would have yet another happy memory of pulling it on and seeing her face as I wore it for the first time. I have been robbed of that moment forever, and no one appears to really understand that, or maybe they do, but they are afraid to say so, as it brings back such memories for them, and actually, all of us that those deep painful feeling of loss are buried within us somewhere.

I took a deep breath and got stuck in, for as long as I had lived, this room had not changed, and if I was to live and work here, which was now looking to be the case, I had to try and take some of the pain of the past away. I did not want to be in here hurting all the time, I did need to move on, but I was never going to betray my memories, I just wanted different ones for my future. The way I saw it, to remember Han's desk in the middle of the room, and me sat by her side, was very special and precious to me, but it had to move, and then new ones I made, would be from a different place, a place not Han's.

I leaned on the edge of the desk, took a deep breath, and moved the corner round, as I pushed it into a different place. It had been here all my life, but I needed it to be moved, I really needed it to be somewhere else, so that my mind would not keep flooding with those moments I had clung to all my life as I was at school.

I lifted one end and dragged it round, and then pulled it over to the wall, next to the plug sockets, I would need power, so it was better placed so that I did not have cables all over the floor. The drawer to the desk was very neat and orderly, as I pulled it open, I sat back on the seat and took a breath.

Her fountain pen, and ink bottle were where they had always been, and I had seen her pull it out to write in her journals a thousand times in my life. Her small scissors and geometry set, made from brass were laid out in a small velvet lined box. She took such good care of everything, and I had always admired that. I lifted her small brass set square, and looked at it. It still shone from her endless polishing, I turned it over, and my breath caught.

On the back neatly engraved it read, 'Amelia Montgomery.' It was my mother's, and I was not even aware of it. She must have kept it for all these years as a precious memory of her daughter, and she had never told me. I placed it back carefully, and closed the drawer, it was mine I suppose now, passed down from my mother through Han to me, and I knew I would use it when drawing up plans.

It is strange in a way, the only reason I know who my mother was as a person, was through Han. I had sat for so many nights listening to her soft voice, as she talked about her, and those were actually my own memories, of the woman who when I was tiny, called mum. They were not mine, they were Han's, and yet because of them, I had been able to really build a picture of her looks, life, and personality. That was the gift Han gave me, she gave me a mother, and so to understand that both of them were now gone, was the struggle within me at the moment, because no one really sees or understands that about me at the moment.

No one can actually see that all that information and knowledge that Han freely gave me to fill in the blanks of my mother, had gone forever. Even my father to a degree cannot talk of her youth, of her struggles as a child, or the joy of what she was like aged eleven. Saying that, he is now the only person who can tell me of those times when she left here with him to live on the outskirts of London. He had years with her here living around the lake, and he holds the key to that for me, but again, if I lose him too, then in many ways, my mother will be wiped out forever. I don't want that, because as insane as it sounds, I still want to feel as close to her, as I did talking with Han about her.

I sat back in my chair as my mind wandered, and my thoughts paused on a moment from many years ago. I had been curious like any child would be, and had asked lots of questions. I sat at Han's side and looked up at her.

"What did my mum do?" Han gave a smile, and leaned back in her chair.

"I won't deny, I wanted her to study history, and especially the folklore of this country, but that for her was a hobby, and she must have read every book written on it, she was probably more knowledgeable than her teachers. She went to university and studied botany, she was very good at plants and the natural world, especially foods and medicinal plants. She would spend hours picking flowers and pressing them. She made up an album of them all, and on each page, she would stick the flowers once they were dried, and write a whole page all about them, she had quite a collection. I suppose your father has them now, he used to walk with her and help her collect them."

"So, she learned about flowers?" Han gave a wide smile, and her old lined face creased up, as her eyes sparkled at me.

"Emmy child, your mother loved this place so much, she wanted to learn what she would need to protect it, after me."

I remember frowning at her, not really understanding all of it, and asked possibly what was the most obvious question for a young child.

"Does it need to be protected?" Han gave a nod, and took my hand.

"Emmy, there is a very rich beauty to this land, and one day when you are of age, I will teach you all about it, and then show you. There is a very delicate balance here, that could very easily be tipped, and your mother knew and understood that, as you will one day. It is up to us to do everything we can to keep this place sacred, and safe from the hands of those with darkness in their hearts, for they would tear this place apart, and we cannot let them do that, can we now?"

I sat back in the chair remembering, lost in my thoughts staring at the wall, she was so sincere with me, and so serious, what was it she was trying to tell me, what was this richness that must be protected, and why did my mum feel that she should help with the task? I heard my own voice in my thoughts.

"Don't worry Grandma Han, I will protect it for her."

Was that why my mum was coming back when she had the accident, my dad had told me Han needed help, but for what, the land has not changed since I was a child? Everything was exactly the same as it had always been growing up, and no matter how hard I tried, I could not for the life of me work out what this thing was that needed to be watched over.

My mind sifted through everything that had happened of late, the incident the other night with the light for starters. I hated admitting it, because honestly without Shelly's video footage, I would have laughed at her, because let's be honest, it was pretty unbelievable. I actually felt guilty that in the past, Pam and myself had laughed at her theories of levitation, and yet, I saw my body floating before it lowered to the bed, leaving a white shimmering image of me above it.

Was I having an out of body experience, or had my dream manifested above me, all of this was new and alien to me and it made no sense at all, as it was scientifically disproven? I had always clung to scientific fact as a sound board for stability, and yet, Shelly had filmed me doing something that was not scientifically possible. You have no idea how much that actually scares me?

As if that was not bad enough, what the hell was the bright white light? I know for a fact light is filled with heated protons, but I cannot deny, I have to ask myself, how much energy was in that light, because it just flooded the room and prevented the camera from filming anything that was happening? All I had was my dream of talking with Han, and it felt so real, I actually felt her touch me, and there is no doubt in my mind that was her voice on the recording, even though I know it is not possible.

I think I am slowly going mad, which to be honest is yet another theory I can add to the many currently floating around my brain, mixing with all the feelings of loss and hurt from losing Han. I really do think my sanity is being challenged, and at the moment, it feels like my sanity is losing.

Somehow, this memory of Han was important, even now as I think about it, and her words, the tone of her voice in my memory held a sense of urgency and importance, but I was too young at the time to really pick up on it. I know without doubt, if this conversation had come up again when I was in my late teens, I would have picked up on it and questioned her deeper. Everything around me felt connected, almost like I was studying an ecosystem, and in a way, I felt like I was. It was not just flora and fauna, there was far more to it, and at it's centre was Han, and possibly my mother.

I held her words in my mind and quietly spoke them out loud as I tried to work everything out in my mind.

"There is a very delicate balance here, that could very easily be tipped, and your mother knew and understood that."

This is the frustrating thing about all of this, delicate balances have been a part of my study and work for almost four years, it is the core of every system I have worked on. That is what drives me so crazy, I am the one person who should be able to spot the obvious, and yet currently I am struggling to gain any understanding of any of this at all. Why did Han need help?

I have lived here for every school holiday I have ever had, and she worked hard, and coped amazingly well. If anything, I had always felt she just blended in to everything and it worked, she was in a way a part of this place. It had always felt like she was at one with everything, and the cottage, the land and Han were simply a part of all of it, she was one with everything here, and understood implicitly without even having to think, so how could she have needed help from my mother?

I tried to put the pieces of the puzzle together. Han always talked about the light, my mum studied botany at university and was a folklore nerd, Han told me the place needed protecting, and my mother was coming back to help her protect it. So what was this delicate balance that could so easily be tipped, and what was this so called richness here? The site was two thousand acres, and yet Han managed it alone from this cottage, how was that possible for a woman of her age?

Nothing made any sense at all, except in just one area, and it had been on my mind for almost a year now, and it all led in one single direction. In my mind as I focused on it, I found it made complete sense, and yet no real sense at all, but I will not deny, it was the only logical direction to look. My voice was soft as I sat back thinking.

"What is it that you really are after Uncle Pete, what is your aim here, because this has to be about more than just the land?"

"I have been saying that all year."

I blinked and came out of my thoughts, and saw a fresh hot coffee on the desk in front of me, and turned to see Shelly sat smiling in a chair at my side, I had not even noticed her sit down.

"Saying what?" She shrugged and lifted her cup as she stared at me.

"He is a bit too desperate to cheat you out of this place, call it a hunch Emmy, but he wants more than just logging and development rights here." It made some sort of sense.

"Like what Shell."

"Emmy, do you remember that job we did for him just after Uni, before you went to Scotland?" I nodded as I lifted my cup.

"What the coastal area over near Southampton, yeah, it was a big site, but once we discovered the wild flowers and rare butterflies, and reported it back, he pulled out of the deal. That was a good job, I have always wished it had lasted longer than a week, but protected flowers and insects he never had a hope." Shelly gave a smirk.

"You skinny dipped there too, that night we got drunk on the beach. Emmy, do you remember how fast he pulled out of the deal?" I frowned at her.

"It was instant, I told him it was a no go and why, and he quit the place, that is normal procedure Shell, why does it matter?" She gave a shrug.

"You have told him for almost a year this place was a no go, and yet when we arrived, he was trying to con a surveyor into surveying the place. Emmy he even paid someone to set fire to the place with us inside, I mean, I know we have no proof, but be honest, we both know he was behind it. That site on the coast was vastly bigger than here, and yet he just dropped it the moment he was told it was not possible. You told him about the newts and the squirrels, and in other circumstance with those two facts, he would have quit. So, ask yourself this, why has he not dropped this place?"

I felt a cold shudder run down my spine, too much had happened in the last year. I was trying to forget the attempted fire the other night, and I was hoping my dad could warn him off as he said he would. I looked at her, feeling a little panicked.

"But Shell, apart from logging and the developing of the land, there is little else here. I am no geologist, but from what I have seen growing up here, there is no evidence of minerals or metal here, it is just land." She raised her eye brows.

"Well, there must be something, because he has been bloody persistent, if it is not on the land, it has to be below it, so you tell me Emmy, just what exactly is he after? If you ask me, staying here is the smartest thing you have done, because there is something here, and Han wanted it protected, which is why she left it to you." I gave a long sigh.

"I get that Shell, but what is it?" She shook her head.

"No idea, but honestly, as far as I can tell, that is the only question you need to answer."

Mad as it sounds, it is actually the only thing in my weird mixed up life at the moment that makes real sense. There is more to this than meets the eye, and Pete is after it. I leaned back in my chair and stared at the wall as I held my cup.

"I think you have point; I need to really research this place, and see if there is anything in its history that might give me a clue. We need to get our things and move them here, I feel that staying close to home at the moment is not only prudent, but probably the safest thing for this place." She nodded.

"Okay, so how will do all this?" I turned and looked at her, I could not help but smile, she was in at the deep end and right by my side, and I was relieved to know I was not alone.

"I want to text my dad and let him know I am staying, and then I think tomorrow, we will take a boat ride, I want to check all is well before we leave for Exeter. Pack your long lenses, I want to really look at the place from the water, it is the best advantage place we have." She smiled.

"Cool, I will not deny, I am a little excited Emmy."

Chapter Fifteen

Lake And Land

It is strange to understand that you are surrounded by deception, and that others have been plotting your downfall. I went upstairs to gather my thoughts, and sat on my bed looking out of the window across the water to the island. The whole lake and surrounding land looked at peace, and yet I knew it truly was at threat, and knowing how sly my uncle Pete was frightened me. Dad had promised to warn him off, but I knew Pete would use others to get what he wanted, and I had to find out why.

I opened my phone and looked at the messages new text box, I clicked dad's number and then wrote. 'Sorry it is getting late, but I thought you should know, I have decided to stay, but I am scared, it is a big step for me.' I took a deep breath and pressed send.

It was done, I had no idea where my future would take me. For as long as I could remember Han had always been there in the shadows, ready to embrace me and hold me close. As I had always looked to her for guidance and wisdom, and as I sat on my bed, having sent the one text message that would change my life forever, I felt fearful, because my future had just lost its certainty. I still felt emotional and a huge sense of loss, but deep down inside, the ray of light that guided me, was knowing Han planned ahead, and this was what she thought was the right thing for me to do. It was a year later than she planned, but nevertheless, I was here, I was home, and I knew in my aching heart, she would be proud of me.

My phone rang and I jumped, as I came out of my thoughts. I picked it up and saw dad on the screen, I swiped up, answered the call and put him on speaker phone.

"Dad, I am surprised you called."

"How could I not, this is a big step for you, and I wanted to say I am proud of you." I took a deep breath.

"I won't say I am not terrified, I am."

"I know, but trust me, you have done the right thing, your mother would be so proud of you Emily. What do you plan from here on in?"

"I have to return to Exeter to move all my stuff, which worries me as I will have to leave this place alone. I will probably go early Tuesday, pack as quick as I can and get back, I am leaving the furniture, I won't need it, so I am just taking my personal belongings. It should not take too long, and I want to be back by late afternoon, Shell and me will clear things out fast, we do not have much stuff."

"Okay... Emily I will put a security team on the cottage for you so that it will be watched whilst you are gone, I do not want you worrying when you are driving. The cottage will be safe, just please, drive carefully Emily, I will not say this does not worry me, it does, I cannot help it after your mother."

I understood that, I could hear the concern in his voice, and I swallowed hard, I cannot deny, it had crossed my mind. My mum was coming back to help Han, when her accident occurred which took her life, and I will not deny, it was on my mind.

"Dad I will not be rushing, I promise, I will take it easy and keep my eyes open at all times." I heard him take a deep breath.

"Emily, let me arrange a driver and a vehicle for you so that I know you will be safe, I am worried, I do not want to lose you." I could hear his worry.

"Dad, I am sure I will be safe, are you really that worried?"

"Yes... I am sorry, but we just finally found our way back to each other, and yes, I am very much to blame for that, but please, let me do this, let me protect you."

It bothered me that he sounded so upset, and so I thought I would let him, after all, in a way he had not really done that much for me, and for the first time in my life since I was four, it felt like he was really trying to be father.

"Alright Dad, if you really are that worried, then I will let you do this, but Dad, you have to stop worrying, honestly I will be fine."

"Maybe Emily, I have told Pete to back off, but I really do not trust him, he is capable of many dark dealings. I want you safe, so I will send a driver for both of you and a vehicle to carry all your things."

"I think you are right; I do not trust him either, and to be honest I will feel safer if others are with us, thanks." He gave a sigh of relief.

"Good, I will sleep better knowing you are safe. I will talk to Kate in the morning, I will work something out to get you a grant and you can take your time, settle in, and just get used to being there. I will take care of everything so you will be financed properly. Emily, that place is of extraordinary value, and very soon I will sit with you, and go over everything your mother told me about it. Get some sleep, and rest, you looked tired."

"Yeah, I am, I will, thanks Dad."

"Alright Emily, leave this with me, goodnight."

"Night Dad."

The call ended, and I relaxed and thought about our call. It surprised me how worried he sounded, did he really think I was in danger, actually, was I in danger?

I slid off the bed and picked up my phone, and walked downstairs, Shelly was sat on the backdoor step sipping a wine. I grabbed a glass and sat at her side; she handed me the bottle with a smile.

"It is a beautiful night, the lake is so calm here, I feel at peace." I smiled; I knew that feeling well.

Randolph stopped on the road and slipped his hand into his pocket, he slipped out a phone and looked at it, he had a message. He swiped it open and read the text. 'She is staying.' He smiled and took a deep breath, and looked back across the lake.

"You were right Han, Barrack will already know, and he will relax, his people will be saved. I have preparations to make as my time to meet Emily is coming." Across the water Barrack smiled as he stood on top of a large rock within the trees and smiled to himself.

"I feel the light, for the first time since you arrived, I truly feel the light within you. I feel joy in my heart to know the daughter of Amelia will take her place, my people will be forever grateful."

He turned and floated down from the large rock, and within the foliage, he walked with a smile towards the stone circled enclosure.

Having talked with Shelly and explained what my dad had told me, she agreed that having someone with us was probably safer, I think it came as a little bit of a relief for her too, after all, if I was at risk, she was at my side and risking herself too. Shelly has surprised me a great deal since coming to the cottage, we have grown to be great friends since Uni, but these last few days, which have been hard for me, she has really hung in there for me. Back in the flat she was pretty free spirited and a little irresponsible, but being with her in the cottage, she has shown another quality of herself, and she actually has been a great strength for me.

Feeling a little calmer, which was probably the wine, I slept well, although I had a lot of dreams from childhood, which were mainly just memories. I woke early feeling refreshed, it was Monday, and a new week, and yet I had done little at the cottage. I was well aware I still had Han's room to face, and I still had a lot to do in her craft room, but considering I had decided to stay here at the cottage in Hempsley, I had the rest of my life to sort out everything.

I headed down stairs and into the living room, Shelly was stood peering out of the front window, I leaned over at her side.

"What are you doing?" She turned to me.

"Your dad does not piss about, look there is a security car down by the gate, and two guards." I leaned further forward and looked out.

Twenty yards down from the gate, a white car with a blue stripe on it had pulled into the side of the driveway. Two men were stood outside in black uniforms talking on a radio, it gave me a sense of calmness knowing my dad was on the job and watching over us. With a security presence, I hoped it would curb any ideas that Pete may have.

I made a coffee and then stood in thought, as I looked out across the island in the centre of the lake, it was bathed in the sunlight, and was for me, a very sacred space. My mind drifted, as I remembered that time from my past, I was six, and we had taken the boat across to it. Han helped me out of the boat into the shallow water, and pulled on the long rope to tie it to the bank, it was a roasting hot day. Holding my hand, we crossed the beach, and walked onto the path under the trees, the whole atmosphere changed.

The canopy was dense, but shafts of light came down in streams of white, and the pollen from the plants was swirling around inside them like tiny dust particles. For me, a little six year old, it felt like a place of awe and wonder, with its warm damp atmosphere, filled with earthy scent, and the hum of millions of insects.

"Oh, Grandma Han, this place feels like a magical forest." She smiled as she held my hand, and we walked slowly on the damp earth path.

"Emily my dear child it is. The true wonder of this place, is what you cannot see, for within the plants and the trees, there is a beauty and magic so deep, it will stir your heart and soul." I remember looking up at her smiling face.

"What I cannot see it, is there something more here?" She gave a gentle nod.

"Emily, a day will come, when the real magic of this place is revealed to you, and will happen at the moment when you decide to embrace the whole truth of life and the light within all things. That will be the day when your eyes are opened to everything." I frowned.

"Do I not see everything now?" She gave a little chuckle.

"Oh, my dear child, you have so much to learn and see, your life will be so precious and special, and yes, one day, you will realise that there are so many things of wonder to see, and in time, you will see all of them." I looked round at the woodland.

"But I want to see them now Grandma Han, I want to see the magic." She gave a little chuckle.

"Emily, if you want to see them, let go and open your heart to everything, that is the only way to see the world as it is. To feel your way with the love you hold, is the only way to really see with opened eyes."

I blinked, and came out of my thoughts, still stood, looking out of the window at the water and the island, the words of Han held in my mind. 'Feel your way, with the love you hold' What did she mean, I was finding it hard to understand, it was as cryptic as the night she told me to look at the stars? I noticed Shelly walk in, she had obviously given up staring out of the window at the security guards, I turned holding my drink and looked at her.

"Shell, do you think I find it hard to love, you know, I am a little emotionally closed off?" She frowned as she approached the kettle.

"How do you mean closed off? I mean if you are asking if you hold back a little, I suppose you do a bit, but hell, you have had your fair share of heartbreak, who would blame you." I nodded.

"I think growing up here as a child, I was more emotionally open to things." She clicked the kettle on, and pulled a herbal tea bag out of the box.

"Children are don't you think? Emmy, you have had to deal with a lot in your life, it has its effects, and maybe you have withdrawn a little. You know, the way I see it, here you have the time and space to relax and revaluate, and come to terms with everything. Be honest, when have you had the time and space to do that really?" I smiled.

"I suppose never really." She sat down with her tea.

"Be honest at Uni, we were too busy studying and pissing about, it was a good distraction, then we did Scotland, and then came back to Exeter and you worked for Harry. He sucked up your time, even in the flat you did not really have time, you were just too tired. What with Ken, and then you lost Han which added to the pile, you have been a state of flux for years."

She made sense; I had felt like an emotional wreck for as long as I could think of, maybe I did need some time out just to take stock and work things out with me, well I certainly had the time and space to do that now. Shelly was watching me, as I thought about things, she gave a giggle as I blinked out of my thoughts.

"What?"

"I asked if we are still going boating?" I smiled.

"Yeah, I want to get out on the lake and have a good look round. I am going to see the security team first though, I will let them know we will be on the lake, you know, just in case." She gave a nod and got up.

"Cool, I will grab my stuff."

Five minutes later, fully dressed in shorts, T shirt, and pumps, I walked down the to the front gate and onto the roadway. The guards noticed me coming and turned to face me, I smiled as I approached, one of them was really tall and broad, but he had kind blue eyes and a nice smile. The other one was not as big, but looked like he could handle himself, I noticed the white estate with the pale blue line that had Duncan Security written on it. The biggest one gave a nod.

"Good morning, Miss Duncan." I gave another smile.

"Good morning, I wanted to thank you for watching over the house for us." He looked at the cottage.

"It is actually our pleasure, your father has filled us in on the goings on, and we are here to make sure you are not pestered again."

"Are you both alright for everything, would you like a drink, or to use the toilet at all?" The tall one smiled and shook his head.

"It is quite alright, we are quite self sufficient, and will be working in shifts, just get on with your normal day, and act as if we are not here." I nodded at them both.

"We will be heading off on the lake in the boat today, we will feel more relaxed knowing you are here, so again, thank you."

I turned and headed back to the house, stopped at the mini bus, to grab a can of fuel for the boat, then headed indoors. Shelly was sat on the floor in the living room sorting out her camera back pack, as I walked through to the back garden to put the can down.

Forty minutes later both of us walked down to the jetty, turned left, and walked the five yards to the boat house doorway. Shelly appeared to be excited as I unlocked the door, and pulled it open, it has been a very long time since I was in here, and I felt like it had been too long.

Shelly was in awe, as she saw the bright blue boat hung above the water, on the boat lift. She walked along the side of it with a huge smile on her face, her eyes twinkling, she turned to me smiling.

"Emmy, this is awesome, when you said boat, I thought you

meant like a row boat or a dingy, I never expected a speed boat."

I put down the petrol can and walked to the power box, and flipped the switch on, and pressed the big green button. The winch whirled into life and the boat began to lower towards the water, I watched it carefully as it hit the water's surface and bobbed off the cradle below it, as it sunk into the water. I released the button, as Shelly gave a happy little giggle, and pulled the rope of the boat to steady it, she was funny, she was so like me when I first went out in the boat age five.

I climbed in with Shelly, and showed her how to check the oil and top up the fuel, exactly as Han had showed me. Once settled in, with a flask and some sandwiches, Shelly settled down as I fired up the boat. It had not run for a year, so I felt a great relief when the engine fired up. We chugged slowly forward, and out through the open end, onto the lake, and I pushed forward the drive to increase the speed.

Standing under the open ended cockpit, and watching through the glass window, as the boat roared along the left side of the lake, and up the side of the island, I felt a huge sense of freedom. Shelly was sat at the back loving every second of it, and looking round through her camera, as she focused on the lake and the land surrounding us, taking shots. I stood, my feet slightly apart, holding the wheel, and watching through the window, as the boat skipped on the smooth water, taking a look at what was now all mine. I owned all this, and it felt insane, this vast lake, all the surrounding land, and the island, it felt so surreal, and also quite frightening, because as I sped along taking it all in again for the first time in years, I understood the responsibility that I had taken on.

I found it hard to really understand, I was young with a whole life ahead of me, and yet Han seemed to manage all this with hardly any effort and she was in her late sixties. We carried on past the island and down towards the far end of the lake, in the distance across the water, I could see the bridge across the river which marked the end of the lake. I slowed slightly and the boat chugged along, Shelly came up at my side.

"Emmy this place is beautiful, we are so lucky, look at what we have, it is paradise."

I had to smile, she was right, growing up, I had always felt the same, this was my playground as a child and I now knew, it was also my mothers. The far end of the lake was new territory for me, I had been around the lake in the boat, but never really explored some of this end. I pointed across the water and got Shelly to take pictures of prominent features, I knew if I was going to document the life here, I would need to understand the terrain, and prepare, her pictures would really help with that.

We slowly chugged back as Shelly poured us a drink from the flask, and at a much slower pace, I got to watch along what was the northern side of the bank, which we had just travelled down. The edge of the lake was quite rocky in parts, and was densely lined with broadleaved trees, it looked like a perfect habitat for wildlife, which was promising. As I scanned along to try to see deeper into the rising sides, I felt my insides give a jolt and turned to Shelly.

"Is that smoke?" Shelly was looking at the island and turned, to look.

"It looks like it, do you think something is alight?"

I wasn't sure, but I did not like the idea, I turned the wheel, and increased our speed and we motored towards it, as I felt a sense of urgency rise inside me. Was it a campfire? I was not sure, but I did not like the idea of people just setting up fires without my knowledge, out here a forest fire would be devastating. Shelly stood at my side as we sped towards the bank, whatever it was, it was set back, slightly up the hill in the trees, and there was some sort of clearing inside the trees.

As we approached, I slowed down, the lake was deep, but close to the edges, it became shallow quite quickly and I did not want to snag the motor, I leaned back.

"Shelly, take the wheel." She looked panicked.

"Emmy, I have never driven one of these before." I pointed.

"When you pull that back, we slow, push it forward, we go fast, the rest is the steering." She nodded, and looked worried, as I let go of the wheel, we were moving quite slow, so I was not too concerned.

I leaned out over the side to watch the clear water, I could see we were still in deepish water, and moving slower, Shelly appeared to read my thoughts and slowed more. Up ahead there was a sandy beach, and the boat was pointed right at it, I moved towards the back of the boat, and looked back to see where were in relation to the bank.

"Shell, kill the engine."

She gave a nod, and pulled the silver lever back, and the engine died, I pulled at the locking clasp, and heaved back on the outboard, and it swung up towards me, and the prop came out of the water, as we drifted slowly towards the bank.

I had never actually done it before, but I had seen Han do a million times, and was relieved it worked, the boat drifted silently towards the bank, and I climbed up on the bow, and gathered the rope as we drifted silently into the bank. The boat drifted softly into the sandy mud and shuddered, I dropped off the front with the rope, and splashed into the water, I was glad I was wearing shorts, and waded the few feet towards the bank, and up onto the grass edge.

With the boat tied off to a tree, Shelly climbed out and handed me the keys, the smoke was somewhere up ahead of us. Parts of the grass were worn, this was a regular path for something, with Shelly at my side, we started to walk. Shelly looked around at the vast woodland of mature trees, some of them with large sprawling limbs, this was a place that had never been logged, which to a degree explained Pete's lust, there was some high quality timber here.

"Emmy, what do you think it is, do you think people wild camp here?" I was not sure as I stared ahead of me.

"I really am not sure, I worry about fires here, one spark and this whole place could go up, I want to know what is happening just to be sure."

We followed the path, that appeared to weave through the rocks and tall trees, Shelly sniffed the air.

"Is that cooking?"

The air hung with dampness and the smell of cooked meat, I rolled my tongue round the inside of my mouth, I could not deny, it smelt good, and I felt my mouth water. We came around a huge rock, and suddenly the whole place opened up into a large open clearing, in which was a cabin of timber, and I gave a gasp.

"What the...?"

There was a fire pit, over which was a large black metal spit, on which was a small pig roasting, a tall man stood up behind the pig, in heavy thick patched pants, and a dark canvass shirt, his long grey hair washing around his shoulders. He smiled as I walked across the grass towards him.

"Oh, good you are here, I saw the boat, I did not think it would be long before you found your way here." Shelly smiled and I was confused, he wiped his hand on his pants as I approached and he stuck out his arm.

"Miss Duncan, I am glad we finally meet, I am Randolph, Randolph Sage Feather, I am the game keeper here on the property."

I took his hand and he shook it gently, he had dark intense, yet kind eyes, set in his dark tanned face with matching grey bristles across his chin, and I felt a little at a loss for words, as I recognised his voice.

"I have a game keeper; I did not know?" He gave another smile, and nodded as he stretched out his arm to offer me a place.

"We have much to talk about, I see you realise who I am now, and that it was I who called you the night Han passed."

I struggled for words, as I felt the surge of emotion build inside me, this was the one person I had yearned to talk to, and now I had finally met him.

"Yes, since that night, I have wished to meet you, I feel you have answers to my many questions?"

"Please... Sit, we shall eat and talk, and yes, we really do have a lot to discuss. I know your father, and also knew your mother, and if I may say so, you are very much her likeness."

I was wrong footed, but walked across to the fire pit where there was a table and three chairs. It was almost as if this had been planned, as there was salad, breads, and plates on the table. As we both sat down, Randolph took out his knife, and started to cut thick slices of meat off the pig, which he laid on a plate, he looked back to see me watching him.

"I believe you have decided to stay, I was the one who brought aid to Han, and I am in your service, and will continue my duty, as I made her a solemn promise, I will guide you, as I did her." He smiled, and even though I felt very emotional, I also felt a huge sense of relief, and suddenly a lot of things made sense.

"It was you who stocked the fresh food, and you who took care of that person who wanted to burn the house? I feel I owe you my thanks Mr Sage Feather, I am in your debt." He gave a chuckle as he filled the plate.

"Miss Duncan, call me Randolph, and you owe me nothing, all my needs are met here, Han ensured it. I feel you have much to learn, and we do not have a lot of time, and that will be my role. I will answer all your questions, and reveal to you the truth of this place, and if I may say, it is not a moment too soon. Your uncle will never stop trying to take this place from you, and until you see the truth of why, you cannot truly take possession here and protect it. My job is to take over where Han left off, but we only have seven days, time is not on our side."

He walked towards the table, and placed down the plate filled with freshly cooked meat. Shelly dived in, but I was confused, he watched me as he lifted a bottle of wine and poured some into my glass, almost as if he was waiting for my question. He sat with a smile as I held the glass, he had handed to me.

"Why is time not on my side, I aim to live here?" He smiled a wide smile.

"Your instincts are very good, and you have no idea how happy I am to hear you say that you are going to live here. There are a lot of lives that hung on that decision, but I can assure you, it was indeed the best decision you have ever made. Please, eat, and will shall talk."

I looked at the plate of meat and my stomach gave a whine, I had not had breakfast, Shelly was happily chewing away.

"Randolph, this is wonderful, thanks." She continued to chew.

Chapter Sixteen

Looking In To the Light

My life has felt like one long series of searching for the missing pieces. It is almost like my life is a jigsaw, as I find and fit each part of the puzzle of who I am, back into place. My history has felt so fragmented for so long, and yet, since arriving home since the death of Han, tiny little parts of my life, had started to slide slowly back into place. I am starting to wonder if Shelly was right, I had to stay here, as this was the only place, I could actually have the time to really understand, not only who I am, but what has really taken place behind the scenes, under the guise of protecting me.

Felix and Esme came running through the ferns, at high speed, and burst out through a tall patch of sedge grass, and skidded to halt in front of Barrack and Chandak gasping for air. Chandak turned noting the two gasping little Nairn, he gave a frown and sighed as Esme swallowed hard.

"Is it true, oh please tell me she is going to stay?" Barrack gave a warm smile as Chandak frowned.

"Yes Esme Honeyrain, the lady Emily will be staying and living in the house across the water." Felix gave a huge smile as he caught his breath and turned to Esme, and gasped out.

"See, I told you, Han's granddaughter would never desert us." Esme nodded, with large blue eyes.

"I knew really, she is too beautiful not to live with us." Felix smirked.

"The fat one will stay now, you should make a flag out of a willow pole, and put a big flower on it, so she does not step on you." Esme scowled and folded her arms.

"You are as rude as you are smelly Felix Dillberry, you should go dip in the dew pool." He frowned lifted his arm and sniffed, Barrack gave out a mighty belly laugh.

"Both of you need to calm down, yes Lady Emily will be staying, but she has not fully embraced the light yet, as we speak, she is sat with Randolph, and she has much to learn about her own life. She will need to fully accept that before walking into the light, so you two, should keep clear, we do not want her frightening off." Felix looked up and frowned.

"We are not scary; how could we scare her?" Esme smirked.

"If she smells you, she will flee screaming." Barrack gave another loud laugh, even Chandak smirked as Felix sniffed his chest.

"I don't smell." He looked up. "Do I?" Esme rolled her eyes.

"Felix, even the stink mushrooms have stayed underground because they cannot compete, come on, you need to bathe."

We sat at the table and ate, as Randolph explained, that he had come to Han many years ago, and he had taken on the role of gamekeeper, and a watcher. He talked of how he had watched the land and lake, and helped her manage the estate, which in a way gave me a great sense of relief, as he understood Han's role here, and could guide me. He talked of all the game on the land, and how most of the meat in Han's freezer was caught and prepared by him for her.

He talked with great fondness, and I smiled as I quietly listened feeling happy in the knowledge that she had not been totally alone when I was at school and Uni. One thing that I did not understand, was why I had never met him before, it appeared odd that he had always been here, and yet he was a stranger to me, he smiled as I asked.

"Emily, I was always here, I have watched you grow, but most of the time when I would call in, you were usually asleep after an excited day with your grandmother. I have stood at your bedroom door many times with Han as you slept, and I saw the great joy in her life due to your presence." I looked down, as I felt a deep stir of emotion.

"I am glad she had someone to keep her company, I always hated leaving her alone, I wish she had told me about you. If I had known she had you, I would have come back sooner." He gave a slight nod as he understood.

"She loved you deeply, as deeply as she loved Amelia."

I felt the surge rush up inside me, and tried to hold it in, but a huge sob came thundering up and exploded out of me, as I stared at the floor, and I saw my tears drip onto the grass.

"I loved her too; she was a mother to me in every sense." He leaned forward and touched my shoulder.

"The loss of your mother, and then Han, has cast a shadow over you Emily, and it was Han's wish that you came here to heal, and unleash the light of who you are. She wanted you to understand that all is not as it appears, and joy will fill your heart and life, for that is the gift of this place."

I looked up and wiped my eyes on my sleeve. I did not know how to say it, I wanted so badly to be able to express accurately what was going on inside me. I wanted to say, how I was always fighting to stay in control, and had been for a year, I guess my thoughts escaped as another surge came up inside me.

"It is not that easy, I have lost more than any of you realise, she was not just a mother figure, she was the only connection I had to my mother. I am trying so hard to be brave and cope with everything, but I have this huge hole inside me, and I feel so utterly empty. I am sorry, I am really trying, but honestly, being here is not filling me with joy, it is heart breaking because she is no longer here."

Shelly leaned in and put her arm round me, Randolph gave a sad looking nod. He stroked back his long hair as he watched Shelly hug me.

"Shelly, can you handle the boat?" She sat up and shrugged.

"Yeah, I suppose so, I mean how hard can it be?" He smiled.

"I need to talk alone with Emily, I will walk her back." I held up the keys, and she smiled and took them. Shelly stood up and put her hand on my shoulder, and gave it a gentle squeeze.

"Take your time Emmy, talk, I will be home waiting when you are ready."

Shelly gave a wave, and walked off down the path towards the boat, I started to gather together the plates, Randolph smiled at me.

"Leave that, it will take but a moment for me to do it later, come, we shall walk on your land, it is time you felt the dirt of your home on your boots again."

My head was so cloudy, my emotions were high, and my thoughts were flowing too fast to make sense of anything. He guided me away from his cabin, onto a path that ran along the north bank through the trees, I could see the boat chugging slowly, Shelly was not really very skilled, she had literally only spent a few minutes at the helm, but she appeared to be making progress.

Randolph had a sense of calm around him, very similar to Han, and even though he was a stranger to me, I felt a sense of safety with him, after all, he had frightened off my Uncle Pete, and taken care of the guy who had been paid to burn the house down. I had never walked this path before, and it felt strange considering I had lived here for every moment I had free from school. I glanced at Randolph, he appeared quiet and thoughtful, with a strong stance, and a long stride. His hair was long and thick, washed grey and white, although I was uncertain of his actual age. He stared forward, and yet I felt it was almost as if he was waiting for me to talk, I looked forward into the tree lined path.

"You and Han were close, I feel that, probably closer than most people realise, am I right?" I noticed his small smile.

"She was a huge part of my time here, and yes, I cared deeply for her. You know, I understand you Emily, it may not show, but I feel her loss deeply. Like you, I also wished she had longer, I can assure you, she wanted to stay simply because she did not want to leave you."

I took a deep breath, I had thought I was dealing with this better, but actually meeting with Randolph, had hearing about Han, proved I still had a way to go.

"I am very emotional at the moment, but I want you to know, I am happy she had you, if I had known, I would have come straight home to be with her. I really regret that I wasn't."

"Emily, she did not want you see her that way, she told me, she had always been strong for you, she got sick, and declined fast, I was there and it was painful to see her that way. Strange as it sounds, I am glad you were not there, she knew her and Amelia would be reunited, and that gave her great strength, because she missed her so much, and never really recovered from her loss." I shook my head.

"No matter how hard it was for her, or would have been for me, I wanted that moment, that small pause, to tell her how important she was to me, and how much I loved her, and I have lost that forever, and it hurts."

He gave a nod as if he really understood that, but I was not sure if anyone really got it, hell, even I was struggling to make any sense of things.

"Emily, you are Amelia's daughter, have you any idea how important that was to her? Why do you think she left this place to you and cheated her other daughter out of the land? Amelia was returning to take over the care of the place when she lost her life. Han knew then, one day all this would be yours to watch over, you are so like your mother, oh you have no idea. I hate to point this out, but there was a time she too was afraid to take this all on." I turned to him feeling the surprise hit me.

"What do you mean, she was afraid?"

He smiled as we walked on at a slow pace, the trees broke at our side revealing the lake as we stood on a large rocky outcrop, and I could see the island across the water. Randolph stopped and turned to look at it.

"Emily, you do not know the whole truth of this place, hell you do not understand who Han really was, but there in front of you, is a prize more precious than all the gems on the planet. It is not obvious, but it is there, hidden from almost all people. The life there is sacred, it meant everything to Han and your mother, she too was fearful at first, for to care for this place is a great responsibility as the whole land is teaming with life. Each and every one of those lives to Han, was as precious as you were to her. Emily, she has entrusted their care to you and me, and we must work together to protect her legacy."

I had a really odd feeling, maybe it was his belief, his sentiment in his voice, I was not sure, but I got a tingle down my spine, and shivered, as suddenly I understood something, I glanced at him.

"Are you talking about what she called her children?" He smiled.

"I loved that she saw them that way, and she truly was a

mother to all of them. Yes Emily, I am talking about her children, Han's children, your instincts serve you well, but she knew they would." I looked at the island.

"What is it that lives there, because I have never seen them?" He turned back to me.

"Of that I cannot say today, but that day is close, for the time for you to embrace all things and all life is upon you, and it will be sooner than you realise. Emily, you must now look within you, and open your heart, for there is a great need for you to understand it, and I am here to guide you. That was Han's last wish, and her heart's desire." Yet again, I could hear those words, and yet no one has ever actually told me what I had to do, in order to do that, I gave a frustrated sigh.

"I know there is something here, I have strange feelings when I look at the island, and yet no one will tell me what the hell is going on. No disrespect, but what is the point in owning the land and the lake, if I have no idea what the hell is contained here?" He turned with a smile, and gave a little chuckle.

"You need to go home to your flat and return with all your things, and then the moment will be upon you, and your eyes and heart will be opened to everything. Be patient Emily, before your next birthday, all will be revealed to you, and then you will truly be the watcher of this whole domain. Come, the day wears on, we should head back to the cottage."

I gave a frustrated sigh, my imagination ran wild as I tried to work out what the hell this whole place was actually about, and to be honest, I was getting frustrated with all the secrets. I just wanted truth, I wanted to be able to relax and not have my mind in constant turmoil and my insides filled with pain.

We were not that far from the cottage, walking slowly along the dirt path, and I sensed there was far more to know about the land, he turned his head as he looked at me.

"What will you do to live here, will you take the offer of your father?" It surprised me he knew; he gave a cheeky smile.

"John grew up around here, he is no stranger to us, he has always helped watch over Han, as he has over you. Han told me of some of the things you thought and felt, but I can assure you, he was watching over you. Losing your mother was the hardest blow he has ever taken, never doubt his love or commitment, he suffered Emily, in ways you will never comprehend. Emily, we all have a time in our lives, where we lose touch with who we are, just like you today, spinning and trying to work out what is the right thing to do, with no clear vision. You father was the same, living in pain and doubt, it has taken time, but he too is awakening to his truth."

I nodded, I understood that, I had seen a very different side to him when he showed me the spot above the waterfall. I had thought about it a great deal since that day, it had stayed on my mind as I felt I had misjudged him, and actually felt a little guilty about it, Randolph walked quietly along at my side waiting for my response.

"He wants to fiancé me to research here and log all the wildlife, so it can be protected forever. Shelly wants to stay on and help me, it is a huge task, and I must admit, I would love it, but I cannot deny, I am a little afraid, especially doing accounts etc..."
He understood.

"I will help you." I frowned at him.

"How?" His face wrinkled and he chuckled at me.

"You look at me and see a game keeper, it may surprise you to know, I once had a different life. I owned my own logging company long ago; I managed many men and had a great deal of contracts with truck companies. I understand your world far better than you realise, I can help you with that, and I know others in the village that can be trusted."

I suppose in a way I had jumped to conclusions, after all, he did not look like a business man at all, to be honest, he looked like some sort of outdated prepper. I smirked to myself, he appeared suited more to this place than an office, after all, I could never imagine Harry living out here. Ahead, I saw the boat house through the trees, we were almost home.

"I am sorry, I meant no offence, but you do sort of have a wild man of the woods look, if you do not mind me asking, why did you quit and come here?"

He took a deep breath as he considered the point, it felt like he was trying to find the right words to properly express his thoughts.

"I suppose I grew tired of the world of money. Working out in the trees was the life I loved, and yet I ended up stuck at a desk and it was not who I was, and then my people left the area, and so I sold up and followed them. I ended up here working for Han, it was a simple life and more suited for me." I nodded, to a degree I could understand that.

"Did you never marry?" He smiled and shook his head.

"No... I had a daughter though, it was quite scandalous back then, I lost her, and her mother, I suppose you could say we have that in common, both of us understand the pain of the loss." I suddenly felt guilty as hell, as I saw the sadness in his eyes.

"I am sorry, I did not know, I did not mean to upset you." He gave a nod of recognition.

"It was not your fault, you did not know, it is part of the circle of life and the light, it was not easy at the time, but you learn over time to handle it better. I have no regrets, my time with them is still a very special part of my life, and one I shall always hold dear, and close to my heart. I was blessed for a time, and that is what was important."

I suppose he was right; he was lucky to be able to see it that way. I was not sure I would ever really get there, the loss of Han even after a year had not lessoned, and I still felt the deep pain of it. Would I ever be able to speak the same words about her, I really was not sure?

We walked down a slight slope that brought us to the side of the boat house, and walked past it towards the jetty. Shelly was sat on the low wall at the bottom of the garden sipping her drink, she smiled at me as Randolph stopped at the end of the jetty. He had a kind gentle old face, and a soft smile, it was strange how I felt completely at ease with him, maybe it was his calmness wearing off on me, he looked deeply into my eyes.

"Emily, open your heart and feel the world around you, for within that is the light you hold. Release it, don't look at the land, feel it, for it is within your inner being that all your answers lie." I shook my head.

"Not you too? Look everyone tells me that, but how... I mean honestly, how do I do that?" I think he understood me, or at least I felt he did.

"Emily, Han did once show you how, all you have to do is remember." He looked to the island, and then back at me.

"Come, I will help you." I frowned, he took my hand and pulled, and I turned as he walked me slowly to the end of the jetty. He pointed at the island.

"I want you to look at the island, empty your thoughts and just look." He moved to my side, and then stepped behind me. "Take deep breaths, and as you breathe out, just let everything within you flow out with it. Think, and focus on nothing but the island, now close your eyes."

I relaxed my mind and felt his hands softly take hold of my shoulders; I stared out across the lake at the image of wonder I had seen all my life. The tall green trees, the lush undergrowth, the soft sand on the edges where the water lapped up, and took a huge breath, and then closed my eyes, and held the image in my thoughts, his words were soft and quiet.

"Think only of the island, and the love within the memories that you hold. Rejoice in those treasured moments walking with Han, asking questions and understanding all the life that was surrounding you. Focus, breathe deeply, imagine you are there, walking on the soft damp earth filled with life."

Shelly swallowed hard and stood up, her eyes fixed on Emily. Randolph stood with his hands on her shoulders, and his hands began to glow. Emily stood still, looking vulnerable and frail, and yet she had started to radiate light of the purest light.

"Oh shit!" Randolph spoke softer.

"Feel the life, feel the love of those living in hope of you, embrace them Emily, embrace all of the life with your love and your heart."

Shelly stood rooted to the spot, hardly able to understand what she was seeing, as the light intensified and became even brighter as it flowed out all around Emily and Randolph.

I stood with my eyes closed, a picture of Han locked in my mind as I walked holding her hand through the trees, and she spoke of a world filled with life and love. I could feel a warmth growing inside me, radiating around me, like the day I lay in just my knickers on the warm jetty, heating my skin and filling me with the heat of the sun. A deep powerful calmness was growing inside me, it was hard to explain, I could not really describe it, but it felt like nothing I had ever felt before. It was safe and beautiful, so beautiful I wanted to cry. I had no idea what it was, but I never wanted it to leave me.

Across the island, Felix sat with Esme on the edge of the water, hidden in the low ferns, and stared out with wonder, as his eyes filled with tears and he gasped.

"She is magnificent." He gave a sniffle as Esme stood rooted, her hands on her tiny heart, tears streaming down her face, her voice was croaky and very quiet.

"She is so beautiful and filled with such love. Felix, I have never felt so adored by anyone, not ever." He swallowed hard as he watched the purest white light grow like a huge ball, blotting out all of the jetty and the garden, he gave another sniffle.

"I can feel her Esme, I can really feel her, and she is everything I wished for." Esme wiped her eyes on a leaf and breathed in, her face a huge fixed smile.

"I love her so deeply, and I really want to meet her."

I felt relaxed and at ease for the first time in a long time, as the calmness washed around me. Randolph spoke so quietly; it was almost as if he was speaking in my thoughts.

"Feel the force of life, the power of the light, feel for them, for they are there."

The pictures in my mind expanded, and I could feel a sense of Han all around me, it was stronger and more powerful, as I stood calm, softly breathing and rejoicing in the wonder of the feelings within me. I sensed everything, almost as if I was there, it felt strange and surreal, and yet wonderful, but there was something else, something more, and I tried to focus on it. It felt like the night of the stars all over again, just like the night of my tenth birthday, I had always remembered it, a sort of sense of something strange to me, something I had never known, a life, a creature, I was not sure?

My thoughts surrounded it and the feeling grew stronger, I was lost to the glory of this feeling, in my mind I could see the path, see the trees and the soft earth, and I could actually smell the damp moist air around me. My whole body felt alive and warm, like there was a heat radiating out of my soul, and it was such a wonderful and beautiful feeling. The pictures of me walking on the island flowed through my head. My arms hung down at my side, relaxed and carefree, as I walked slowly through my thoughts, and breathed the wonderful scent filled damp air.

Something took hold of both of my hands and I looked down into the bright blue eyes of a small frail looking child she smiled. Her voice was soft and loving and very quiet.

"I love you, Emily."

I gasped in shock, and opened my eyes, and suddenly I was back on the jetty. I turned quickly, and Randolph stood with tears in his eyes, and they were running down his cheeks, my voice was shaken and panicked.

"What was that?"

He smiled, and then threw his arms round me, and pulled me into a hug and almost crushed the life out of me.

"You are so like her, oh Emily, you are Amelia through and through."

He gave a huge sniffle and I was completely caught out, and lost for words. I looked over his shoulder to see Shelly stood staring at me with huge wide eyes, she looked completely freaked out. She blinked, and swallowed, and was struggling for words. Randolph pulled back and looked at me, he appeared happy and sad at the same time, it was so strange. He lifted his hand to his face, and wiped his eyes with dirty fingers.

"Emily, there is no doubt you belong here, I felt it flow through you, I know you felt the life of them, and I know all the life in this place felt you. Your mother gave you a mighty gift, a beautiful gift, you have no idea how special you are, no idea at all. Go and collect all your things, I have much to do, we will be busy on your return." He smiled. "What I saw and felt made me so happy today, Emily, I know you do not understand, but take me at my word, you put great joy in an old man's heart this day, thank you." I blinked completely lost in all of this.

"Okay... You are welcome... I think?"

He nodded and gave a sniffle, and without another word, he turned and walked quickly down the jetty, and headed back to his home. I felt confused as I looked at Shelly who was simply standing and staring with tears in her eyes, her cup limp in her hand and half of it spilled on the floor.

I walked towards her, she did not move, just stared with a fixed stare, I came up close to her and looked at her, then frowned.

"Shelly, are you alright, you look pale?"

She blinked, and took a huge intake of breath and jerked slightly, her eyes appeared to focus more. She swallowed hard and spoke softly.

"How the hell did you do that, what are you?"

"Huh?" She blinked again.

"Emily, you just made a ball of light the size of a house, how the hell did you do that?" I frowned at her.

"Ball of light, what do you mean, I was just meditating on the island?" Shelly shook her head slowly.

"Not from where I was standing, you lit up like the other night, only this time it was a hundred times more powerful. To be honest, it hurt my eyes, but I was so captivated I could not look away. Emmy, I felt you, weird as it sounds, I could actually feel your inner presence, I have never felt like that before." I stepped back.

"Okay you are being weird again, Shelly please, don't freak me out again, I actually feel calm at the moment. I really need a drink, considering you spilled most of yours, do you want a top up?" She looked down at the floor, as I walked towards the steps.

"Shit, all over my trainer as well." I headed for the house, as Shelly turned and came after me.

"I mean it Emmy, I do not know what the hell it was, an aura, energy, psychic projection, honestly I have no idea, I just know you did it and I saw it, and it was amazing and beautiful, honestly, it made me cry."

I shook my head as I walked inside where it was cool, my whole body felt overheated, as pictures of two small children holding my hand were fixed in my thoughts, one of them had the biggest and most loving blue eyes I had ever seen, and her quiet words still reverberated in my thoughts. 'I love you, Emily.'

I clicked on the kettle and leaned on the unit looking out at the island, what was that, what had I seen, it was not a normal being? I really had no idea why I had even pictured that, none of it made sense. Shelly came in through the door, she was still very pale as she held her cup, her hands were trembling and shaking.

"I know you saw them, be honest with me Emmy, you saw

Han's children, didn't you?" I felt my breath taken for a moment as the shock hit me, and I turned and our eyes locked on hers.

"Why would you ask that?" She smiled.

"I felt them too Emmy, the ball of light was so big and so bright, it expanded out of you and touched me, and my mind exploded with pictures. I have no freaking idea how, but I saw them and I heard them, Emmy please, tell me, you saw them too."

I just stared at her, and I had no idea what the hell was going on, how could she know, how could Shelly possibly know what I saw in my thoughts, it was not possible at all."

"Shelly you are freaking the shit out of me, please stop, something really weird is happening and I am nowhere near ready to have this conversation at the moment." She nodded, and looked at the table.

"Yeah, I am freaking the hell out, but I am also more excited than I have ever been." She leaned over the table and grabbed her pad, yanked it open, and flicked through the pages, she gave a nod and then looked at me.

"Honestly, is this messed up? Hell yeah! But do not lie to me Emmy this is too important, just look at this and tell me honestly, you saw them, didn't you?" She slid the pad across to me, and I looked down and my heart almost stopped.

There on the pad was the same face, the same small little creature with bright blue eyes, and suddenly I felt weak and my legs started to shake. I reached for the chair and almost did not make it, as my eyes were locked on the picture, and I had no idea how to confront my feelings. Shelly stood looking hopeful, I lifted my eyes, and I had no idea what to make of it all.

"Shell, it is not possible, how could you draw this?" She gave a long outward flow of breath, and flopped down in the chair at the end of the table.

"I knew it... Emmy that night I told you I took a picture, that is what I saw, so because the photo went weird, I drew it and painted what I saw. I hate to say this, but I know you saw it too today, and I know because whatever the hell that light was, when it touched me, I saw it too. Emmy, whatever that is, it is a young life, a childlike form, I saw it, you saw it, and looking at his reaction, Randolph saw it too." I had no idea what to say, none of this was logical, nothing was making any sense at all.

"Shelly, it is impossible, have you any idea how crazy that sounds?" She shrugged.

"I hate to point this out Emmy, but the impossible just bloody happened... Oh hell, I need alcohol, I am shaking like a leaf."

I nodded, momentarily lost for words, I think she was right, coffee was never going to fix this, I needed something way stronger. None of this made sense, and to be very honest, I felt afraid to admit what I had seen and heard, because honestly, I think if I admitted this, and actually said the words out loud, I would need locking away with the other crazy people.

Chapter Seventeen

Secrets

It was a strange night, I had so many mixed emotions, and even more questions than I had started the day with. I curled up under the covers of my bed, in hope of an early night, and as a way of getting away from Shell, who had hundreds of questions that I simply could not answer. In truth, I had no understanding of what I had done, in my mind, I had closed my eyes and thought about the island and Han, which was all. Shelly's constant chatter of large white orbs of light made no sense to me at all. I had not seen it, my eyes were shut, and it defied any logic which I could apply, simply put, what she described was impossible and against any known principles of the science I had studied.

I lay back and closed my eyes, and I could see her. The tiny face, with soft light skin, and the golden curls that flowed from her head, and the tiny little petite mouth with fine lips. Her smile was so radiant, and her eyes the deepest blue I had ever seen, and so large and round and filled with love. Who was she, had I met her before?

I had no idea, her soft quiet voice echoed through my thoughts, and I had no idea why, I simply knew, I thought it was beautiful.

"I love you, Emily."

She knew my name, she knew who I was, and yet I had no memory of every meeting her, or even seeing her and yet, the strange thing was, I wanted to see her. I wanted to meet her and talk, there was something about the feeling I felt, almost as if I had the most powerful urge to hold her and protect her, but I had no idea of how or why I would feel that way to someone who was an apparent stranger. Nothing about this made sense to me, nothing felt logical and easy to follow, and all I could think of, was she who Han talked about, was Shelly right, did Han really have other children?

I have no idea when I slipped into sleep, I think the wine helped. My dreams were strange and surreal, of plants and trees, and Randolph's tears, and I was so hot. When I woke, I had kicked off the covers and was lay naked dripping in sweat. I sat up and rubbed my face, it was still early in the morning, and I had a long day ahead of me. I stunk of sweat, but needed coffee, I felt groggy and smelly, but needed to be awake more, so opted for drinks, and then shower.

I felt apprehensive today, going back and leaving the cottage worried me. It is odd really, I had always intended to only stay for a short while, and yet now I had decided I would stay, I did not want to leave, it somehow felt wrong to me. I stood in the kitchen sipping and leaning against the sink, when Shelly entered looking rough. She looked at me through bleary eyes as she approached the kettle, I slid sideways out of the way. She sighed and clicked it on.

"Hey, how are you this morning, were your dreams as weird as mine?" I nodded.

"Yeah, I have no idea what they all meant, nothing today makes any sense to me at all, if anything I am more confused than ever before." Shell appeared to understand, she stirred her drink, and turned.

"I am still a little freaked out, and honestly, I have no idea why, but I am dreading today. Emmy is it wrong that I think leaving is not a good thing, even though we will back soon?" Okay so that was weird as hell, because I was feeling the same. I gave it a moment to consider the question.

"Shell, we will back quickly, it is just one day, that is all, I mean, how much damage can Pete do if he finds out?" She sat down in the chair.

"I suppose so, to be honest, let's just get this done and get back and settle down, I could use some calm normal at the moment."

Yeah, I got that, it is all I had wanted for a year, but I was starting to think, nothing about my life was normal. I turned to head for the shower, when Shell looked up at me.

"Who is Esme?" I stopped, turned, and saw her looking at me

and shrugged.

"No idea, I have never met one, why?" She put her cup on the table.

"You called out to her in your sleep, I thought she was someone important." I shook my head.

"No... I have never met anyone called that before, how strange." She smirked.

"Our whole bloody life at the moment is strange."

Boy, she had that spot on, I thought I would get out of the kitchen before it got weird again, I was not sure I could cope with weirder today. I left her alone and headed for the shower quickly, before yet more of her strange questions began.

It felt nice to stand in the shower, and feel the hot water running over me. It probably sounds strange, but I felt like my body temperature was running slightly higher than normal, and I hoped I was not getting sick. Washed and cleaned, I wrapped in a towel and dried my hair, and then dressed in a vest and jeans, and slipped on a long denim shirt with the sleeves rolled up, and I felt so much better.

I headed downstairs, and as I turned into the living room I heard voices. I walked slowly through to the kitchen, where Shelly stood talking to a tall blonde haired woman, she turned as I entered and smiled, and I felt a little wrong footed.

"Emily, nice to see you, Kate will be here soon, she will be your driver today, but I have a few legal things we need to discuss, I hope that is alright with you?" I felt a little awkward, Shelly looked at me.

"I need a shower, you two talk, I will give you some space." I nodded, as I looked at Jane, dad's legal eagle, and now, my new step mother. I took a deep breath.

"Hello Jane, sorry, if I had known you were coming, I would have been faster." She smiled.

"Emily, let's clear the air here. Look, I am your father's legal counsel and wife, I understand that is not an easy thing for you, and you should know, I have no issue with it. I married John, because it was something I knew would enhance my life, I did not marry him to take over from your grandmother, of which, I am sorry for your loss. Emily, I am here in a legal capacity, you need help setting up the research and all I want is to guide you through the paperwork to make the whole process smoother for you, nothing more." I nodded.

"Yeah, sorry, it just caught me by surprise, if you must know, it was nothing to do with you, I was pissed off with my dad. I see now I was childish, and I do wish you both well." She smiled again, wow she actually smiles a lot, she lifted her case onto the table.

"I have some papers I would like you to look at, I believe Matthew Higginson is your representation, you can have him look them over with you, if that is what you wish. Your father wants you to consider some things, and I have all the papers for the banking which you will need to sign, and I will need a few personal details if that is alright?" I nodded feeling even more awkward.

"You better come through to my desk, I have everything you may need in there." I lifted my arm and she smiled again, and I turned at the door.

"I still have a lot of things to get from the flat, but I will be using Han's work room as my office, it is not posh, it is actually pretty basic." She followed me through back into the living room, and round to the office.

"If you want my advice, keep things as basic as possible, you have no idea how some business become so elaborate, they become chaos to run. Simple works Emily."

I walked into the work room, and over to my desk, and sat down, and slid back my seat, to make room for her to sit on Shelly's chair. My office was one desk and a laptop, that was about it. Jane sat down and made herself comfy, she opened her case and pulled out some papers.

"Emily, shortly after your mother's death, your father wanted to help Hannah, and he set up a trust, which he named the Amelia Montgomery Trust, Han did not want to get into all the legal logistics of it, she was getting old, and as she said at the time, had enough to deal with. He spoke with me yesterday, and the trust is there, it is set and waiting, all the legal side of it is done, and it is a not for profit organisation, purely for conservational purposes. I have all the details here, and your father would like you to consider it, and become the trustee of the trust, of which, he will be one of the board members, and you can appoint others. The way it will work, is the trust will be run by you, but will be appointed to the land, and in doing so protect it forever, and will contain the funds to pay you a wage, and also fund every aspect of the trust. Ultimately, the decision is yours, and again, you may consult with others, I understand this will take some time to organise, so think it over, there is no rush."

I looked at the thick wad of papers, and felt completely out of my depth, I understood none of this, I opened it and glanced at the paperwork, as I nodded at her.

"It is a lot to take in, I won't deny, this is the part that scares me the most, I am an ecologist, I am usually doing drawings and study flows, all of this is a whole new league to me." She gave a slight nod.

"I can understand that, I would say, if you really want the very best advice, then talk to Kate, she did most of the revamp work on this for John. I think you will find, she is very knowledgeable, I would even say possibly the best to advise you. You know, I work with her a lot, and I never understood why he asked me to marry him, and not her."

That really surprised me, I looked up at her feeling a bit shocked, Jane smiled, and shrugged.

"She is younger than me, and very pretty, and they work really closely, honestly, I always thought that they would end up together, and when he asked me out for a drink after a business meeting, I will not deny, I was surprised. Emily, I had a huge crush on him, but I always thought Kate would be the one for him, and as it appears, I was wrong." I was not sure how to respond.

"I am the last person to ask, I hardly know him, I am his daughter, but to be honest, you probably know him far better than I do." She gave a soft smile.

"Emily, he adores you, I will let you into a little secret, the other day, it had a huge impact on him, and he is so happy at the moment. I would not lie to you, Emily, he has beat himself up for a long time about you two, he wanted to make amends but did not know how to. You just showed up out of the blue, and reminded him that you truly are Amelia's daughter, and it blew his mind. You know, in his line of work he is brilliant, but when it comes to feelings and opening up, he is hopeless. Emily trust me, keep forcing him to talk, if you wait for him, you will wait forever, be a little pushy, it will do wonders for both of you."

I smiled, I actually liked the idea of that, it made me happy to know it had such a huge impact on him, it had on me, and I had felt a little less alone.

"I want to know him Jane, I want us to be closer, I too struggle at times, maybe I have grown too independent. I am not sure, but it made me very happy to actually sit and talk, and not be at war all the time. I needed him, and in a strange way he came through for me." She smiled a big smile; she does smile a lot.

"I am happy to hear that Emily... Right back to business, Kate will be here soon, so let's get this done. Okay you have the trust papers to consult, and don't forget, any ideas and we can make changes. These are the banking forms, when you have made up your mind, these will need filling in, I am available if you need to talk. Emily, you do understand don't you, this is your ship, your view, you will be in charge of the trust. It is set up to run here, but the land and property remains yours and yours alone, the trust is just a way that allows you the space and funds to work here. You will control everything, not your father, he is just a board member, an advisor, nothing more, he wants this to be completely you." I understood that, she got out of her seat.

"There is no rush, take your time, talk this over with others, and then get back to me, here is my card." She slipped a card out of her pocket and handed it to me.

"The security detail will be here for as long as you need them, when you feel comfortable and safe, just let them know, and they will return to base. Good luck, relax and just settle in, and if needs be, call me." She closed her case as I stood up.

"Thank you for everything, I do appreciate it, and I am sorry I did not attend the wedding, it really was not a statement against you, I was really angry with him." She nodded.

"Emily, I knew that, and honestly, I did not blame you, he should have done more in the past for you, he simply had no idea how to. Emily that was then, and this is now, let us say this is a new sheet clean sheet." I smiled at her, she was actually quite pretty for her age, I could see why he liked her.

"Yeah, fresh start, I can do that." She turned for the door.

"I think we all need one, so let's make this place safe forever, and keep that slithering lizard of a man as far from here as possible." I gave a slight chuckle, as she gave a shudder, she grinned at me as she walked to the door. "I realise he is family, but I cannot deny, I find him quite distasteful." Now that I understood.

As Jane walked to her car, Kate drove in, as always, she was right on time, I waved to Jane as she got into her car, and she waved back as she reversed, then drove off. Kate got out with a big smile, she looked back as she walked towards me, and then turned to look at me.

"Hey you, I brought gifts." She held up two bottles of wine, I smiled.

"Hi Kate, it is nice to see you, I did not know you would be driving us." She smirked.

"A day out of the office with you two, a girl's day out is just what I need. Your dad is having a day off, so I volunteered, hence jeans and a t shirt, you have no idea how much I hate business suits. I see you met Jane and she lived?" I giggled.

"I do not hate her Kate, to be honest I do not know her." She smiled.

"She is alright, she can be a little strait laced, but she is livelier than your dad, so maybe she will soften him up a little bit. She was nervous this morning, not quite sure how you would react to her. I mean, come on Emily, you ignored the wedding invite, that was a pretty big thing for her, she did actually want you there." I giggled as she stepped in.

"She seems nice enough, I don't have an issue with her, I was angry at dad, not her." Kate looked round the house.

"Wow Emmy, this place is stunning, I do hope you have a house warming at some point, I am definitely crashing for a night."

I like Kate, she is really down to earth and friendly, although I have heard that she runs dad's office with ruthless efficiency. She is thirty six, pretty, very clever, and a lot of fun, her humour can be very twisted. She gets on with Shelly like a house on fire, and they love to bounce jokes off each other, and she has always cheered me up.

She came through into the kitchen and I clicked on the kettle, Shelly was still busy showering, she stood by the kitchen door and looked out at the land with a huge smile on her face.

"Wow Emmy, you have a small piece of paradise, John was not wrong, this place is beautiful, I have often wondered what it was like, so this is where Amelia was born, I totally get it now." I turned and looked at her.

"Get what?" She turned back into the kitchen, and pulled out a chair and sat down at the table.

"Her free spirit, the wild earthiness of her, he has told me often of her joy in the simple things, and her love of nature. To be honest, if this was her garden growing up, I can really see where she got it from."

It made sense in a way; I suppose I saw the same in Han. I put down her coffee and sat with her talking until Shell was ready. She talked of her latest crush, and a few of her more recent escapades, and she was really funny. Kate liked to be single, she had no intentions of settling, she was career minded and lived for her work. For her, it gave her a good life and some amazing holidays all over the world, where she did not deny, she enjoyed a few liberated flings. I like her a great deal, in a way much of her life made sense to me, I did not want to get tied down, although, I just inherited two thousand acres of property, so in a way, I now was.

Shelly arrived and we had another coffee, and then shortly after she explained our day, which was, she would drive, and in Exeter there would be a team to help pack and carry it all into a large van, as we supervised. We would then have a meal, paid for by dad, and then head back. I did point out, all my equipment was in the lock up at Harry's place, so she worked that into our plan, we would leave Shelly as head supervisor at the flat, and she would accompany me to Harry's to help and give support, which to be honest, came a great relief. In truth, it was the one part of my day I was dreading. It was just ten in the morning when we set off, I sat up front, and Shelly lounged in the back, for the drive of just over an hour.

As we zoomed towards Exeter, Randolph worked on his old Austin A55. The bonnet was up and he was bent over tinkering on the engine, when behind him, he heard the gravel crunch under the wheels of another car. He looked up, and saw John Duncan walk from his car towards him, he stood up, and grabbed the rag to wipe his hands, John smiled.

"My God, are you still patching up that piece of junk, Randolph, why the hell don't you just put it out of its misery and scrap it?" Randolph smiled, and threw the rag on the car wing.

"I like value, and with this I have had it. The thing can play up a little, but all in all, it has always run well, it just stumbles occasionally." John gave a hearty laugh.

"I admire your dedication, I brought you some decent beers, it is better than that weak slop they sell at the store." Randolph gave a titter as he threw down the rag, and walked out from under the carport.

They headed into the cabin, and Randolph washed his hands, John looked round at the carvings and handmade furniture. He had always liked this house, so had Amelia, he moved over to the table and placed the eight pack of beer down, then pulled out a chair. Randolph turned and looked at him, as he lifted the towel to dry his hands.

"What is on your mind John, she is staying, is that it?" John gave a sigh.

"You and I know well what is on my mind, Randolph, if she walks in the light, you know she will learn everything, you saw the effect on Amelia, is that what you want for Emily?" He nodded, as he slid into his chair.

"Amelia handled it well; do you not think Emily will? I have to add here John, you too have kept things from her, the light will reveal all." He reached for a can and pulled on the ring tab, and lifted it up, he looked over the can at Randolph.

"She is still very vulnerable, I fear for her, I am not sure she can handle the truth." Randolph shrugged.

"If she wants to commit to the land, she will have no choice, the moment she walks in the light, she will remember everything, including the crash. John, she will be twenty two next week, and her time will pass, and the Nairn will be forced to leave, and I will leave with them. It is up to you, if you want to prevent her from doing this, all of us will understand, no one better than me understands trying to protect a daughter."

John stared at his can for a minute, and took a deep breath, as he looked back at Randolph, he was so unsure of himself, and needed advice, and he was looking to Randolph for guidance.

"I fouled things up between Emily and me, and I doubt every decision I make in regard to her. Randolph seeing her there at the cemetery, hurting as badly as she was, broke my heart. I looked at her, and all I saw was Amelia in pain, and knowing I was a part of that, was soul destroying. What should I do Randolph, what would you do?"

It was a difficult question, he sat back, and stared at John as a long breath flowed from his lips.

"I saw her powers last night, she is drawn to them John, I am not sure we have any say in how this will turn out. I helped her focus, but within seconds, even though she did not realise, she was the one in command as she opened her heart and the light just flowed, and John, it was Amelia's, and it was glorious and as beautiful as she was. John, it brought tears to my eyes, I could feel her, for the first time in years, I felt my daughter, I felt Amelia." He wiped his eyes and John smiled.

"I have seen my old friend, I saw it in her at the waterfall, and later in the house, she is her mother's double, of that there is no doubt." Randolph nodded.

"John, she needs to know that Abraham was only father to Jessica, and not her mother. Right or wrong, Han and I created her mother, and she has those gifts her mother had, and honestly, after last night, I have pondered if Amelia did more than just shield her in the car." John frowned and leaned forward.

"How do you mean?" Randolph took an intake of air.

"John, the light should have protected them both, everyone knew she was coming back, she should never have lost her life, and yet she did. For years I have thought and tried to understand why only Emily lived, and yet last night I felt my daughter, and I have to question, if Amelia gave her gifts to Emily to ensure she lived?"

"What did Han think?" Randolph shrugged.

"It was hard for her to accept, it broke her heart, and for a long time she was distant from everyone except Emily, even me. I always thought she knew more, but on the few occasions I tried to talk with her, she just cut me off, and told me it was the natural way. She talked only to Emily of Amelia, never anyone else. I suppose Abraham's death, and then five years later Amelia's, she withdrew, I always thought she felt she was protecting me, and feared I was next, and in many ways, it took its toll on us. From that moment on, she focused on Emily and we became the closest of friends. I never stopped loving her John, I miss her deeply, and now Emily is back and I have to be a stranger to her, it is hard on me." John nodded; he could understand that.

"I can see that, but I am grateful to you for watching over and protecting her. I feel so caught, and for the first time in my life, I doubt myself. I want what is right for her, and only her, and I am trying to do that, I am trying to be the father I should be."

Randolph drained his can, and put it back on the table, he gave a sigh and lifted another, then pulled on the ring.

"Whilst she is busy, I aim to talk with Barrack, she saw Esme, and I think maybe Felix in her mind, she is connecting to the Nairn of her own will. I feel he may offer me some good advice, after all, he has led his clan for four hundred years, his wisdom is superior to ours."

John leaned back in his chair and looked out of the window, and stared at the sky, as his thoughts drifted through his mind, Randolph sat quietly watching him, as he slipped into his own thoughts. Moments drifted in silence, and then John sat up, and broke the silence.

"The way I see it is this. Amelia had a natural way, and I always stepped back and followed her instincts, because they always guided us right. She was returning because her instincts were telling her, that there was darkness on the trail of Han, and to a degree I think she was right. I will maintain more contact with Emily, and so should you, between us both, if something feels off, we will know. If we need to, we will act together, if as you think, Amelia is guiding her, she will be well watched over by the light. Talk to Barrack, share our thoughts and let me know what he makes of all of this, and please Randolph, stay vigilant, I have warned Pete off, but I do not trust him. He has had his sights on this land for over twenty years, I do not believe he will walk quietly away, and I will put nothing past him, he works in the darkness, and should never be trusted." Randolph gave a nod.

"You still think he tampered with Amelia's car?" John nodded.

"I do, but like all things with him, it is proving it which is hard, I have not forgotten how he leaned on Abraham to try and get Han to sell the place. I would put nothing past him, if Abraham had not died in his boat in the thunder storm, I would have looked to Pete for that too. The only way to prove any of this, is to catch him in the act, and that is the problem, he never gets his hands dirty, just like the kid with the fuel, he pays them off to stay quiet."

"And yet you got him to talk." John nodded.

"I am Pete's weakness, I am far richer than he is, whatever he pays, I can double it." Randolph chuckled.

"I take it you cancelled the cheque?" John smiled.

"Kate cancelled it before I walked in." Randolph gave a large belly laugh, and shook his head.

"I like your style; I take it he told you who paid him?" John nodded.

"It was his builder, who paid him in cash, I know the guy, and made it clear I want to speak with him, for now he has gone underground, so I know it was Pete." Randolph gave a nod.

"If he shows up here, he will most certainly go underground, I know caves no man has walked, and he will find himself wandering alone in the dark down there."

The two men sat and talked, and moved on to other subjects, they whiled away the morning chatting and catching up. It had been a long time since John had taken some time out, working closer to home and close to Emily. For now, he was putting other teams on the overseas projects, and staying close to his office in Plymouth.

As my father sat with Randolph, we arrived after a long drive of jokes and chuckles back at the flat. As arranged, a large white van with the Duncan logo was parked outside, and there was a team of five young men armed with empty boxes, I took them in and told them what was going and what staying. It felt strange to walk in, and see all of my things, the flat had only really meant to be a temporary base, and yet I have lived here for over a year.

In many ways, it was my home from home, which for the last year I had spent sharing with Shelly. Those first four months alone had been nice, but once she moved in and I became accustomed to her strange ways, I had enjoyed having her company, and our friendship had deepened. I walked into my bedroom, which was as immaculate as always, and placed some boxes on my bed, in the living room, which was also the kitchen, Kate oversaw things, as men started to pack up our pots and pans. The furniture was staying, well most of it, there were a few things Shelly wanted, and so she guided the men as to what she needed on the truck.

I emptied my bedside cabinets and boxed up my books and plans, and then moved to my wardrobe. Carefully I folded up my things, and placed them neatly in a large box, and considering most of my clothing comprised of jeans, vests and thick jumpers, it did not really take that long. I labelled each box carefully, and stacked them at the side of the bed, which I stripped and boxed up all my bedding, to be washed back at the cottage. It did not take too long, I did not own a great deal, I had lived a quiet simple life, and not really spent a lot of money.

As I finished stacking the boxes to be moved to the van, Kate walked in with a smile, I was holding a picture of my mum and dad taken on a beach in Florida, she smiled as she saw it.

"They were a lovely couple, he looks so happy, I do not think I have ever seen him smile like that before." I looked down at the picture, my mum looked really happy, and he was wearing a huge smile.

"What, not even with Jane?" She shook her head.

"No... I mean, don't get me wrong, they work well as a couple, and he does laugh with her, but that, look at him, he is radiating joy. I never met your mum, she was before my time, but when I first worked for him, a lot of them told me about her, and how she would turn up and they would have a picnic in his office." She chuckled.

"Apparently, she would tell the girls to hold his calls, then throw a blanket out on the office floor, and they would sit and talk as they ate. The girls told me he loved it, all of them agree he doted on her, she was special Emmy, no woman could replace her." I smiled.

"What, not even you?" She stood back and gave a sly smile.

"I cannot deny, we have very close working relationship, he is like my best friend, but had he asked, I would have turned him down. Emmy, Jane has a big job on her hands, you know she really is in love with him, but she is also smart enough to know, he loved your mum more than he could ever love another. In a strange way I admire her, because I could not settle for that, I would never want to be second best with the man I love."

"Yeah, I really understand that, you are good friend to him Kate, I am glad he has you with him, I am glad he has not been alone." She patted my hand.

"You know, it is a two way street, Emmy, he may not admit it, but he needs you in his life, trust me, on that particular subject, I really do know. Right, Shelly seems to be enjoying bossing the men around, so, let us face the demons, you need your equipment from Harry. Prepare for a war of words, because he will not be polite, so let's get this over with."

I took a deep breath, put the photo in the box, and folded the lid down, then taped it up, I was packed and ready to leave. I grabbed my jacket and lockup keys, and with Kate at my side, we headed out to the car, and the thirty five minute drive to Harry's offices, and my stomach was twisting and churning. I sat back in the car seat and closed my eyes, I needed to calm myself, this was not going to be easy at all.

Chapter Eighteen

Moving on

I sat in the car and looked at Kate as she drove.

"While I have you alone, what do you really think about this idea of a trust in my mum's name?" She watched out of the window, as she drove.

"Emily, the trust was actually your mother's idea. Your dad had a hand written proposal that your mother had done, before she headed back to the cottage. It was her intention to convince Han to create a trust around the land to protect it. Apparently, at that time, she was afraid, because Jessica and Peter were putting a huge amount of pressure on Han. After her death, John decided to try again with Han, but she feared losing control. I got the original document a few weeks ago, and looked it over, and made a few changes." We pulled up at a red light and she turned and looked at me.

"Emily, I made it so the trust has only your say of who controls what is done on the land, it has nothing to do with the title, call it a blanket of protection. All I did was change Amelia's name for yours, the land is your sole property, and you have complete control of the management, it has nothing to do with Duncan Developments and Design, although your dad will be a board member simply to help advise you. Emily this will be funded through a grant from Duncan, so you own everything, and can work unhindered, but your dad has ensured all the cash it will cost. In a way, this is him trying to honour your mum's final wish, it is a good deal, and will give you freedom, and protection from Pete and Jessica. It is up to you, but if I was in your shoes, I would do it."

"Thanks, you explained it much better than Jane did, and if

you think it is right, I will consider it." She nodded as we moved off.

"Emily, I wrote it so only you would benefit, think carefully and read through it, then decide. You know there is no rush, you have had a lot to deal with, so just go at your own pace, and if there is anything you do not understand, call me."

I looked forward and out of the window, the buildings were high, the road was full, and people were all over the place running about their daily lives. It all seemed so rushed and so busy, and it was hard to imagine that after just a week away in the quiet and peace of the cottage, I had actually lived and worked in this and liked it. It all felt too much to cope with now, and it seemed strange, how could I have changed so much, so quickly?

I had worried so much about walking away from this, but why? The city looked like it was overflowing, and felt grimy compared to the empty clean air and wide open spaces of my property, it shows how stupid we are in accepting this as a good life. Kate turned towards the industrial estate, and I gave a sigh, I knew what was coming and felt my insides twisting. I was not ready for this, it had been such an emotional and challenging week for me, and I knew Harry, and his abrasive behaviour, and really wanted no part in it. Kate noticed me watching the road.

"Just go in, get your things and leave." I closed my eyes.

"I wish I could, but with Harry it is not that easy, every chance he has, he has a go at me, and you know what, I have no idea why. I have always worked my hardest and done my best, and yet nothing I do is good enough. For me, it is like he only gave me the job because he hated me, and needed someone to bully." She frowned.

"Is it really that bad, he has always spoken highly of you to John?" I took deep breaths to prepare myself.

"I am not sure he has ever said anything remotely nice about me to anyone else, honestly, I despise him."

"Then why work for him, when you could work on any large scale restoration project?" I gave a chuckle.

"Mad as it sounds, I loved being out on location and doing the work. It really appeals to me Kate, I have no idea why, I just get a thrill out of being out there alone doing the work and recording what I find. It has always been something that makes me happy, you know, doing my bit to preserve the diversity of a place. I also love the fact I am the barrier that land developers like Harry get stopped with, it has meaning to me." She nodded at me.

"Yeah, that makes sense... Look at this way, for him you survey and report for him to bulldoze, what you will be doing with the trust, will be to protect and nurture, whichever way you look at it Emily, the trust will be far more rewarding. Okay are you ready for this?" I shook my head.

"Not really, but it has to be done."

The car swung to the right, and past the large sign that read 'Scott Developments and Land Scaping,' and there it was, my own idea of hell. The red brick, pretty boring bog standard building, on to which was a large hanger, filled with building supplies. Harry made out like he was something special, he lorded around his business giving out his orders, but compared to my dad, he was a nobody. If anything, he was simply a supplier of labour, this company designed nothing, they built other people's designs. Harry found the sites, brought in architects and then supplied the labour and materials to construct the developments, most of which were box houses with barely any gardens, all cramped in, to fit as many as possible.

His policy was to build it as cheaply as possible, and then charge ten times the value for them, by adding some bogus bullshit about the benefits of living in a high class home, he was an utter fraud, and I knew it, and he hated me for it. I was the daughter of his Uni pal, one who had outclassed him every step of the way, and because of that, he never left me alone and took every chance he could to humiliate me.

Kate pulled up, and I unclipped my belt, and opened the door, I grabbed the box off the back seat to empty my desk into, I looked at Kate.

"I will not be long." She frowned at me.

"I am not staying here; I am coming in with you." I smiled at her.

"Honestly, you do not have to." She winked at me.

"I want to, I want to see him as he really is."

She had no idea of what Harry was really like, and maybe my dad needed to know, so I closed the car door and headed across the car park. Two of the lads on the forklifts waved, and I smiled and waved back. It is sad really, because Harry has some good people working for him, and he is not even aware of them. I reached the door and pulled, it swung back and I walked into the office through reception, towards my desk. I had not even made it to my desk, when he saw me from his office.

As I reached my desk and put the box on my chair, he was at his door. He stood with that smug smile, on his stupid face, his thin wiry greying hair combed badly, in his badly pressed suit, wow, he thought big of himself. He looked at me and smirked, and in a loud voice announced right down the office.

"Oh, what have we here, has little miss hurt feelings come to say something? Tell me, is that a tail between her legs, as she arrives to beg for her job back?" I gave a sigh, and tried to ignore him as everyone stopped and looked at me.

I pulled open my drawer, and lifted out my camera equipment, and grabbed my keys to the lock up. I dropped the camera in the box and looked up.

"I came to clear out my desk as instructed; I assume that is alright?"

He started to walk towards me, with that arrogant air of superiority, God, I hated him, strutting like he was commander in chief of his sad little army, a man who dreamed big and fell very short of the mark. His powder blue shirt was dull, with a dirty collar, his green tie was stained with food, and his pants really needed to meet an iron, and yet he walked like he was perfect.

"You have a nerve, just skipping off and leaving us all in the lurch, and now what, you want your gear back? Remember missy, that desk and equipment belong to me."

I stared at him with hate, as I felt the embarrassment of being stared at by everyone in the room. I was determined he was not going to get the better of me, and stood my ground.

"The camera and some of the papers and books are mine, bought with my own cash, and all the surveying equipment belongs to me, it was a gift from my father. It is alright Harry I won't steal your pens; I would hate for you to lose out. Oh, and just to be on point, I booked the week off, just because you are too lazy to write it in your diary, do not have a go at me. I called in and explained how I had to take care of my gran's estate, and I am allowed a holiday. I still have three unused weeks, which is my right to take."

He reached the desk and I could see the smirk on his face, he was enjoying this. His pale lips enjoying the taste of his superiority, I could smell the cigars on his breath as he breathed out, he made me nauseous. My hand shook a little, as I lifted my wooden name plate and threw it in the box, and lifted my fern plant, and placed that carefully in, he put his hands on his hips. His eyes narrowed as he stared at me.

"So that is it is it, just saunter in without a word, and lift your gear? Wow, after all I did for you, what an ungrateful bitch you really are, the perfect little daddy's girl, we can see how that works can't we lads, the little billionaire's daughter all upset and having a tantrum because granny died."

That hurt and I felt it, but he knew it would, which is why he said it. I looked down at my seat, and felt the pain in my chest, I didn't want to, but the tears filled my eyes, and I gave a sob, I was angrier at myself than him, I did not want to cry. I bit my lip and took a deep breath and then stood up and faced him, as the tears ran down my cheeks, he was really enjoying this.

"Yes... Yes, I lost her, and it hurt, not that an unfeeling shit like you would understand, but if you really want to know, she was my world. I loved her, she was there for me after my mum died, and you have no idea of the beauty she held in her heart. I miss her and that is not a crime Harry, but how would you know, I mean really, is that what this is? You are so fucking shitty and twisted no one has ever loved you enough to make you actually feel? I pity you Harry, because you are cold, and vile, and you will never find one tenth of the love I have felt growing up with Han."

He blinked at me, and then smirked, as the tears dripped off my chin, some of the others in the office looked uncomfortable, and looked down, I pushed him back out of my way.

"I will get my gear and be gone soon enough, so just leave me the hell alone." He turned and watched me walk to the lock up.

"I want to check everything you take, nothing from this company is yours to take, go on, go cry in the lock up, honestly, you are pathetic, I don't know why I bothered hiring you."

"Ah hum!" Harry turned round.

"What... Kate... What the hell are you doing here?" She smiled.

"I am with Emily, tell me, is this how you always treat John's daughter, he would really be interested to know?"

Harry swallowed hard and went pale, he stood rooted to the spot, as she glared at him with narrowed angry eyes.

"I... I... Er... I am just having a laugh, you know, keep the spirits up, you know what it's like, all harmless fun."

Kate nodded and looked at the door, where I carried out my long plastic case containing my surveyor equipment, her eyes moved to Harry.

"Yeah, I know how it is Harry, but when a person has tears in their eyes, that is not fun, that is harassment and intimidation. I will be talking to John about your behaviour today, and informing him of the unacceptable working conditions of his daughter. Thank God, she has something far more rewarding to move on to, and a better working environment. It is probably a good job John was busy today, because if had seen what I just did, he would have beat the shit out of you." He lifted his hands up, in front of his chest.

"Look Kate, this is all just a misunderstanding, that is all, I will make up for it." She nodded at him, her eyes glaring.

"It is a misunderstanding alright, John thought you were taking good care of his child, and he was wrong." He turned to me as I arrived back at my desk, shouldered the big case on the strap, and lifted the box off my chair.

"Emily love, tell her, this is just a bit of fun, tell her I meant nothing by it." I lifted the box and looked him.

"Screw you Harry, I am done with your shit." I turned, and walked towards the door, he panicked as Kate turned to follow.

"Aw, come on Emily, no hard feelings, it was a good run for you."

I walked through the door and said nothing, I gave a sniffle to clear my nose and felt a huge sense of relief. Shell was right, I detested him, and had hated working for him, and I was glad to finally be moving forward. I had no idea what the next few years would bring, but anything was better than working for Harry Scott. Kate opened the back of the estate, for me to load my things.

"Are you alright, hell Emily, why didn't you call, if John had known it was like that, he would have done something?"

I took a deep breath and looked back at the building, Harry

was stood by the big window watching us, I gave another sniffle and cleared my nose, my emotions were all over the place, and I was fighting to hold everything inside.

"It was not dad's business, I have to fight my own battles, normally I do not cry, but it has been a hard week, and I am trying, I really am. I am holding it together Kate, and I am doing my best, Harry knows my weak spots, and he hit the most sensitive, I will be fine when I am back home in the cottage." She looked at me and gave a sigh.

"Will you though? Emily, she meant the world to you, Han took over from your mum, it is massive, you cannot hold it all in, not forever." The tears filled my eyes, and I nodded, I was fighting like hell to hold everything in.

"I know." She lifted her arms and pulled me close, and I felt a huge surge inside me, and more tears flowed as I gave a huge sob.

"I am sorry, I'm really trying Kate." She squeezed me tight.

"I got your back Emily, let some of it out."

I felt the shake and I wept, it was hard to explain, and hard to control, there was so much connected to all of this, so much pain and loneliness. I was trying so hard, but if I was completely honest, I was so frightened at the moment, and felt like a huge part of me had gone forever, and I missed it so badly, and yet I simply could not find the right words to express it. All that made sense was that Han had gone, and I would never see her again, and I had never felt so utterly lost as I did at the moment.

I gave a sniffle and took a deep breath and pulled back, and tried to wipe my eyes, Kate's eyes sparkled as she looked at me, she tried to smile, but was visibly upset.

"Feel better, Emily don't hold it in, trust me, it does a lot of damage. Look, we are done here, let's head home. I will grab some takeout coffee on route, and we will have a short break, and then head back to the cottage." I gave her a nod, and sniffed up.

"Yeah, I want to get as far from here as possible, thanks Kate, thanks for being here."

We jumped into the car, and headed back to the flat, which was looking empty, all that was left was the sofa. Shell had hoovered every room, and the place looked desolate and abandoned, it was so strange. It reminded me of the day and I first moved in, I just had a bed, nothing more, and I rang Han filled with excitement.

"Han, it is so amazing, I have a kitchen in my living room, and I love my bedroom, and I finally have my own bathroom after having to share all through Uni and work hostels. Han, this is mine, my first real home and I am so excited."

"Emmy my child, I am so happy for you, I wish I was there to celebrate with you."

"Shell is coming over later, and we are going to have takeout and drink wine." She gave a little chuckle.

"Emmy, I am so thrilled, what will do for furniture, you know if you need help, I can talk to your father?"

"No... I don't want that, Han is it wrong that I want to do this myself, I have just over a week before I start my new job, so I want to go out and buy the things I want for here? Han, I want this to be just me, all my doing, my new start in life, that is not silly, is it?" She gave a little chuckle.

"Not at all Emmy, I do not think there is anything wrong with wanting to create your own world and your own life. I think this is the best thing on earth for you, and it will be a good reminder in the future. Emmy, carve your own road, follow your heart and be guided by your light, and if you do that, the happiness you deserve will come to you. Emmy, I trust your instincts, follow them."

"I will Han, and thanks, you know, without you, I never would have done this, you gave me the inspiration to try, and I love you for it."

"I love you too Emmy my dearest child, and never forget, you will also always have a home here if you need it."

I came out of my thoughts, sat on the sofa, which no longer had extra cushions, Shell was stood I front of me smiling, and holding a polystyrene tray of food.

"Hey, you need to eat." I smiled and took it.

"Sorry, I was just thinking about that first day here when I took over, and I rang Han, and then you came round and we celebrated with wine and tacos. It was a special time Shell, for me anyhow, I really felt like I was moving forward again and starting to live my life." She knelt down on the floor in front of me.

"You still are Emmy." I shook my head.

"No, I stopped Shell, I lost Han, and Harry just got so intense, and I got lost and stopped moving forward. Shell, I walked out of that office today, and I felt a huge pressure lift off me, staying at the cottage is right for me. I know it took me a year, but I have important work to do there, and I feel that is the only place I will ever really know as home, that is where my heart is Shell." She sat back and smiled a soft smile at me, and her eyes twinkled.

"I am happy to hear that Emmy, I really am, you belong there, and I know it freaks you out, but she is there, and she needs you."

"Yeah, I think she does."

We sat and ate takeout, and drank coffee, and I settled down, but felt restless, I wanted to get home. The van was loaded and set off ahead of us, they would have to drive slower on the roads, so they needed a head start. The final moment came, and I locked the door, and said goodbye, then turned and headed for the car.

I took the back seat, and let Shell sit up front, and soon as the car moved along and Kate and Shell chatted away, I closed my eyes and just drifted in the back, feeling exhausted.

Grief is a strange thing, I thought I was really doing well. It has been a year, and it has taken a lot to come back, but I have done it, I have faced my biggest fear, and I thought I was coping. For most of the first few days in the cottage I cried pretty much all the time. I had a huge ball of pain inside, and it just got bigger and bigger. As the week moved on, I still felt the pressure inside me, but felt I had cried enough, and yet several times in the last few days, I have suddenly and unexpectedly burst into tears. Harry today was cruel, and it really hurt me deeply, even now, I cannot understand how anyone can be so cold and cruel. Has he really got no one to love or be loved by? If anything, I pity him, his life must empty and shallow, and all his money will not bring him cheer, if anything, he will die alone counting his cash.

I cannot understand that, I could not live without compassion and empathy. Things have not been good with my dad for a long time, and yet standing with him at the grave sides, or listening to him talk of his meeting with my mum, I could see the pain in his eyes. I am twenty one, almost two, and my mum died when I was four, that was seventeen almost eighteen years ago, and yet my dad is still feeling the pain of her loss.

Maybe it never goes away, looking at my dad it just hangs there in the shadows, and when that moment arises, it floods back in, like it did with me today. Is grief like a tide, flowing in and flowing out? Will there be moments in my life where the beach is clear and warm so I will bask in the joy of the moment, and then out of nowhere, in will come the tide, and it will all surge back up inside and explode out? I think that is probably right, it is how it feels for me.

I once read that time heals all wounds, but at the moment, I really am finding that hard to accept. Maybe it is like a scab, time is just the cover, a temporary fix to help us all heal a little, and become accustomed to the loss. I remember cutting my leg on a barb wire fence when I was eight, even to this day, I still have a white line of a scar to show where it happened. Is that what happens to us, we have a scar inside that helps ease the pain, but really if you think about, the wound is still there, lying hidden below the surface, as a reminder that it will never truly go away.

I slipped into sleep as I thought about my life, and I drifted peacefully, until I jerked awake with a start. Shelly was smiling at me, I had lay down on the seat, so sat up and blinked.

"Sorry, did I fall asleep?" She giggled.

"We are home and safe Hun, Kate has gone in to put the kettle on, the guys are going to start unloading the van, where do you want stuff?" I yawned and slid to the door.

"What do you think, living room or office? I will take the stuff with my name on up, I don't have that much for my room, although it will be nice having more clothes."

Once again, it got busy, as the guys unloaded the boxes. Shell and myself carried boxes up to our rooms to be unpacked, and some of the stuff was stacked up in the office. My PC was placed on the desk with my printer, and my drawing board, which was the biggest thing I owned, was leant against the wall, as it came in two pieces and I would have to set it up again. The good news was, we brought our desk chairs, so we now had three. I took the small fern from my office desk, and placed it on my bedroom window bottom, it was a bright and airy place, and I felt it would grow better there, and then I set to work, unpacking my clothing.

My bedroom here was pretty empty, I had taken most of my stuff with me when I moved out, and so I had plenty of space to fill. I hung all my clothes in my wardrobe, and finally refilled the empty chest of drawers, which had an empty top, so I displayed my pictures of my mum, dad and Han. I also had one of me with

Pam and Shell, which was taken on our last day of Uni. The room felt more like home when I had finished.

I wandered down and thanked the drivers, and gave them some cash as our way of thanks, and suggested they had a beer on us, as they had worked very hard, they appeared very happy as they left. Kate sat back on the sofa and smiled as I sat down.

"You appear much more at ease here; you really do fit the place. I enjoyed today, it is nice to get out of the office, how are you doing now, I hope you do not let Harry get under your skin? Emily, you do realise it is his way of taking out his frustrations because your dad did much better than he did?" I understood that.

"Maybe Kate, but why pick on me, I have nothing to do with what my dad does, and I worked hard and gave Harry some high class work. He did well out of me, he charged much higher fees on the jobs I took on, he could have kept me there, but he chose to humiliate and ridicule me, and it is his loss now, he blew it." She agreed with me.

"Things will be better for you here, you have plenty of space and a good project to work on, be honest, you have years worth of work and funding here. Emmy this could be the making of you, I would imagine you will be able to write and publish a lot of papers on this place, it is important research, all you have to do is set it up."

Shell came in with glasses of wine, and handed me one, and then one to Kate, she flopped down at the side of Kate, I curled up my legs as I sipped my wine, and took a moment to think carefully of my words.

"Kate, I am going to take your advice, I want the trust to carry the name of my mother, I want her remembered. I know dad is on the board, but I would like you on it too, I trust you, and I trust your instincts, you have been there for me, when my dad was busy, and I respect your advice. I want Shell on the board as well, and I am going to talk to Pam, she knows as much about environmental studies as I do, she will help with some of the decisions."

Kate sat back and thought for a second, she sipped at her wine as her eyes watched me, she gave a slight smile.

"You have thought about this much deeper than I thought, I

am actually quite surprised. Jane only delivered the papers today, but it is obvious this has been given a great deal of consideration. Pam would be a good choice for advisor, not only does she understand the work, she understands you, I am sure your father will be very pleased with your thinking. I cannot accept without your father's permission, I am contracted exclusively to him, but I will talk with him about this. Emily, the piece of advice I would give you, would be do not rush. Look, after what I saw today, I think you need more time, take a break, do as little as possible, focus on the house and focus on you. I do think you need to let more of your grief out, holding it in will cloud your mind, so rest, sort out the house, and sort out your feelings, and carefully plan everything out."

It was hot, and had been a long day, so with our wine, we headed outside, and walked down the garden with some of the cushions, and sat out on the jetty, I slipped off my jeans and just relaxed, Kate appeared to be enjoying herself, and I looked at her dangling her feet over the edge in the water.

"Didn't you say you have a couple of days off?" She gave a nod, as she wriggled her toes in the water.

"Yeah, I have enjoyed today, it will be nice to chill out for another day." She did seem to be far more relaxed than she ever had in the office."

"Why not stay over and hang out with us, this place is so peaceful, take your chance to make the most of it. We have a spare room, and we are not short of bedding now, so relax, have another wine and just destress." Shell agreed.

"Yeah, chill out girl, and let go a little, this place is perfect for it." Kate gave a little chuckle.

"I will not deny, I love the place, it would be nice to really get a good feel for it."

It looked like the decision was made, I lay back and looked at the sky, which was a beautiful pale blue, and completely clear, and I just lay back and let my mind drift, as the stress of the day washed out of me. Han was right, she had told me often how this place held the power to heal, and simply knowing I was now completely free of Exeter, and had all the time in the world here in this place of tranquillity to rest and recover, which calmed me more inside.

Shelly was also right, Han was here, she was in my dreams, walked through my memories, and was held cherished within my heart. It was hard to not see her each day as she did her chores or gave me her take on life, but just knowing she lived here, and lived a good life was for now enough. Today I had thought of her, and that special memory of her had popped into my mind, so in a strange way, I had not lost her, I could still talk to her through my thoughts, and again, that did make a huge difference.

Across the island on the water's edge, hidden slightly from view, Randolph stood and watched. At his side was the figure of Barrack, who was sat watching and leaning against an old stump, Randolph turned and smiled.

"See, she has returned, you felt the power of her light, Emily is as big as part of this land as you or I. Your concerns were unjustified, Han was right." He stared across the lake towards the jetty deep in thought.

"I am happy to be wrong Master Sage Feather. Chandak has raised good points which I have considered, her youth and inexperience still concern me, I would have been more at ease if Han had presented her to the clan. Her emotions are not completely in control, and they will need to be, we have little time, she has not faced her full future yet."

"I can understand that, give me this time, and I will guide her through it." He turned to look at Randolph.

"If she embraces the light, she will know the truth, what have you decided to do, will you tell her first, because that may create great emotional turbulence?" He watched across the water from under his hood, his eyes locked on her.

"Han never told her, and I never understood why, maybe now is my time to walk beside the new watcher, as she had intended to do, and maybe that is my place now. If she is to learn the truth, I feel it should be from my lips and no others, although it will be a fine line to walk." Barrack understood, as he watched across the water.

"Maybe, but the truth always has been, it is good you want to do this, she will need you if the predictions are right." Randolph gave a slight nod.

"She is in my care now; I will not fail her as I did my daughter."

Chapter Nineteen

In The Light

I woke early and the sun was shining, although as I lay in bed and looked out of the window, I could see white fluffy clouds drifting slowly across the sky. I had slept well, but once again I had dreamt of strange things, and always about things surrounded by light. In the peaceful surroundings, snuggled under my duvet, I let my thoughts wander. I felt like everything had happened so fast, that I really had not been given the time to fully understand what was happening, and I had so many questions about this place.

Who was Randolph really, and where had he come from, who was the little figure I had seen when with him in my thoughts? Was Shell right, did I make the rainstorm stop, and how did I float above the bed, like some sort of glowing soul like entity? Actually, how did I create a ball of white light that allowed Shell to see my thoughts?

All of this appeared to have something to do with Han, and possibly my mother, and yet I did not know what. Was it really Han that came to me in my dream, and how was that even possible? Everything happening around me made no sense at all, and pretty much all of it was impossible according to science. The insane thing was, as sceptical as I was, some of it I could not deny had happened, and it really did bother me, as I had always made fun of Shell for talking about it, and now, I felt a little guilty.

In many ways, I was no better than Harry, he had ridiculed and humiliated me, for my feelings, and in a way, I felt I had done the same to Shell, I had ridiculed her beliefs, and I felt I should not have sat in judgement of her so easily. The one thing I realised that Shell and I had in common, was both of us sought the truth, both of us wanted our questions answered, and somehow, I felt that was something I really needed to resolve. As I lay in my bed, I knew, this was not just about Han and the cottage, this also had something to do with the island. My answers lay across the lake, that was where my truth lay, and I was determined I was going to find it.

I finally got up, and headed down to the kitchen, I made a drink and noticed the kitchen door open, I wandered out and stood at the bottom of the garden, Kate was sat on a cushion on the jetty. I wandered down quietly, she was looking out across the lake, and looked so peaceful. I walked quietly up at her side, and she came out of her thoughts, she turned and smiled.

"Emily, this place is so beautiful, you have no idea how lucky you are to have all this, hell, I could live and die here. It is so peaceful and tranquil; I feel completely at peace with myself." I sat down on the edge of the jetty.

"I think I did not really understand this place as a child, in a strange way, coming back after losing Han, I have really started to understand why it was so important to her, and in a strange way, it has brought me closer to my mother, knowing she too felt the same." She smiled and nodded her head.

"Most things take time, appreciation I have always felt was an act of hindsight, we need to stop and take stock occasionally, and it is at those moments, we see the truth of all we have been." I gave a chuckle.

"You would have loved Han; she has said many similar things."

At the top of the garden, Shell came out of the back door, she was wearing just her knickers, she held up the loaf bag.

"Guys we are almost out of bread, when are we going shopping?" Kate gave a giggle.

"Sorry I had a couple of slices, if you want, I will drive, and you can show me the village?" She nodded.

"Yeah, give me a few to have a coffee and some toast." Kate smiled as she got up.

"You hang out here, this place and some alone time is good for puzzling out things, I will keep Shell busy for a while."

She left me alone, so I sat down, holding my cup and stared

at the island. I had been back for a week, and not yet been over there, although, I had not even opened the door to Han's bedroom either. I had many memories of being on the island as a small child, walking with Han, although as I got older, especially during my Uni years, Han took a back seat and sent me over alone.

Last night as I lay in my bed, I had wondered why she left me to roam alone on the island, what did she want me to see, or what did she want me to feel? Both Han and Randolph referred to the life that lived here, I guess, because I was studying ecology, I just assumed they meant the flora and animal life, but after the other night and my strange vision of a child like creature, I was starting to wonder.

I sat for a while lost in thought, when Shell appeared at the door dressed, and shouted she was off, and would be a while, and knowing they would be gone, I made my decision. I got up and headed back to the house, and made another coffee and then headed to my room. I pulled off my top, slid off my knickers and walked into the bathroom to wash.

Feeling cleaner and wrapped in a towel, I dropped the towel, and sprayed myself with deodorant, slipped on pants with clean knickers, and grabbed a vest, and noticed the bra hanging on the end of the bed post. I had not really worn one since I had come here, I had every day for work, I left it and slid on the vest. To be honest, this is my land my rules and skinny dipping was also a part of that, and I no longer cared what the outside world thought, this was my world, and that was all that mattered to me.

Once dressed, with a travel mug, I headed to the boat house, and jumped in the boat, and I had one task in mind, what was it Han wanted me to know, why did she insist I spend time alone on the island? I reversed the boat out, gunned the engine, and made a dead straight line for the island.

Esme gripped Felix by the hand, and squeezed it hard, he jolted awake, and looked up with sleepy eyes. Esme stared out across the water.

"Felix, get up quickly we have to go, she is coming."

He blinked and jumped to his feet, and looked out across the water where the boat was heading straight towards them.

"I don't want to go; I want to talk to her." Esme shook her head rapidly.

"No Felix, we promised, we swore an oath, we have to wait until Randolph says so, we do not want to scare her, we want her to stay." Felix gave a sigh.

"It's not fair Esme, we could show her why she must stay, Esme, she is filled with love, she would listen." Esme looked panicked.

"I will not break a vow Felix, a promise is sacred, and I don't want my wings to fall off for lying." Felix looked at her and sniggered.

"Esme, do you still believe that tall tale, that is for children?" She shook her head and let go of his hand.

"I am not going to risk it, you can stay here and walk everywhere, if I lose my wings, I will not be able to cross the water and see her when she knows of us." He gave a frown.

"I did not think of that, is the fat one with her?" Esme looked out; the boat was getting closer.

"I don't know, the boat is too big and I cannot see." He gave a quick nod.

"We better hide then, she has big feet and might step on us, and I don't want to be squished."

Esme smirked, she knew that Emily was alone, she could feel it, and so she turned, and holding Felix by the hand, she pulled him under the ferns, and ran with him towards their secret hiding place.

The boat came close and I killed the engine, and unclipped the bracket to raise the motor out of the water, as the boat glided towards the bank and low water line. I rolled up my jeans, and slipped off my socks, then made my way up the boat, and grabbed the long line. The boat glided onto the soft sand below the water and slid to a halt, I swung my leg over the rail, straddled it, then slipped down into the cold water, and pulled the line up onto the bank. On the bank there was an old fallen log, I watched Han tie the boat to it a hundred times, so I looped the rope round and tied it off.

The earth was warm under my cold feet, as I stepped onto the path, the grass was longer here, it had been a while since anyone had walked here. I knew the way, Han had taken me up this path a thousand times as a child, and it led right up the centre of the island.

The air was warm and damp under the trees, with bright patches where the ferns grew, as the light flooded down through gaps in the canopy. I had always loved this place, it was a virginal place, untouched by man, where the squirrels jumped from tree to tree and the few boars on the island hunted at night. The whole place was a hive of life, from the plants to the insects and the birds in the trees, and a surface that teamed with small animal life. It was untouched by modern man.

I breathed deeply, absorbing the scents in the air, it was so peaceful here, so calm, and with each step I felt the whole atmosphere absorb into me, almost as if I was soaking it up from the ground through my feet. My mind was calm, although I was also alert, call me crazy, but if anything moved, I wanted to know why. I followed the path, taking my time, and looking around at the landscape, many parts of which were really overgrown. The occasional rock loomed up from the floor, rising half way up the height of the trees, solid and light grey, filled with cracks and, grooves that had splintered off and fallen.

The island was beautiful, above me, red squirrels ran from branch to branch, almost as if they were following me, interested in what I was doing here. I had a place in mind, a place Han had shown me many years ago, and a place I had visited often alone, and a place Han had told me my mother often sat to think things out. I am not really sure why I thought about it, but it had to come to mind as I crossed the lake, and hadn't Randolph told me to follow my instincts?

Both Randolph and my father had told me I was her double, like her in every way, and I knew this was the one thing my mother did on a regular basis when she was home, and so today, I wanted to follow in her footsteps, and try and find out why. I arrived at the circle, and looked round, it had not changed much, a wide circle of empty space, bathed in sunlight, around which, there were stones that rose two feet out of the ground. The stones were old, and carved with strange markings, I assumed they were Celt, Saxon, or maybe Viking, I had no idea really, I thought Shell would probably know, she is after all into this kind of stuff. I took a huge breath, and walked right into the centre.

"Okay mum, let's see what this is all about. Han told me you were close to me, and always in the light around me, so if that is true, help me to understand why you did this." I sat down, and flicked open the top of my travel mug, and took a sip, then placed it on the floor at my side.

"Close my eyes and feel, that is what Han said, so, let me see what I can feel here in this sacred place."

I crossed my legs, and closed my eyes, breathing in deeply to try and relax more than I currently was. It was not that hard, after all, this place was tranquil and silent, there was nothing to disturb me. With just the sounds of the island, which was the quiet rhythmic hum of insects, and my thoughts in my head, I felt calm, and thought of Hans words.

"Emmy my child, just feel with your heart, open it and allow the light of your love to flow."

I breathed out softly, and then inhaled, and my mind filled with pictures of Han, as she smiled at me, and her soft voice echoed through my head.

"You are so like her, filled with love and light, she would be so proud of you Emmy, you must feel her within you, look back to that small span of time when you two were together. Emmy, look through your black out, remember."

I breathed in deeply and felt like my whole body was as light as a leaf, and then slowly breathed out feeling the calmness wash through me. A picture filled my mind, it was hazy and dark, but a voice I did not know spoke.

"I cannot say if she will remember, the shock of what she saw may permanently damage her, and she could lock it away forever. Mr Duncan, this is one area where we cannot predict the science."

"So, she will never remember it, it will just be a blank forever?"

"It is possible, we just cannot say."

I breathed in, drawing the air in slowly, what would I not remember? I was not sure, I focused my thoughts, and whispered to myself.

"Tell me, tell me the truth, you owe it to me, tell me what I forgot."

I drew a deep breath in and felt more calmer, and even more

relaxed as the sun warmed my body, my eyes closed tight as pictures flowed through my thoughts.

I turned and saw my mother, she was unclipping her seat belt and outside the car there was such a loud noise, I was breathing fast, and very scared.

"Mummy I am frightened."

"It is alright Emmy, I am here, don't be scared." Her belt came away, and she slid up from her seat and leaned over towards me, I felt her warmth around me, felt her holding me.

"Shush, we are fine, the car lost control in the storm, that is all, I am going to take your belt off alright sweetheart. Emmy I am here, we are in the light."

I could feel the sweat on the back of my neck, I was breathing faster and faster and my nose was filled with her perfume as she struggled to unclip me, I pulled at the belt, it was not coming off.

"Mummy, it is stuck, Mummy I cannot pull it." I felt a shudder vibrate through me, the car was moving sideways, I felt her jerk as she pulled on the strap to get me out of my child seat, and she looked frightened, as her face contorted.

"WILL YOU JUST BLOODY COME ON!"

She screamed at it as she pulled, outside the car there was I deafening cracking noise, and she looked back through the side of the cars broken window.

"Oh God no."

Her body came down and she looked at me, and tried to smile, and I felt myself shaking in the seat, for a moment everything felt quiet, as I looked into her hazel eyes.

"Emmy, I will not leave you, not ever, I love you, I love you with all of my being and will forever, do you understand me?" I could not talk I was so scared, and just shook, she smiled at me.

"Take my light, take my love and my joy, I will be with you forever my precious angel, I love you, Emmy."

The thunderous crack and groan, and thunderous crash, and the pressure of her soft scented body slammed into me, and all I could see was light, bright beautiful radiant white light. I felt the gasp within me, I was not sure if it came out, and felt the cold tears as they rolled down my cheeks, and I was afraid, I was afraid to open my eyes.

I was breathing much faster and tried to control it, was that what happened, was I with her when she died, did I see her die, why had no one told me? I felt the sob deep down inside me, and shook where I sat in the open green circle.

Stood on the path twenty feet away, the silent figure of Randolph bowed his head, as the white light radiating out of the circle touched him, and he felt Amelia, his hood shook silently, he had always known what happened, he had never seen it, and now he had. I sat with my head down, and my eyes closed sobbing and shaking, not knowing what to do. Randolph stiffened and then looked up.

In my darkness with only my thoughts, lost and unable to understand why Han had never told me of this, I felt utterly wretched. She died trying to save me, if I had not been with her, she would have got out and lived. It was my fault, I was the reason she died, and my shoulders shook as I wept, my thoughts running wild inside my brain. Randolph stared in shock at the light.

"Emmy."

"Emmy my precious child." I took a deep breath, and in my mind a picture started to form.

"Emmy listen to me, look at me." I gave a huge sniffle and opened my eyes and looked up, and my breath caught in my throat.

The whole of the circle was drowned in white light, and none of the island was visible, and yet there was something, a shape, a figure, and one I remembered.

"Emmy I am here in the light, I always have been, Emmy we share the same light, I gave it to you, we are connected always, and I have been at your side always. Emmy I am still here." I breathed in a deep breath and swallowed.

"Are you really there, or is this just another mind game?"

"I am here, this is not trick, Emmy, open your heart, feel me." More tears filled my eyes and I felt like a little frightened girl again.

"Mum?"

"Yes, my darling, I am here, I always have been."

"Mum it was my fault, I am so sorry, I wanted you to stay, and Han has gone as well." I felt another huge sob. "Mum, I feel so alone."

"Emmy, you have never been alone, I am there within you. Emmy, it was not your fault, it was a terrible storm, and the car lost control, all the peddles stop working, and I could not control it, it was never you. I asked the light to save you, do you understand that? Emmy, I begged the light in those last few seconds to protect you and save you, I wanted you to save the children, I asked it to save you. Emmy, look deep within you, remember everything, it is time my precious child, it is time for you wake up and save all of Han's children, they need you, they are depending on you."

I stared into the light and hazy shape of a person before me, I had no idea who the children were, how could I save what I did not know about?

"Mum there are no children here, I would have seen them, and I have not seen any."

"Emmy, open your heart, let go of the pain, because it is blinding you to the truth, we did not leave you, see I am here, and Han is with me. Emmy we will remain here forever, we will never leave you alone, believe in me and trust me, trust in the love I showered on you."

"I do love you, I have always loved you Mum, and I want to remember you always, I am staying here to save the land. Mum, I need you, I need you to help me, because I don't know what to do."

"Talk to your grandfather, he was sent to you as your guide, listen to him Emmy, and he will bring you into the light to join with us." I shook my head not understanding.

"Mum my grandfather died in a boat accident; he is not here."

"Emmy, Abraham was not your grandfather, and Jessica is only my half sister, your grandfather stands waiting before you, go to him, and I will walk in the light with you soon." I frowned.

"Wait… What, that makes no sense?"

The light began to fade, almost as if it was flowing down and soaking into the floor, and as it diminished, the island came slowly into view, and her voice sounded distant.

"I await you in the light, walk with truth, and open your heart to the land, and protect it. Listen to the words of the wise Emmy."

I swallowed hard as I saw the hooded figure on the path staring at me, with a look of complete surprise, I really did not know what to say I just stared at him, and lifted my sleeve to wipe my eyes. I suddenly felt awkward, and I think he did too, we were related, and he had not told me, and I could not understand why, it would really have helped knowing. He took an uneasy step forward.

"Emily, are you alright, how the hell did you do that?"

I blinked, and came back to full reality, as Randolph walked towards me, I was struggling to make sense of what my mum had told me. None of it made sense, like everything since I had come back to the cottage. He knelt down in front of me, and looked astounded, I stared into his eyes.

"Is it true, are you really my grandfather, because if it is, I need to know how, because it makes no sense to me at all, tell me Randolph, was Han really my grandmother, or is that a lie too?"

Randolph sat back on the grass, and took my hands in his, I could see him looking for the right words.

"Emily, I was going to speak to you today, firstly yes, Han was your real grandmother, she gave birth to Amelia in what is now your home. I have no idea how you did that, but unbelievably, your mother came to you and walked in your light, but she did not lie. Emily what I did was seen as wrong, but I will not deny, I loved Han with all my heart, I love her still as deeply, and I miss her. I had a relationship with her behind her husband's back, it was never planned, it just grew from the friendship we shared."

I gave a nod as if understanding, but this was not something I had ever expected from Han. I slipped my hands out of his, and lifted my travel mug, my throat was dry, and I needed liquid. I took a long swig and rolled it round the inside of my mouth, Randolph looked uncomfortable.

"Amelia was my daughter, Abraham was not a kind man, and life was hard for Han, he tried to make her sell the land, and she came to me for help to stop him. Emily, Han owned the land, it was her fathers, and his fathers before. Abraham tried to take it away from her, and I helped her prevent it, and we grew close, and as a result she became with child, with Amelia. I faced Abraham, and told him the truth, and asked him to let her go, but he refused and threw me out of the house, and banned me from the land."

I took a huge breath inwards, this was a startling revelation to me, and I was struggling to come to terms with it.

"We talked the other night, we were alone, you knew how I was feeling, I told you how lonely I was, my mum knew, why didn't you tell me, it would have made such a difference, and helped me?" He gave a long sigh as he watched me.

"Would it though? Emily, I did not want to add more to the burdens you were shouldering, it was there on my mind, and I was so unsure of myself. Since I left you that night, it is all I have thought about, and today when I saw your boat head for the island, and I saw you were alone, I decided to come here and tell you."

"Yeah, well my mum beat you; she came to me first." He gave a solemn nod.

"I am sorry, I let you down, it was wrong of me, I should have been more open with you. Emily, I always turned to Han for advice, and like you, I no longer have her and miss her. I lost my daughter and Han was all I had left, and then she took you in, and I watched you grow. I have always been there in your shadows watching over you, but Han asked me to stay silent, she asked me not to confuse you more. Emily, you remembered nothing of the accident, you do not even recall it was I that helped cut you free. I carried my daughter to the ambulance helicopter, and then carried you. They whisked you away and I had to wait, and it was awful, and unbearably painful."

I saw the tears in his eyes, and the pain he felt, I knew that pain well, and it felt heart breaking to see what I felt in another person, and I really did not want that. I felt the tears again and shook my head at him.

"Randolph, we have to let it go, my mum told me, we have to move forward and we have to live. I do not know how I did what I did, but I do not regret it, I felt her Randolph, I felt my mother for the first time since I can remember. I do not know how she did that, but I needed it, I really needed it." He smiled at me.

"I am glad she came, you had a very precious gift today, Emily, you got something I have yearned for. I am so glad she came to you, it was typical of her, she found a way against all the odds and reached out to you, and I am so grateful she did." I sniffed up and wiped my eyes again.

"Yeah, me to." I gave a smile. "Randolph, she felt wonderful, I felt her in my heart for the first time. Randolph, you knew her, you talked to her, will you tell me about her, tell me your stories like Han did? I miss Han, I miss the joy in her when she spoke of my mum, so talk to me, tell me of your daughter, my mother." He gave me a smile, and I could see how emotional he was.

"There is so much to tell, I really do not know where to start." I nodded understanding that.

"I do not mind, start anywhere, I want to see her through your eyes, and listen to your heart as it opens. Randolph, I am thrilled that I can share her with you, and in doing so learn more about her, so just tell me how you saw her."

Esme sat alone in the low shrubs, and watched from about fifty feet away, her large bright blue eyes locked on Emily's face, and her soft smile, as Randolph talked to her about Amelia. She leaned on her hands and smiled as she watched, and whispered to herself.

"Oh Emily, you are so beautiful, I am so happy you are staying, I am going to live my whole life knowing you, and that makes me so happy." She gave a long happy sigh, and smiled to herself.

Shelly walked up the aisle lifting things into her basket, Kate followed grabbing a few things for herself, Rachel Hannity eyed them with suspicion. Shelly grabbed a loaf and then walked towards the counter, Rachel looked her up and down, as Shelly put the basket down with a smile.

"Good day to you, may I enquire as to if you have recently arrived here?"

She came over as being a little bit starchy and judgemental, Shelly was quite used to it, she gave a big smile.

"Hi, I am Shelly, I live with Emmy." Rachel frowned.

"Emmy, I have no idea who that is?" Shelly nodded her head and smiled again.

"Sorry, Emily, you know Emily Duncan... Oh actually Montgomery, yeah, I am her house mate." Rachel gave her a strange stare.

"You live there, I heard she was returning to Exeter?" Shelly nodded.

"Yeah, I live with her there too, or at least I did, until we moved all our things here yesterday. We are living here now, you know, me and Emmy?"

Rachel was very surprised, she took a step back and then smiled, and suddenly her whole attitude changed.

"Emily is staying, oh that is such good news, Hanna really wanted her to take up the cottage, I am so relieved to hear she will be around more. You know, there has always been a Montgomery in this village, it is a long standing tradition of the village. I am so pleased to welcome you to the village, both of you." Kate gave a giggle and shook her head.

"I am just a visitor, I work for Emily's father in London, but I will not deny, I think your village is truly delightful and beautiful." Rachel appeared very pleased and happy.

"We are very proud of our village, and it is always nice to have our hard work noticed. So, Shelly did you say, tell me, what will Emily be doing at the cottage, I take it she works?" Shelly nodded.

"I am a writer, well author actually, and with Emily being an ecologist, she will be freelancing, she is very well regarded and sought after, so she will be fine for jobs. For now, we are taking some time out and just settling in properly." She gave a nod as she tilled up the goods, and Shelly slipped them into her backpack.

"Well, all of us in the village welcome you, and wish you well, we are sure she will do very well here, Han thought very highly of her, and we believe that she is very like her mother. Amelia was a very lovely girl, we thought very highly of her too."

Shelly smiled, and put her card on the machine and it bleeped, Rachel handed over the till receipt.

"Now you are a resident, don't be a stranger." Shelly smirked.

"This is the only store, so that is probably a definite, but nice to see you and I will again, thanks."

Rachel smiled, and Kate handed over her few things as Shelly stepped back, and waited for Kate, and when they were done, they headed out across the street giggling, Shelly looked back and saw Rachel watching through the window.

"Wow they are nosey; they want to know everything." Kate

smiled.

"It is the same wherever you go, their lives are so dull, they live off the gossip." Shelly chuckled.

"I loved how her attitude changed when she realised I was a resident now, before that she was a little off, but say the magic word Montgomery and all the doors open."

They both laughed as they walked towards the car, the florist shop door opened and Heidi came out holding her phone, and hurried across toward Shelly.

"Is it true, has she decided to stay?" Kate gave a giggle.

"Wow the gossip does travel fast." Heidi came up with a huge smile on her face.

"Oh Shelly, I am so delighted, Amelia would be so happy, Emily belongs here, she belongs in that cottage. Tell her when you see her how delighted I am, tell her we need a night in the bar with a few drinks." Shelly nodded with a big smile.

"Yeah, I will, we moved everything down from Exeter yesterday, so we have a few days of getting sorted, but you are welcome for a brew anytime." Heidi nodded.

"I won't keep you; I have flower arrangements to make, but just tell her how happy I am, will you?"

"Yeah, I will, she will be happy to know."

Heidi ran back with a smile, and Shelly and Kate got in the car, and headed back to the cottage, it was going to get busy, there was a lot to organise.

Chapter Twenty

Making Sense

As we walked back towards the boat, having spent well over two hours talking, I felt a deep sense of ease within me. I had smiled and cried, listening to the beautiful way in which he saw and interacted with my mother. He really came across as a doting father, he certainly loved her very deeply, and I liked that a great deal about him.

It is strange, that the only way I have a decent understanding of my own mother, is through the interactions and words of others. I learned a lot today about her, and how when first confronted with the fact that Randolph was her father, she had not made it easy for him. She had been greatly upset, which caused a big row with Han, and Randolph explained how he managed to convince her to visit his house and sit and talk.

He talked of that day, and how they sat outside and he cooked for her, as he explained the full truth of his secret affair, and how Han had conceived as a result. Randolph spoke of how she questioned him thoroughly about every detail of how it all happened. My mother wanted a reassurance that Randolph played no part in the death of Abraham, Han's husband. I will not deny, I sat up and listened as he talked of how Abraham had ignored the weather warnings, and argued with Han, then left in the boat to fish, and whilst out in the middle of the lake, he was struck by lightning and fell into the lake and drowned. He assured me, the autopsy agreed in the manner of his death, although Randolph did admit to my mother, had Han asked, he would have taken care of him.

Randolph told me of how hard Han's life was, as she had to battle her husband, and the father of Peter to save and protect the land. The pressure on her was unbearable, and in private with him, she faltered, and almost broke. In many ways Randolph felt, that was why my mother was in such a hurry to return, as Peter took over from his father, and began again to apply a lot of pressure. He talked of the night of the crash, and his heartbreak, and he cried a great deal as he told me of how devastating it was to find the car all bent and crushed, with my mother braced over me to protect me. I cried with him, as I remembered the memory that had flooded back to me as I sat alone in the circle, and I was still feeling the aftershocks of that moment.

I have a sadness within me, is this me grieving properly after seventeen years of not knowing? I feel so much has happened, and I feel the weight of it, but I am also reaching a point where my exhaustion from it all, has reduced my ability to cry anymore. The island has given me peace to think and let out more of the pain within me, yet walking at the side of Randolph, back towards the boat, I know I have to return to the cottage, and the distractions that have interfered with my focus recently. My mind was clearer today, and it helped, I can only hope I will have the chance to find more clarity as I move forward.

We finally reached the boat, and I turned and looked at him, with his hood down, and his long grey hair lay across his shoulders. He looked tired and worn, as if today had taken a huge toll on him, I gave him a smile as I looked into his eyes.

"Thank you, you have helped me a great deal today, I am still sort of trying to work everything out in my head, but seeing your love for my mother has given me more of her, and I am grateful to you for that. It appears we are family, it is unexpected, and not something I was prepared for, but I have loved that you sat with me, and spoke of past events, because that has added yet more pieces to my fragmented life. You are my grandfather and I am a little shocked still, but I would like to see you more and talk more. We are family, and I think Han would have wanted us to work together to save this place from the likes of Pete." He smiled and I liked it, he had such a kind face.

"Emily, if I may, would you allow me to embrace you, as my thanks for listening to the wittering's of an old man."

I gave a giggle and held out my arms, and he came forward and gently pulled me to his embrace. I felt his arms wrap around me, and it felt nice and safe, as I snuggled into him.

"You are so like her Emily, it stirs my heart to see you, for I have missed her so much." He gently kissed the top of my head, and then released me. "Jump in your boat, and I will push you off the sand bank."

"Today helped me, thanks Randolph… Grandfather, what do a I call you?" He smiled and gave a nod.

"Your mother asked the very same thing, and I told her use what makes you feel most at ease, it is not the name, it is the quality of the relationship that is important." I smiled at him and understand that.

"Okay, I will go with the flow, and see where it gets me."

He gave a nod as I turned. I untied the rope, and coiled it as I paddled through the water to the boat, then pulled myself up on deck, and sat at the back ready. Randolph waded in and gave the boat a mighty push, as it glided backwards into deeper water, I dropped the motor, and headed for the wheel. The engine fired up, and I reversed back round, as he stood in the water, and watched me push the throttle and move off, I waved as I turned, and he waved back with a smile, and I felt a sense of sadness leaving him there, but I also felt a little joy growing within me, as I motored back towards the boat house.

I arrived back and tied up the boat in the boat house, to find Shell and Kate sprawled out on the jetty, topless and enjoying the sun, it was another hot day, and I had hoped this hot spell would last longer, but Shelly informed me storms were coming at the weekend.

I slipped off my vest, dropped my pants and knickers and dived into the cool waters, and I felt my skin tingle as I surfaced. Kate was not far behind, and stripped and dived in, she surfaced with a smile.

"God, I love this place, today has been such a wonderful experience. Honestly Emily, I have not felt this calm in ages, I envy you having this place all to yourself."

It was nice to swim and cool down, I was starting to understand that when I create what everyone calls my light, my body temperature rises. Under the trees in the dappled shade, it had been fine, but once in the boat exposed to the hot sun, I had felt like I was cooking. I swam around, feeling calmer and cooler, as I enjoyed the feeling of being free for a while from the heavy weight I carried inside.

Once out and drying, we spent the afternoon, sat on the jetty sunbathing, I had a huge list of jobs to do, but was really enjoying the company of Kate and Shell. We made some salad, and added lots of different meats which Shell had bought at the store, and headed back to the jetty, for the rest of the afternoon, with food and wine, and talked. I filled them in on my time with Randolph, although I edited out the white light and remembering my mother in the accident, but it was enough, and we talked and relaxed, and I felt calm inside. As we headed towards the evening, Kate had to leave, she had to get home and get ready to return to work tomorrow, I walked out to her car with her, and thanked her. She made such a difference being at my side at Harry's place, and I made sure she really understood that. I was sorry when she drove off, and walked slowly back into the house, and headed for the chaos that was the work room, although, it would also become an office.

The room was an utter tip, and so I rolled up my sleeves, sorted the boxes into piles, as close to the craft shelves along the far wall. With enough space to move, I put together my desk from the flat, and fitted it next to the Han's desk. Shell joined in and put hers together, as I set up my PC, and after an hour, more wine and some giggles, we had quite a decent work space with our computers all set up and working, it looked very much like a hub of operation.

Next came my drawing desk, it was big and heavy, and we were a little bit drunk, so we giggled as we fell about struggling, wow, I never realised how weak I had become. We finally manged to get it back together, and then laughed as we pushed and grunted to move it into place on the back wall, and I felt a lot happier, knowing I could plan out the plots I would work on. Shell handed me an OS map of the area, and that was a great start to understanding the size and scale of what I faced.

By the time we had done, we were really hot and sticky, it was cooler outside, even though it was starting to go dark, but it felt really nice and cool, as I wiped my neck, and looked out across the lake. I walked down the garden to the small bench, and sat back, and I took a deep breath, the difference in air quality compared to Exeter, was really noticeable. The air felt so fresh and clean, and I sat back simply enjoying the feeling of this beautiful wide open space.

I had a lot to process, and felt a little calmer and in a place I could reflect. I remembered my mother's words, and her telling me the pedals did not work, and I found that weird. I could not fully remember that day, from what I understood, such was the trauma I had mentally blocked it out, but just sat here thinking, I voiced my thoughts.

"That makes no sense, she drove from north London here with no problems, and I do not know a huge amount about cars, but for all three pedals to fail at the same time, is that even possible?"

I have heard of peoples clutch going, or an accelerator cable snapping, even brakes failing, but all at the same time made no sense at all. Was Randolph right, was someone trying to prevent my mum making it home? In a way, it is probably a good thing I am not into conspiracies, because days ago someone tried to burn my house down, was that a message to me, to watch out?

Across the water at the heart of the island Veda White Shell walked down the path to the large open circle, where Aubrianne stood in thought, the wise old woman watched her carefully.

"She has surprised you, even before embracing the light, she uses it?" Aubrianne turned to see the leader of the wiser elders walking into the circle.

"I cannot deny, even though she should not, Esme witnessed it and told me what she saw. Veda, Amelia came to her, how is that possible?" Veda gave a little chuckle

"Amelia was always a rule breaker, and I did once tell you, she was capable of far more than we realised. If you ask me, the simple act of pure love for her daughter, strengthened her powers. It does appear that even the white wall cannot contain her when it comes to her love of Emily."

Veda walked up to her side and gave her a smile, she looked around the circle lined with stones, and the low soft green grass.

"I can still feel her power all around here, it is impressive, although I must make a single point to you, about your thinking." Aubrianne gave a slight frown.

"My thinking, I was questioning how Amelia managed to actually walk from her realm into this one, I feel they are the right questions to ask." Veda shrugged.

"It can be done, we have seen that this day, the question I want answered, is if she has so much power, why did she die?" Aubrianne blinked.

"What?" Veda looked at the soft grass below their feet, and could feel the energy still running through the floor. She lifted her head and looked deeply into Aubrianne's eyes.

"With that kind of power, the tree that fell on her should have been deflected, why did her light not do that and protect both of them? I cannot deny, it has occupied my thoughts all day."

"She gave up her power, and gave it to Emily." Veda turned with a smile and saw Esme standing alone outside the edge of the circle, Veda smiled.

"I do believe my little leafling, you are right, but I also believe it was a miscalculation on Amelia's part. A watcher cannot give their power away, it must be taken back by the light itself. There is no doubt Emily was enhanced by her mother, and sadly Amelia's miscalculation cost her, both should have lived." Esme nodded as she understood.

"I did not meet Amelia, I saw her once when she came to visit, and I was very young and struggled to fly. I never forgot the feeling from her that crossed the water to me, and I felt that today, I also felt her love for Emily, and it was exactly the same as that day I watched her. If she had lived, she would have been more powerful than Han." Veda gave a chuckle.

"Aubrianne, I feel your daughter has learned much wisdom from you, even for her young years. I agree with you my little leafling, I also think her love for Emily was vast, and also her abilities within the light."

Aubrianne walked round the circle slowly lost in thought, she paused, looked at her daughter, and then continued to pace. She stopped at the entrance to the circle of stones.

"This place is ancient, it was here long before we came, is it possible that it enhanced the power of Emily to connect with her mother?" She looked to Veda. "Even Barrack is unsure of its purpose." Veda nodded as she looked round.

"I met men in the northern lands before we came here who had strong beliefs in circles such as these. I know some of them saw them as a doorway, and maybe in that sense, Emily reached through without knowing. Although, Han did show Emily this place, and instruct her to use it. I do ponder if Han was aware of its purpose, I know like myself, she felt the light sealed away the memories of the accident within Emily."

"Did Han think Amelia would know how to open it?" Esme looked down at the floor. "Sorry, I should not speak out loud." Veda gave a slight chuckle.

"Never fear speaking up my little leafling, it is what defines future leaders. Sadly, the only person who could answer that would be Han." Esme shook her head.

"Not really, Randolph would know, Amelia was here when she was younger. He watched as she grew, he knows a lot about her, I heard him talk about her with joy in his heart." Aubrianne agreed with Esme.

"He is her father, she was hostile when she first found out, but he worked hard and they grew close. It has been a comfort to me knowing Emily still had one grandparent around to aid her. I was relieved to find out she understood and did not react as her mother did, her acceptance of Randolph, may serve well our clan in days to come. It is clear we will need his counsel on this matter where is he?" Veda turned and looked to the shore.

"This day wore hard on him, and brought forth feelings he had long since buried, he will take this time for him. There is a lot to heal for him and Emily, and it is good that the process has started."

He was, as the darkness fell, up at the cemetery on the hill above the village, he knelt at the side of Amelia's grave, and whispered words of love, and shed many tears. The words he spoke were precious and heart felt, and meant only for the ears of the lost spirit of his daughter, as he told her of his love, and pride in the woman she was, and the joy in his heart at watching her grow and create a new life.

He talked of his day with Emily, and how he tried to show her the truth of her mother and the vast love she held for her, as he remembered his moments, sat on the grass and watching her face as he talked to her, and of the joy it gave to him. In many ways, today, Emily had filled part of a large hole that had lived within Randolph, where his daughter once lived, and he felt, the hole within was less as Emily accepted him as family.

Whilst Randolph shared his secrets with his daughter, I sat at the bottom of the garden, with my eyes closed picturing the white blur that was the shape of my mother, and remembering the powerful feelings I had received from her. I finally had a memory, one that was mine and not handed to me by another, and it filled me with happiness. I felt a disturbance and opened my eyes, Shell smiled as she sat beside me.

"Sorry, I did not want to disturb you. I brought you a coffee and Han's shawl, it is getting cold out here."

She was right, I was only wearing my knickers and a vest top, I wrapped the shawl round me, but did not really feel cold, Shell handed me the cup.

"Are you alright Emily, it is a hell of a lot to take in?" I lifted the cup and watched through the steam as I sipped at it.

"I am actually okay, but I have to say, it has been a really weird day." She gave a slight snort of a laugh.

"Hell, every day here is weird, but to be honest, I kind of like it."

She did have a good point. It is strange really, for a year I have never really considered her to be completely sane. I have laughed at her conspiracy theories, and yet here, in this world of Han's, filled with secrets and mystical happenings, I felt like she was probably the only person who would understand me. How strange can life be?

"Shell, promise you will not laugh?" She frowned at me.

"Okay, that is weird, but alright, I promise." I looked at her, and hoped I did not sound like a mad person.

"Shell... Today... Oh shit, how do I say this and appear normal?" She shrugged.

"You just say it and hope." I nodded.

"Shell on the island there is a circle of stones, you know, old stones with markings on them? When I was young, Han told me to sit in the centre and concentrate, and open my heart, so today I did." She nodded at me.

"Yeah, I worked that out when I saw the light in the trees, although I said nothing to Kate."

"You saw it?" She nodded.

"So, you sat in the centre of an ancient circle, possibly a circle of some sort of sacred belief, and you glowed white again, so what happened?"

It astounded me that she was so bloody calm about all this, it felt really strange, like this was just some normal everyday thing we all do, like go shopping, fill the car, or conjure up a spirit from the other side to converse with.

"Shell, my mum came to me." Her eyes opened wide, and then she smiled.

"Emmy, that is so cool, I am thrilled for you." I leaned back and looked at her.

"Is that it? Shell, she appeared before me and spoke to me. Shell, she died when I was four." She shrugged.

"Well yeah, I know that, but hell, you sat in a doorway with your white power sort of thing, and thought of her, what else did you expect?" I stumbled for words.

"Are you not shocked?" She shrugged.

"Why would I be? That is what doorways are for, they are the ways to the spirit world for the ancient shamans, and let's be honest, this white light thing is pretty spiritual." She took a sip of her drink, and then looked at me. "So, what did she say?"

It happened to me, and yet I was finding this the hardest to comprehend, I looked at her casually sipping her drink, like this was a completely normal conversation.

"She was the one who told me about Randolph being my grandfather, she also helped me remember the accident. Shell, I saw it in my mind, I felt her as she hugged me and leaned over me to protect me. All I saw was a bright white light, and then I woke up in hospital. Shell, I could actually feel her like she was holding me, I smelt her perfume, and heard her voice." Shelly, smiled a beautiful smile and her eyes filled with tears.

"Oh Emmy, you have a real memory of her, I am so thrilled for you. Oh God, that must have been the most amazing thing to have happened, Emmy, that is so beautiful." I nodded feeling emotional.

"Shell, it was a car crash, and pretty horrible, but yes, it was my memory, not Han's, Randolph's, Heidi's or my dad's, it was mine, just mine."

She gave a little gasp and giggled, and reached out and took my hand and squeezed it softly. She snorted a little and just kept smiling.

"You felt her, and that is what counts, Emmy she came all that way back, just to be with you. I am blown away and so happy for you right now, it is a good thing you know?" I frowned.

"It is, how?" She gave a big sniff up to clear her nose.

"Emmy, you know where she will be if you need her, you know, you have a grandfather and you have me, but now you also have her. Emmy you are not as alone as you think here."

She was right, I had not thought of it, for a year I had been racked with grief dreading returning here. Yet here I was, with no job, sat in a garden on a land I owned, and I had Shelly, and Randolph, and also my dad was talking to me, and if I needed her, I knew I could sit in a circle and feel close to my mum. It had taken just over seven days, and yet my whole life felt like it was changing and moving in another direction, and I had no idea at all of where it would go from here, but I was not as afraid as I had been arriving. If anything, I was feeling more hopeful than I had been in a long time.

We sat out and talked for a long time, and it was pretty late when we finally staggered up to bed. I slid under my duvet, and snuggled down, and looked across at the two pendants hanging on my mirror.

"Night Mum, Night Han." I closed my eyes, and drifted in my thoughts of my day alone in the circle with Randolph.

At the far end of the lake, where the river came down from the hills and moors, and poured into the lake, across the road bridge, several trucks drove slowly along. They moved as a small convoy and made their way along the deserted lane, then turned onto the road that wove its way up to the side of the lake.

The trees broke on the side of the road, revealing a large section of flat rock, surround by smaller younger trees, where a white pick up truck waited, to guide them in. Men in yellow hard hats, directed each vehicle into position as the trucks backed off the road into place. The air brakes hissed, and the engines turned off, and their lights went out.

The men in hard hats stood closely together and unrolled a plan, as a man with a torch pointed out specific points on the plans, and they all appeared to understand, and agreed with him. Across the lake, the water was calm, and still, On the island, Esme curled up in a leaf with a smile on her face, behind her, Felix snored and made tiny little happy noises as he dreamed of his days sat talking with Han.

Far across the lake, up the bank inside his cabin, Randolph sat in his chair snoozing, lay open on his lap was a small brown paper book, onto which were stuck pictures of a young girl with long wavy brown hair, and the white teeth of her happy smile. His album was only small, but his collection of just nine pictures, meant more to him that anything else in the world, especially the one of him with Han and Amelia, sat on the grass in front of his cabin.

Everyone was asleep, except Shelly, she was sat downstairs at her desk, scrolling down pages on her laptop, looking up all the mythology of stone circles, and all references to gateways through to the other side. She sat back in her chair staring at the screen, lost in thought.

"I knew it, she is a watcher and a guide. It is a force of nature passed down for generations in a direct family line? Oh my god, she is the meeting of two lines of watcher, Han's, and Randolph's. Wow Emmy, you really are pretty special, hell, I could write a whole book about what you could do if you put your mind to it."

She lifted her pad and started to rapidly make notes, as she mumbled to herself, and her thoughts emptied from her mind onto the paper, her hand moved like lightening. Deep down inside an idea was forming, as thoughts and pictures flashed through her mind, and she knew the feeling well, she had the start of something, the start of a new book on folklore, and it would focus on the power, not the creatures.

Chapter Twenty One

Han's Habits

It was early morning and the sun had not been up for very long. Esme bent down and picked up some more rabbit fur, and slipped it into her sack, and gave a sigh, she stood up and looked up the path to where she saw more.

"How much do we need Mother, we have enough to spin yarn for ten tops?" Aurbrianne turned and looked back, her sack had five times more in it.

"Esme, I have told you, I will share the yarn, Eulah has three children, and they all need new clothing they are growing so fast. Esme, she did promise to make you something too." Esme looked down at her small green knitted top.

"Why, there is nothing wrong with this one, I like it, it is comfortable to wear?" Aunbrianne smiled as she shook her head softly.

"Esme, you are growing, it will not last forever, and she did say she had a nice blue to dye the yarn."

"But I don't want blue, I like my green clothes, they suit my golden hair, and curls, Felix thinks I look pretty like this." Aubrianne gave a sigh.

"You need to stop listening to Felix, he lives for mischief, and will get you in trouble. Where is he anyhow?" She looked to the north.

"He is collecting wild bilberries for Barrack over near where Randolph parks his raft." Aubrianne scowled.

"What does he hope to achieve by that?" Esme shrugged.

"He idolises Randolph, you know that, he will want to talk to him."

"What about?"

"I don't know, man things I suppose." Aubrianne looked at Esme, with a shrewd look.

"What sort of man things?" Esme looked at her puzzled.

"I don't know, what do Nairn men talk about?" Aubrianne looked to the north.

"When it comes to you, that is what I worry about."

I woke early, and headed down for coffee, I grabbed some toast and sat out on the doorstep, it was still a little cool, but the sun was warming up slowly. In the last week, I have learned to really love the mornings, I love the peace and serenity of living at the cottage. My mornings before had been get up, rush around, sit in traffic, and finally arrive at a job I hated, and now, all that was done with. Sitting on the doorstep, I have the sounds of the birds, the sun on my face, and the most wonderful view, looking out over the island, and oh, the quality of the air here, is simply beautiful, it is so clean.

The last week of my life had brought with it so many new facts, that my mornings in peace, were perfect for sitting and reflecting on it all. Having what is possibly the most intense conversation with my father, I finally got to see the mother I loved, and it was a strange moment, because all my life I had seen him as cold and emotionless, and it was a big eyeopener for me.

Finding out about Randolph was a shock, and I am still really trying to get my head round that, he is my grandfather, and everything I had ever known about my life, has been a little tipped upside down. It is going to take time to really get used to that, but I decided there and then, I was not going to be like my mother and explode, I was going to talk and listen, and try to understand him, and I am glad that I did. It may appear strange, but in an odd sort of way, I was happy to know that Han had some important moments of love in her life. I knew how hard things were, I had as a young teenager on a few of the rare occasions I stayed with him, overheard her talk of how hard she had it with Abraham, so I knew Randolph was telling me the truth.

Sitting in the circle, meditating as Han showed me, is still a bit of surprise and a mystery to me. I did not for one second expect my mum to appear, let alone speak to me, and as for finally seeing the night of the accident, I was not even aware I was there. To be honest I had never actually thought about it, I think in the back of my mind, I simply assumed, I was with my dad. Thinking about it now makes so much sense, dad was going abroad to work, and mum was coming to Han, I was four, where else would I be, apart from with mum?

My life has felt so fragmented at times, and I have always thought that there were too many gaps. I had constantly asked questions of Han, and she had as far as I knew been honest with me, but I have come to realise, I had asked the wrong questions, and maybe I should have started with, why was it I could not remember my mum aged four?

I understood now I had suffered from trauma, and had to a degree blocked out my memories, I can only surmise that for four year old me, it was simply too painful, and some mechanism in me kicked in to blot it all out. I had to a degree, allowed my subconscious to deny me from seeing my early life, and I had been living in denial ever since. It posed a big question, which was one I was asking myself this morning, which was, what else was I living in denial of?

I gave a sigh and stood up, there are days even I get tired of my thoughts. I was half way into my second week here and still feeling a sense of loss inside, but I cannot deny, being here I had begun to deal with it better. I still had her bedroom to do, which I was dreading and putting off, but I knew soon I would have to pluck up the courage and do it, just not yet, I felt I was not ready, but I was aware of it. I walked back into the kitchen to make more coffee.

I was lost in my thoughts humming to myself as the kettle rumbled, and I slipped a couple of extra slices of bread in the toaster, I really was hungry this morning. I filled my cup, put down the kettle and turned to the fridge for the milk, when I noticed movement by the door, and jumped out of my skin with a squeal, and felt my heart pound inside my chest.

"Jesus Heidi, you scared the hell out of me." She was stood in the doorway and giggled.

"Sorry, I thought you had heard me knock. I did knock at the front, but it appeared no one heard me, so I looked through the window and saw your back door open and came round." My heart was still racing as I looked at her smiling face.

"Yeah, I was out back, I came in for a new coffee, it has just boiled, are you having one." She smiled and walked in.

"I would love a tea, thanks." I turned back to the kettle and lifted a new cup off the rack.

"It is nice to see you, Shell told me the village now knows, I hope it has been received well?" She sat at the table and smiled as I glanced back.

"To be honest Emmy, they all appear to be really happy, something about there always being a Montgomery in the village." I nodded, they were a funny old lot, but in a way, it was nice to know I was actually welcome, I had seen in the past their distrust of strangers.

"I am happy to hear it, because I am going to be here for a while." She gave a chuckle, as I opened the fridge and grabbed the milk.

"Your mum would be really happy; she really loved this place." I poured the milk in the drinks and put the milk back then turned to her holding her tea, and passed it to her.

"I would not know... Heidi, I remembered the crash, I know what really happened." She froze with her cup against her lip.

"Really, you actually remembered?" I nodded and sat down.

"We skidded off the road, my mum told me the peddles were not working, and unclipped her belt. Heidi, my belt was seized, she could not get it open, she was tugging at it, when the tree cracked, and she threw herself over me to protect me, the next thing I remember was I was in hospital." She looked white faced.

"Jesus Emmy, none of us knew what happened, we just found the car with you two inside. Are you alright?" I nodded; my stomach had twisted.

"It was a shock, and scared me, and I will not deny, I am a little shaken to be able to see it in my thoughts, but I can remember it now." She looked pale.

"Does your dad know?" I shook my head.

"Not yet, I needed a little time to put it all in place, I will talk to him soon about it." She gave a soft nod.

"You should, you know he has the car, don't you?" I felt a jolt to my system.

"No, I didn't, why the hell would he want to keep it?" Heidi sighed.

"Emmy, he really lost it when your mum died, he had it transported to a garage, and it is still there. He was convinced it was foul play, we did everything to try and get him to realise it was just a bad accident in a really bad storm, but he was obsessed with the notion that it was deliberate. Honestly, even now, he will not let it go, just be careful how you tell him, when it comes to Amelia, he gets lost in his pain."

I understood that, I had seen it at the graveside, and later at the falls. I had no idea about the car, and it did weird me out a little, just thinking about it, why would he want it, she died in there, it felt more than a little bit morbid. But I cannot deny, the fact he thought it was a set up interested me, my mum had said in my memory dream, whatever the hell it was, none of the peddles were working, which was why she ended up off the road. Heidi watched me closely as I sat sipping and thinking.

"Are you sure you are alright Emmy?" I came out of my thoughts.

"Yeah, sorry, I was just thinking, it does seem weird he would keep the car, if I am honest, it feels a little creepy to me." I think she understood, I smiled. "I am doing alright, it has not been easy being back, but I am getting used to it. I do miss Han, it still feels a little strange, but I am coming to terms and trying to get on with things."

"Emmy, if you are living here, what are you going to do, you know, if you need work, I can ask around the village for you?" I shook my head.

"No, I am fine. Heidi I am an ecologist living on two thousand acres, I am going to survey the whole place and chart its diversity, and look into maybe having the place protected. I know my mum wanted it safe, and so for now, that is where my thoughts are." She gave me a big smile.

"Oh Emmy, she would be so thrilled to know that, you know, that was her dream, she was afraid the developers would move in, and all she wanted was to protect the place. In a way, you will be picking up where she left off, she would be so proud of you if she was here knowing that." I smiled.

"Yeah, I would love that."

We sat and talked, as Heidi filled me in on the village and life in Hempsley today, and how her shop, which was being manned by Angie today was doing so well. She began to talk about Han and her visits to see her, when I had a sudden thought. I had taken a drink and put my cup down, and was nodding at her agreeing with her last point, when the thought hit me, and quite out of the blue is asked.

"Heidi, did Han ever talk about her children?" She gave a smirk.

"Emmy, you know what she was like, she loved all creatures, even the mystical, and she saw joy everywhere. You should know, you grew up with her stories of the Nairn's, sprites and elves. She had such a wonderful imagination, it made all of us titter how she would buy bags of dried fruits for them, and would tell us how much they loved her for it." I looked at her and did not understand, I mean, I pretty much knew all of her stories off by heart, but I had never heard any of her feeding them.

"She never told me those stories, are you sure she talked of feeding them?" Heidi gave a giggle.

"Oh Emmy, you missed out, every Easter she bought pineapple for them, at the summer solstice she bought blueberries, and over Yule, she bought them mango, and for in between, she always bought large bags of cranberries, she often told us how much they adored them, she was so lovely, we all miss her."

It stuck in my mind all through the next hour, as we had another coffee and then walked round the garden. I cut her a cabbage and bagged it up, and she was delighted, and left shortly after with a huge smile, and many hugs. She jumped in her car and headed back to the village, and I came back in as Shell came down the stairs yawning.

While Shelly ate her breakfast of toast, I sat with another coffee watching her, she noticed as she scratched her head and yawned with a mouth full of toast.

"What?" I thought I had better just ask, even if I did risk looking like a basket case.

"Shell, is it true that, you know, fairies, Nairn's, elves and such, like dried fruits?" She chewed and then swallowed, and lifted her tea and took a big swig.

"Fairies and Nairn's are both Fae, elves are obviously a different breed altogether. Although your average Nairn, is a little taller than your traditional types of Fae, they stand at about eight inches, whereas your average Fae is about five to six." I nodded at her.

"So, they like dried fruit, yes?" She gave me a weird look.

"How come you are so interested, I thought you were sceptical about all this stuff?" I gave a long sigh; I knew I had to come clean.

"Shell, Han always talked about her children, today I found out she used to buy dried fruit under the guise that she was treating her children. Am I mad, you know, considering everything that has been happening?" I looked at her and shook my head. "Am I becoming a basket case?"

Shelly gave a little giggle and smiled at me; I think she was really enjoying this. For a long time, Pam and me had made fun of her, I assume it must be really amusing for her seeing me like this.

"Emmy, if you must know, all small natural creatures eat wild foods, if you had to pick something as an offering of peace and friendship with them, then I suppose dried fruits would be an ideal thing. In the world of these creatures sharing food is seen as a sign of deep respect, and peace."

"So, if Han was feeding these creatures, then she was on good terms with them?" Shelly giggled.

"You know this is weird right?" I nodded at her feeling a little foolish.

"Yeah, but come on Shelly, things here have been weird as hell, even for you?" She shrugged.

"It is only weird if you do not understand or believe in this stuff. If like me, it is your life's work, then this is a normal sort of conversation." I sat back in my chair with my coffee.

"Honestly Shell, I am so glad you are here, some strange stuff has happened and I am not sure I would have coped very well on my own. I know this all sounds bonkers, but after the lights and your photo, and all the things Randolph told me, I am honestly starting to think that Han had some sort of secret life." She looked over her cup at me.

"Would it bother you if she did, you know, does it matter to you?"

It felt like a strange sort of question, or maybe it was just the look in her eyes, or call it instinct, but I felt Shelly was holding back a little, I narrowed my eyes as I watched her.

"You know something, don't you?" She a gave a little giggle.

"Emmy, I know nothing for certain." Okay so that was not a complete answer.

"Okay, so you think you know something, so come on, you are not one for holding back, give me your theory." She gave me another little giggle, and then looked seriously at me.

"Look Emmy, I know what I saw last week with my camera, if you are asking me if that island has something living on it, as mad as people may think, my answer would be yes. If you are asking, can you make friends with them using dried fruit, well, that would be up to them?" That was not the answer I expected.

"You really do believe in all this don't you?" She nodded at me.

"Yes, I do, I am open minded to all aspects of life. Look Emmy, I know you and Pam think I am nuts, but ask yourself this. You sat in a circle of ancient stones, and out of you came a huge burst of light, and in walked your deceased mother who told you her side of the story. It made you remember something that you have blocked out of your memories for what, seventeen years? Emmy, no which way you look at it, compared to my belief in mystical creatures, you sort of win hands down."

Why did that feel like a burn? Hmm, I think there is a little bit of I told you so going on here, she did look smug, and I was feeling like the idiot and conspiracy nutter. She gave me a smile.

"Look Emmy, if you are asking me do I think you have some sort of spiritual gift, then I would say yes, and if you think that island has life on it, my answer would be if you want proof, go look for it. It does not matter what I say, at the end of the day to be truly in the know, go and test your theory and see if it gives you results. If Han really did take care of some sort of creature, then that means for a year it has been fending for itself, and it might just be in need of a compassionate friend who will not harm it. My only question is, if it is true, can you handle it mentally, you know, you have been really emotional since we got here, and taking care of yourself first is really important?"

"I understand that Shell, and it has not been easy returning, but I have been thinking a lot as I do stuff, and I think, if I really am going to live and work here, I need to really understand Han's life, and why it was so important that my mum came back in such a rush to help her."

As I sat airing my thoughts with Shell, over in Exeter, Harry was as always busy complaining at the sight of my empty desk. In order to replace me, he had brought in two others, and he was unhappy at double the cost.

He stormed to his office and sat back in his seat, muttering to himself, as he flicked through his diary, crossing my name off his jobs, and filling in one of the replacements names. His door opened and he muttered bent down, ignoring what he assumed was his secretary.

"I am busy Liz, give me an hour." The cough alerted him to a male presence, and he looked up and froze. "John!?"

John Duncan smirked as he looked at Harry, and sat down in the chair opposite him.

"Harry, I have been hearing a great deal about you of late, I thought we needed a chat." Harry gave a nod, the colour running from his face, his voice was low and very quiet.

"Alright... What exactly do you want to talk about, I am a little busy today?" John smiled at him, his confidence showing.

"Then get unbusy." Harry slid back in his chair and sat up straight.

"Look John, if this is...."

"No, you look Harry, and listen to me, I asked you if I could help you, and you said you needed the jobs, so because we are old friends, I got onto Kate and asked her to prepare some work to come your way, after all, what are friends for? It is strange how news comes my way, so firstly, hearing about the way you abused my daughter, has angered me greatly, and secondly to find out that Pete had a second co-investor in his little project to con Emily out her land, and create a luxury tourist development, and it was you, has pretty much pissed me off more than you will realise. So, here I am, looking you square in the eyes, and I want to know why you humiliated my daughter, and why you are part of trying to con her out of her home? Start talking."

Harry looked panicked as John stared at him. John had a fierce reputation in the industry, he did not mess around, and had at times in the past been very confrontational with people who had tried to fool him. Harry knew better than to mess him around, he felt pressured as he looked across his desk.

"Look John, I did apologise to Emily, you know I had a high regard for her work, and maybe our joking around went a little too far, and for that I am sorry, I really am." John relaxed back in his chair.

"Kate found none of it funny, she heard everything you said, and she felt it was harassment and humiliation. My daughter was in tears and I do not appreciate that, I trusted you Harry to take care of her, and you do what, intimidate her?" Harry took a deep breath in.

"I did not mean it like that John, I can assure you. Look I meant nothing by it and yes, I went too far, and I truly am sorry for that... Honestly John, I would not do a thing to hurt her." John nodded; his eyes locked on Harry.

"She has three weeks holiday still due; I expected it paid, and I expect you to show her your gratitude financially, I have enough evidence here to cost a lot more in a tribunal, and you should thank her and consider this just a warning. Harry, I do not work with people who cannot be civil to their staff. Right, tell me about your involvement with Peter."

He was very red in the face, and looked very worried, John sat back, his eyes locked on him. Harry dithered in front of him, he wiped his mouth, and swallowed as he looked at John.

"What does it matter, Emily is living there now and not going to sell, all deals are off and my cash was returned? John, I had no idea it was the same property your daughter inherited, when Peter approached me, the old lady was alive, and he told me she was about to sell. I saw the plans, it looked like a good investment, so I jumped in. You know the deal John, we get offered all kinds of things, hell, I was going to ask Emily to look it over until Peter informed me he would prefer me not to. He told me had already lined someone up." John nodded.

"So when did you find out it was Emily's property?" John gave a long sigh, he was sweating.

"The day before you met us in the pub. I asked to meet him as I panicked, I told him this was insanity, but he said she was going to take her grandmother's things out and sell them, then you waked in, and he shit himself. Honestly, I was as panicked as hell, and I quizzed him later that night, he gave me a hard time and told me he had other investors, and if I wanted out to say so, so I did. I promise you John, as soon as I realised, I pulled the plug and got the hell out. I would not do that to Emily, you know, okay, I was pretty shitty with her, but she had fire, she stood her ground just like Amelia did. I actually really admired her for it, Emily can really step up to the plate, I respected that about her." He gave a nod.

"You went too far." He put his head down.

"Yeah, I know, I am sorry, and I will make it up to her, I promise." John Duncan stood up from his seat.

"You keep quiet about my visit Harry, you tell no one I was here or what I was asking, I need to do some checking out of things, and if I find out you have been straight with me, my favour will show. I will warn you, if you are trying to cross me on this, I can promise you, this company will not make it through the year, are we agreed?" Harry swallowed hard as he stood up.

"Yeah, I won't say a word, I promise." John held out his hand and Harry shook it.

"Good, you will be hearing from Kate as soon as a few things have been confirmed, and think on, change your manner around this place." He nodded.

"Yes... I will, thanks John."

John left the office, and Harry felt a huge sense of relief, he had got out just at the right moment, and he knew Peter would cop for a lot of anger. He sat at his desk and pressed the button on the phone pad, it bleeped and then he heard his secretary's voice.

"Yes Mr Scott?" Harry sat back in his seat.

"Liz, will you check Emily Duncan's file for me, and make sure she has her holiday pay for three weeks awarded, and I would like her to get a bonus, she brought a great deal of extra cash into the company, so inform finance, to award her a one thousand pound bonus for me please." She looked at the phone with a frown.

"Er... Yes... Really?"

"Yes Liz, I overstepped the mark with her, and to be honest, she brought a lot of extra revenue in, I think it will settle things between us. I am sorry to lose her, I regret that."

"Yes Mr Scott, I actually think that is a very nice gesture, she will be really happy to find that in her pay. I will get right on it for you now."

"Thanks Liz." She smiled as she pressed the button to connect her with accounts, the power of John Duncan, was not to be trifled with, and she was actually very pleased to see him stand up for his daughter in such a way.

We had not cleaned up much, Shelly had been up late on her computer, so she headed up to her room to get ready and have a shower. Whilst she was up there, I cleaned up in the living room and ran the hoover round, and polished everything. It reminded me very much of being a teenager living here with Han. I would clean up whilst she took care of the wood store and the boilers.

I moved into the kitchen and scrubbed down the large table and washed all the pots, we had been a little lazy and had built up a pile. Once done, I cleared the units, we had packets of cereal and salt, pepper etc to place in the cupboard from the flat. I opened the door and looked up, and on the top shelf there was a large glass jar, filled with red berries.

I reached up, and slid the jar off the shelf, and lifted it down, and placed it on the table. It was clear, she had quite a stash. I could not deny, it got me thinking, I pulled the chair over and stepped up on the seat to look at the back of the shelf, and to my surprise, there were four more jars, a pineapple, a blueberry, another cranberry, and a mango, I stared at them.

"What is this Han, did you eat them, or did you really use these for children, I wish you had told me?"

Behind me came the sounds of Shelly, as she wandered into the kitchen wrapped in a towel, she saw me on the chair, peering into the back of the top shelf.

"What you doing?" I turned and looked back down the kitchen to where she stood next to the open door.

"Look what I found, she has quite a large stash, there is mango, blueberry and pineapple, exactly as Heidi said. Is it me, or is this weird Shell?"

She gave a shrug and walked down the kitchen towards the large jar of red berries, she unscrewed the lid, dropped her hand and pulled out a handful.

"I must admit, these are really big jars for one old lady to eat, but I don't know, maybe she had a real passion for them, you did say she always ate only the best healthy food. Maybe she was a health nut, did you never eat this stuff with her as a kid?" I stood looking down on her and shook my head.

"I don't ever remember doing so, I mean, when I was really small, I might have, to be honest, I am not sure." Shelly chewed.

"Wow these are good, I love cranberries. Well, whatever they were for, we have shit loads left, no harm in having a few is there?"

"Shell, what if these were meant for the children?" She swallowed and considered the point.

"The way I see it Emmy, she must have fed them here or on the island, so maybe you should think of where would be the best place to put some out. I say go and I don't know, display them and see what happens."

"Won't the squirrels just eat them?"

"Possibly, to be honest I have no idea, Han left us no clue, so I suppose you will just have to follow your gut and see what the result is." I understood that.

"Is that what you would do Shell?" She gave a giggle as she dropped her hand in the jar.

"Oh, Christ no, honestly, I would not make it to the island without eating them all. Emmy, these are really yummy." I smirked.

"Weren't you complaining about gaining weight?" She smiled as she nodded.

"This is health food, I am safe." I started to chuckle as I climbed down off the chair, honestly, she was priceless.

Chapter Twenty Two

Revelations

It was strange to find all the dried fruit, and I cannot deny, it bothered me, I sat in the garden thinking about it all, in hope of understanding Han. All my life she had told me the truth, well, okay, she had also hid the details of my accident with my mum from me, but in a way, I could sort of understand that.

Han has told me stories all my life, and they were beautiful, and added such joy to my youth, but as crazy as it sounds, and I do think I am slowly going insane, I was now wrestling with the notion, that they were not stories of fiction. See what I mean, she talked of her children, which I think was some sort of mystical creature, and she was telling me the truth. So, I think I am having a breakdown, and who would blame me after the last week of my life.

Shelly came down the garden with two cups, she sat at my side and handed me a cup. She knew me well enough to know what I was thinking.

"Emmy, the way I see it is this. You need to put your mind at rest, either Han was caring for some form of creatures, or she really loved dried fruit. So, trial it, go over there and I don't know, lay a trail, and then sit back and watch, and see if something follows it. Whatever the result, you will get an answer one way or the other. I must admit I am really interested in finding out, I will come with you if you want?" I turned to her.

"Honestly, answer me truthfully, do you one hundred percent think this is even possible, because I got to tell you Shell, I trust you, but I am really struggling with this?" She smiled and gave a

nod.

"Emmy, call me insane, but I really do believe this stuff, if I doubted it for one moment, I would not be writing books about it." I gave a long sigh.

"Shell this is challenging every belief I have ever held, which has always been very scientifically rooted." She patted my shoulder, with a giggle.

"Welcome to reality."

As we sipped our drinks, we talked, and she actually made some sense, I suppose I had to know, I had to find out the truth. We sat together and made a plan, it was warm but overcast, and looked like rain, so we hurried and prepared for our field trip. I filled two medium sized freezer bags with the dried cranberries, and then headed for the boat house and topped up the fuel. We fired up the engine, and headed for the island.

It may seem strange, but I felt nervous as we tied up the boat, and walked onto the path, that led to the centre of the island. Shell looked like she was in heaven, as she gazed around with a huge smile on her face.

"Emmy, this place is beautiful, oh wow, I should have brought my camera."

It was fun to see her so happy, but my mind was fixed on my sole aim of the day, which was to lay to rest the theory of whether Han was taking care of something, which was not to date, recorded. I watched the path that led to the central path down the island, my mind swirling with crazy ideas about what I was trying to achieve.

My brain is telling me this is not possible, there is no scientific evidence for any form of mythological creature, and yet my heart, or intuition, whatever you call it, was telling me trust Han and believe in her, which I always had, but seeds of doubt had been sown. I really wanted to believe in her, I wanted so badly to believe she had never lied.

We arrived at the path and I pointed along it, showing Shell where I wanted to go. Which was back to the circle, although, I knew for a fact, I was not going to even attempt to meditate in it this time.

"Shell, it is this way, we follow this to around halfway down the island, and that is where the circle is." She turned and looked down it.

"Awesome, I really want to see this place and get a sense of it." I started to walk towards the circle, and Shell happily followed me.

As we walked away down the path, Felix popped his head up and grabbed Esme by the hand, and started to walk towards the boat, Esme pulled back on his hand.

"Felix, where are you going, I want to watch Emily, she is really beautiful?" Felix shook his head.

"Esme it is too dangerous, the fat one might step on you, we need to be careful." Esme pulled her hand back hard, and it slipped out of his.

"I have told you, Shelly is a nice person, and you need to stop being mean about her." Felix nodded.

"Esme I am not worried about her being nice, I worry about where she puts her fat feet, she is clumsy, and we are too small to risk it." He pointed at the boat tied to the bank.

"Esme, we can hide in Han's special place, and that will be closer to her than you have ever been. Can you not smell what they have on the boat?" She frowned and sniffed the air, and her eyes sparkled.

"Does she have the red berries too?" Felix gave a big smile, and his green eyes twinkled.

"Of course she does, she is Han's granddaughter, they all have the berries."

Esme grabbed his hand with a giggle, and with Felix, they both happily ran towards the boat, where they knew there was a small hidden panel, that Han used to let them ride in with her.

It was warm under the trees, but it felt darker than last time I was here, because the sunlight was not streaming down through the trees, as the sky today was cloudy. I could make out the large circle of stones on the path ahead, and I felt my nerves intensify in my stomach. Shell got very excited as she saw it, and walked at my side, her face was a picture, she was loving this, and I was terrified, because if Han was right, I was not completely sure how I would react.

We were five steps away when I stopped and looked at the space where I had sat, and my nerves bubbled inside me.

"This is it Shell."

She walked ahead and looked round the circle, with the neatly cut stones that stood about two feet proud of the earth, and were covered in strange carvings. Her voice was soft and filled with reverence.

"Holy shit Emmy, this is fantastic." She crouched down, and looked carefully at the slightly green stones, and then looked up at me.

"Emmy, these are exquisite, but I can tell you for sure, these symbols are like nothing I have ever seen before." I gave a frown.

"I thought you would know, I thought they must be Celt or Saxon or something like that." She looked blown away as she shook her head.

"I never seen anything like this, they are not Celt, and I don't think Saxon, they are definitely not runes, well, not any I have seen."

That bothered me, I was really hoping she would explain them to me. I know she had studied Celt symbols at Uni, and had hoped she would take a look and explain it all to me. The fact she didn't really bothered me, I wanted an explanation. Shell took out her phone, and started to take shots as she walked round the inside of the circle, getting up close to the stones and taking picture after picture. She was way too much into this for my liking, I had expected an answer.

I stood watching, with the cranberries in my bag, unsure of how I was going to do this. I watched her taking her pictures, she was really in awe of them, I took a breath.

"So, what do I do now Shell?" She looked back and smiled.

"Emmy these are spectacular, just give me a few minutes, I want shots of all of them."

I will not deny, I was nervous, the last time I sat here, my mother came to me, and then Randolph appeared and my whole world changed, or at least my perception of it did. Deep down inside I was afraid of another terrible memory coming back, I had been shaken by it, although feeling my mother, actually feeling that sense of her had awakened a sense in me I think I had forgotten. It was for me, such a powerful moment, and I had simply been elated from feeling it, but since that day, hidden away in the back of my senses, the sadness had been growing that up until that moment, the only real memories I had, were those given to me by Han, and then Randolph.

Shelly made a full circle taking her shots, and then stood at my side smiling, her whole body felt like it was bubbling with joy, I looked at her huge smile.

"So, what do we do, scatter them and stand back?" Shelly shrugged.

"Probably better just to make a pile and focus everything in one spot."

It made sense. I took a deep breath, and walked into the centre of the circle, and crouched down. I slipped my hand into my bag, and grabbed the bag of cranberries, I felt my hand shake a little as I lifted it out, I looked up as Shell stood in front of me, but she was distracted gazing at the stones.

I opened the bag, and tipped some onto the palm of my hand, and then looked back up at Shell.

"How many?" She looked down.

"Not sure, I would say a good handful, I mean, we want to attract a few." I frowned.

"A few, how many do think there are?" She gave another shrug as she stared at the stones.

"She said children, that infers more than one, because if not she would have said child."

It made sense; I filled my whole hand with what I thought was a good pile. I put it down on the floor in a neat pile, and then resealed the bag, and slid it back into my shoulder bag and stood up.

"Okay, so they are there waiting, so what should I do now? We cannot stand here, they may be shy, most small mammals are." Shell agreed.

"Yeah, we should probably move away and hang out where we cannot be seen."

I nodded and took a few paces forward, Shelly stopped and pointed at my side, and I looked at the stone which formed the gap to the opening of the circle.

"Look at these Emmy, they are the only two that match, you

know I am sure they form a doorway; I think I was right, I mean, look at them, these things are ancient."

I stared at the stones, they were old that was for sure, I am no geologist, but I know lichen, and it was obvious from the size and formation, the lichens were very old indeed. I was a little fascinated, even I had not seen them this big before, I crouched down to take a closer look, Shell crouched at my side and pointed at the intricate swirls and patterns.

Neither of us were fully focused, and did not see as behind us, small creatures rose from the dense plants and shot to the centre of the circle at high speed, snatched up the berries and shot back into cover. Shelly was so engrossed.

"I am telling you Emmy; I really do think these things predate Celts. I do know a few people, and I am happy to get their opinions on these, I am sure these are pretty unique." I was not sure and felt a little nervous.

"To be honest Shell, I am not sure, Han kept these secret for a good reason. Call it a gut feeling, but I want to keep quiet about them for now."

I stood up and she stood up with me, I think she understood me, I was really feeling a sense of urgency, and she was picking up on it, she gave me a nod.

"Okay Emmy, I can look into symbology and see if I find anything similar, and keep it to myself until we do actually know what we are dealing with." I smiled.

"Thanks, it might just me being paranoid, but honestly, I really feel a strong sense that we need to protect this place. Han and my mum really cared about keeping this place a secret, and I think we should too."

"Yeah, I get it, don't worry about it, I will keep this under wraps." I looked at the opening.

"Come on, we need to find somewhere to stay concealed." I looked back at the circle and felt a jolt, and griped Shell by the hand.

"Where the hell have they gone?"

"What?"

Shell turned, and looked back into the circle where the grass was bare, all the berries had gone, there was just an empty patch of grass where I had placed them, I looked at Shell.

"They are gone, did you see anything?" She shook her head and looked round the circle.

"I saw nothing, oh God, please don't let it be an invisible entity." I felt the goosebumps run up my arms, and felt a panicked, my voice was a little strained.

"Shell, what do you mean... Invisible?" She swallowed hard.

"Emmy, I have heard of things, you know, creatures you cannot see that lurk in dark places like this one."

I was already feeling freaked out, I saw nothing, and yet my eyes did not lie, the whole of the circle was empty, the cranberries were gone, I looked at Shell, as the goosebumps ran up my arm.

"You need to be quiet; I am starting to freak out. Shell, they are not there, they went right behind our backs and we heard nothing, and I know I am really going to hate myself for asking, but where the hell did they go?" She looked pale.

"Honestly, my mind is filled with a million answers, and I do not like any of them." I nodded.

"Yeah, screw that, I am leaving."

I turned quickly, and walked out of the circle, and I just kept on walking, my whole insides filled with hidden fears, and I was completely sure of one thing, I was never going to look back.

I am a scientist for God's sake, I operate on logic and recognised theories and processes, and fruit evaporating behind me without a sound was definitely not a bloody scientific process, and it freaked the hell out of me. My problem was, that since I came here, the unscientific had been happening all around me, and all I wanted was just a slice of quiet normal.

Shell hurried up to my side, and we both walked at a fast pace away from the circle, and I will not deny, I was shaking, and nervous, and all I wanted was to be in the boat heading away from the island towards the safety of my house. The fact that she was freaked out, and she knew all about this shit, rattled me even more. I think had she been calm and rationale, I would have been okay, but the fact she was as freaked out as I was, she had no idea how much that added to my terror.

I was massively relieved when we reached the boat, I untied it as fast as I could and hopped in. Shell pushed the boat off the soft sand, and climbed on, and once in deeper water, I fired up the engine, and we reversed back into deeper water and I sighed a huge breath of relief. I swung the boat round and pointed it at the boat house, then gunned the engine and we picked up our pace. I was shaking at the wheel, and looked back at Shell sat on the seat at the back, looking pale.

"I have no idea what happened, but hell Shell, I am having a stiff drink when we get back." She leaned back and breathed a sigh of relief.

"I will tell you what Emmy, whatever these children of Han's are, they are without doubt mystical."

Yeah, I really was not ready at the moment to cope with that, I pushed the stick forward to speed up, I wanted to be as far from here as possible at the moment. We cruised across the water towards the house, and I felt my panic easing just a little, as I started to breath in a more regular fashion.

I pulled into the boat house, and Shell jumped out and pulled the lines to tie up the boat. I cut the engine, grabbed my bag and climbed out onto the deck. I was still trembling as I walked towards the garden and up the steps to the back door. I slipped out the key and walked into the kitchen, grabbed a bottle off the rack, and opened it. Grabbing two glasses off the draining board, I poured out the wine, then lifted mine and took a really long swig.

I swallowed it and leaned on the edge of the table, my hand was still shaking, as I closed my eyes for a second and just took long deep breaths to calm down. It is crazy, I saw nothing, and so why did I get so terrified? My God, I am becoming neurotic, although Shell did not help me at all, I honestly thought because she knew about this stuff, she would be calm and stable, I realise I thought wrong. I should have known really, after all; she did faint and pee herself when she saw Han at the window of my room.

Shelly sat on the wall and placed my bag at her side, she noticed the clear bag sticking out of the top, and reached out and pulled the bag of berries out of the top with a smile. She placed the bag on her knee and opened it, and took out a large handful put them on the wall, then slipped the bag of berries back into Emmy's bag.

Shelly relaxed and took one and popped it in her mouth and chewed, and gave a happy sigh as she calmed down, half way up the garden, a large cabbage leaf lifted up, and a little head popped out.

Felix was fidgeting and jumping about under the leaf, Esme was slightly panicked.

"Felix, sit down and stay still, they will see us and we must not be seen, or Barrack will be really angry." He peered through the gap in the leaves and saw Shelly lift out the bag of berries, he gave a little whimper, and looked back at Esme.

"That fat one has got our berries, what do we do?" Esme shook her head.

"I don't know, but Felix, we cannot be seen, you need to calm down."

Felix watched as Shelly placed a pile on the wall, and the scent wafted up the garden, and he felt the juices in his mouth build. Those berries were a delicacy, a delight for his face, and prized above all other fruits. His stomach groaned loudly as he watched her place them down on the wall.

Just the sight of the pile of big fat red berries, just left there sent him close to the edge as he yearned to fly down there and grab some. His little legs dithered, as Esme sat almost holding her breath, afraid of what Felix would do, but she too could smell them, and it was teasing her beyond her imagination. Shelly looked at the pile, and picked one up, she smiled as she held it in front of her face, and Felix went into melt down with a whimper.

"SHE IS EATING THEM, THE FAT ONE IS EATING THEM!"

Esme panicked, he was leaning through the gap pointing and raising his voice, he was irate, and his eyes were huge, as he looked back under the leaf at her.

"Esme, that fat one is eating them and they are not hers, Han brought them for us."

Esme grabbed the top of his small pants and yanked back hard on him, he was going overboard, and she was starting to get really scared, she had never seen him like this, even his face was going red with his anger, and she pulled him as hard as she could to keep him from exposing their position.

Shelly chewed and swallowed, and reached for another one

of the plump cranberries, and there was a tiny, but high pitched squeal up the garden, she looked up, as she lifted the berry to her mouth, to see me coming out of the door with the wine glasses, she slipped the berry into her mouth and reached for another.

Esme yanked hard, as Felix jerked, and her hands slipped, and she went sprawling backwards into the chunky stem of the plant with a crash, as Felix's wings exploded up his back and he squealed in a high pitched voice.

"THAT FAT ONE IS EATING THEM ALL, AND THEY ARE NOT HERS!" He exploded at speed out from under the cabbage, and zoomed down the garden raging at Shelly.

"YOU PUT THAT BACK, IT IS NOT YOURS, YOU ARE FAT ENOUGH!"

Shelly stood up holding the berry tight, her eyes wide open, as the yelling tiny six inch, bright green eyed, enraged, Nairn headed straight towards her. She stepped back quickly, walking backwards along the jetty as Felix flew right up in front of her face, ranting.

"IT'S NOT YOURS, THOSE WERE BOUGHT FOR US, NOT TO FILL YOUR FAT BELLY. YOU PUT IT BACK NOW AND LEAVE THEM ALONE!"

Shelly stared at the ranting little figure who bobbed in front of her nose, and gave a shriek, she moved back quicker.

I was frozen on the steps staring in utter disbelief, as Shelly back tracked along the jetty looking petrified.

To my left, a leaf moved, and out from underneath, another little figure appeared, I felt my wrist go limp, the glass tilted, and the wine began to pour out onto the step, as the little figure from under the cabbage screamed in a very high pitched voice.

"FELIX, NO... YOU MUST NOT DO THAT!"

I swallowed hard, not understanding anything I was seeing, I turned to see Shell, she was almost at the edge of the jetty, with who I now knew was Felix, raged in her face. I was losing mind, that was it, I had finally gone mad and was hallucinating.

Shelly over balanced with a squeal of fear, and from nowhere a really loud voice shouted.

"FELIX STOP THAT THIS SECOND!"

I took a breath and breathed in, as Randolph appeared at the side of the boat house, Shelly flapped her arms, dropped the berry, and went backwards. Across the water on the island there was a blinding white flash, and Shelly froze parallel with the edge of the jetty, and just hung there in mid air. She stared at Felix, as he dropped to the floor and picked up the berry, he leaned over the edge and looked at Shelly, as she breathed at an alarming rate.

"YOU FAT THIEF!" She just stared at him feeling panicked, and swallowed hard.

"I am sorry, honestly, I did not know."

I wanted to move, but I could not put words to my feelings, I looked to the cabbage bed, as the little figure suddenly realised I was there. She turned and looked at me, and just for a second our eyes met, and I felt a really strange sensation. She gave a little squeal, and shot back under the cabbage, and the leaves fluttered, she was running away under the cover of the cabbages. I have no idea why, but I suddenly spoke loudly.

"Please don't leave, don't run away, I beg you, I will not hurt you, I want to help like Han did." The cabbage leaves stopped moving.

Below in the garden Randolph stormed across the jetty, his eyes fixed on Felix, and he was really angry, Felix felt afraid and stepped back away from him, Randolph looked down at him, his temper obvious.

"Have you any idea of the damage you have done? WELL, HAVE YOU?"

Felix trembled and stepped back further away from him, Randolph pointed at him, with a shaking finger.

"You have no right to be here, you were told not to come back, and yet once again you disobeyed the laws of our kind for this. Barrack has every right to take your wings and condemn you to the walnuts for life."

Felix dropped to his knees shaking with tears in his eyes, and from nowhere, a pair of hands came round to protect him.

"No Randolph, that is not your call, it is Emmy's. Han loved these children; you will not hurt them."

Felix sniffled, and turned back with big tear filled eyes and stared at Shelly, as she perched on the edge of the jetty, she was staring at Randolph and shaking her head. She looked down at Felix and smiled.

"I am sorry, I did not know they were yours, you are right, I am too fat, I should not eat them." Felix burst into tears.

I knelt down on the step, and looked at the tiny little figure, as she peered out at me from under a cabbage leaf, I smiled, she was cute.

"I know you; I saw you in my dream." She swallowed hard and gave a nod, she had the most beautiful blue eyes, I gestured to her.

"I will not hurt you, I am Emily, I am the daughter of Amelia, and Han's granddaughter, I now own all this land. I promise, you are safe here, no one will hurt you whilst I am here."

She stepped out and I breathed in and swallowed, she was amazing, I could not believe what I was seeing, she gave a tiny little bow, and looked up at me, her voice was soft and very quiet.

"Lady Emily, I am pleased to meet you. I know who you are, I have watched you grow. Han was our friend, we used to visit her and we miss her."

I felt the tears in my eyes, and I had to swallow as I breathed in, she was real, she was living, she was a tiny human being, or at least human like. I took another deep breath.

"I miss her too; I miss her a great deal."

The tears rolled down my cheeks, as the little figure took another step forward. She was a perfect copy of a human, but only five inches tall. She had long blonde hair, that flowed from under a tiny knitted hat, and her hair had little curls at the end, as they touched the base of her back. Her top was like a little crop top, and it looked knitted, as did what looked like a small skirt, that had grasses attached, I was in awe of her.

I was on my knees and lost for words, as I watched her walk along the bed towards me, she looked up, and I noticed the almost transparent wings on her back, she gave a smile, and I noticed her tiny little nose and quite chubby cheeks, she was utterly unbelievable and beautiful.

"I am sorry about Felix, he gets carried away, those red berries were Han's treat for us. He did not mean to shout, he has missed

Han more than he says, he loved her very deeply. Please do not be angry with him."

I lifted my hand and wiped my eyes, and sniffled, then looked to the end of the jetty, where Randolph had pulled Shelly up to her feet, and Felix sat on his shoulder with his head down. I looked back at the little figure.

"Was it Esme, is that your name, sorry, I am feeling a little overwhelmed at the moment?" She smiled.

"In your language, I am Esme Honeyrain, I am the daughter of Aubrianne Evening Flower, one of our clan's elders. We should not be here, we will be in trouble, but I am glad we spoke, Emily of the clan of Han." She was so adorable; it was impossible not to smile.

"I will talk to Randolph, and ask him to put a good word in for you."

She gave me a huge and beautiful smile; I was utterly captivated. Randolph came up the steps looking very stern. I stood up, and Esme scurried behind my leg, and peered round it, she was obviously afraid. Randolph gave a sigh as he looked at her, and then lifted his eyes to me.

"Emily, I am so sorry, they were told not come here until I had spoken with you, but they are young and foolish, and disobeyed the head of their clan. I will sort all of this out and then return to explain it all to you." He turned to look at Felix sat on his shoulder with his head down.

"As I was already on my way to do today."

It was a lot to take in, and I was still reeling with the surprise, but as I looked at the little brown clad figure of Felix, I felt a tug at my heart.

"We have all been foolish at times Randolph, it is a feature of youth, I dare say I still am at times, where will you take them, and what will happen to them?"

"I will head to the island and seek a counsel with their Clan leader Barrack, and explain what has happened here." I nodded understanding.

"Was that him on the island, was it him who saved Shelly from the water?" He gave a nod.

"He will be greatly displeased, they have rules that they adhere to, for the safety of their clan, and these two have broken them and risked everything." I looked down at Esme as she hugged my leg.

"I am glad they broke the rules, I went looking today for Han's children, I wanted answers. They have helped me to understand why it was so important for my mother to return, and now I fully understand. Pete wants to destroy their habitat, and my mother was joining Han to stop him, and if I had been older, I would have been helping them both. Take me to this Barrack, I own this property, it is my land and my fight, so show me who I am fighting for." Felix looked up and smiled at me, and I winked at him.

"If we have a fight on our hands, we need everyone to stand in unity, what say you young Felix?" He gave a soft smile, and nodded, Randolph looked very concerned.

"Emily, this is not how things are done, there are rules to follow." I understood that.

"Randolph, normally I would have no issue with that, but those so called rules are for normality, and let's be honest, losing Han, has disrupted the balance and Pete is more determined than ever to take this place. I would say, for now, we need to act, we can worry about the rules later. Han's children are my priority, it is the reason she left me this land, I am coming with you, and I am going to speak to this Barrack."

Chapter Twenty Three

The Light Within

Esme flew up and sat on my shoulder, it was strange, and yet I found it made me feel delightfully happy. She gently held my hair, as I turned and walked back to the house, I realised I had one glass half empty, and one completely empty, I lifted the half filled glass and swallowed the lot. Then took a deep breath.

"I hope I am doing the right thing; Han has never mentioned any of this."

"Does it feel right?" I glanced to the side and saw the big blue eyes looking at me.

"I think so, I think Han would have stood by you and defended you." Esme smiled.

"She would, I feel her around you, I think you are as strong as she was."

"You do? To be honest Esme, I don't feel it, I wish she was here to advise me."

"She will be, she walks in the light, I know, we all helped her to come to you. We asked the light, Felix nearly hurt himself he asked so hard, he slept for two days after that."

I felt a little shocked, there was something about her innocence, her vulnerability that really stirred deeply within me.

"You all did that for me, why?" She gave me another big beautiful smile.

"We love you Emily, and you were so sad and hurt, so we all decided to help Randolph reach out to Han to help you."

I swallowed hard as a huge wave of emotion crashed over me, and I felt yet more tears rise into my eyes, Esme smiled, and leaned over to touch my cheek.

"Han always said, it was our job to stick together, and always be there for each other, so we did as she taught us." I tried to talk, but found the words hard, my voice was a little squeaky.

"It really helped me, thank you." She gave a little nod.

"I am glad it helped. You know, Han told us, that one day she would walk in the light with Amelia, and you would need us, and no matter what, we had to be there for you, and guide you." Oh God, this little person was so cute, she was breaking my heart. I gave a big sniffle and reached for the paper towel.

"I need to calm down, today has felt like a strange day, and I need to present myself properly, if I am to talk with your clan leader. I will not deny Esme, I am a little bit scared about all this." She gave a resounding nod.

"I am glad to know it, I am terrified, Barrack can be really scary."

"He can?" Her eyes went huge as she nodded.

"He scares me to death when he is angry." I reached for the half filled wine bottle.

"Oh hell, I wish I had not asked now." I poured out a good measure, and lifted the glass, and looked at her. "You are under age; this stuff is not good for you." She nodded rapidly.

"I know, Felix tried some once, and he ended up flying upside down, and he blew up the broccoli. It was scary, but I also laughed a lot, especially when he flew into a tree." She put her hand on her mouth and giggled.

"I am so glad we don't fly; I would be forever pulling Shell out of trees. Okay here goes." I downed the wine in one gulp, and took a deep breath, picked up the keys and headed out of the door, and then locked it.

Randolph was prepping the boat, Shell was still looking a little shocked, she looked at me and then Esme sat on my shoulder.

"What do I do?" I frowned at her.

"What do you mean, you are coming, this is your life's dream isn't it?" She blinked and looked a little lost.

"Well yeah, but Emmy, I cannot walk in the light." Randolph leaned out of the boat.

"They will not be happy, they are very secretive, they do not take well to guests in their domain Emily." I understood that.

"Well, they need to understand, that Shell is with me and it is together that we will all stand up and protect this land. As for their domain, I own this land, so technically, they are guests in my domain and so need to pay attention and listen to me." Randolph looked worried.

"My God, you are like your mother, Barrack found her hard to deal with at times too. Okay, both of you get on board, Esme, you know where to go, Felix is waiting for you."

Randolph drove the boat out of the boat house, and I sat at the back with Shelly, I took her hand in mine. Felix and Esme had a little hiding place behind the dash, which was padded with cushions. I felt a little frightened, and needed some reassurance, I turned and looked at Shell's white face.

"Are you alright, you are a hell of a lot quieter than I thought you would be?" She took a deep breath, and turned to me.

"Honestly, I feel so amazingly happy, I am overwhelmed. Emmy, I was right, have you any idea how weird that is? Emmy my dream flew at me and yelled at me, and yeah, I was scared and freaked out at first. But as I lay there, floated, whatever the freaky hell it was, I just stared at the little guy, and I thought he is unbelievably remarkable and my dream has come true. I honestly though Randolph was going to hurt him, and there was no way I could allow that, I think I surprised the little fellow, as I protected him. Emmy, we have to protect these people, we have to keep them safe, Pete will destroy them if he finds out." I squeezed her hand.

"I aim to Shell, I am a little lost at the moment, what science says is not possible is alive and well and has been hiding in the cabbage plants. I am surprised you have not said I told so; you have every right to." She smiled at me.

"That is not who I am Emmy, you have seen them, and that was all I wanted, just for you see that this world is an amazing place filled with so much we have not really discovered. Emmy you are an ecologist, well you know what, this is an environment that now supports unique life."

I sat back and thought about it, how long had they lived here, had they carved the stones in the circle? Had Han known all her life, did her parents know, and those parents before that, the questions just kept coming? I looked at Shelly.

"Do you think the stones are fairy stones, have they been here since the ancient times?" Shell shook her head.

"No, in my last book, I briefly covered the story of a race of Fae that moved from the lowlands of Scotland to an undisclosed location. I think this is that race, and since earlier today, I have thought about it, and I have wondered if it is the power of the stones that attracted them here. Look I have no idea how old the stones are, but I think they were around long before civilised life. The way they stand, even though they are only small, and the carvings on them, they are really old Emmy, I can only say ancient."

"My mum studied folklore; I wonder if she knew about them?" Shelly shrugged.

"Unless she wrote it down, I am not sure we will ever know."

Randolph slowed the boat, and I felt very apprehensive, I really had no idea what I was walking into, but the one thing I knew for sure, was no one would hurt the two children. From the moment Esme told me she had visited Han, I had felt a bond with her, even though I knew little of what she called the Nairn, but why would I?

In truth, up until today, I had thought fairies were a myth, even now actually seeing two, I still could not believe they were real, and yet they were. I felt like the tables had been flipped on me, and I was starting to come to terms with it all.

We slowed to a halt, and I slipped off my plimsoles and rolled up my jeans. I got up and walked to the cockpit, and took the tie line, as Randolph handled the motor. We drifted slowly on to the sand, and I slid over the side and dropped into the cool water, and waded towards the bank, and fallen tree I always tied the boat up to.

Felix and Esme flew over to my shoulders, it made me laugh as I now had two, one on each side. I pulled on my shoes and stood up; Randolph gave a nod at me.

"You still want to do this?"

"Yes, I am not sure how to treat these people, or how to address them."

"It will be fine, show respect and stand tall, they admire resolve, your mother never showed any weakness in front of them, she was always firm, but fair." I nodded at him understanding what he was saying, and I prepared as he turned and led the way.

"Randolph, where will we meet?" He looked back.

"There is a place, but for now, that is out of the question, and so I feel the circle will be more suited. Han had many conversations within the circle, she used it a lot for informal meetings, as did your mother."

"So, my mum was quite involved with these Nairn?" He gave me a sharp nod.

"She embraced the light the day after her twenty first birthday, and for five years, she spoke often with them."

As we walked down the path, I found a little comfort in knowing my mother was a part of this life. I watched the path, and realised the Nairn's were quiet, I glanced to Felix, who was sat with a big smile.

"Are you guys alright; you are pretty quiet?" Felix looked at me.

"We have a lot to think about, we broke a big rule, you saw us when we were supposed to stay hidden. Esme and I will get in a lot of trouble for this."

I glanced at Shell, she was watching Felix carefully, I could see how she was studying him. I suppose in a way it made sense; she had been looking for proof for as long as I had known her. This must be mind blowing for her, in a strange sort of way, I admired her, and her total belief in her research. She had always been adamant she was not wrong, and at times I had ridiculed her, which at the moment, with two mythical creatures sat on my shoulders, I was regretting saying anything.

Randolph stopped, and I almost bumped into him, we had arrived, I stood on the outside of the circle, he looked at me and smiled.

"This is your ball game, I will follow your lead, so as the future of this land, establish yourself in a way that you would mean to continue." I nodded, and then looked from left to right at the two Nairn's.

"Stay on my shoulders, I want your clan to see that I care for you. It is important to me that your leader understands, that even though you broke the rules, I am happy you have done this, it has helped me a great deal." Esme looked terrified, I smiled at her.

"Be brave my little friend, I am scared too, but I am going to try my best." She nodded, but I could feel her trembling on my shoulder, hell, I was a little. I took a step forward and turned to Shell.

"Stay close, no matter what happens, Shell I need you with me."

She smiled, and stayed stood just in front of the circle. I walked past her, and into the very centre, and stood still. I closed my eyes and tried to clear my mind, I needed to be calmer, Shell sat on the path in the opening and watched, nothing appeared to be happening. Felix leaned in and whispered in my ear.

"They are here, they are watching, sit down on the floor, so you are not too tall, it will put them at ease."

I lowered myself down, and crossed my legs, I had an idea and hoped it would work. I pulled my bag round, and lifted out the bag of berries, and sat it on the grass, and undid the zip tie. The woodland appeared empty; I whispered as quiet as I could.

"Are they still here, it's very quiet?"

I slipped my hand into the bag, and pulled out a small handful, with my free hand, I picked a couple up and offered them to Felix, he took them with a happy chuckle, then I handed some to Esme, she smiled and gave me a very polite.

"Thank you, Emily." I thought I would try to hurry things up, I looked at Randolph who was watching from the path.

"I am here waiting Randolph, do they really fear me that much, I came to talk, is that so scary as to hide in the bushes?"

I heard the rustle behind me, but did not turn round, they were obviously hiding in the ferns. To my left and right, there was more movement, and yet no one had appeared.

"This is not their way; they feel intimidated by your boldness to confront them."

Randolph stepped aside, and I caught my breath. Up the path was a woman about eight inches high, she wore long white robes and had hair of gold, she was beautiful. She walked with confidence down the path towards me, Esme shook more on my shoulder.

"Mother!"

Shelly looked awestruck, as she slid out of the way, and the small figure with great confidence walked towards me. Honestly, she was tiny, and yet her presence was powerful, and I was actually a little afraid. I really did not know what to say as she stopped two feet in front of me, I could the resemblance to Esme. She looked up at Esme.

"Step down from her shoulder Esme, you are not a pet for her to play with, you are Nairn, take some pride in your line." I swallowed hard.

"I asked her to stay with me for comfort, I would never insult her by asking her to be a pet. She is a life, one of great intelligence, I would never compare her to the level of a common mammal. I have no idea of your custom, but my mother taught me that introductions should be observed when meeting." She gave a chuckle.

"I see much of the spirit of Amelia within you, Lady Emily. I am Aubrianne Evening Flower, in your tongue, and one of the council of this clan." She gave a tip of her head, and I copied her.

"I am honoured to meet you Aubrianne, had Han told me of you, I would have made a sooner introduction." She smirked; I held out my hand filled with red berries.

"Would you care to join me, in a snack?" Esme gasped.

"Too forward, much too forward Emily." I turned to her and gave her a wink.

"Where I come from, the sharing of food is a token of peace and high honour for a guest, and so with that tradition in mind, I wish to honour your mother and share what I have with her." Esme swallowed hard, and looked very nervous, I turned to Aubrianne.

"Are you offended by my gesture?" She gave a quiet giggle, and reached forward and lifted a berry.

"I am unaware of your traditions, but will honour you in them, in the spirit they are given." I smiled and slipped a berry into my mouth, I noted Felix fidget, and offered him another, then Esme.

It was strange, and I was reminded of my childhood reading Gulliver's Travels, except I was not in Lilliput, they were in my world. Aubrianne looked at me as I chewed.

"Emily, we all realise that Han did not have the chance to talk with you about us, but there is a certain way that we do things, and there is a place, a sacred place where we gather together and embrace the light." I nodded as I chewed slowly.

"I can understand that, and given time I would have been able to learn more, but when I heard there would be a harsh punishment for my two companions here, I wanted to come to this place, and plead for their rights and explain the benefit to me of what they have done."

A white figure suddenly popped up out of the ferns and I jumped, Esme gave a little shriek, and Felix tensed. He landed on the stone near the entrance, and Shelly leaned back in surprise, he was obviously angry. I felt afraid, he glowed bright white and then stretched in front of me, and he grew to about five feet high. He stepped off the rock, walked towards me and leaned right over me. As the light faded around him, I could see his detail, his golden hair and bright blue eyes, his face was contorted slightly, and he shouted at me.

"You have no right to interfere in the affairs of our land, it is I who decided the fate of those who live on our land."

Wow talk about rude, him and Harry would love each other. I felt angry, I was trying my best to show respect to him. I saw Randolph tense and lean forward, but I was not completely helpless, and had no need of his assistance. I stood up, and I was just a little taller than him, I looked him up and down.

"Your land, may I remind you that you are indeed a guest on my property?"

He blinked, and looked a little startled, Aubrianne gave a little titter, I scowled at him as the ferns vibrated. Esme slid under my hair and was hiding; Felix was shaking so hard I could feel the vibrations running down my shoulder. The Nairn scoffed.

"Your land, we were here long before you were." I folded my arms and stared at him.

"Really, and just how long have you resided here, because if I am correct, this is a second home, are you or are you not originally from the northern lands of this country?"

He stepped back and looked surprised, Aubrianne blurted out a laugh, and lifted her hand to her mouth. I stared at him defiantly.

"I would request your response sir?" Esme squeaked in panic in my ear. He lowered his voice and appeared surprised.

"We came to this land ninety and six of your years ago. I am impressed you have some knowledge of our line." He gave a bow. "Lady Emily, I am Barrack, the leader of my clan." I returned his bow, I was shaking in my shoes, and trying to remember Randolph's words.

"Lord Barrack. I am Emily Montgomery Duncan; I know you know of my mother and my grandmother. The Montgomery family have been on this land for ten of our generations as the land owners and protectors. It saddens me greatly that neither my mother or grandmother are here to introduce me as I feel would be proper and right. I had no knowledge of your clan before this day, but your young clan members may have broken your rules, but I can assure you, without their exposure to me, I would never have understood the importance of my place here. So, with that in mind, please accept my apology for not knowing your rituals, but let me also add, this land is in great peril, and your clan members may have saved their race by coming to me, as I was unaware of the life that lived on these lands. We have common ground here, both of us may lose everything if we lose, and so I will not withdraw my request that you show lenience towards these two younger members of your clan, coming to me was an act of bravery to save their lines." I bowed before him.

He stepped back and bowed to me, and I felt terrified, Esme was shaking so hard, I could feel her within the folds of my hair, vibrating against my ear. He looked at me and gave me a nod.

"I thank you for the honour you have shown me, with you indulgence, I would wish to consider your response with Randolph, for he is known to me, and had many interactions with Han. I will also consult my clan?" I felt it was fair.

"That would be agreeable to me, I shall await you here, and present an offering to any of your people who would wish to indulge." He bowed and withdrew to Randolph, I watched feeling nervous, Esme slipped out from my hair and looked down at her mother.

"Please let Felix keep his wings mother, I would be heartbroken if he lost them." She fluttered her wings, and flew to the floor, and stood before her mother. "He is so special to me, please, I beg you, help him mother."

She gave a smile and lifted her hand to her daughter's cheek, and cupped up it.

"I will plead on his behalf for you, stay here with Emily, and behave, Barrack is very angry at what you did." I smiled as I saw the love between them, Esme watched her mother's face.

"We did not mean to mother, but look, we helped Emily understand. Mother she will take care of us like Han did, she will not hurt any of us, we are safe here, please listen to Randolph, he knows Emily, he watched her grow up here." She gave a soft smile, as she looked at Esme's shaking little figure.

"I will do what I can."

She turned and walked out of the circle, I watched as further up the path, Barrack stood with Randolph talking. Aubrianne walked towards them, and I noticed others rise from the undergrowth, and walk toward him. Shell got up and walked over to me, with a smile.

"Emmy, this is mind blowing, have you any idea of how important this is?" I shook my head.

"Not really, I am trying to hold it together, Shell this might appear normal to you, but for me, it is freaking me the hell out. Shell, a fairy just shouted in my face, honestly, I was so frightened, I almost passed out." Felix leaned in to my hair.

"Fairy is not technically correct, we are Nairn, and a little taller and a much older race." I nodded.

"Good to know... Thanks."

Shelly's eyes were bulging they were so big, she leaned in and took the bag of berries out of my shoulder bag, she walked to each of the stones, and put a small pile of the berries on it, and slowly went round the circle. As she placed down the pile, small faces appeared above the plants and peered out, I was so surprised at the sheer number, I felt my legs weaken.

I sat back down, and watched in amazement, as little figures appeared at each stone, bowed to me, and politely lifted a berry. There were at least a hundred of them. Shelly pushed the empty bag back into my hand, I felt numb as I watched, this felt surreal how was it even possible?

Felix flew down from my shoulder, ran over to one of the stones and grabbed two more, he returned with a smile, and handed one to Esme, who sat on the grass in front of me to eat, Felix plopped down at her side. All around me on every stone the berries had gone, and on the outside of the ring, every fern, small shrub and plant, were covered in tiny figures all sat eating, their wings occasionally fluttering quickly to keep them stable, and the only way I could describe it in my head, was this was a miracle of evolution.

All around me there was activity, on the path quite a distance away, Randolph was crouched down talking with the group of older Nairn's, and Shell had stepped over a stone and was sat in the grass talking to a group, who were sat on the branches of a small beech sapling. Felix and Esme were tucking in in front of me, and I was just sat here, surrounded by what could only be described as the impossible. Yet here I was, feeling slightly out of place, awkward, insecure, and I think in the midst of some scientific crisis. I swallowed hard and tried to calm myself, and closed my eyes and just breathed in allowing what little calmness I could glean, surround me, talking to myself in my head.

"It's alright, just stay calm and relax. Emily for fucks sake, fairies are real, what the hell is happening? I know Emily, I am not going to freak out, I am simply going to sit here calmly, and get my shit together, this is explainable, there is a perfectly rationale and scientific explanation, so relax. Emily, there is no science to explain this shit, they are bloody fairies." I took a deep breath, and tried to relax.

"It is fine, this place is special, that is all, these creatures, children, whatever the hell they are, needed a home, and they came here to live free and safe, and I will allow that. Emily, they are not travellers looking to camp out for a bit, they are fairies, you know, the ones we have always said were not possible? Oh hell, am I having a nervous breakdown, has all the pressure been too much, am I hallucinating?" I took another deep breath and tried to focus, as my thoughts continued.

"Just calm down, this is happening, it is not what I expected, that is all. Remember Han, and all the things she told you about relaxing and opening my mind, yeah, that is all I need to do.

Simply remember all those cherished moments and find my inner calm... There... Just breath and let everything flow with the natural rhythm of life... Yeah, this is it, just relax Emily, calm your mind and settle your feelings, and open your heart and see with your love, that is what she told me when I was ten, just open up and flow with it... Oh yes... This feels so much better..."

Randolph felt it first, he turned and looked back as Barrack spoke, and he smiled as he saw Emily sat with her eyes closed in the centre of the circle radiating white light. Esme and Felix had stood up and walked backwards towards Shelly, as the light around Emily intensified. Randolph tapped Barrack on the shoulder and he turned to see Emily serenely sat flowing with the light, Randolph gave a happy nod.

"You may have little trust or uncertainty of her Barrack, because she has not embraced the light, but I would argue, she has. Maybe not in your ceremony, I would argue she has in her own."

Shelly sat with Esme and Felix on her knee, smiling as she watched the light radiate out of in a large orb. Nairn sat on their plants watching with huge eyes and bright smiles, and Randolph simply nodded, and understood my inner calm. I was seeing with my heart, although my eyes were closed and I was not aware of anything. I was simply following Han's advice to quell my insides and find my centre of quiet peace.

Barrack stared at me unable to fully understand how I was even doing this, he walked forward, as all the others turned and watched him approach the circle, which was now completely filled with light, his voice was soft and filled with wonder.

"How is she doing this?" Esme looked up from Shelly's knee.

"See, we told you, she is Amelia's daughter, that's how."

Veda walked up to his side, and stood on the outside of the circle, she gave a smile and lifted her hand into the light, nodded to herself and walked into it, as soon as she did, I felt her, and opened my eyes, and the light went out. I looked at her smiling.

"What has been decided?" She gave a little chuckle.

"Emily, I am Veda, an elder of this clan. I take it you feel calmer and less afraid now?" I gave her a wary look.

"How do you know how I am feeling?" She walked a little closer, and stood in front of me, she was a great age, but she had a beautiful and kind face.

"Emily, when Han was younger, she was afraid of the light, and one day, her mother rowed across the water to this island, and told her to walk here alone until she understood the power of the light and lost her fear." I was surprised to hear it.

"Han was afraid, but she always talked about it, and even told me she would wait for me in it?" Veda gave a nod.

"She walked around the island lost, alone and afraid, not really knowing what she should do, and I watched her from below the undergrowth. She reached this circle, and when she saw it, she became so afraid she started to cry."

I gasped in surprise; I could not believe what she was telling me. I had never known Han be afraid of anything. All my life she had been so strong, confident, and self assured. How could Han be afraid of a circle of stones, it made no sense? I shook my head.

"Han was always there for me, I was always falling apart, always afraid, she was so strong she inspired me. It is one of the reasons my heart is broken, I miss her, and I do feel at times I need her, I need her strength and for her to tell me all will be fine, and we will deal with it." Veda gave a gentle nod and smiled her kindly smile.

"None the less young Emily, I speak the truth. You are very like she was, and if I may say so, have the same fears she did, and also your mother, she too was scared to enter the light at first. Emily to fear the unknown is not something to be ashamed of, but to fear it so much, you prevent yourself from doing something that is right for you would be foolish. Many in your race have unfounded fears, but they allow them to control the choices they make, and in doing so, they take much joy from their lives. I told this to Han, I broke our rules, but in doing so I helped Han face the truth."

"How did you do that, because I will not lie, all of this, it is alien to me, and I arrived here today afraid? I have sat here doing what Han showed me to calm myself, and I do feel better now, but I still have a great fear within me."

She clearly understood me, and I felt grateful that she did, Barrack scared me, and my nerve had failed as he walked away. I did not want him to talk to me again, I was really struggling with this reality, it challenged my every belief. Veda felt to me like she understood that, she looked back at Barrack and then turned to me.

"Emily, it was I who showed Han this circle, and I was the one who sat her in the centre, and taught her as she has your mother and you, how to open your heart, and look with it. She too sat here surrounded in the warmth of the light as you just have, and within that, she found the strength to embrace the light, and the knowledge and understanding that came with it, as you will soon." I smiled, somehow knowing Han felt like it did helped.

"I think I made Barrack angry with me, should I apologise?" She gave a little chuckle.

"Not in the slightest, you stood up for two of my kind and defended them, hold yourself up, you acted like a watcher should." I nodded and took a deep breath.

"Alright, I am not sure he likes me too much though." She shrugged.

"Possibly, but I can assure you, he respects you for what you did." I felt a little relieved.

"Thank you, Veda, I do feel a lot better now." She gave me another smile and turned to Barrack.

"What path will you take in this matter Lord Barrack?" He looked down at Esme and Felix, and then directly at me.

"They broke our rule and revealed themselves, Esme is blameless as she only acted to stop Felix. Felix under the laws of this clan should be punished, an example must be made. I have taken advice from Chandak, and both of us have deemed, the penalty for this crime has been to have the tips of the wings removed."

I swallowed hard, it felt so cruel, and I could not accept that, Barrack looked round at all the frightened and worried faces of the other Nairn.

"However... Lady Emily has pleaded on the behalf of Felix for leniency, and we have considered it. It is true, the earth below our feet is in her care, and so we must consider her wishes deeply. This Clan has met, and it has considered, and so, in order to save his wings, we will impose two conditions. The first condition will be, if the Lady Emily seeks our approval of her request, she too must offer something in return, and so we respectfully ask that on the day of the human sun, Lady Emily is brought forth, and attends the ceremony of embrace." I had no idea what that was, but I gave a nod at Barrack.

"I have no idea what that is, but I will seek guidance from Randolph, and I will attend on the behalf of your people in good faith." Barrack gave a nod, and then looked down at Felix who looked terror stricken.

"To save your wings, then you must brave a task. You will deliver, thrice your body weight of comb and sweet paste for the ceremony of embrace." Esme gave a squeal, and pulled her hands to her face, and shook her head in terror, I felt alarmed.

Felix slipped off Shelly's lap and faced Barrack, he gave a regal bow to his clan leader.

"I will complete my task, my Lord and Master, and I will honour Emily at the embrace." Esme looked absolutely terrified. Barrack bowed to Felix.

"Then it is done, and we will meet on the day of the human sun. Felix, come with me, and we shall talk. All of you, to work, we have a celebration to prepare for."

Barrack turned, and walked away, and all the Nairn lifted into the air, and scattered in every direction. I was left sat alone not at sure what the hell had just happened, but it frightened the hell out of Esme, what the hell was going on? I looked at Randolph, as he watched Barrack leave with Felix, Esme was nowhere to be seen.

"What has happened, why is Esme so afraid?"

Shelly was looking as puzzled as I was, she shrugged as Randolph turned and walked back into the circle.

"Your agreement is that on Sunday, you will enter their sacred circle, and will embrace the light as your mother and Han did. Barrack is aware that you already to a degree have, but it is a deeply sacred ritual of his people, and he wants you to respect that and participate."

"Okay, so why is Esme so terrified, is this ritual dangerous?" He shook his head.

"It is merely a ceremony, and I will talk you through it and prepare you for it, it is time, and should be done before next

Tuesday, when you pass from twenty one to twenty two. Esme fears for Felix, for his task is a dangerous one." I frowned at him.

"What do you mean, how dangerous is this task?" Randolph gave a sigh.

"Emily, he agreed within the confines of the circle, he cannot go back on his word, you need to learn when to step in, and when to hold back. This is their custom, and their ritual, it is important that Barrack saves face, as he commands this clan. I am sure Chandak would like to see him slip and jump at the chance to replace him. Stay out of this Emily, it is their way." I felt he was not telling me everything.

"Randolph, how dangerous, tell me, do not treat me like a child and try to talk round it?" He gave a long sigh and looked me in the eye.

"That was not what I was doing. Emily, Felix has to collect thrice his body weight in comb and sweet paste, to you, that would be honeycomb. For a young Nairn, that would involve at least six trips to the nest." Shelly swallowed hard.

"You mean wild bees? Randolph, he is tiny, those buggers to him will look as big as large dogs to us."

"Shelly, this is their law, if he lives, then he will be redeemed." I felt the alarm rush up through me.

"IF HE LIVES, WHAT DO YOU MEAN IF HE LIVES!?"

"Emily, a sting from a bee to most of us is painful, but not deadly, for a Nairn, it can be fatal. Emily, Felix has agreed to do this, you cannot stop him, or you will dishonour him and his entire family line. To have cut wings is dishonourable, he will live on the floor in danger from every rat, mouse or squirrel, he has to meet that challenge and live to prove his value again to the Nairn."

The thought terrified me, I did not want anyone dying for my wish, especially Felix, it was clear Esme was very attached to him, and I could not bear the thought of her losing him. Shelly looked equally as upset as I did, the thought of a bee that big horrified me.

"Randolph is there nothing we can do?" He shook his head.

"This is now the fate of Felix; all we can do is hope he is brave enough to endure his task. Come we should leave, the day is drawing on, and I smell rain approaching."

Chapter Twenty Four

Pause For Thought

When we finally arrived back at home, I was feeling exhausted, and worried. I was coming to terms with the understanding that the Nairn, a type of fairy from what I could fathom, were real. To the scientific side of me, which was pretty much most of me, I had just witnessed an evolutionary impossibility, and I won't deny, I was struggling with the whole concept of it.

I sat on the end of my kitchen table, and poured a drink, hell my life had just got weirder and weirder, Randolph stood in the doorway.

"Emily, I know your mother, and you are very like her, please listen to me, do not get involved." I held out the bottle to him, and lifted the glass to my lips.

"I am involved, I stood up and asked for him to be treated less severely. Randolph, he is facing possible death because of me, you cannot stand there and say I am nothing to do with this. Tell me, are you happy about this? I saw your face, even you do not agree, admit it." He looked uncomfortable.

"Emily, I understand you I do, but we cannot disrupt their way of life, you more than anyone should understand that. Emily you are an ecologist, you literally study life and do everything not to disrupt it, can you not see that?" I gave a sigh and lifted my glass and took a long swig.

"I did not say I would stop this, but if you are telling me I cannot help him you are wrong, I aim too. I need to talk to Esme, I want to see her and talk, and I know you are aware of how to get hold of her, so, it is up to you. Are you going to support him, because if you are not, then as your granddaughter, I am asking you to turn your back and walk away, and let me do what I can to protect him?" He gave a small smile.

"Amelia and Han would be so proud of you. You are so like them, and Han would actually approve of this, she too broke many rules and riled up Barrack, I think he enjoyed sparing with her." I really got that, Han had no fear, well none I ever saw.

"I need Esme, and I know you know where I can get hold of her, I cannot do this task for him Randolph and I won't, but I can advise him on how to do it successfully. I understand bees, well, better than many others. They are massively important to ecosystems, and in that I have knowledge that will help him, and I want to try." He gave a nod.

"I will do what I can." I smiled.

"That is all that I ask."

It was getting late, and I was hungry, and so I started to prepare a meal, it was nothing fancy, but I asked Randolph to stay, he appeared to really like that. Shell joined in, and we prepared a stir fry with a pot of Han's preserved sauce, it was actually really tasty. As we sat at the table, Randolph gave me a rough idea of the ceremony I was to attend, and if I understood him, it was not much different from my time in the circle. I had to swear an oath, to protect the land and the Nairn, and then the Nairn would bring forth the light, and I would accept it.

There would be a feast afterwards and a sort of fairy party, which okay, I could deal with, and all of this, had to happen on the coming Sunday, and it was Thursday, so I had two days to prepare. I had to be bathed before the ceremony, and dressed in white, Randolph told me, I would find robes in Han's room, which unsettled me. I had still not plucked up the courage to enter, and so I was dreading what was to come.

We talked and drank wine, and by midnight I was slightly drunk and falling asleep, and it was throwing it down with rain. Randolph flicked up his hood and said his goodnights, and once again, I pulled him into a hug. I felt we had moved forward slightly, and I felt a little less awkward around him, although that was probably the booze. I locked the door as he walked through the rain home, and I swayed up the stairs to bed, I remembered little after that as I crashed out, and was in a deep sleep within minutes of hitting the pillow.

I slept reasonably well, I did dream, but it was filled with bright lights and tiny people, so they were not horrible or frightening dreams, if anything they were peaceful. I felt a lot more refreshed than I thought I would, as I walked down the stairs, the house was quiet and peaceful. Shelly would be out for the count, which suited me, as I enjoyed my morning coffee alone. The day was dull and grey, and there was a lot of drizzle, but with the door slightly open, it smelt fresh and clean, almost as if the rain had washed the whole place clean.

As I sipped my coffee, my thoughts were upstairs, I had to go into Han's room before Sunday, and I could feel that ball of hurt growing inside me again. The last few days had been so involved and busy, in a strange way it had helped me to calm down a little. I knew I had been avoiding it, Shelly had brought it up last night, and her voice reverberated through my thoughts.

"There is no pressure Emmy, I can go in for you, I mean, Randolph said they were white robes, so they will not be hard to find. Emmy, I know it will hurt, but you know, no matter what you do, that day will come when you have to go in there, and to be honest, I think the longer you put it off, the harder it will be."

I understood that, and I know she was right, but it did not make it any easier. Han's room in my mind was a sacred space, to me it was the place she lived the strongest, all of her most precious and personal things were there. Yes, I had her knitting bag and shawls downstairs, but her room had the more personal things, like hair brushes, makeup, jewellery, and most of all, her clothing.

I find it strange, that out of all the things we own and do in a life, nothing is more intimate than those really close personal items. For me, it is those things that identify us more than anything else, a picture on a wall, or an ornament that stirs memories, but to hold a brush, or a comb with strands of hair in them, or the smell of scent on a pillow, really hits home hard, my biggest fear though, was her journals.

I know about her journals, I watched her every day I was here, sit and write about her life. I know, that somewhere in her room, are her words, her thoughts and joys, written by her hand on a book she held. In many ways, they held the very essence of the woman I knew. I absolutely was sure that if I lifted one up, I would open it and read, and that would break my heart all over again. I knew Shell was right, I knew I had to do this, but I was dreading it, and it was there in the back of mind, slowly wearing away at me.

Since returning from Exeter, the feeling had grown stronger, Harry's comment had stayed with me. Yes, Han had died a year ago, and maybe I should be over it as he said, but the truth was, I wasn't. I have read a lot of blogs on grief in the last year, and most of them reflect on how the loss faded into the back of the mind, and it gets easier in time as you reshaped your life. People tell you to move on, change your focus, and do your best to cope, and in many ways, I have had all of that said to me, and to a degree, I can understand it. The problem I have, is not so much related to her death, but more to her life, and no one appears to understand that. You see, the truth is, there has not been a single day since I was four years old, that I have not either been with her, or had her in my thoughts.

No matter what occurred in my life, my first reaction was always, I must tell Han, and that is my biggest problem. I no longer can, and I so desperately want to talk to her. I want to call her up and say hey guess what, I am doing fine, because that is what I have always done. I cannot call and tell her, Han, oh my God, fairies are real, I had one sat on my shoulder and talk to me, oh hell, she would have loved to have that conversation with me, it was right up her alley. When I say I miss her, that is what I miss, phoning her and hearing her reaction to my joy. I phoned her almost every day when I was in Scotland or in the flat, each night I would come home and crash, and lie on my bed or sprawl on my sofa, and phone Han, and for a year, I have not been able to. For me, it is not just about the house, or the garden or visiting here, it is so much more than that, it is about simply ending my day with a conversation, and the joy that gave me.

In Exeter, I often walked in the park, luckily it had quite a few, and one was close to the flat. I loved to go there because of the open spaces, I suppose deep down I am a big of a country girl after being at Han's. It was a place I could breathe and walk, and sort out my mind alone in the cleaner air. A great deal of the city was built up and so busy with endless noise, and the park gave me a quieter space to simply be me. I was a regular most evenings in the summer, I would walk from the bus stop through the park, and linger in thought. I got used to seeing the regulars, the dog walkers and the joggers, and there was one man in particular I saw a great deal. He always sat alone on a particular bench, and he always appeared so at ease and calm, and at times, I had sat down on the other end of the bench, and simply sat quietly watching the world as he did.

One day he turned and smiled as I sat down, and introduced himself as Frank. I had been polite and told him my name, he commented how he had often seen me, and he thought it was a shame, such a pretty girl would sit alone looking sad, and then he turned to me.

"I realise this may appear inappropriate, because I do not know you, but is there anything I can do to help?"

It really surprised me, and I am not sure why, but for the first time since her death, which had been three months prior, I sat and talked about Han, and how much I was hurting. I cried a little and wiped my eyes and apologised, and he smiled with a really kind smile at me.

"Never apologise for the tears, for they are the truth of who you are. I understand your pain, I too lost someone, and it still lingers after ten years. Oh yes, I am told it will eventually fade and become easier to live with, but the simple truth is, I do not want it to, I do not want to forget, it was the most joyous part of my life."

He was talking about his wife, he had been married for forty two years, and she had been gone for ten, and he was still missing her. I really understood that, and as he talked of how they would walk in the park and talk every evening, I could see that he was not breaking that routine, he was keeping it alive, and in doing so, keeping her alive. He missed her, he could not hold her or touch her, but he could talk in his mind, in the place they always sat, and he could continue to keep a very important part of his life alive. He chuckled as he told me.

"My son thinks it is morbid and I need to move on, he has no idea of the love and joy I had in my life. To him, we have to move on and forget, but how can I, she was the reason I lived? So, I come here, and I sit in silence, but in my thoughts, I still talk, and in a strange way, she answers me, and it gives me peace. My son thinks I am a silly old fool." I shook my head.

"You are not, I know for sure, for I do the same, I cannot call Han anymore, so every day I walk home from the bus stop through the park, and I too talk to her. I have that precious moment still, and I am so sad to lose her, but it does help me get through each day." He smiled, he understood, he probably is the only person I have spoken to since her loss that has.

"Take my advice, no matter what anyone says to you young Emily, keep talking to her, honour and cherish her memory, and she will never truly leave you alone, trust me I know."

I stopped and talked to Frank every night after that, and for over a month, I found he was possibly the only person who fully understood me, and it helped me so much. One night I walked up and he was not there, and I felt so sad. I watched out, but I never saw him again, and I really have no idea what happened to him, yet his words stuck fast in my mind. 'Honour and cherish her memory, and she will never truly leave you alone,' I have done that, and I have also done that for him. I have no idea if he died and had been reunited with his wife, of if his son simply took charge and moved him away, but every day after that, because he really was a sweet old man, as I walked past each night, I would look at the empty bench, and simply say, 'Hi Frank,' in my thoughts.

When the winter came and the weather got bad, I would hurry home and grab a hot drink, and then sit on my bed, look at my phone, and talk to Han. I know it sounds insane, but Frank was right, talking to her kept a sense of her around me, and it comforted me in my times of deep sorrow. I still talk to Han now when I am sat in bed, I look at the mirror and see her pendant hung by the side of my mum's, and I wish them goodnight, or tell them of my day, and it helps me cope.

In a way, I think my biggest fear, is if I clean out her room, I will feel like I am cleaning her out of my life, and I do not want that. Leaving her room as it is, simply means, she still has a place that is just hers. Yes, I own the house now, the land around it is all mine, but that room, that is still hers. That is a place that is untouched from her final moment, and as long as it is there, to me, she still has a part of her here. I get it, no one understand it, but that is not the point, I do, and it matters to me, and that is all that counts.

I have been told by countless others to let her go and move on, they have no idea at all what that even means. The truth is, I am not ready to, I do not think I ever will be, I want her with me no matter what I do or where I go, and honestly, telling me to let go, why the hell should I? She was a massively important part of my life and she still is. I will live my life, I will move forward, and I will do it at my pace, but there is one thing I absolutely know, and that is, I will never let go, and I will never leave her behind. She will always be a part of the person I am, and I will carry her in my heart for the rest of my life. If you don't like it, ask Frank, he knows, and one day, if you are really lucky to have that kind of bond with a person, you will too.

I got up and made an extra coffee, and headed into what was now my office and shared craft room of Han's. It was a lot tidier than it had been, and we had both mucked in and really cleaned it up, and it was now more office like, well one side was. I sat down with my coffee and looked at the screen, I had emails to deal with, and on the front of the desk, I also had all the paperwork for the trust.

Having decided to go ahead with it, I opened the drawer and took out my pen, and started to fill in all the details for the trust and banking. It was pretty detailed, and it took a hell of a lot longer than I thought it would. My dad really does cover everything, and I had to stop a few times to look stuff up. I am used to this sort of stuff, I have dealt with it as a part of my job, but my dad was really thorough.

I needed to get the papers to Kate, so I slipped them into a large envelope, and wrote on the address of dad's offices in Plymouth, where she was. It would have to be posted, and I was putting off Han's room, and Shelly was still in bed, so I left her a note on the kettle, locked the backdoor, and headed off towards the village with my umbrella. I did not fancy driving, I wanted the walk, so followed the path my thoughts drifting back to my dealing with Han's death, and just letting everything wash around in my brain, whilst enjoying looking at the trees along the footpath.

I reached the edge of the village, and stood for a few minutes simply watching. In a way it had changed quite a bit since my childhood days, modern life and practices were very much on view. The village once had a bank and a post office, both were gone now. The bank had been replaced with a mobile one, and since the closure of the main post office, Brian and Jean Coulson, had managed to get sponsorship, and ran a scaled down version from the side of the Milking Gate Inn. It was only open until one each day, so I was in good time, they also had a deal with a courier company which allowed express packages, although you had to collect those from the post office, there was no deliveries to the houses.

I stood watching, this tiny place that was again my home, with its quaint shops, hotel and church in the background, it was beautiful, and precious to me, I had simply never expected to be living here. I breathed out as the drizzle ran off my umbrella.

"I am here Han, I did it and came home for good. I hope it is enough to protect the land, and your children, because if it is not, I have no idea what else to do."

I came down the end of the road and back into the heart of the village. I say heart, because right in the centre of the village is a strange, almost heart shaped patch of grass. It was once a pond, until two children tried to walk on it one December when Han was younger. It had frozen over and appeared stable, so they walked onto it, and yep, the inevitable happened, the ice cracked, the kids fell through and almost drowned. They were saved at the time by one of the local farmers.

Shortly after that, it was drained and filled in, and has been a lawn ever since. The shops sort of are arranged around it, in a higgled piggled sort of fashion. They are not really uniform, they are just placed all out of line and slightly off kilter to each other, but I actually like that about them, it feels more unique. I crossed the road, and walked alongside the edge of the grass, Heidi was out filling her flower tubs, and she saw me and waved, I held up my envelope and pointed to the Inn, and she gave nod of understanding.

Back to village life, Han's life, I must admit, I do wonder if I will be as accepted as she was, this lot can be a difficult crowd at times, and I wonder if I will have to grow as old and eccentric as Han, before I will be truly part of the village. I am sure at some point, Shelly will raise an eyebrow or two, especially if she starts talking ghost hunting with this lot, they are already a superstition riddled lot. I smiled to myself as I reached the inn, and walked down the side to the open blue door.

I was greeted with a smile from Brian, as I slipped the envelope under the window.

"Emily, it is nice to see you back in the village, I heard you came back last week?" I gave him a smile.

"Yeah, I am still adapting back to life here, it has been hard to see the place empty, so I am slowly adjusting." He gave me a smile as I pointed to the envelope. "How fast can that go; I need it at my dad's place as quickly as possible?" He looked at it, and then popped it on the scale, and tapped on his digital screen.

"The fastest will be first thing in the morning recorded, it will be eight pounds twenty five, will that be alright?" I nodded and pulled out my purse.

"That is fine Brian, thanks." He printed out a stamp, and peeled it of the backing and stuck it on.

"Your dad has done well, I remember him and your mum running wild round the village, he has really made something of himself, not bad for an old farmers lad from the sticks." I smiled, Han often told me how proud his dad was, Brian looked up from the counter. "Will he be selling his dad's land like the Johnson's have?"

I gave a slight frown, I had known the Johnsons for years, their land bordered mine, as did dad's, his father owned most of what ran up the side of the lake. I owned all of the lake, and an acre along the side of the road, as far as I knew, my dad still owned all his family's property. The Johnson's property was at the far end of the lake, across the road from my land, and on the end of my dad's. I looked at Brian and shook my head.

"He has not said anything, I do not think he will ever sell his dad's land, he grew up there and loves that place. I did not know the Johnsons were selling, they always told Han it was for their two children." Brian shrugged.

"Apparently the developer offered him double the price, so he is going to take it, I must admit, it was too good to be true, he is no fool, and said when he meets them, he will be taking the money." I pressed my card on the machine and it beeped.

"I don't suppose you can blame him really, although it has a beautiful orchard, Han and I often picked apples there. It will be sad if they build over them." Brian nodded.

"There are a few round here not happy, they say it will end up with rows of tiny boxed homes filled with young families, and in other places where that has happened, it has always brought trouble to the village." I smiled.

"I better be careful then; I would hate to be lumped in with them, and labelled a young thug." He gave a giggle as he handed me a receipt.

"I doubt that will happen, you are very like Amelia, I was at school with her you know? She was a nice girl, quite a few of us asked her out, and she turned us all down flat, and then John came along, and those two were destined to meet. I was always sorry you all lost her so soon, she really was a lovely person, and I see a great deal of her in you." It was a nice compliment, and I smiled, and blushed a little.

"Thanks Brian, we miss her too. Han has talked to me all my life about her, and so does everyone I meet around here, it is nice she is so well thought of, it makes me proud of her." I think he understood.

I said goodbye and walked out, and lifted my phone, I hit speed dial, and it rang.

"Emily, how lovely, what can I do for you?"

"Dad, did you know the Johnson's are selling to a developer?"

"No, I have not heard a thing. Who are they selling to?"

"I don't know, I just came out of the post office, Brian asked me if I knew. Dad, they have offered twice its value, and honestly, it worried me. If they have offered double, that means they really want that land, and it borders mine, so you can guest where my thoughts went?"

"I am already there with you, it does not take a lot of working out, and it also explains why Harry may have been in on the deal. Pete will use a front to buy it, but he will be behind it."

"I get that, but it is across the road, and at least an acre away from the lake, I mean, I am not selling ever, so my place is safe right?"

"Emily, do not worry, I am on this, and if it is Pete, I will be all over it to make sure you are not troubled. Leave this with me, and I will look into it. Do not worry, I told you, I will not let him near you." I smiled, why did it sound so wonderful to hear my dad saying he would watch out for me?

"Alright Dad, I just thought you should know, because it is right next to your place, I don't trust him Dad, I really don't."

"You shouldn't, you have your mum's instincts, and that is a very good thing. Emily leave this with me, I am on this now, alright?" I nodded.

"Yeah, thanks Dad."

"No problem, I will see you soon, so just relax, and focus on you, alright, I have to go and see into this for you, I will let you know as soon as I hear something."

"Alright Dad, see you soon."

I ended the call, his voice had sounded concerned and that bothered me, but he was aware of this now, so I thought it best to wait until he rang me. I suppose it is silly really, but just the world developer had my heart beating. Pete was up to something, call it a gut instinct, but the way my stomach was churning, and my heart was racing, I knew I was not wrong.

I walked slowly back through the village lost in thought, it does appear that since returning, my mind has been a whirlwind of spiralling thoughts, all blowing around in my head, as I endlessly try to process my life, whilst understanding the reality of losing Han. I stepped off the road onto the tree lined path heading in the direction of my home, completely unaware of my surroundings, as my mind raced and I tried to puzzle things out.

Why had Pete been so hell bent on owning the land, and why now was he after the Johnsons property, it made little sense to me, after all it was on the other side of the road from my land. Was it so he could make fast cash, or was there more to this? Mum's car, the attempted house fire, were these something to do with Pete? I paused in thought.

"No, she was his wife's sister, as shitty as he is, he would not do that... Would he?"

Okay, so I am biased, I really do not like him, in a way he frightens me, but he has always been about the money and the power associated with it. Han had once said, once he started throwing around the cash, Jessica changed, before that she had been a happy carefree girl, but Pete had corrupted her. I had to wonder, because honestly at the funeral, considering it was her mother who was being buried, she had not appeared that emotional. I had cried buckets, and felt broken, and yet she was cool, calm and composed for the whole event.

How could a person be changed so much; can money really do that? Well, for a time I had thought my dad was the same, and yet, I had seen another side to him recently, and I really liked it, I felt a little closer to him because of it. In all honesty, it had helped me come to terms with things. Simply understanding I was not completely alone and still had a connection to my mum, had to a degree eased a little of my inner pain. If you think about it, in the last seventeen years, Han changed my life, just by being Han, In the last week as I fell apart, my dad walked in, and his influence has caused a big impact on me and really helped.

Considering that, then it makes sense to me that Pete could have such a corrosive effect of Jessica, that she may well go along with his plans, which does actually really worry me. His obsession with this land concerns me, and I have to ask, what is it he really wants, is it the land to build on, is there something more to this land I am unaware of, or... I suddenly felt a feeling of dread wash through me?

"Oh hell, does he know about the Nairn?"

I looked to the trees, I was not that far from home, and I had a feeling of sudden dread. I picked up my pace, and hurried towards home, suddenly I wanted to be as close to home as possible. If the Nairn were at risk, I had to protect them no matter what.

Chapter Twenty Five

Going on Instinct

By the time I got home, I felt a little panicked, and honestly, I am sure my mind goes into overthinking mode deliberately. As soon as I walked through the door, I calmed down a little, and breathed a sigh of relief. Shelly was up and sat in the kitchen, she was playing around with tin foil, and making little bowls. It is Shelly, I accept she can be weird, but did not even think about asking about what she was doing.

I sat at the table and told her of what I heard, what I thought, and what my dad had said, she listened as she messed around making her tiny little bowls. She had a row of them on the table as she looked at me.

"You did right Emmy, your dad is probably the best placed to sort this out, and find out what is going on around here. To be honest Emmy, he has the clout, he has the team, and he has the money. I do not know a huge amount about him, but be honest, you do not get to his level by being an idiot. He is top of the pile at this stuff, I mean, when I first met you and I found out who he was, I was blown away. I sat there thinking, holy shit, this girl's dad is a billionaire, why the hell is she hanging out with me?"

It really surprised me to hear her say that, and I could not help but ponder, was that how people saw me, some sort of rich guy's kid?

"Shell, I hang out with you because I like you. To me you are an amazing friend, I might be his daughter, but I am a normal person. I grew up here with Han, not him, I have lived a pretty simple self sufficient life up to now. Shell you saw the flat, I did not have that much, we moved in a day it was so little." She gave a giggle.

"Hell Emmy, do not be so defensive, I did not mean anything by it, I was just saying I was a little surprised, mainly because you were so down to earth." I gave a nod.

"Okay, sorry, I am a little rattled today, I really do not want any more grief with Pete. Shell, I just want things to calm down, so I can deal with everything." She put another little cup down.

"Yeah, it has been mad, I will not deny, it has been really different here, not at all like expected."

"Now that I understood." I watched her start another cup and simply had to ask.

"Shell, what the hell are you doing, are you like making a tea set for the Nairn?" She gave a giggle, and put another one down on the table to add to the row.

"It is your fault, last night you started talking about smoke to subdue the bees. I figured Felix was small, and the bees would probably be a tree variety, so he would need to get the smoke to the bees. In my mind Emmy, if he can lift something light with smoke in it, he can calm the bees, and it might make it easier for him." Weirdly enough she made sense.

"Okay, so what do you intend to use for smoke?" She gave a giggle.

"No idea, I thought you would be smart enough to come up with something."

I should have known, how many times had I seen her have half an amazingly good idea and stall? I took a breath and leaned on the table as I looked at them.

"Well, it has to be lightweight, but it has to produce enough smoke, but not too much, if he over does it with the smoke, they will get angry. A lot of people never understand that, you need just enough, too much really pisses them off. Shell he must not make them aggressive, if he does, they will attack him, and I am terrified he may get stung." She appeared to understand.

"So, I know little about this stuff, but I have seen pictures of big balls of crawling bees, is that what he will be dealing with, or do they build a nest like thing?"

"It depends on the bee, I have seen swam nests here before, so I am hoping it is a wax structure. If it is open, he may be able to smoke them to quieten them down, and then somehow cut a piece off, and let it drop. Oh God Shell, it scares the hell out of me just thinking about it. I feel so guilty about all this, and that poor little fellow is being forced to risk his life because of it." She shrugged at me.

"Do not underestimate him Emmy, he came at me with quite the rage, he may just surprise you." I breathed out and gave her a nod.

"Yeah, he is a tough little bugger, and I will not deny, he is pretty brave." I had an idea and turned to the kitchen drawer.

"You know, Han has a lot of incense cones if I am right." I gave a chuckle. "She would light them when she cooked cabbage, she loved to eat it, but hated the smell of it cooking."

I reached over, and pulled open the drawer, and there they were, it made me smile seeing them. I had always laughed at the look on her face as it cooked, she was lovely, and a funny old stick at times. I pulled them out of the drawer and put a box down on the table, Shell winked and lifted it up.

"Citrus, well that will help, it wards off flies, I wonder if it works on bees?"

She opened the match box, and lit one, let it burn and then gave it a shake, and placed it in the small foil bowl. It appeared to fit, and the smoke rose up out of the top. I did not look that much, it was thin and wispy, I was not sure it would be enough. I picked up a glass from the draining board, and held it upside down over the cone, and it started to fill with the smoke. Shell looked hopefully at me.

"Well, if it is a closed nest, we know he can fill one up with smoke, not sure about the open nest though, it may not have the impact."

"Yeah, but at least it is a start. It is a shame he is not bigger; he would be better placed to do this. I wish bees lived on the ground; he may have an easier task."

I was not that sure, up in the air or on the floor, the hazard was the actual bees, and he could not injure one, because I knew for sure that would be fatal, as bees gave off a pheromone to warn all the others. The last thing he needed was anything getting hurt, especially himself. This was looking harder and harder as I tried to work it all out for him.

It was frustrating, and I got up and walked around, I opened the back door, the rain had fizzled away, and I took a really good deep breath of clean air. Talking about Felix, just worried me even more, and it was upsetting me, because even though I had only actually met him once, for not really that long, I found myself really caring about him and Esme.

It is insane, right up until yesterday, I would have sworn blacks white, there was no such thing as fairies, and yet here I was one day later and struggling with my emotions, because I felt responsible for the life of one, I did not want to die. I stepped out and felt the air stirring around me, my voice was low.

"Mum, Han, what should I do, I cannot let him die?"

"He won't."

I spun round in surprise, and Randolph stood smiling, his hood up, and his rifle on his shoulder. I took a deep breath and put my hand on my heart.

"Jesus, you scared the hell out of me, wear heavier boots so I can hear you coming." He gave a little chuckle.

"Your father rang me, he was concerned about you, and asked me to look in on you. I was heading this way anyhow, I wondered if you fancied a boat ride?"

I looked at him stood there with a smile on his face, call it intuition, but I felt he was up to something, I eyed him carefully.

"Firstly, you have a phone? And secondly, it has been raining and if you have noticed, it is pretty choppy out there, I do hope you are not expecting thunder? Okay so I am intrigued as well, why would you want to go for a boat ride today of all days?"

He looked out across the lake, and then turned back and looked me right in the eyes, and I knew he was up to something, he just had that air of mystery around him that Han used to have when she was trying to surprise me.

"I trust your hunches, and I trust your father, and when both of you think the same, I know you are guided by the light. Your boat is faster than my raft, and can drift in safety for a good period of time. Emily, all I want is to take a look along the lake banks further down, just to be sure, and it is a long walk."

Well, he was not wrong about that, the lake was huge, the boat would be ten times quicker than walking. I gave a nod to him.

"I need a coat and some boots; I will get changed."

I hurried into the house and grabbed my boots, Shell had heard us, and was getting her things on. I grabbed a coat and slid it on, and then both of us joined Randolph and headed for the boat house.

Randolph took the controls, and we sat back, I was not a fan of guns, so seeing it on his shoulder bothered me a little. I really had no idea what he expected, in my mind, my uncle was trying to buy a house, as far as I could tell, the sale had not gone through yet, and so for now, I had assumed I was safe from whatever twisted plan he had.

The boat raced round the island, Randolph was really pushing it, it was a fast boat, yet neither Han or myself ever pushed it this hard. The water was choppy, and the boat bounced up and down, and yet it felt refreshing and thrilling as we skipped along, although, I was hanging onto the rail for dear life. We came round the top of the island, and Randolph headed for the bank, just up from the waterfall my mother and father met at. He turned the boat and followed the bank, and then slowed the boat down, so we just chugged along slowly, his eyes fixed on the window, staring forward.

I got up from the seat at the back, and left Shell, and walked up to the cab, and held the rail as I stood at his side.

"Why have you slowed down, what is going on?" The engine was chugging along, and we moving at a snail's pace.

"I am just being cautious Emily, I am not about to rush in on anything, especially with you here." I frowned.

"Rush in on what?"

"Emily, vehicles have been spotted up here, all I want is to check things out. Trust me, this was normal at one time for Han and me." I was a little surprised to hear that.

"It was... Is this a frequent thing?" He nodded at me, and then looked back out of the window.

"Look Emily, a long time ago, your uncle was hell bent on getting this place, and he put a lot of pressure on Han. Abraham was gone, and your mother was with John. Pete took over from his father, and he really turned the screws and made life hard for a while. Han was struggling, and doing her best to cope, but he really was intense. I had hoped those days were gone, but since we lost her to the light, he looks like he is back to his old tricks. I want to make sure he is not; I do not want you going through what she did."

I understood some of it, for a year he had not left me alone, and I had suffered an endless string of emails and phone calls. I had thought coming back and deciding to stay here would put him off, and it now appeared that Randolph and my dad, were pretty convince it would not. I looked at Randolph as a thought occurred to me.

"Is that the reason my mum was coming back, Han was not coping with it?" He did not look at me, he just kept his eyes out of the window.

"Yes, it is Emily, and it cost her greatly, she paid with her life." I felt a cold shiver run down back.

"Randolph, he is a shit, but seriously, you cannot think he had something to do that? He would never have the guts to try something like that, he is a coward at heart that hides behind his money." He continued to stare out of the window.

"You are pure of heart, just like your mother, and my best advice would be keep thinking that Emily." I have no idea but that shocked me.

"Randolph, I mean, come on, Randolph we are talking murder here, there is no way he has the stomach for that, it is insane to think it. I mean seriously, how would someone even be able to prove that?"

"That is why he is still alive Emily, if I could prove it, trust me, I would have stuffed him where no one could find him." I swallowed hard, and felt a little panicked.

"Randolph, do not say things like that, do not even hint at it, that is not a joke."

Randolph turned and looked at me, his eyes were as sharp as an eagle, and he looked so resolute it was a little intimidating.

"No Emily, it was my daughter, and your mother."

Okay, so now I am terrified, that look scared me to death, and also his tone of voice. Randolph was a game keeper, a tracker, a man used to living outdoors and taking what was needed from the land. I have known one or two, the one I worked with in

Scotland was not unlike Randolph, just not as intense. I decided I was not going to pursue the current conversation and decided to stay quiet. He turned the boat and he headed for the bank; it looked like he was going ashore.

"Take the wheel, and I will get the line. I want you to stay with the boat, and I am going to take a look ahead." I shook my head.

"I am coming, this is my property, and I defend it." He smiled and nodded his head.

"Alright then, just stay a few feet behind me, and watch everything, let me know if you spot something." I frowned at him; I had honestly thought he would stop me.

"Are you not going to order me to stay in the boat?" He chuckled.

"Would you stay if I did?"

"Well, no, I would still come along." He looked at me and smiled.

"And you are her double, you have no idea how like her you are, and knowing her, she would not stay put either. I just assumed I would give it a shot and see, and I was right, you and her would both disregard me and follow me anyhow." I smiled at him.

"You are wiser that I thought." He winked at me.

"I got to know her well in our brief time, all I have to do is predict her, and I understand you."

It was a good point, and I know it is silly, but somehow, I love knowing I am like her. I had four years with my mum, and the rest was with Han, so I suppose I always felt I would end up more like Han, and not so much like my mum. It is strange to know, that even without her influence, I turned out like her anyhow. Actually, I am little bit thrilled about it.

The engine was cut, and he jumped out and pulled the boat into the bank, and tied it off, and Shell and myself clambered off into the shallow water, and walked onto dry land. We were a lot further down that I realised, and up in front, I could see the large white rock that ran out from the bank, into the deep water. This side of lake was very rocky, and the drop from the rock into the lake was quite high.

It was very wide, and the top formed a large rough plateau of the white stone, onto which trees had rooted, in a thick dense woodland. Randolph slipped his rifle off his shoulder and my heart skipped a beat; I touched his arm.

"You are not seriously thinking of shooting someone, are you?" He shook his head.

"Doing it, or letting someone think I will do it, are different things. Relax Emily, a warning I find makes for a persuasive argument." I breathed a sigh of relief.

"Good... I panicked a little for a second." He smiled.

"Emily, if I meant to use this on a human, you would not be here." I nodded.

"Good to know, thanks."

Randolph slid his hand inside his jacket, and brought a thick black metal object, Shell was very interested.

"Wow, a silencer, you know, I have to ask, you are not like, ex SAS or anything like that are you?" He screwed the object onto the end of his rifle.

"No... I do have a few friends who have served though." Yep, him and his mates... Scary as hell. Shelly was impressed.

"I figured as much. I dated a para just before Uni, clever bloke, but he told some scary bloody stories. I figured I was best off where he wasn't." Randolph nodded and turned to the path.

"Probably a wise choice. Okay stay a few feet behind me, and stay quiet from now on."

He walked off slowly, and I looked at Shell, she was enjoying this, she really appeared to think all this was fun. I was scared shitless, and I had no idea at all why. I was not hanging around, Randolph walked quite fast, with long strides, and I hurried to catch him up. I felt nervous and tense, Shell appeared to be quite calm, but he had a rifle, and I was still worried about that. I hurried along watching everything, it was still quite some distance to the rock, and Randolph slowed to an almost halt, I came up at his side.

"What is wrong?" He slid his rifle slowly off his shoulder, which worried me, as he tensed up.

"Listen!"

"Huh?" I could hear nothing but the lapping of the water on the bank.

I stood completely still holding my breath, and had no idea

at all why, as my ears strained as I tried to hear anything. There were birds tweeting, and the sound of the wind blowing through the leaves, but apart from that everything appeared to be as it normally is. Randolph lifted his rifle, and his hand came across to me.

"Emily, you and Shelly get in the trees, and stay out of sight." I looked at him.

"Why... Randolph, what is happening?" He lifted his hood up.

"It is alright, just stay hidden until I say so."

I have no idea why, but I felt panicked, and grabbed Shell behind me by the hand, and slid back in amongst a patch of young birch trees. It was overcast but really warm, and I felt the perspiration on my brow. Shelly huddled in close and talked quietly, her eyes were sparkling.

"You know Emmy, Randolph is cool and all that, but I got to say, he is freaking me out."

I understood that, I was watching him, crouched low on the path, with his rifle up and ready. The fact he had rifle bothered me so much, and he still had not told me why exactly we were here. I sat still in the damp birch trees, smelling the pine further up the hill, I felt really scared but I had no idea why, as I strained my ears.

It took a few moments, and then I heard a strange kind of buzzing noise, I sat still listening, it was quiet, and I could not believe that Randolph had heard that already. As I watched, I saw a drone come over the trees above the rock, and out across the water. I could not believe my eyes, who the hell was flying a drone over my property?

Okay so that really did not take a lot of working out, and I was there already, and starting to get really pissed off, what was he up to now? Randolph lifted his rifle to his shoulder, and squatted down, as the drone hovered above the lake, he pulled the rifle and up, I held my breath, and then, I heard his rifle make a sort of puff, muffled sound. I watched as the drone gave a pop, and then fell down into the water with a small splash, and disappeared below the surface.

I pushed my head through the trees, and looked round, I spotted Randolph crouching, with his hood up, back against the trees. I kept my voice down, but I had no idea why.

"Randolph, was that what I think it was?"

He nodded and waved me back into the trees, I had no idea what was really going on, although, I had guessed, it was something to do with Pete, and the Johnson's house.

I slid back and looked at Shelly, she was smiling, so nothing new there, she was enjoying this, she was sat back in a huge fern, simply watching and enjoying all of it, she is weird.

"Shell, are you enjoying this?" She nodded.

"Yeah, pretty much, he is a bloody good shot, I doubt I could hit a moving target like that."

She made a good point; I looked back and noticed a man in a yellow vest holding the controller. He had stepped out from the trees and was looking down into the water, obviously looking for his drone.

He did not look familiar, if anything I had no idea who the hell he was, all I knew was he was trespassing, and on my land, and I wanted him off. His yellow vest was no protection, he did not belong here, and I wanted him gone. I looked round, oh crap, Randolph had gone, I looked up and down the path, there was no sign of him, I looked back at Shell, and noticed movement in the corner of my eye, and realised.

"Oh hell, Shell, Randolph has gone rogue on us, and he is moving quick, come on, we have to try and stop him shooting someone."

I grabbed at her wrist and yanked hard, and pulled her off the floor. I spotted Randolph, moving quickly half way up the steep banking, and yanking Shell along, I raced after him, the last thing I needed was a pissed off game keeper with a rifle. My feet slipped on the wet grass, why did this have to happen today, it had been dry all week and would have been so much easier?

My boots slid sideways, and I let go of Shell, and lunged at the small saplings on the bank, pulling myself forward, and dragging myself up, to try and catch up with Randolph. I gasped and panted, but pushed with all I have, he was fast for an older guy, and I was pretty fit and strong, but I was no match for him. I looked back, Shell was doing her best to keep pace, as I moved up at a much slower rate than Randolph, hoping to hell, he would not do anything stupid.

Randolph reached the top, and his suspicions were right, through the trees he could see a man in long black woollen coat, walking at speed towards the guy in a yellow vest, he took his time and breathed in, he was not as young as he once was, but he had made to the top without being spotted. He lifted the rifle and looked down through the telescopic scope as he advanced slowly. Pete was stood just outside the trees, staring at the man in a yellow vest.

"How the hell could you lose it? That drone cost almost a thousand pounds, it is the best of the best. You told me you could fly it with no problems, well what do we do now, it will be days before we can another out in this God forsaken place?" Randolph lifted the rifle and stepped forward.

"You won't be needing another, I am sure Miss Emily made it perfectly clear to you, that you are trespassing." Pete turned round and saw the face below the hood, and gasped with a little horror and fear.

"Randolph!?" He nodded at him, as he pointed the rifle right at him.

"That would be me." Pete swallowed hard, and took two paces back, he was close to the edge of the rock, and the colour was draining fast for his face. Randolph gave a snort.

"Why are you here, this is private land and you know it?" Pete lifted his hand, and his voice wavered slightly as he lowered it.

"This is nothing to do with you, this is family business, stay out of it." Randolph gave a nod.

"Family eh! Funny that, because Miss Emily knows nothing about it, and considering it is her land, I would have imagined, she would have told me, and yet, she has not. Explain to me how this is a family thing, and be fast, my arm is tired and needs to pull this trigger." Pete looked at the man in the yellow vest, and then back to Randolph.

"Look, this is just one big misunderstanding, nothing more." Randolph smirked.

"That it is, you misunderstood her last time, she said never come back."

I heard the voices as I got near to the top, and hoped Randolph did not shoot anyone before I arrived. I did not want to explain a death on my land, not ever. I pulled and tugged and saw the top, I was almost there, I could hear the branches and twigs snapping behind me, and knew Shell was not far away.

I reached the top panting and covered in mud with slimy boots, and staggered in the direction of the front of the rock top. I saw a path of freshly cut small saplings, it did not take a minute to work out why, and it was then that I heard the voices.

"Look mate, I know nothing about all this, I am getting paid to do a job, nothing more."

I moved quickly into the opening cut between the trees, and right into the eyes of Pete looking at me over Randolph's shoulder. Yeah, he looked worried, I saw him, and my anger flared up instantly, once again he was on my land and up to his devious tricks. I marched at speed towards him.

"I TOLD YOU TO STAY OFF MY LAND, WHY ARE YOU HERE!?"

Randolph turned back and saw me, he lowered his rifle as I marched, filled with anger towards them all. God, you have no idea how much I have come to hate this man in the last year, I stormed up to the side of Randolph.

"How many times do you need to be told before you will finally leave me alone, this place is not, and never will be for sale."

I tried to march past Randolph, but he was far more agile than I had thought, and he grabbed at my waist, and pulled me into him. I tried to swing at Pete, but Randolph had me held firm and tight, as he pulled me back into him. Pete smirked.

"Emily, overly emotional as normal I see, you know, you really need to calm down, you are as emotional as your mother was." That just about pissed me off more.

Randolph was good, but not good enough, I pushed my feet into the floor and pushed hard, and as Shelly came gasping up at our side, I pulled my legs up high, and then kicked out with my feet together as hard as I could.

"Screw you Pete, you want the lake, then take a good look."

I hit him full on in the waist as threw all my anger into my legs, and he lurched backwards, with two large slimy muddy footprints of the front of his pants and coat. He gave an almighty squeal, and with his arms flailing out at his sides, he yelled out in panic, and disappeared out of view. I heard the almighty splash, and smiled. Shell burst into loud raucous laughter as my feet landed back on the floor, and I heard Randolph give out a huge sigh, as he released my waist.

I peered over the edge, to see Pete gasping and splashing in the deep water, and smiled at him as he looked up, with rage in his eyes.

"Maybe now you will cool off, and stay the hell off my land. I mean it Pete, next time I will tell Randolph to shoot you, this place is not short of quiet spots to hide your pathetic body. Just understand, stay away from me, and this land, otherwise I mean it, you will suffer." I turned as Pete swam towards the edge of the bank, and saw Randolph looking at me with a smile on his face.

"Not what I was planning, but I feel it served its purpose."

I gave a chuckle as Shelly leaned over the edge watching and still laughing at the soaking wet Pete, as he pulled himself up onto the bank. I shrugged.

"Look on the bright side, I saved you a bullet." Randolph looked at the pale looking guy in the yellow vest.

"Why are you here?" He looked over the edge and back at both of us.

"Honestly, I want no trouble, I was just paid to do a job." I nodded.

"Okay, so what is your job?" He frowned and looked at me as if did not understand why I did not know.

"I am here to drill a hole, nothing more, I wanted an idea of the land fall, so was filming it. The other guys take care of everything after that." I frowned and looked at Randolph.

"A hole, what is the point of drilling a hole?" Randolph gave a sigh and nodded at me.

"Now I understand... Not here Emily, I will talk to you in while." I could see his face, and had to ask, was this yet another secret of the land? I looked back at the guy in the yellow vest.

"He does not own this land, I do, I am the sole owner, if you are gone within the day, I will not prosecute, now go."

He did not need telling twice, he fled past me, leaving me alone with Randolph and Shell.

"Okay, we are alone, tell me what the hell is going on?" Randolph shouldered his rifle, and slipped down his hood.

"Emily, the geography and the rock compositions, imply, there may be shale gas below the land. There are deposits along this ridge, two other locations five miles away have been tapped. Han knew, or at least suspected, Pete wanted to drill it out, or at least buy the rights to drill it out, and she refused. So, he pushed her and would not leave her alone. He is also aware of certain mineral stones, and high quality quartz, he made life hard, and finally he gave up. It looks to me, like he wants to revive an old plan, Emily there is so much more to this place, far more than you realise, and Han wanted it all left untouched, your mum was heading back to stand with her." I should have known better, if it is Pete, there is money.

"Randolph, it will stay right down there where Han left it, nothing has changed, I aim to preserve and protect this place, and honour my mother and Han's wishes. As long as I am alive, no one will ever drill in this place."

He knew that, but that was why he was worried, Amelia had said the very same thing, one week before she died.

Chapter Twenty Six

Negotiation

Randolph wanted to hang around to oversee things, but he wanted Shelly and myself to go back to the boat and leave. He took my arm and led me back down the slope to the pathway, where Pete was being helped, as he was pulled out of the lake, soaked through to the skin. He stared at me with utter hate.

"I promise you Emily, this is not the end." I sneered at him.

"Get the hell off my land, or I will have my gamekeeper shoot you." Randolph stared at him with hate.

"I warned you years ago, I meant it then, and I mean it now, stay clear of me, or you will regret it." Randolph turned to me and lowered his voice.

"Emily, go home, let me deal with this, I want you safe. I gave your message to Esme; she will come to you." I nodded, my eyes still on the soaked figure of Pete as he was helped up the bank.

"Okay, just watch your back." I looked at him and he smiled.

"Thanks." I frowned.

"What for?"

"Worrying about me." I smiled.

"I do that a lot; you know we all have to be careful; Pete is far more dangerous than he looks." Randolph gave a nod, and looked back.

"Emily, do not worry, I know him a lot better than most people realise." I could sense that, but none the less, I wanted to say it, and I had.

We headed back to the boat, and as I looked back, Randolph was heading back up the banking towards the trees and the rocky top. I turned the boat, and headed back towards home, feeling really angry inside, was he ever going to stop? Shelly came up at my side, and looked out of the window.

"Are you going to be alright, you were pretty bloody angry, and I know you, I know how you internalise everything?" I stared through the window, watching the lake.

"I am so tired of him Shell, I mean, what the hell do I have to do, to get him to just leave me alone? Shell it has been over a year, and yet once again, he pops up trying to sneak a pipe into drill for gas. I understand now what he is up to with the Johnsons property, he is going to buy it, so he can pull it all down and drill for gas. Shell he will use fracking techniques, have you any idea of the chemicals they pump into the ground? If that comes up in the ground water, it will poison the lake and kill everything." She slid up to my side and slipped her arm round me.

"It will not get to that Emmy, Randolph and your dad will never allow it, trust them, they will do something."

I wanted to believe that, but just seeing his smug face and listening to his threats, somehow, I felt like he would be back to do more harm. We approached the boat house and I slowed down, as we ran up against the side of the covered wooden deck, and I killed the engine. I needed to sit with a coffee and just calm the hell down, and think everything through and gather my thoughts.

At the lower end of the lake, the line of trucks stood silent, backed onto the lake side of the road, as a group gathered. Still dripping, Pete wrung out his coat, and then threw it is the boot of his car, his anger was more than apparent as Randolph stood leaning on a tree trunk watching.

Pulling out a blanket, Pete put it on his car seat and climbed in, and then spun the car round with a scowl, and drove off back to his hotel in the next village. The foreman on the job approached Randolph.

"Look mate, we were told to park here until we were allowed on that piece of property over there, which is taking longer than planned. These guys have come a long way to be here, we have to go somewhere." Randolph nodded at him.

"That is the problem with working for criminals, they put you in difficult situations. The land owner was quite clear, you have to go. Honestly, I am doing as requested, so it is up to you where you head to, all I know is it will not be here for a minute longer than it has to be. So pack up, and leave." The foreman gave a frustrated sigh and looked back at the crew and shook his head.

"This stinks." Randolph nodded at him.

"Crime does." The foreman walked back slowly, and raised his voice.

"Pack it up lads, there is no hope here."

All the drivers looked annoyed, they kicked at the ground, and then headed for their trucks. Randolph smirked as he watched them climb up into their cabs, and very shortly, engines were running as the trucks warmed up ready to leave.

Down the road came the black BMW of John Duncan, he slowed as he saw the trucks, and then Randolph. He came to a stop and his window slid down.

"What is going on?" Randolph leaned off the tree and walked onto the side of the road. He came up to the side, his eyes still on the trucks.

"We caught this lot and Pete surveying the lake with a drone, it appears Pete is after the gas under here." John looked round.

"Where is he?"

Randolph smirked and noticed Jane sat on his other side, and nodded a welcome.

"Pete got a little wet, Emily kicked him, and he went off the cliff top." Jane smirked and bit her lip, even John gave a little titter.

"I take it he lived then?" Randolph smiled.

"He is certainly a lot cooler, Emily is very like her mum, and has that slightly aggressive streak she did. He is fine, his pride is hurt and his blood is boiling. Emily had demanded all these trucks get off her land, they are a little unhappy, but will be leaving shortly. Apparently, Pete informed them they could park here until he had done the deal with the Johnson's. John, it looks like he is going to buy them out, and then drill the land for the gas, you know what that will do to the lake, don't you?"

He gave a nod and looked really angry, he looked at Jane, and she nodded back, it appeared John had something in mind. He turned back to Randolph.

"Where is Emily?"

"She has gone home in the boat, I let her know I would stay here until the place was clear. John, we need to do something, he has to be stopped or he will destroy everything."

"I am aware, and I am working on it. Make sure this lot leave, if not let me know, I will have a security team up here tonight to make sure they stay off. I am going to see Edgar and see what can be done, one way or the other, I want Pete kept off that land." Randolph gave a nod and stepped back.

"When it is all clear here, I will look in on Emily, she was pretty angry when she left." John smiled.

"Yes, I might swing round myself in a little while, I am going to phone her before I speak to Edgar."

He gave a wave, and Randolph smiled, and he pulled off to drive the twenty yards down to the gate to the road of the Johnson's property. John pushed the pad on his phone that was attached to the dash board, and it dialled and then rang. My phone was on the kitchen table, it lit up as it rang, and saw dads name, and I snatched it up.

"Dad!"

"Emily, I am at the Johnson's property with Jane, we are just about to drive in. I have spoken with Randolph, so I am aware of the recent activities. Emily, I do not want you to worry, I aim to stop Pete from drilling, I just need a few more hours, and then I will call at your place and fill you in." I breathed a sigh of relief.

"Dad he will poison Han's lake, we cannot let that happen, I have seen the damage that can happen, I must find a way to make sure that never happens here."

"Emily, we will stop him, so please, I do not want you worrying yourself to death, I am on this, I promise, I will protect the lake at all costs."

I breathed a huge sigh of relief, never in my life had I needed him on my side more than now, and I was so glad he was. Alone, I would never have been able to stop Pete, he really had come through for me in my hour of need. It is strange how much my life has changed in the last few weeks, considering a year ago I was afraid to return here.

My father had always felt like a stranger to me, and I cannot deny, I had not had a great deal of trust in him, and yet in just fourteen days, I find myself glad, knowing he was there helping, and I actually have no idea why, but I feel I can trust him.

I am not good with trust, I have been let down so much in my life, Han had been the only person I had ever really felt safe with, and yet here I was with Randolph, my dad, and Shelly all standing with me, and it felt new and different, yet nice. Han always told me life could be complicated and messy, well she was not wrong there, and she was so right, and yet out of all the chaos and pain, I have found something that was actually far more important to me than I realised.

With the right support and encouragement, I had somehow changed, and gone from being nervous of everything, to feeling just a little more confident, so much so, I was making decisions that would shape the rest of my life, and they were actually pretty good ones. I still think I have a terrible ability to pick men, the obvious example being Ken, but in a way, even though I had arrived filled with panic, I did feel a little better inside, I did feel I had a little more belief in myself.

It had felt like a long day, and Shell wanted to cook, and I felt wasted. Pete worried me, and I was worried about Felix, and Esme had still not appeared, yet Randolph had told me he had told her, so where was she?

Back on the road down the side of the lake, John Duncan drove up the driveway of the four acres site owned by Edgar Johnson. He pulled up outside the large ornate six bedroom house. John sat back and gave a sigh as he turned to look at Jane.

"This guy is a decent guy, and Pete will rip him off. One way or another, we need to find a way to protect him." She smiled and lifted a hand to his cheek.

"John, we will protect her, just talk straight, and tell him what you know, he will see reason." He nodded.

"I hope so, it has been quite a few years since I lived here."

He pulled on the lever and the door opened; Jane made her way out of the other side. As he walked towards the front steps, the large front door opened, and a tall balding man stood with a smile on his face.

"Well, John Duncan, now this is a surprise." John gave a smile.

"It has been too long Edgar; I am happy to see you looking so good." Edgar smiled.

"I cannot say I am surprised really, I wondered if you would hear about the sale and follow in your father's footsteps, he always wanted this place also."

"My father always said you were a wise old buzzard, but there is a lot more to it than that, but I do need to sit and talk to you." He pulled back the door and opened it wider, and John introduced Jane to him.

There was some small talk catching up as Edgar led them into the main living room. They sat down and chatted for a while, about the land and the forest that they both shared, and John's dad's instincts on the farm, and Edgar appeared happy and relaxed as he talked with great fondness about the house and land around him. He even mentioned Emily and Han spending their late summers picking apples in his orchard. Edgar sat back with a smile.

"Emily has grown into a lovely girl John; she reminds me greatly of Amelia. Han was a good influence on her, I was in the village yesterday, and a great deal are talking about how nice it is to have her back here. I was going to call round at some point in the week and welcome her home." John smiled and gave a nod.

"She would love that, Emily is one of the main reasons I am here, I am not sure if you are aware, but she finished university, and is a fully qualified ecologist now?"

"No... I knew she went, Han was very proud of her, good for her." John gave another nod.

"Edgar, it is why I am here." Edgar frowned.

"Really, I thought this would be about your brother in law trying to step on your toes. What does this have to do with young Emily?" John looked at Jane, and she shrugged. He turned back to Edgar.

"Edgar, Emily is going to enact the trust that Amelia planned, she is going to preserve the whole of her property under Amelia's trust, and carry out studies, in the hope of keeping it the wild beauty it always has been." Edgar nodded understanding.

"I am glad to hear that, too many places are being lost to developers." Jane frowned.

"Excuse me, but if you feel that way, why are you selling your property?" He turned and looked at her.

"Peter McDougal assured me, he wants the house and to save the land, and his price is far more than I thought it would be. I have seen a house in the village that suits me and the wife better. The way I see it, I downsize and the kids get a helping hand with their own aspirations. Our Paige has some great ideas for her own textile business, she wants to expand, and I can help with that." Jane shook her head.

"He has a house in Hampstead, and it is bigger and set in far more land than this plot. Edgar excuse me for being forward, but you are aware he only wants this land for his new fracking operation are you not?"

Edgar sat back and looked at John, and then Jane. It was very clear he had no idea, he lifted a hand and rubbed his chin, then looked straight at John Duncan.

"John, I have known you since you were a kid, hell, I let you date my daughter once. Look me in the eyes and tell me you are on the level, and this is not some sort of family competition thing, and I will believe you." John looked him square in the eyes, and did not flinch.

"Edgar, I know you are aware of the gas below this land, and I also know it was you and my dad that stood up with Han, and refused to sell. I will not deny, there is professional competition between Pete and myself, but this is not about that. Edgar, if you must sell, as a friend and neighbour, I would ask you sell it to Emily's trust, so it will be preserved forever. Hell, sell it to her and live here rent free, and if you do not believe me, then fine, sell the house to Pete, but before you do that, sell me the rights to drill the gas on your property, so that I can ensure no one ever goes near it." Edgar smiled as he looked at John.

"Hell lad, you are as wily as your dad, he always had a way of making sense that put others out of the frame. So, this Pete, he wants to do what here exactly?"

"Look I do not know his exact plans, but what I do know, is his drill team are primed ready, and he has a demolition company ready on standby. The way I see it, as soon as you are out, he will scrape this site clean, and set up two drills at each end. I have worked out from those who are working for him, he will go deep under my land and take what he can, and go deep under the lake for what is below Emily's. Edgar, you know what that will do to the lake, you saw the damage that could be caused twenty three years ago. Now I ask you, is that the legacy you want to leave to this village?"

Edgar Johnson sat back and gave the matter a great deal of thought, he was not a man to rush, he liked to take his time and consider every point before he made a decision. One of the reasons that land had not officially sold yet, was that he had spoken at length to his wife and children. He wrinkled his face and looked back at John.

"Alright lad, I know you are good sort, and I trust you. The problem is I have made an agreement with Peter, now the way I see it, you are telling me this Peter has lied, and as you know, that will not go kindly with me, so, show me your proof." John smiled and turned to Jane.

"Show him."

Jane reached down and opened her case, John was very on the ball, he knew his neighbour better than Edgar had realised, Jane lifted out copies of paperwork, she looked at Edgar, and her professional face on.

"My Johnson, John made it clear you would want to see everything, so I made copies of everything we have for your file. We are still awaiting some things, but I will have copies sent as soon as I have them. Let me see now, this is the copy of his agreement with Expo Drilling, whom I believe was the company who approached you last time?" Edgar frowned; he clearly was no fan. Jane continued.

"This is a copy of Cartwrights Demolition, and as you can see, it lists house and landscape removal. Macmillan Waste Removals, to remove all debris off the site, and here we have the adverts for a crew as labourers from Simpsons Recruitment Agency. Now I will add, you cannot divulge the source for this information, as we have flown under the radar to acquire them, but all of this is strictly legitimate, and you may check for yourself." He gave a frustrated sigh.

"So, this Peter thought he could double cross me on the deal. I should have known the deal was too good to be true. John, I want to confront him on this, before I decide anything." John gave a

nod.

"I would expect nothing less of you. Look Edgar, this is not a loss, we still want to purchase if you are set on selling, but we want to preserve the whole area in one large trust, if Pete falls through, you have lost nothing, I will match his price for you."

"It means that much to you?" John smiled.

"Yes, Edgar, my daughter wants to honour her mother's dream, and I want to see that happen." Edgar gave a slight nod.

"Yeah, she was a lovely girl was Amelia, and I see it in little Emily. Give me a few days to sort things out. No matter what happens, you will have the gas rights to keep the lake safe." John gave a long sigh of relief.

"Thanks Edgar, Emily is worrying herself to death, she will be so pleased when I tell her, I owe you big for this."

"Your dad taught our Pat everything he knows; I was always grateful to him. He has done well working the land because of that, I reckon we are even now."

It took a further forty minutes of talk, before John stood up and shook Edgar by the hand, he had not got a full deal, but he had what it would take to stop Pete, and that was all that mattered. He came out and jumped in the car and closed his eyes for a second.

"I hope this is enough, I know Pete, he is a slimy operator, if I do not save that lake, what little I have rebuilt with Emily will be shot to hell." Jane took his hand and gave it a squeeze.

"You know, I think she gets the overthinking and worrying from you. John, you did good, trust him, Edgar is no fool, he will make the right choice." He gave a nod, as he pushed in the key.

"I hope so, Emily will never forgive me if I do not pull this off."

I was lay back on the bed letting my thoughts drift, when I heard the door open, and looked down between my boobs, to see Shelly stood in her black knickers, crop top, and holding a large silver spoon. She looked confused; I watched her staring at me.

"What?" She frowned.

"Do you like, or really like rice?" I sat up.

"I don't mind it, why do you ask?" She considered the moment, and waved her large spoon.

"I am not a great cook, and I usually buy rice from the take out, but the nearest is thirty one miles away... I looked... The thing is, I put some in a pan, added water, and it really expanded." I frowned.

"Expanded, in what way?"

"The pan filled up really fast, so I had to use the bigger pan." Okay, so that made sense.

"This may be a stupid question, but what pan did you start with, and what pan is it in now?" She frowned and looked even more confused.

"Well... You see, at first it was the smallest, because you know, it is just us two." It made sense.

"So... You went a size up; it is no biggie really."

"Yeah, actually, I had to use the largest, it went mental and would not stop, and now I am looking for a very hungry Chinese village to join us for dinner." I smirked.

"You can freeze it, and it looks like rice will be on the menu for a while. Shell, I use half a tea cup per portion, and a little bit more." She nodded.

"Yeah, I wish you had told me sooner. I will freeze some, and use it up with other things, and you know, it will speed up meal making in the future."

I slid off the bed and grabbed my phone, I felt it was better to oversee her cooking. I followed her down to the kitchen, where she was cooking curry. I looked at her.

"How hungry are you, it is probably a good thing we can freeze curry as well. You know Shell, for someone who lived alone before you moved in with me, your potions sizes are a tad large."

She looked in the pan, and then down at her stomach, then mine, I looked down at my flattish belly.

"What?"

"You may have a point, I look at you, then the pan, and then my stomach, and I am starting to think Felix has a point, I eat too much." I chuckled.

"God Shell, life is about living and enjoying yourself, you like food, why worry about it?" She shrugged.

"I look at you with your pert boobs and flat belly, and you know, I looked like that once, I had the figure of a ballerina when I was sixteen, and now I am heading towards Sumo."

I could not help but laugh, she really was fun to be around. I walked down the kitchen and pulled open the pantry door, and reached in for a bottle of wine, and looked the label. 'Elderberry flower Chardonnay.' Han certainly made some different wines. I headed to the table and picked up the cork screw, and wound it in to the top.

Behind me in the living room, I heard the door knocker, Shell turned and frowned.

"Who the hell is that?" I shrugged.

"Not sure, but we are topless, hold on." I had my shirt on the back of the chair, I lifted a t shirt out of the wash basket and threw it to her. "Wrap up just in case."

I pulled on my shirt and walked into the living room, and over to the door, I opened it a little and smiled as I saw my dad, then pulled the door wide.

"Dad!" He smiled, as Jane came up the path towards us.

"I had some free time so thought I would grab that coffee on offer." I smiled a big smile. I stepped back to free up the door.

"You are always welcome, both of you, come on in, have you eaten, we were just making a meal?"

Dad and Jane smiled as I led them through the kitchen, where Shell stood in her t shirt cooking, she gave a smile.

"Hey guys, we are having chicken curry and rice, lots of rice, yell out if you want some."

Dad appeared really happy, and he joined in as the four of us sat down to eat, and drink Han's, actually really nice wine, as he filled me on the events with Mr Johnson. I listened carefully as I ate, and sniffled, the curry was pretty spicy, as he laid out his ideas. I looked up from my plate.

"Dad, the trust is not even set up yet, I posted the papers today, Kate will have them in the morning. Outbidding Pete or matching his offer is a going to be a lot of cash, he would have set a high bar, he is that desperate to get hold of this land." Jane lifted her wine glass.

"That is why we got him to agree to selling the rights to the gas. Even if Pete gets that land, he will not have rights, and will have a property useless to him, either way Emily, it will tie his hands." I nodded.

"Yeah, that was a really smart move, I never would have thought of that." My dad smiled at me.

"That was Jane, even I missed it. Look Emily, Edgar is going to talk with Pete and then he will let me know what he will do. His property is good land, and for you a bonus if we can get it." I frowned.

"How?" He chuckled and shook his head.

"You will need staff, Emily, with you Shelly and Randolph, you will still need more to protect the trust. The way I see it, anyone you bring in will have quarters and a base to operate out of, even you will need extra wardens at times to watch the place."

It was something I had not thought of yet, I suppose he was right, and I realised I really had to sit and work out a full plan for what the trust was going to achieve. I had plenty of time to really work everything out, I had text Pam, she would give me some great advice, after all she had run a full operation for over a year in the states.

We finished the meal, and relaxed, I was nice to have dad here with me and I kept smiling, it is so weird. A month ago, I would never have seen this at all, and yet here he was for the second time in two weeks, and we had spoken a lot on the phone and in text. I think I had spoken more with him in a week, than I had in the last three years. We finished the meal, and with another bottle open, dad was driving so only had a half glass, but I topped up Jane, and with Shell, we headed out into the garden.

Jane loved the place and was blown away by the island, and walked down the steps with Shell to take a look from the jetty. I walked slowly with my dad at my side, he glanced at me.

"I have spoken with Randolph, he told me about what happened on the island." I stopped and turned to him.

"You know about them?" He nodded.

"Emily, your mother was my wife, of course I knew, why do you I think I encouraged her to visit as much as possible?" I felt shocked.

"Why have you not told me this before?" He understood.

"Emily, Han wanted to take you through the process of learning, it was her duty to teach you. She made me promise to say nothing until she had filled you in, sadly we lost her before she could fulfil her task." I guess I understood that, I suppose he was aware of everything.

"Okay I can understand that, so, it really is true about Randolph, mum and Jessie have different dads?" He nodded and looked me in the eyes.

"Emily, Jessie is aware of them too, and if she is, so is Pete. Han was convinced he was dark of heart and planned to subvert Jessie, never forget that. Pete will still covert this land, and to be honest, your mother also thought the same. We never knew what his real intentions have been, but Han honestly believed it was to destroy the Nairn, you must ensure they are protected." I gave a sigh.

"Nothing is ever easy or simple is it?" He smiled.

"There is great value to be found within the struggles of life Emily, and the reward for that, is endless." I smiled.

"You sound like Han." He winked.

"Well, that was your mother, but I assumed Han taught it her."

"Dad... You know... This, me and you, I like this." He gave a soft nod and his twinkled.

"I do too, I can be a stubborn old fool, and at times stupid, but I made it, and I am here, and I am behind you."

It felt so nice to hear that as I looked into his eyes, there was such kindness behind them, and I could really understand why my mum had loved him. Once you took away his status and his houses and all of his global empire, he was at heart just an ordinary man, a man who had loved an extraordinary woman, and from that, I had been born. I turned to see Jane stood on the end of the jetty talking with Shelly, I was hoping it was not ghost stories, I reached out and took dad's hand.

"Come on, come and see the island, and watch the sun set with me."

I gently pulled, and he followed, and somehow, I felt if my mum really was watching with Han, she would be smiling to see him protect and love their child.

Chapter Twenty Seven

Night Guest

It is hard to put to into words, my joy at having my dad come round and stay for a meal with us. Sitting at my table and watching him eat food we prepared, and sharing my table, felt very special and gave me a huge thrill. It is strange to see him, sat with another woman, but I cannot really blame him, a life alone and isolated can at times feel like a prison, I know, I have felt alone a great deal in my life.

It was nice to sit in the garden and just talk, as Shelly kept Jane company, and it gave me a chance to discover aspects of my father that I had never really known about. I could not help but feel that maybe in getting married, she had opened up a little of the man he lost after the death of my mother, and through that, he had found a way to open up to me. I have wondered in these last few days, if I had to come back here, back to my mother's roots, before he could really understand who I was.

I had been so afraid of returning, and yet I am starting to wonder, if coming home and standing in my mother's footprints, has in a way, repeated the past. Did I have to complete the journey she was making when she died, fulfilling this role in her stead? My father and I have been so distant from each other for all of my life, and yet suddenly he is here, almost as though the parts of me that are my mother have called to him, is that what all of this is really about, the connection of the land, myself, and my father? Are we all bonded by this house and the island in some sort of strange connected way, did I have to be here in order to be seen as the person I am? I had no way of really knowing or fully understanding, all I know is, tonight meant something, it had meaning, and it deeply mattered to me.

As the night wore on and we had to say goodbye, it felt a little sad, but I had the joy of knowing, I would see him again soon. Gone were the days where I could wait eighteen months between his appearances, and something I had never thought possible, was I could pull him close and hug him, and he would respond. The smile on his face as he walked to the car, was such a thrill, it is ridiculous really, as I am almost twenty two, and yet for me, I was the biggest thrill, and I felt a great deal of happiness and joy within me as I closed the door.

Shell and I were tired, it had felt like a long day, and I made us both a coffee. We headed up to our rooms, her to work on some editing she had to do, and I just wanted to relax. I sat back on my bed and let my mind wander as I thought of the night, it had been so lovely, although it had started to rain, which brought an end to the night's events.

Outside the wind picked up, and the rain tapped as it bounced off the glass behind the drawn curtains, and it had a gentle relaxing rhythm to it. I looked at the mirror and smiled as I saw Han's and mum's pendants hanging together.

"Mum, dad came tonight, and he had a meal with me, and it made me so happy. I wish you could have been here with me too, but sat talking with me in the garden, he told me a lot more about you, and it felt special and nice."

I sat back and lifted my cup, and sipped feeling happy, when suddenly there was a bang against the window, and I jumped almost spilling my coffee. I put my coffee on the bedside unit, and slid off the bed slowly, now I know it sounds strange, but honestly, it has been so weird since I came back, as I approached the curtain, I was afraid there was going to be a ball of white light outside. To be honest, my mum had appeared to me in the circle, and Shell had filmed Han's visit. I pulled back the curtain carefully, the rain and wind were lashing into the window.

At first, I did not notice, but as I pulled closer, I saw the small figure getting drenched with their back to the glass, as they balanced on the narrow window ledge. Seeing the wet blonde hair, I understood it was Esme, and I reached for the latch, and pushed the window open. The power of the wind was strong, and I had to really strain to hold it open, as it felt like it wanted to yank my arm, and swing wide open. I held it firm and leaned out enough to look at her, she looked afraid.

"Esme, come on, get inside, it is not safe for you there."

She looked like she was using all her strength, just to stay on the ledge, so I opened the window wider, and reached out with my hand, whilst the window rattled on my other arm. It was not the easiest position to be in, but I manged to get the back of my hand against her front.

"Esme, hold my hand, and I will guide you in."

She clamped on to my hand, and I could just about hear her faint voice, but the wind was so strong, I could not really understand her words properly. She side stepped slowly towards me, holding onto my hand firmly, as I held the tugging window, and felt the jerks on my arm. Slowly she edged nearer looking scared, and finally, she stepped back over the lip of the window onto my inside sill. I heaved and pulled the window closed, and gave a relieved gasp, as I looked at her dripping.

"Are you alright, you should not have flown up in weather this bad, Esme you could have been very badly hurt." She nodded and was trembling.

"I am sorry, I could not get away until now, Barrack has told all of us to stay away from you until you embrace the light at the ceremony. I have a lot of jobs to do in preparation." I looked round the room, she was really shivering.

"The radiator is on, see that big thing below the window, it gives me heat. Sit on the ledge there and warm up, I will get you a towel... Flannel, something to dry you off faster."

I turned to my drawers and pulled open the bottom one, it was where I kept my beach towels and spare sponges and flannels etc. I pulled one out, and turned back to her, and draped it round her.

"Here, rub yourself dry." She pulled it round her and smiled at me, as I crouched in front of her.

"You are so kind like Han was."

I smiled at her, in many ways I was fascinated, she was so tiny, and yet so perfect, a doll sized human like being, with the added bonus of wings. Her thoughts her feelings and emotions were perfectly the same as any human, and yet there was a child like innocence to her, and all the other Nairn, and I felt it was like a part of the humans that we had somehow lost or forgotten.

"Is that better, are you warming up a little?"

She gave a nod, her eyes were so large and filled with life, and it was clear, they held a wealth of emotional intelligence.

"I am alright Emily, we get wet a lot, it is part of our life, I was a little scared. My mother has told me not fly high in the big winds, but I wanted to get to you, and you were in the top of your box." I gave a little giggle.

"We call them houses." She nodded as she looked round.

"Your house, has lots of boxes inside, and they are pretty, but very large."

"This is my bedroom; it is where I sleep. Inside our houses we have different rooms, for different things. I sleep here, Shelly has one on the other side, and in between that, I have a room where I wash and clean myself." She frowned.

"You do not clean in the lake; I have seen you do that?" I shook my head.

"I swim in the lake not to clean, but to cool down and have fun." She appeared to understand that. "See, I will show you."

I held out my hand, and she carefully slid onto it, and sat in my palm as I walked to my door. I could feel the warmth of her body on my skin, and it felt strange to know that I had a living tiny human sat there. I walked through my door and pointed.

"Shelly has her room down there." I pushed open the bathroom door. "This is the room where I wash, we call it a bathroom."

Esme looked round in wonder, I suppose for her, a creature that lived outside in the woodland on the island, this must all be really strange and interesting. To be honest, the bathroom needed an upgrade, it was very out of date. I showed her the shower above the bath and tried to explain how it worked, but she appeared confused, she watched as I turned it on, and her eyes grew huge in her face, and her voice was filled with awe.

"You can make rain, Emily, that is powerful light."

I could not help but giggle, as I turned it off and tried to explain, that it was not me, but a pump, which sucked the water up into the pipe, and allowed it to fall as rain on me. I am not sure she fully understood, but she appeared happy with my explanation, and I could think of no other way to explain it, so left it. I lifted my hand, and Esme crawled onto my shoulder, still wrapped in her flannel, and I walked back out onto the top of the stairs. Shelly popped her head out of her door.

"Who are you talking to?" I turned to her, and she saw Esme on my shoulder.

"Greetings and well met Lady Shelly." She came out of her room.

"Hey Esme, we were worried because we had not seen you, are you alright?" She walked up to Esme and me.

"I am alright, Emily is showing me the rooms of this box, and it is very strange to me, but I find it very pretty." Shelly smiled, I turned to look at Esme sat near my cheek.

"Have you eaten, or do you need a drink of anything?" Once again, she looked as if her eyes would pop out of her head.

"You want to share food with me?" I was not sure what to say.

"That is alright isn't it, I have not broken another rule, have I?" She gave me a big smile, and shook her head.

"Emily, to offer food is a great honour to a guest. To share food in your box, would be the highest honour to all Nairn."

I was not sure why, it was just food, but it appeared I had hit the jackpot by accident, after all, if Esme told her people, Barrack may think better of me.

We headed down to the kitchen, stopping briefly in the living room so she could see it. The pictures of my mum and Han were a huge hit, although it was not easy trying to explain that I did not paint them, I decided to point out other stuff and distract her. It was strange, this was all so new and wonderful to her, where as to me, this was home and normal life, it really was quite odd, but cute at the same time.

I find Esme fascinating, I am an ecologist, and I have dedicated my life to the study of living environments, and the interactions of all who live there, in order to protect and preserve them. With Esme, a creature I had always stated was not possible in the scale of evolution, I had a million questions which I was yearning to get answered, and as we entered the kitchen, I knew, this was day one of a life time of study for me.

I set her down on the kitchen table, and let her look round, it appears she had never been in the house, but had spent hours sat with Han and Randolph outdoors. For her, all of this was as new and as magical as it was for me, and her excitement bubbled away as she saw what to her, was a huge table.

"Your eating plane is huge; it is like an island of its own." Shelly gave a giggle as she sat down.

"We call this a table, we sit at it to eat, but we also sit here and talk a lot, it is sort of a meeting place for people who come in the house." She nodded happily, her eyes wandering as she took everything in.

"We have one in the temple circle, but we do not sit at it, we sit on it."

She slipped off her flannel, which on her looked as big as a blanket, and walked around the top of the table, and I smiled at her, but noticed her wet footprints.

"Are you still wet Esme?" She smiled up at me, her blue eyes twinkling with excitement.

"I am alright Emily; I am used to it." I frowned at her.

"But you were shivering, are you sure?" She nodded.

"I was very scared, the wind took me and I had to fight hard, I still need to grow, I am not as strong as Felix."

Shelly got up and headed into the living room, she returned a few seconds later, as I tried to work out, just how exactly I could serve food to a Nairn, who was no bigger than a doll. Shelly smiled as she held up a hair dryer.

"Here, this will dry you off."

She plugged it into the wall socket and pointed it at Esme, and then flicked the switch as I turned to look. The warm air blasted out, and Esme staggered back with a squeal, as she slid along the table, and I panicked. Understanding Shelly lifted the blower, as Esme sat up looking positively thrilled.

"You can make wind too, oh golden blooms, the light with you two is so strong." Shelly shrugged and smiled as she clicked the power down, then pointed the blower back as Esme.

The warm air streamed out, as Esme sat back, leaning on her arms, with her long blonde hair wafting around behind her, and she shrieked with laughter, as the air blew over her. I had to giggle; she had the most amazing high pitched happy laugh I had ever heard, it was so sweet and happy, and it made me feel so warm inside. Shelly lifted the blower and looked at Esme.

"Do you feel drier?" Esme touched her top, and looked up with bright blue wide eyes, it was a look of pure innocent amazement.

"I am dry, oh light of lights, I have never known such things, this is indeed a magical place."

I spooned out some curry and rice into bowls, and put one in the microwave, set the timer and turned back to Esme.

"I know you eat fruit, but what else do you eat?" She sat smiling on the table.

"We eat many things, there is a bounty of food on the island. I love the red berries that Han gave us, but there are many fruits, seeds and grains, as well as many roots and leaves that we harvest." I looked at Shell.

"Rice is a grain, I guess she will be fine with that, what about curry?" Shell shrugged, as Esme looked round at her.

"What is Carry?" Shelly looked down to the table.

"It has veg, meat, and spices in it, we boil it to cook it." Esme looked a little confused.

"What is boil?" I lifted the pan and tipped it slightly to show her, Shell had made a lot, so even with a second helping in the microwave, we still had a lot left.

"We put everything in a pan and then add water, then we put it on the fire and heat it up, and let it bubble for a while." Esme understood.

"You heat kill everything like Randolph does." Shell looked at me.

"Heat kill?" I smirked, I felt it was a pretty good description of Shelly's cooking. Esme looked at me.

"Veda says it is wrong to add the heat to kill the food, it should be taken into the body in its natural state." It made sense to a degree, I loved salad, so I completely got that, after all, no one would boil lettuce, or at least I hope not. Esme looked at the huge pan.

"I will try heat killed Carry."

I really did not have plates for fairies, so I grabbed the blue top off a two litre milk carton I had washed out, compared to her size, it was still quite large, but it was the best I had. I took a tea spoon, and grabbed a little of the cold curry, and put it on one side of the blue top. I then spooned a little cold rice onto the other side, and then something occurred to me.

"Esme, have you ever eaten spices?" She was sat on the table watching me, and she shook her head.

"I may have Emily, we may call them something different to you, what do they taste like." Now there was a question, I looked at Shell, who appeared as nonplussed as I did, she shrugged.

"They are spicy, I have no idea how to describe it." It was a good point, I looked at Esme.

"I think the best way to describe them, would be, they can heat you up without fire." She appeared very impressed and got very excited.

"REALLY!?" I nodded.

"I suppose they taste like the sun does."

I could see she understood that, or at least I hope she did. Explaining human life, suddenly feels very difficult, which is strange, as I can talk about any habit and way of life for any British creature. Esme appeared very keen and excited, so I thought, what the hell, give it a go. I placed the top with the food on down in front of her.

"The rice is the white grain and is cooling, because you are smaller than all my other guests, you are probably better off, picking up a rice grain, and dipping it in the curry." She looked very excited and nodded at me, and then she stood up and bowed very politely.

"Emily, and Lady Shelly, I am deeply honoured by this gesture of food sharing, and I vow a bond of eternal friendship to you both for this act." I smiled, and felt I should reciprocate, and bowed back, Shelly giggled.

"Young Mistress Esme, you honour us both greatly by accepting this gesture of our equal bonds in sisterhood."

She smiled, sat down, and lifted a grain of rice, and dipped it in the curry as the microwaved pinged, and I turned and opened the door, to grab our food. Shelly sat down, and lifted her fork ready, I turned back as Esme popped the rice grain in her mouth and chewed.

I handed Shelly her hot bowl, grabbed mine and sat down in front of her, Shelly handed me a tall glass of water. I lifted my fork and scouped up a mixture of rice and curry and glanced at Esme, who had suddenly stopped and her face was turning beetroot. My heart almost stopped she looked so red, and her eyes were growing huge, I panicked.

"Are you alright Esme?"

I could almost see the heat rising from her head. She swallowed and opened her mouth, and out came a long almost painful gasp. I looked at Shelly who was staring at her, she looked at me as I stared at Esme feeling panicked.

"Emmy, she is not going to explode or anything is she?"

I was not sure, and as she turned even redder. Esme suddenly shot into the air, and at high speed. She flew around the room above our head making little strange gasping sort of squeaks. She had her tongue sticking out of her mouth, as she flew so fast, she was becoming a blur, and I went into instant panic mode, and jumped up and flapped around not knowing what to do.

"Oh God Shell, she is overheating, what the hell do we do...? Oh Christ, I hope she does not melt, I could not handle that."

Shelly gave off a giggle, stood up, lifted her tall glass of water, and then whistled loudly. The tiny blur in the air came to a screeching halt, Esme saw the water, and flew like a possessed hornet towards it. She snatched it out of Shelly's hand, lifted the huge glass and stuck her head in the water, and I flopped to my seat with a bump, as I watched her flying and holding a full tumbler of water, as she gulped. I blinked feeling relieved and completely surprised.

"Wow, for your size, you're are pretty bloody strong Esme, that would be the equivalent of me lifting the boat out of the lake and drinking from it."

Shell took the glass as Esme returned to a normal colour, she hovered for a moment making little panting noises, and then dropped to the table next to her plate, and sat down. She panted a little, and then looked at me with a huge smile.

"Emily that was wonderful." I blinked for a moment feeling stumped.

"Huh... You enjoyed that?" She nodded, looking very happy.

"I have never tasted the sun before; it gave me a lot of energy. I like your carry, it is wonderful."

Shelly started to giggle as I felt a little lost for words, mythological creatures were far more complex and confusing than I had thought they would be. I looked at her smiling at me.

"Are you alright, I mean, was that not too hot for you, Esme, I do not want you harmed, it is alright to say if it burned you?" She shook her head looking really excited.

"It is wonderful, never in my life have I felt food come to life inside me, and I felt such energy, it was wonderful. Can I give some to Felix, with energy like that, no paste beast will get him?" I shrugged, feeling a little lost in all of this.

"Yeah, I want to help him, I will wrap some up for him."

It all felt very strange to me, but there again, not much of my life had been normal compared to other people. We talked to Esme and I explained the work I did, and how I knew that bees, or 'Paste Beasts,' did not like smoke, it made them sleepy. She understood, but the Nairn never touched fire, as they knew it harmed the life of the plants, animals and trees.

I advised her only to eat the rice, and she had quite an appetite, considering her size. We talked and ate, and she explained that Felix was much stronger and had more power with the light than her. She told me the rice grain and carry, gave her a big energy, and she wanted Felix to have some before he went to get the comb of sweet paste for the ceremony. Apparently, honey was a delicacy of the Nairn, and it also gave them great energy, but because it was so dangerous for them to collect, it was rarely eaten.

I suppose that made sense, I would not be in a rush to take honey off a bee that was angry and the size of a large dog. We talked of Han, and Esme told me how she and Felix would sneak off and fly to the jetty to meet her, and she would sit on the wall and tell them stories of Amelia. It pulled at my heart strings, and yet I smiled, as I remembered the hours I sat alone with her listening to her stories of my mother as a young girl.

In a strange way, I knew the life of my mother through Han, and I had never realised before, but that was her way of dealing with the loss of her. In educating me on the truth of who I was and where I had come from, she was easing her own inner pain. Hearing Esme tell me of how Han told her the same tales, made me sad, because it was only now that I was starting to see that at times, Han had felt as lonely as I did, and she too missed her daughter, which appeared a great pain to her.

I never noticed growing up, she always seemed so calm and so relaxed. Han for me was always a rock, the stability and the assurance I needed when I was in pain. Suddenly, sat the table, I could see that she had kept strong for me, when deep down inside, she must have been feeling the same as me within.

It was getting late, and I felt very tired, the rain was still lashing down, and the wind was even stronger, and I felt it was not safe for Esme to return just yet. She told me she would sleep under the cabbage plants, but I would not have it, I could not bear the thought of her out there, although it was silly really, she lived in a woodland.

I took her back to my room, and put a soft cushion on the chair, and she curled up on it, and I laid her flannel over her. I crossed to bed and slid my off top, and she smiled at me.

"You are a pretty colour, and you have nice shapes to you, I think you are very beautiful."

I have no idea why, but as I looked down to my naked breasts, I felt my face burn, it was crazy, a fairy was looking at my boobs, and I blushed, oh dear, my mind is messed up. I grabbed my duvet and slipped into bed, and Esme looked at me.

"Is the Carry starting to work on you now, does it take longer to work with the big people?"

I felt my face go even redder, and swallowed hard trying to find a road out of my embarrassment, I took the easy route and gave a nod.

"Yes Esme, with us big people it does take much longer." She smiled and gave a nod.

"Oh, that is good, I had thought you had felt shamed because of your big lumps."

She put her head down and closed her eyes, and I slid down under the duvet, feeling stupid, but I smiled. I loved their simple innocence and pure honesty, how wonderful the world would be, if the humans could be similar.

I leaned on my pillow and closed my eyes, and gave a long sigh, the bed was soft and warm and I relaxed feeling a little more relieved to know, that Esme would talk to her friends, and tell them of her great adventure in the box of Emily, with Carry and rice. I smiled, she is cute and lovely, and I could really understand why Han wanted so desperately to protect them.

Two minutes later I peeped over the top of the duvet, she was curled in a tight ball, under the flannel, with her eyes closed. She was breathing softly, as outside the rain poured, and I felt happy to know she was safe with me.

Across the lake, under a large outcrop of rock, hidden by the thick undergrowth, Aubrianne sat in a chair woven from reeds and looked at Veda sat opposite her.

"She was told not to go." Veda shrugged in her chair.

"We both knew she would, come on, you cannot be that surprised? Esme has bonded with her just like she did Han, and no matter how you look at it, great good has come from it." Aubrianne looked irritated.

"Barrack will not be happy about this, how can good come from it?" Veda sat back and pulled her robes around her for comfort.

"Emily lived in doubt, without Esme, she would never have excepted the truth. Esme has a light within her that will one day glow to match hers, and she will guide a very powerful Watcher. Our clan will benefit greatly from the bond that grows between them." Aubrianne nodded, she understood that, she had seen it with Han.

"Emily will grow old and wither and die, Esme took the loss of Han deeper than most could see, and in time, it will ache in her heart. I never wanted this for her." Veda nodded softly.

"Even now after all of the years that have passed us by, you still feel the loss of Rachel, I understand your concerns for your daughter. Answer me this honestly, I remember how Hosta warned you, and yet you still bonded with Rachel, and cared for her deeply, tell me, did you honestly think you could prevent Esme from doing what you were also incapable of?" Aubrianne gave a sad sigh.

"Veda, you cannot blame me for not wanting my child to suffer as I did?" Veda shook her head softly.

"No, I do not, but I also know that the bond you shared protected our clan for many years, I saw it, and like Emily, Rachel would have never found her belief, if like your daughter, you had not gone to her and revealed yourself. Aubrianne, I had many conversations with your mother such as this one, and she too understood that it was your bond and your love of our watcher that ultimately saved us, for without Rachel, all would have been lost. I have often thought of those times of struggle, and how Rachel risked everything to save us, and I find, that it is within your line our salvation has come to us twice now."

"As I said, I understand what you say, but that does not make it easier for me." Veda gave a chuckle, and her old lined face wrinkled.

"You had the means to stop her, you know the danger of the winds, and yet you closed your eyes and allowed her the moment she needed. Such trust in the ability of your daughter is remarkable, I seem to remember something similar with Hosta." Aubrianne gave a slight chuckle.

"I have no idea why I tolerate your madness?" Veda smiled.

"Neither did Hosta, and yet we were friends through her whole life."

As the rain lashed down, and Esme dreamed of Emily and her strange beautiful box house, Aubrianne and Veda sat in safety, as the weather pounded the island, smiling and chuckling sat in their chairs made of woven reeds. The Nairn were at ease, and waiting for the ceremony of Emily embracing the light, and taking on the role of protecting the clan.

Chapter Twenty Eight

Time to Move

I woke up around ten, I had slept better than I had in years and felt fresh and alive, and happy, as I slipped out of bed and headed for the stairs. I was not fully awake, but just felt good, as I arrived in the kitchen, and my memory came back, Esme was sat on an up turned egg cup, eating tiny slices of toast with Shelly. She gave a big smile as I walked in, her bright blue eyes twinkled.

"Greetings to the new rising of the day to you Lady Emily." I smiled.

"Good morning, Esme." She chewed her toast.

"I am eating the fire killed and burned bread, which is the mixing of your seeds, I have never known seeds be killed by fire before, I like them." Shelly giggled as I poured a coffee, I blinked as I turned around, I may have slept deep, but my eyes felt a little hazy this morning.

"Esme, when will you see Felix?" She smiled.

"I will take the carry and rice seeds to him this day, he will be in the temple preparing with Barrack until after the sun hangs right above the trees."

I sat down and sipped as I watched her eat, I cannot deny, I am fascinated, especially with her language. It really does surprise me to hear many of our human words mixed in with the language of the Nairn, and I could not deny, had to wonder how much human interaction the Nairn have had in the past for their language to develop on a parallel with ours. I looked as Esme as she ate.

"Esme, has your race known other humans, you know, your people use the word sweet paste, and yet you are called Esme Honeyrain? Esme, honey is the word we use for the sweet paste?"

She blinked and looked surprise.

"It is?" I nodded.

"Yes, it is a human word, and you have it in your name, and there are other words you use, like tree, and grain." She frowned and I felt she was thinking.

"My mother had a human friend called Rachel, she told me often of her, I know she was a human, and all the watchers are, so I think, we have learned some words of your word. We all can speak in a human tongue; we are taught it at the start of our life so we can talk with the watchers."

It made sense, I had just not realised, all of their clan knew Randolph, my mum and Han, I gave a sigh, as I watched, I had so much to learn about this race, because I really needed to protect them. Another thought occurred to me, as Esme finished her food and sat smiling at me, she was really enjoying her stay here.

"Esme, is Felix important to the clan, you know, Randolph said something yesterday about the one called Chandak, he said this Chandak would be happy if Felix failed?" Esme nodded; her bright blue eyes wide open with the wonder of her situation.

"Lady Emily, Felix is the son of Berrendock." I looked at Shelly, she shrugged, I had hoped it would mean something, but it didn't.

"Who is Berrendock?" Esme giggled.

"Lady Emily, he is the son of Barrack." I suddenly realised, and I think Shelly did too, I nodded to Esme.

"This Chandak is a rival to lead the clan, but Felix and his father stand in his way, I fear the politics of your clan are similar to those of the humans." She smiled.

"I know nothing of this polllticki you talk of, but they spar for leadership, if that is what you mean?"

Shelly giggled, she was so cute and lovely, and again I could see the innocence of her race showing, which made me want to protect them more. It was clear they had a structure of their society, which was not unsimilar to our own. To a degree their secret life, meant aspects of their lifestyle which was to protect them, and so there were subtle differences, but none the less, they were very human like in many things, and it fascinated me. Esme slipped off the egg cup, and walked across the table to me, she looked up and smiled.

"I will have to go soon, could I ask something special of you?" I looked down at her and smiled.

"Esme, I would hope you felt confident enough to ask me anything." She smiled, God, she was so gorgeous, I adore her.

"Lady Emily, could I please see the painting of Han and Amelia again?" I smiled, it was such a beautiful moment, she loved Han deeply and missed her a great deal. I nodded at her.

"Of course you may, you know where it is, go on, go have a look, and I will prepare the curry for Felix. Her faint little wings flapped at speed as she gave me the most beautiful smile, and then excitedly, she zoomed from the kitchen, and through the doorway into the living room. Shelly sat with a glazed dreamy stare and a big smile on her face, I giggled at her.

"Remarkable aren't they?" She gave a long happy sigh.

"Emmy, you have no idea of the emotions I have felt in the last twenty four hours, for me, this is my most longing dream come true. I have to tell you, I absolutely love this place, I would give my life to protect it."

I did actually, I was feeling the same, for her it was a dream come true, for me it was something that I never thought could exist, and yet it did, and I was facing it in my ordinary life, and it had sent ripples through my entire being. I served up a portion of the curry and rice, and placed it in a small tinfoil bowl, I was uncertain to how Esme would fly with it, but last night she proved to be stronger than I realised. It was quiet, so I walked round the table, Shelly got up with me, and we leaned round the door to see what Esme was up to.

Esme sat cross legged on the side unit in front of the photo of my mother with Han, I smiled, she was simply sitting and staring up at it. I noticed as she lifted her arm, and wiped her eyes. She had been silently grieving and it hurt to know that, it hurt that she felt as I did. She was trying to be brave, just like me, but inside hidden away, she felt the sorrow of the loss. I walked quietly up to her, Shelly stayed by the door, I think she understood, and I crouched down to bring me eye level with her. Esme swallowed and looked at me, her eyes were still very watery.

"I miss her, but this painting makes me feel better, I swore I would never forget her, and your painting helps me remember."

It was such a simple statement, filled with the purity of innocence, and yet it adequately expressed the huge internal feelings that had lived within me for a year. I nodded at her.

"I see it every day Esme, and like you, I will never forget her and always love her deeply for the life I shared with her. I was once told by Han, to remember is a great tribute, and I believe she was right." Esme gave a small smile and nodded at me.

"You have her heart, I feel it, you have a powerful light, I knew that when you called to me to stop, it is why I came to you, I feel Han inside you." I took a huge deep breath and swallowed, and felt tears in my eyes.

"I want to be Esme, I want to be like her, and I want to protect your people, Han was the mother of my mother, and everyone says I am very like my mother. I have always thought she was like Han, and so to be like my mother, I learned from Han." Esme looked at the picture.

"You look like Amelia, but if what my mother says is true, then you have the same light, and that is a beautiful thing Lady Emily."

She smiled at me and I smiled back, is it crazy that I want this tiny little human like creature to be my friend for life? There was sniffle behind me, and I turned to look back to see Shelly wiping her eyes, I smiled, she was very emotional, but there again, this was her dream come true. Esme stood up, and lifted into the air.

"I have to go, I have tasks to do, and then I must take the carry to Felix." I stood up and headed back to the kitchen, Esme flew at my side. She landed on the table next to the tiny foil bowl, and I looked down at her.

"Go with peace in your heart, and the knowledge that Felix will come through this to stand once again at your side. I gave him a little more than I did you, I feel he will need more of the taste of the sun to get him through this." She smiled a big smile and stepped back, then gave a regal bow.

"I pledge thee my watcher, Emily of the clan of Han, and I will serve thee from this time onwards." It felt somehow a serious moment, and so responded.

"So shall our bond be Esme Honeyrain, daughter of Aubrianne, and you shall have my allegiance always."

She gave me a huge smile, lifted the bowl, and then sprung into the air with it, she hovered in front of Shelly, and she almost went cross eyed trying to focus on Esme. Esme gave a nod of her head.

"I name thee friend always, Lady Shelly of the house of Han." Shelly swallowed hard and teared up.

"I am honoured, and likewise Esme, you are my friend forever."

Esme gave a little giggle, and shot through the open door at high speed, and by the time we got to it and looked out, there was no sign of her, wow, she could fly fast.

Shelly was quiet, far quieter than I had expected, but in a way, I understood that, this was after all her life's ambition. For her, having had her work laughed at, just knowing she was right must have been a massive relief. In a strange way, I also felt it was a bit of a shock to her, after all, she had lived in doubt for so long, striving to prove she was right, that maybe, getting what she always wished for, must have blown her mind completely.

I sat on the doorstep with a fresh drink and stared out at the island, yet again my mind felt cluttered, as it slipped to the ceremony, and also the fate of Felix. It felt unfair I could not help him, and my mind slipped to the words of Randolph again, and pondered what he had said as such as casual remark. Would Chandak be happy to see Felix fail, why would anyone want that? It struck a chord with me, after all hadn't Harry wanted me to fail, or even Pete for that matter? Both of them were hell bent on pushing me to breaking point so I finally broke and lost everything. Was that what was going on in the Nairn, were they so human like, and had their interactions with us worn off on them? It made me think, if they had adopted our language, what else had they learned and embraced from humans?

I felt a cold shiver run down my back and shuddered, simply knowing that even in a race of the ancients, the same qualities and traits of humans existed, bothered me, especially considering, I had vowed to protect all of them.

It is strange how the world works, for a year now, I feel I have been on a journey, as things just happened out of my control, and yet somehow, I feel they were guiding me here. I have started to recognise things without really understanding why, as I thought I was trapped in some sort of unreal cycle. A year ago, I was shocked by the loss of Han, I felt numb, in denial, and kept exploding with emotions, and I have no idea why, but I felt so angry at the world, and afraid of everything. I think I have gone through the whole spectrum of emotions, filled with panic and guilt, and I felt so alone and lonely. Shell pushed me to get anti depressants, but I did not want them, I think I felt I had to go through this, and yet I still do not understand why.

Taking the plunge and returning has not been easy, but it has not been as hard as I had imagined it. I think it has given me a new inner strength I did not know was there, and I have changed everything about the life I had. Here, it feels almost like I am living in a different routine, a different pattern, and as weird as it sounds, I think it suits me better. I feel less jaded today, almost a little hopeful for the future, maybe I needed a purpose in my life, and here I have found it as I start my journey to help the Nairn and save this beautiful idyllic landscape. Today is the first day I have felt like I am actually coming to terms with my new life, a life that will include Shelly, my father, Randolph, and Esme with Felix, and within that knowledge, I feel some joy.

I suppose we all have to grow up and move forward at some point, and maybe this is my time. I suppose, I am still very young and have a lot to learn, not just about life, but also about me, it strikes me that Han told me so much about my mother, but only now, am I really starting to understand the things she said. I am starting to think this was Han's plan all along, she was always a few steps ahead of me, always looking out for my best interests. I think she knew I would take my time and travel a long road of suffering, but maybe she knew that this was the finish line, and having gone through it, she knew deep down, here I would finally find inner peace.

Shelly came through the kitchen behind me and made herself a herbal tea, she came to the door and stepped through at my side, then stood in front of me looking out at the island, I looked up at her.

"It is a lot to take in, isn't it?" She turned with a smile and sat on the path in front of me, her short scruffy hair wafting in the soft breeze, her eyes were alive and with excitement.

"Emmy, my head is filled with thoughts, honestly, I am finding it hard to contain it. I spent most of the night rambling into my voice recorder, because I have observed so much, I could not write it down quick enough to keep up with my brain." She took a huge deep breath.

"You will never understand the significance of this for me, Emmy it is mind blowing, and amazing, and..." She breathed out and I giggled, I had not seen her this happy ever.

"I am glad you got your dream Shell; you deserve it, you really do." She smiled and gave a soft nod; her voice was soft.

"You know Emmy, it is all because of you... You doubted me, and yes at times you laughed with Pam, but you still allowed me to keep searching, you kept pushing me to get my book finished. If I had never met you; I am not sure where I would be, I just know, that being at your side has guided me into my destiny, and I will never forget that, never forget now, this moment, us."

I swallowed hard, she was so sincere it really touched deeply inside me, I smiled, as the emotion surged.

"Shell it is the same for me too you know? I have struggled and you were there, you have stood by me for a year and kept me going. Hell, if it was not for you, I would still be in the flat hating my job and crying myself to sleep every night. I think it has been a team effort... No, it has been an equal partnership."

She gave a nod and smiled at me, she knew, and I understood, she truly was the most remarkable of friends, and I am so lucky to have had her at my side. Shelly gave a sigh.

"When is Randolph coming?" I took a sip of my coffee.

"Not sure, it's Randolph, he just sort of appears, and I have other things to consider." Shell gave a nod, and then looked at me.

"You know if it is too much, I will go in her room and get the robe?" I smiled and shook my head.

"No, Shell, I have to do this at some point, I have left it too long, I think I need to do it, and do it alone." She gave a soft nod.

"Yeah, it is probably for the best, it is good though, you know, first steps and all that, moving forward. I do think it is time to move on a little Emmy." I knew that already.

"Yeah... I am going to bawl like a bitch you know?" She gave a smile.

"We have tissues." She gave a chuckle leaned forward and patted my leg. "I will be here if you need me."

Mugwump sat on the old log, his green clad legs slightly apart allowing room for his large belly. His grey tufts of hair stuck out from under his cloth hood, and he gave a sniffle and wiped his nose on his filthy sleeve. He was one of the oldest of the clan, many thought he was mad, as he preferred to live alone near the edge of the water, eating slugs and talking to himself.

Berrendock was one of a select few, who really spoke to him, after all, he was a distant uncle, and in the past, as crazy as Mugwump could sound, he had always given him good advice. With Felix at his side, he needed the best advice he could get, to try and help his son through his trail of bravery. He looked at the old fat Nairn, with his long nose and wide happy smile, and gave a sigh, and scratched at his short brown beard in frustration.

"Mugwump, this is serious, I need something to help him, he will not survive an attack." Mugwump nodded, and then leant to one side, and let the gas exit him in a noisy fashion, he gave a smile of relief. His voice was high and squeaky.

"I told thee, tis those with whispers that bring the problem, the little leaf will have to find some sting like a nettle and prove him wrong." Berrendock gave another sigh.

"Sting, what sting, he has a blade of crystal, and it is my finest?" Mugwump gave a stern nod.

"AND THAT IS A GOOD THING, NOW NEVER FORGET." Felix frowned and pulled at his dad's robe.

"What is he talking about?" Mugwump rolled his eyes, leaned back and gave a loud hearty laugh, he nodded forward and stared at Felix.

"Twen the light is there, passed ye go little leaf, and then again ye goes, and until thy beasties no longer know." He learned back and gave another huge roar of laughter, and looked up at the trees.

"I tellin em, and they are as deaf as slugs."

"Felix... Felix!"

He turned as he frowned at Mugwump and saw Esme flying

along the path holding something round and shiny. Berrendock turned to see her heading at speed towards them.

"She was told to stay away, and yet she still comes."

He gave a sigh, but smiled as he watched his son watching her, he gave a chuckle and softly nodded his head. He understood the friendship better than any, had he not once had that as a child with Aubrianne? They were more like their parents as children than they realised.

Esme landed softly, and looked over Felix's shoulder as Mugwump was still laughing and looking at the trees, her eyes moved to Felix and she smiled.

"Felix, I bring a gift from Emily, she has food that holds the sun, you can use it." She pulled a leaf off the top of the bowl revealing the curry and rice inside, Felix looked at suspiciously.

"What is it?" Esme smiled.

"It is Carry, Emily heat kills it, and it has the power of the sun and the light." Mugwump slapped his leg and screamed out in laughter.

"Twen the light is there, passed ye go little leaf, and then again ye goes, and until thy beasties no longer know."

Esme handed the bowl over to Felix who was looking unsure, it had a very strange smell and one he did not know, and it looked fire killed. She walked past Felix and right up to Mugwump as he sat laughing on his stump, he calmed down and winked at her, she smiled as she looked at him.

"Mugwump, did you say he should put light in the crystal, and fly past fast?" The old Nairn gave a huge smile and looked up at Berrendock.

"This little flower blooms stronger than all of them." He looked down with a smile. "Esme Honeyrain, ye are the brightest flower of the wooded glade." He looked at Felix.

"Sunshine always blinds those who whisper.... Off, off.... Tis sleep now." He flopped back on his stump, closed his eyes and started to snore, Esme looked really surprised, as she turned to Berrendock.

"That was fast!" Berrendock gave a giggle, he had seen it so many times he was used to it, but loved how impressed Esme was.

"Esme, how does my son use this, did the Lady Emily say

anything?" Esme gave a nod, and looked very serious. Her eyes got wider and wider as she spoke

"You dip the grain in the Carry, and then eat it, and you will taste the sun. It is magical, and the sun will burn up through Felix, and he will be filled with light, and have the power of the whole clan." She frowned.

"Jump in the lake after, you will need it." Berrendock frowned.

"Why?" Esme swallowed.

"The sun inside makes you feel fire killed." Felix's head snapped round.

"WHAT!?" She nodded.

"It is powerful light, only water nulls it." He looked even more nervously at the bowl, and his voice dropped to a whisper, and contained awe.

"Wow, Emily is really more powerful than we thought."

Esme nodded in agreement, and Berrendock looked on confused, Mugwump snored loudly behind them all, and his beard rose and fell as he breathed out. Esme took a deep breathe, and looked at Felix.

"Felix, promise me now, if it is too hard, stop." Her eyes filled with tears, and she gave a tiny sob.

"Please don't die, please come back safely, because Emily and Shelly need you... I need you." Berrendock smiled.

"Esme, I will be with him, and I will make sure he returns, dry your eyes, Chandak may whisper in the ears of the council, but I will not let him win. Felix will come back to you, I swear it." She took a huge breath in and swallowed it, and then nodded, as her bright blue eyes held Felix in her gaze.

"Berrendock, Felix is a very special Nairn, take care of him for me." He gave a nod and rested his arm on Felix's shoulder.

"It is time son." Felix looked terrified but nodded, he turned back to Esme and tried to smile.

"See you soon."

Felix and Berrendock walked away along the path, as Esme watched with tears running from her eyes, she breathed in to calm herself down.

"Felix, don't forget, dip the grain in the Carry!"

He looked back and smiled and gave a nod, and she breathed

a sigh of relief. Esme watched him walking away, and held her hands to her heart, her voice lowered to a whisper.

"Please don't leave me, when the day comes, and the choosing ceremony happens, I choose you Felix.... Felix, I love you." She dropped to her knees and wept, Mugwump continued to snore.

The time had come, I had put it off for too long, I really was not sure I could do this, but deep down inside I knew I had to. If I was going to live here forever, then I had to sort out her room, I could not walk past a closed door for the rest of my life. I looked at Shell.

"I am going to do it, I have to Shell, I have to take a step in the right direction." She simply nodded as me and smiled.

"Hun, go do it, but remember, I will be in my room if you need me."

I turned and walked into the living room, and through to the stairs, I could feel my heart quicken inside me, I was scared, and I am not sure why, but I knew in my heart of hearts this was something I had to do in order to move forward and start my life all over. I looked up at the steps leading up to the top floor as Shelly came silently up to my side, I glanced at her, she looked as nervous as I did, which did not really help.

BANG.... BANG.... BANG!

I leapt in the air and squealed with terror, and Shelly joined me. Both of us got the fright of our lives, I turned to the door, who the hell was that, and what were they trying to do, break the door down?

I took a huge breath and took a step forward feeling more than rattled, grab the door, and pulled it open.

"SURPRISE!"

I felt the shock ripple through me, as I stared at the very sun tanned, long blonde haired and grinning like an idiot face of Pam. I was for a moment completely lost as she stepped in and dragged me into a tight hug. Reeling in shock, I lifted my arms round her and she giggled.

"Pam... What the hell are you doing here?" She leaned back with a smile.

"I quit, Martin has taken over the project, and I jumped on the plane and shot back here... Well, I stopped over with mum last night, after all, if we are going to work on this project, I figured I would need Stan. I grabbed him, threw my shit in the back, and here I am." She smiled.

"I also missed you, and knowing you two crazies were here alone, I thought what the hell, I am going to party on the lake." Shelly burst into laughter and pulled her into a hug.

"Welcome home Hun, it really is great to see you." Pam winked at me, and lifted a bottle.

"I brought wine to get the party started, so... Where is my room?"

I could not help it, my heart was calming down, and I just burst out laughing, she was madder than Shelly, but oh God, it was good to see her.

"I will grab the glasses, come on through and welcome home. I cannot believe you still have Stan, does he even run?"

Shelly leaned out of the door and saw the beat up old green land cruiser, and smiled, we had got up to a lot of fun in Stan at Uni. As I walked through to the kitchen with Pam on my arm, I had to smile, somehow it felt the old team were back together, Pam gave a squeeze of my arm.

"How are you doing, I have been worried about you?" I smiled as I lifted the glasses.

"I am doing okay, I have had some tough moments, and I am sure I will have more, but honestly, I am doing better than I expected." She let go of my arm and put the bottle on the table as I turned for the glasses.

"I am glad to hear that Emmy, so, tell me all about the Amelia Montgomery Trust. I have to tell you girl, it is an inspiring project, I will not deny, I am really excited about this." I smiled at her as I put the glasses down.

"I am glad you are here Pam, there is a lot to do, and I will not deny, I am scared to death." She winked.

"That is what makes it fun, if we are not terrified, how the hell will we enjoy it?" She gave a happy giggle and lifted the bottle.

"First things first, WINE! Shell, get your fat ass in here, we are pouring, and this is one spirit I will help you research."

And suddenly, I had another problem!

Chapter Twenty Nine

Confronting reality

I cannot deny, seeing Pam was so amazing, and knowing she had quit her project, which to be honest, was really well paid, added to my joy, because she wanted to be involved with me. Knowing she would be working at our side, came as a huge relief, she is so much better at all the organising, I had only ever worked on small scale projects, but this was going to be a huge amount of work.

The Amelia Montgomery Trust was a multi million pound operation, and everything would be on a far bigger scale than I had been involved with, apart from the forest replanting scheme in Scotland. Pam was so much better at the daily stuff, my real interest was mainly in the science, and to be honest, Shelly was a wonder at photography and documenting things, so together we technically, were a well matched unit.

The big problem was, Pam was a hard core none believer in fairies, sprites, elves or any other mystical being. I was about to do a ceremony where I would be on the island, dressed in white, and swearing my allegiance to the protection of a so called mythical race, who inhabit my land. No matter which way I look at it, I am never going to sell her on this.

The moment came, when she wanted to grab her stuff out of Stan, I had to chuckle as we walked out of the door, and walked towards the matt painted dark green four wheel drive off roader, with huge chunky tires and a jacked up suspension. I was impressed it was still running, it was covered in dents from some of our off road adventures. She pulled open the back door and dragged her bags out, she took two as I leaned in for some of her technical equipment. She looked back as she headed onto the path.

"Emmy which room is mine?" I pulled my head out of the back.

"Up the stairs, go right, and it is the first door on the right. Pam it's only a single, will be that okay until I can get you something bigger?" She gave a smile.

"Yeah, no problems, if I need to, I will get my bed from home, it is a luxury double."

She giggled as she headed inside, and Shelly was at my side in an instant looking really panicked, she kept her voice as low as possible, but she was freaking out.

"Emmy, holy shit, what are going to do, if Esme shows up, Pam will freak the hell out?" I gave a sigh as I pulled her large metal case towards me.

"Shell, what choice do we have, she is here, she is staying and working with us? Honestly, at some point Pam is going to have to face the facts, we do not really have a choice do we now?" She shook her head.

"Emmy, I am not sure, do you remember that holograph stunt we pulled, she freaked the hell out, and honestly, I thought she would faint? Pam does not want to believe, she really doesn't, and if Esme just pops in, she will either ignore it and pretend she is not there, or will have the melt down of the century?" I understood that.

"Shell, Pam has quit her job and come all the way back from America, and be honest, we could use the help." She dithered on the spot; her dark eyes fixed on me.

"Emmy... Look, you know I love her, she is a great mate, but I am telling you now, she is not going to be able to handle Nairn's just popping in for breakfast. Seriously, do you remember that moment when Felix just exploded out of the cabbages, because I am telling you now, I knew they existed, and I still freaked the hell out?"

I understood that, but felt trapped, I knew her strict code for science, I knew her inability to accept myths and legends, but I did not see how I could avoid it. I had already made a commitment to the Nairn, and I aimed to fulfil it as Han and my mum had. I gave a long sigh, feeling the tension building inside me, I needed to think this through.

"Shell, please, just give me some time; I will try to get her to understand what is going on here." She gave me a nod, but I am sure she did not believe I could.

"Yeah, okay, just for God's sake, do not glow white under any circumstance, oh hell, what have we got ourselves into?"

I was really starting to wonder, I pulled her work case out of the back of Stan, and shouldered the strap, and turned to walk into the house.

"Grab her stuff and help, I would rather we were both in the house when she is." Shelly nodded and leaned in the back, as I headed for the door and the office, and was trying to think of some way, I could achieve the impossible.

"Yeah, oh boy, this is going to be one weird as hell ride, us, Nairn's and a totally freaked out science freak.

Felix walked along the path with his father, and he was feeling terrified, Berrendock talked quietly.

"Felix, remember what Mugwump told you, focus your light into the crystal blade, and fly past as fast as you can, the light will increase the power of the blade and just slice a chunk off. Just keep flying and make sure you are well away before you turn. Watch, take note, and when safe, fly past again and slice another cut. The weight of the paste should help tear it free and it will drop. The paste beasts will stay close to the nest up the tree to protect it, so let things settle before you pick up the paste."

Felix nodded, although his legs felt weak, and his insides felt they had turned to liquid, and were sloshing around inside him. He took a deep breath and looked up at his father.

"I am scared, what if they attack me, I don't want to leave Esme alone, she will not do well without me?" Berrendoc gave a nod.

"You will be fine, you are of a line of leaders, you have what it takes to do this, I have every faith in you." Felix felt surprised.

"You do?" Berrendoc nodded.

"I do." Felix was not sure what to say.

"But I mess up a lot." His father smiled, and ruffled his scruffy hair.

"Felix, we have all messed up at some point, even Barrack, but when the need was there, we have always come through for our clan, and I believe you will too." Felix smiled.

"Thanks Father."

I left Shelly to help Pam unpack and settle in, it was nice to hear their laughter, as I walked down the stairs to make us all a drink. As I arrived at the kitchen I noticed through the door, as Randolph came up the steps, and hurried to get outside and meet him. I was five steps down when we met, he frowned as he looked at my face.

"Is everything alright, you look worried?" I gave a sigh, as I looked back at the house.

"Randolph, Pam has arrived, she wants to join us and move in, what the hell do I do?" He gave a shrug.

"I thought she was a close friend, is her living with you such a huge problem?" I actually felt my eyes open wide.

"Well, hell, yes of course it is, Randolph, you will never find a bigger sceptic when it comes to the mystical, and she will be living right here, what the hell do we do?"

His mouth widened into a broad smile, and then he started to chuckle, his shoulders gave a rapid shake, and eyes his twinkled with mirth. I did not understand and frowned; I was trying to keep my voice as low as possible.

"What the hell is so funny, Randolph this is a huge problem, what if Esme or Felix show up unannounced?" I could feel the panic in me growing and he just smiled.

"Emily, if they show up, well, Pam will know for sure, won't she?" He really was not grasping the stick at all; I nodded rapidly and checked the house again.

"Well, yes, Randolph, that is the bloody point, Pam will freak the hell out." Randolph lifted his hand to my shoulder; I thought I was going to have full on panic attack as my heart was racing yet again.

"Emily, calm down. Look this is not that big an issue, tell me, can she be trusted not to say anything?" I took deep breaths and nodded.

"I trust her with my life." He smiled.

"Well then, we will work slowly with her to bring her round to our way of thinking, and then if she meets them, it will not be that a big a deal, will it now?"

Oh God, he had no idea who he was dealing with, and I was

trusting him more than I had ever trusted anyone else to be right about this. The last thing I needed was for my best friend to see me as another of the raving looney club, where Shell was the president. I breathed out slowly.

"Honestly, I had planned out my day and all was going well, I was going to sort out Han's room, then have a swim, and hopefully hear from Esme that all was well with Felix. Randolph, I have got to say, living here is hard bloody work at times." He smiled at me.

"So you did her room, that is good?" I looked at him and felt crest fallen, I gave a sigh.

"I meant to, then Pam showed up out of the blue, and I got side tracked, so no, I have not started yet." He understood.

"Emily it is not the huge task you think it is." I frowned.

"Well probably not for others, but this is Han, her room, and I will be the one in there alone, it is a huge thing for me." He shook his head.

"Emily, do you not think Han knew that? She was the most precise person I have ever met, and as I have already said, she left behind some very detailed instructions that took into account all of you every needs. Trust me, Han prepared everything to make life here easier for you."

He did not make any sense at all, it was her room, regardless of what she had planned. I know Mr Higginson had a detailed list to follow, but I was about to clear out her room, it was her life, how could any list change that? I would have to move her most personal things, and decide their future. I was not too sure as to how Randolph could not see that any other way, other than heart breaking. Randolph smiled and took my hand.

"Come with me, and I will show you."

He led the way, and unsure of what exactly to do, I followed him as he guided me up the stairs, and I felt my insides twist as we approached the door.

"Emily, Han raised you, she knew this would be devastating for you, and so she left me a detailed plan of what she requested me to do, and once everything was sorted out, I followed her instructions to the letter." I was finding all this confusing, he gave a sigh, and pushed open the door, I felt my heart skip several beats.

"See, take a look, Han did everything you could not, well, to be honest I did it on her behalf. Emily, she wanted to spare you as much pain as possible."

I stepped into the room, and felt my breath catch in my throat, it looked almost as it always had, except her dressing table had nothing on top of it, her brush set, perfumes, all of it was gone. Her bed was stripped and was simply a mattress, her wardrobe door was open exposing her empty rails, and all that remained were two white robes and a pale grey cloak. I walked up to it and opened the door, and there was an old green canvass jacket, which I knew straight away, it was my mother's, I had a picture of her wearing it.

I lifted my hand and touched it, I knew it so well, and yet I had never actually seen it in real life. There was a patch on the top of it, which had the words embroidered on it, 'The world needs more trees and less arseholes' I smiled and turned to Randolph.

"This was my mother's." He gave a soft nod.

"It was, I bought it her, and she made the patch and sewed it on, no matter where she went, she always wore it. I was always so happy to see her in it, Han gave it me back after her death, I felt it should be passed on to a person who would wear it with the same attitude, her daughter." He smiled, and I felt the lump in my throat.

"Randolph, it is an important possession of hers, you have kept it." He shrugged.

"It is, but nowhere as valuable as it will appear to me watching her daughter wear it as she fulfils her mother's dream."

I was lost for words, I really did not know how I could respond, although I knew for sure I would be wearing it when I was out in the field working. I was finding it hard to be in here and see it so empty, I was unsure of which was worse, seeing it empty, and seeing it as it was the last time I was in here. I looked at the wall, and saw all the large silver framed pictures of my mother and father together, there were even some of me, I smiled.

"Even now after her death she has left me the memories of my mother. I know every story attached to these photos, she has sat me on the bed for years and told me about each of these days, and what my parents were doing when she took it."

Randolph stood at the end of the bed, it was clear he too gained a lot of pleasure from looking at them, it felt nice that in a way, Han left him the same memories. I gave a sigh and looked slowly round the room, it just felt so barren, Randolph noticed as my eyes fell on three large heavy looking wooden trunks.

"Han instructed me to place all of her things in those, she told me that you would allow nothing to leave here. Han said, once you knew those contained her life, I was to take them up to the loft, and store them, so her things were always close where you would want them." I nodded, and felt the tears.

Just knowing everything was in there hurt, it felt so little to show for her life here, somehow, I would have thought a life came to more, and yet once all her personal items had been gathered together, it felt like so little. I wiped my eyes on my sleeve.

"Her knitting should be in there as well, I will never finish it, I want it to remain as she left it, but honestly, seeing it in the living room, is painful, because I know, she wanted me to wear it when I came down on my twenty first birthday." Randolph gave a solemn nod.

"Alright, I will take care of it for you, is there anything else you want packing away?" I shook my head.

"No, everything else will stay as Han left it. Randolph this was my home, it was always the way it is downstairs, and I want to keep it that way. I want my home to be the same as it always has been, because that way, Han will always be here with me." He nodded.

"Yes, I understand that, and I feel you are right to have it that way. What will you do with this room, you know, it was once your mother's room, the room you actually sleep in was Han's. Emily, this, how you see it now, this was how it was after your mother passed. Those pictures are hers, she framed them, she hung them there, Han only added the one of you. The cloak, the robes, they were also your mother's, and in the dressing table, you will find her jewellery. Han wanted you to live in the room your mother inhabited, this was Amelia's Montgomery's room... See."

He opened the wardrobe door, and there on the back was carved into the wood, 'Amelia was here.' He smiled, as he looked at it.

"I remember the day Han saw that, she went so mad at your

mum, she was fourteen at the time. Your mum just shrugged and responded with, 'It is my wardrobe, I can do what I like with it, at least I didn't say I love a guy or anything stupid like that.'" He gave a chuckle.

"Han looked so lost for words, and your mum just smiled and kissed her cheek, and told her she loved her, then went out in the garden. I think it is the only time I have ever seen Han lost for words."

I sat lost in all of it, not really knowing what to feel, or what to do. Han stayed in this room to remember my mother after she lost her, and now Randolph had told me to take this room, as it was Han's wish, I had the same room my mother grew up in. the problem was, it did not feel like my room, and also, I could not see the lake and the island from the window in here. I looked up at Randolph.

"I will swap wardrobes, I want that, and I will move my mothers' things and pictures into the back room. Randolph, the back room has always been my room at home, and I cannot change it now, I feel at ease there, Han came to me there. No, I will make some changes and then Pam can have this room, I don't want to be in here, I want to be where I feel safe, and that is facing the island where I can watch over it. Han gave me that room when I came here, and I am staying there."

"I understand Emily, and I think Han knew that, I will move the wardrobe for you, and take her things to the loft store." I felt more at ease with that.

"Randolph, where are her journals?" He gave a smile.

"They are where she told me to put them, in a box, under your bed in your room, she knew it was the one place you would not look straight away. Emily, she told me to tell you, that you should embrace the light before you read them, and I agree with her." I gave a sigh and nodded, this was so much to deal with, and my insides were swirling around.

"If that was her wish, then so be it, I want to leave this room now and go downstairs." He nodded as he looked round.

"Go on, you take care of you, and I will fulfil her wishes as she requested."

I got up off the bed and slowly walked round the room, to be honest seeing it stripped and empty felt shocking, but in a way,

I was glad. Han was right, I would have preserved the room as it was, and she knew me well enough to know, it would have haunted my life. Han wanted me to live here, but she wanted me to be happy, and as long as her room had stayed as it was, I would have always been sad, yet again she was looking out for me as she always had, and in a way, it made me smile. I turned at the door and looked back as Randolph stood watching.

"Thank you for all you did for her, thank you for loving her so deeply. Thankyou Grandfather."

He nodded, and I smiled and left the room, Randolph swallowed hard, and then wiped his eyes, she had no idea how much like Amelia she was, even her tone of voice was the same, and it hurt, but at the same time, it gave him joy. He looked to the wall and the one picture of Han stood alone and smiling on the jetty with the island behind her.

"Thank you, my love."

Esme sat on the path weeping quietly, when Aubrianne walked up, she saw her daughter sat crying and felt a tug to her heart, she had expected this. Esme had her head down and her shoulders shook, as her tiny tears fell into the grass and were lost between the blades. Aubrianne knelt down, and lifted her daughter into her arms and held her close, Esme gave a big sob and buried her face into her mother's shoulder.

"This is wrong mother, no one has ever gone up against the paste beasts when they were so young. Felix is going to get hurt and I cannot do anything to stop it. I asked you mother, I asked you to help him, why does he have to do this, he is risking his life when it was Felix that showed Emily we were here? She thanked us mother, Emily thanked us and was happy to meet us, it helped her understand, and because of that the clan are safe."

She gave huge wail, and Aubrianne felt the pain of her daughter within her spirit, she pulled her tight and rocked her gently.

"Esme, Felix agreed to this, he chose this task."

Esme swallowed hard, and pulled her head out of her mother's shoulder, she looked up at her with huge blue, tear filled eyes.

"Felix did not choose this, Chandak did, and Barrack should not have listened. All Chandak cares about is making sure Felix never leads the clan, because he wants to." Aubrianne gave a sigh.

"Esme, you should not say such things, Chandak is a respected member of the clan, and he only has the best interests of this clan at heart. Esme, Felix broke a very important rule, and for that there is a law we must follow." Esme shook her head.

"I know you do not believe that, you know it was Chandak that sent Berrendoc, Thornrock, and Rosespire down that path knowing they would get attacked and killed, all of us know, and yet no one says anything. Mother, Berrendoc was your best friend, you know how he spoke up for Rachel, you know how he protected her to save you. He accused Chandak and faced him as a true Nairn would, and yet none of you spoke up for him, and he was left alone raising his son grieving the death of Rosespire. He was your friend, why did you not stand up for him?" Aubrianne bit her lip.

"Esme how do you know all this, that is not how it was, I spoke out at the meet, I told Barrack not to condemn his son." Esme gave a big sniffle.

"Do you remember that day, did you ask the light to guide you?" Aubrianne gave a nod.

"I did Esme, and I spoke with the light inside me." Esme wiped her eyes; she was calming down and her voice dropped a little.

"Then you know the truth, Mother, the light does not lie, and now Felix is facing his death, and it is happening all over again, because Barrack only listens to Chandak. Mother, I need Felix, he has to live, Mother a day will come, when I will choose Felix or no other." Aubrianne smiled.

"Is your heart so strong and your mind so sure Esme, you are still young in the ways of the ladies of the Nairn?" Esme gave a nod, and she looked really resolute.

"It is Felix, or no other, I mean it Mother, my life path is chosen, and it is the same path as Felix."

"When you smell the flower, you see the truth, and that little flower has much more light than most of the other flowers. Only light flows in her heart, and that is why she knows of the whispers." Aubrianne looked up, and Mugwump was awake and smiling.

"Hosta was the same, this you know Aubrianne, the silver haired Lady of the Nairn. Pull that long hair out of your ears and eyes, for there before you sits wisdom, and it chatters freely as a Nairn should."

Everyone thought Mugwump was mad, and yet, she had known Veda consult him often as she considered him to be sharp enough to spot the simple things that no one noticed. She felt doubtful, and yet she trusted her instincts and knew in her heart, her daughter was pure of heart and filled with love and truth. She had asked Berrendoc many times what happened that day, but he had always refused to talk of it, saying only it was past history.

It had always bothered her that he walked away from the council to raise his son alone, and as a result, like Mugwump he had become a loner taking little interest in the affairs of the clan. Hadn't she always thought he would be the next clan leader, hadn't she always wished he would come back and stand at the side of his father as an advisor? She knew he was the best one to fill the role, and yet such was his stubbornness, he had always side stepped the issue and walked away, but why? She looked up at Mugwump sat on his stump.

"I will talk with Veda; she will know what to do." Mugwump shook his head and looked round nervously.

"I did not ask, I never did, she told me not to ask, and I left it and hid, but she never forgave, no, oh no she never forgave." He slipped off his stump and landed with a thump, and he quickly waddled into the tall ferns muttering to himself.

"I did not... No, oh no, I never asked." Aubrianne gave a long sigh, and looked at Esme.

"Alright, I will talk again to Barrack and see if something can be done." Esme smiled.

"Please try, Mother you must save Felix, you simply must."

What choice did Aubrianne have? She loved Esme with all her heart, and seeing one of such innocence and love, sat alone in tears, had broken her heart.

I had a lot to think about, yet again, a little more of my past was uncovered and I faced the reality of my life. I have to wonder if I was blind to me, was I so lost I could not see the obvious, and had lived most of my life missing the importance of each moment? The last year of my life had been filled with pain and loneliness, as I had just existed from moment to moment, struggling to cope and understanding anything happening around me. Yet, here I was facing the truth of my reality, and trying desperately to start again, and it felt like history kept repeating and I was dragged back yet again to face my life.

Was this all serving some purpose, was I in sync with the Nairn, as they rebuilt their life here always hiding in the shadows, hoping their past did not return, and that the island was their final sanctuary? It was an interesting thought, and as I sat there my thoughts drifted back across the island and they were with Felix. He was so small, and so filled with life, not unsimilar to me as a child with Han, and yet today, he would face a trial that could take him into the darkness, or the light. I had to smile, was that not me also? I too sat on the edge of darkness hoping my future would be in the light, it is a strange topic of contemplation, Felix could die today, and I was afraid for him.

My life is so surreal, up until twenty four hours ago, I could never believe in any kind of mystical being that could have evolved, and yet one had, and I was really concerned for his life. Everything the last day has shown me, is against the principles of science, which I have clung to for years. At the moment, I feel, I have been clinging to something that was not real, not definite, as the proof to prove it was wrong had slept in my room last night and then sat on my table eating the smallest piece of toast I have ever seen. My reality, is very different from the one I had assumed was real, and it was not, and I was about to take on the task of covering a secret that would rock the evolutionary world, I do feel I am going quite insane at the moment.

Shell appeared and sat at my side, I turned to her and saw her watching me.

"Any news?" I shook my head.

"No... I wish there was, I really need to know he is safe, where is Pam?" Shelly looked back up the garden towards the house.

"Jet lag, she is pretty tired and is taking a nap, she has not unpacked much, we talked mostly and just had a catch up. I told her I wanted to write here and muck in with the project, she is actually really keen and excited you are doing this." I nodded.

"She will be a valuable addition, Pam knows her stuff, she did well in the states, I doubt that idiot Martin will be as thorough as she is." Shelly looked down into the water as her legs swung off the edge of the jetty.

"She will be, as long as she understands the Nairn are real. Emmy, I am not sure she will be easy to convince, you how she feels about the mystical stuff, we will have our work cut out for us."

"Probably, but really Shell, what can we do, the Nairn are here, and so is Pam? I am going to try and stall things, and come up with something, but at some point, they will meet. Esme and Felix have been here long before any of us, this place is their home, and this house has been a part of that, they are not going to stay away, at some point, Pam will have to wise up and face the reality of this place." Shelly sniggered.

"Yeah, good luck with that."

Chapter Thirty

Dire Situations

Aubrianne approached the tall rock, where Barrack sat in thought, at the base of the rock Chandak watched on, dressed as always in his long cloak of velvet, and his rich burgundy robes. His long sleek white hair, braided to the sides, hung down in front of him, as he smiled at her, his distaste for Aubrianne in private was clear.

"Lady Aubrianne, may I say, what a pleasant surprise, tell me, what brings such a pleasant, yet unexpected visit?" She smiled.

"I would seek to talk in private with Lord Barrack." He looked surprised.

"Really, and what would be the nature of such an audience?"

He studied her pale blue eyes, soft features and slender figure, it was widely known, Aubrianne even for her age, had retained much of her youthful appearance, and she was considered to be a great beauty to the Nairn. Chandak gave off his appreciation of her form in the manner in which he studied it. Aubrianna felt the discomfort of his gaze, but was steadfast in her objective, and smiled sweetly.

"If I was to inform you, it would lose its ability to be private, wouldn't it? I need but a few moments alone with Lord Barrack, nothing more." Chandak looked usure, and looked up at the rock.

"He is busy, he is contemplating the ceremony." Aubrianne smiled.

"Then maybe I have arrived at the right time, for I feel as a council elder, I may be of some service."

"Aubrianne." She looked up and smiled, Chandak stepped back and looked up at the rock.

"Lord Barrack, Lady Aubrianne was enquiring as to a moment

of privacy, but as I was explaining, at this time you are concerned with other matters." Barrack smiled.

"It is fine Chandak, the silver lady of the council is always a welcome distraction, I will come down." Chandak looked displeased.

"But my lord, you have much to prepare." Barrack turned, and came fluttering down, and landed before Aubrianne with a smile.

"I am fine, the good lady may be of some service as I mull over recent events." Aubrianne smiled at him.

"I thank thee, I feel to aide you would be a satisfaction, and I do have a topic of private concern, if we could be alone for a moment." Barrack nodded, and looked at Chandak.

"We will be fine, we have many duties, please if you may, could you go check on how the preparations are going for me?" He was clearly displeased, and gave a bow, then walked off abruptly muttering. Barrack smiled and held out his hand.

"Come, we shall walk a while, your visits of late have become less frequent, tell me, what is this matter you wish to discuss?"

Aubrianne slipped her arm into his and began to walk with him, this had been a familiar ritual many years ago, but with the selection of new council due to the losses they had suffered on their journey south, things had changed and changed drastically.

"Barrack, we have known each other since birth, so I will not stand on formality, I have concerns that I feel should be raised before the ceremony." He nodded as he listened.

"If you feel concerned, and especially at this time, then I will take note, for your wisdom in the past has helped guide us." Aubrianne gave a sigh and stopped, she turned to him, and her eyes met his gaze.

"Barrack what has happened to you? I am sorry, but as you know, I once considered you in the choosing, and I did so because I could see you were a man of vision, of wisdom, and may add, a man of action. You were so decisive, you were inspiring, and yet of late it appears you do not know your own mind unless it is whispered into your ear by Chandak?" He appeared displeased and frowned at her.

"It is not like that, and you know it, we meet in the council, it is an open debate, all of us input our opinions, and then we choose, Chandak is merely one of the seven." She nodded.

"And yet there used to be eight... Barrack, you turned your back on your own son, he lives alone, raising Felix, and grieving the loss of Rosespire, and for what, because he disagreed in public with you over Chandak? Barrack for the sake of all the trees, you have sentenced your grandson to death, Felix is brave, of that there is no doubt, be he is no match for one paste beast, let alone a swarm. What were you thinking, where was your wisdom, without Felix, Emily would still be unaware of us, and we would be leaving here? Barrack, Felix may be irresponsible at times, but his actions have created the moment where Emily will walk into the light and embrace it on the rising of the next sun, how can you risk him, he is the future of this clan?"

He did not like her words, but she knew, this was the only moment she would ever get to speak her mind. He gave a frustrated sigh.

"That is not how things are, come on, you of all people know the responsibilities of the clan, they weigh heavy on all of us, we cannot allow disruption, we have to remain focused on the survival of our race. Chandak has proven his value since the loss of Han, he rose to the task and served all of us well." She shook her head.

"How did you become so blind? I remember you Barrack, I remember your great talks of reforming the clan, and building harmony between us and the line of Han. I remember how you snuck off as child to watch the other world and learn its secrets to aide our survival. Felix is no different than you, and yet you stood there, in the glade before the next watcher of our line, and you publicly sentenced Felix to death. For what, the soft whisperings of Chandak, the man who ensures Felix never rules because he has already set his eyes on the seat? You talk of customs and tradition, and all whilst destroying our greatest, the true line of our ancestors, and the rule by the staff. You are fool Barrack, and you have betrayed yourself, your family, and the ancestral line of your blood. I will be no part in this foolishness, I aim to stop Felix, and then will resign my seat, and you can listen to the whisperings of that witless idiot and replace me."

Her large wings exploded up from behind her, and she shot at speed into the air, and left Barrack looking shocked, as he watched her fly off in a streak of white light. He watched until she disappeared, and looked down at the path, with a sigh, his task of late had weighed heavy upon his shoulders, and he was unsure of what to do.

Felix looked up at the tall tree, and took a deep breath, there were many bees flying around the nest, but it was fat and swollen, and he could see, it was possibly a hundred times his own weight. Berrendoc crouched down at his side, and looked up at the large inverted pear drop shape, hanging down from the branch.

"Felix, this is the easiest one from all of the ones I have scouted, it is a lower branch, with nothing to obstruct you, look at it, study it. All the others are within the branches and hard to fly around, but with this one, you can sweep past, and slice as you continue to fly. The Paste beasts will not understand what happened." Felix looked up and studied it, he understood his father, but he could feel himself trembling.

"It is high up, and they have a good view, they will see me, they will know who is there." Berrendoc took a deep breath.

"Felix this is not a game, on this day, you will stand up, and start your journey to becoming a man of great stature. Take your time and think clearly, there is no time for fun and frolics, you have to be focused and calm." Felix nodded, his legs were shaking slightly, but he was determined to prove his worth.

The rain had stopped and the sun was out, and within the forest the temperature was rising, and the bees were very active, he breathed in, determined to do this, and felt his stomach whine.

"I will eat first." Berrendoc sighed.

"Even in the midst of crisis you think of food, be wary young Nairn, that is the path Mugwump took, and look at the size of him now. He is so heavy; he constantly bumps his rear end on the ground when he flies. Why do you think he patched his pants with bark?" He smiled as Felix looked at the Carry, Esme had given him.

Felix sat down and took the leaf off the top of the silver bowl, he looked at the strange food and was unsure, and yet Esme had told him, that it tasted of the sun. He was actually a little excited, he had never tasted the sun before. He lifted a white grain and looked at it, gave a shrug and then dipped it into the strange red coloured mixture.

He popped it into his mouth and chewed as Berrendoc looked on unsure. Felix smiled, and lifted out two grains and dipped them into the carry, and put them in his mouth and spoke as he chewed.

"This is really nice, I was not sure, but it's good, try some."

He lifted a handful and pushed it in as he chewed greedily, he was hungrier than he realised, and lifted another handful. Berrendoc reached out and lifted a grain to look at it, he viewed what looked like an ordinary grain, shrugged as Felix crammed in more, and then reached out and dipped it into the red coloured mixture. He lifted it to his mouth, and was just about to put it in, when suddenly, Felix stopped chewing and looked really worried. Berrendoc froze, the grain still in front of his lips, and frowned.

"Felix... Are you alright, you look strange?"

Felix was sat utterly still, as his eyes began to widen, Berrendoc leaned in and stared at him.

"Felix, you are going a strange colour, you are as red as a poppy."

Felix made a very strange wheezy breathing sound, and his eyes were so big, Berrendoc was afraid they would pop. A trail of sweat ran down Felix's face, and Berrendoc began to grow really concerned, and leaned back afraid Felix would explode.

Felix grabbed the crystal blade and it exploded with blinding light, and Berrendoc gave a squeal of surprise and fell back flat on the floor, honestly believing his son had exploded. The white bright ball, which was Felix, shot into the air at high speed with a wail like a squirrel that was being fire killed, as he watched the supersonic flash of light shoot up at the tree, and zig zag faster than anything Berrendoc had ever seen, and he gasped out in utter surprise.

The speed of Felix was mind blowing as he shot through the air wailing like an injured bird, and each time he passed the nest of the Paste Beasts, another slice appeared. He was so fast Berrendoc could hardly keep his eyes on him, as he darted left and right slicing off pieces bigger than a Nairn, it was utterly bewildering, and yet all he could do was smile.

Esme came running through the ferns to where Berrendoc lay on the ground watching, she saw the hyper speeding light and clutched her heart and took a huge gasp of air.

"FELIX, BE CAREFUL!"

Her bright blue eyes darted left and right watching him, and then suddenly, he shot through the trees heading for the lake, as the bees flew frantically round the nest filled with rage. Esme saw him heading for the lake, and shot into the air with a gasp, and flew as fast as she could to catch up with him.

Mugwump looked up as he swallowed a fat slug, and saw the streak of light come out of the trees and shoot straight down with a wail into the water, where there appeared to be a huge sigh and a strange quiet hissing sound. Esme shot of out the trees and landed on a pebble, looking terrified.

"FELIX... ARE YOU ALRIGHT?" The water where he had hit, bubbled.

The bubbles increased in speed, and then with a huge gasp, Felix popped up, and Esme gave a gasp of relief. His face was scarlet and his eyes were huge as he panted like and exhausted squirrel, but he was wearing the hugest smile. He waded towards her holding the crystal blade.

"ESME, I TASTED THE SUN!" She giggled, and then threw her arms round him and held him tight.

"Felix, you did it, you tasted the sun and it gave you more light, and you did it, you defeated the Paste Beasts, and got more of the comb of the sweet paste than anyone ever has."

Felix simply stood there, breathing a little faster than normal, soaking wet and dripping, as Esme hung from his neck, and he smiled. He noticed Mugwump watching him, the old fat Nairn smiled.

"Tis the light ye see, the sun has many gifts, and one is in the heart of the youngest leaf, and it shines so brightly for the flower." He shook his head. "I never did, no, oh no I never did, she said not and I never did."

He dragged his large rump off the floor and scuttled into the trees with a waddle, and Felix just smiled as Esme slipped back, and looked up at him with those big blue eyes, and she spoke very softly.

"You proved them all wrong, and you became the man who will lead. Felix, I will never leave your side again, I choose you." He smiled, and his eyes bubbled with excitement.

"I can taste the air." He breathed in and out, and got very excited. "Esme, I can taste the air."

Aubrianne looked down at Berrendoc sat on the floor, and she smiled, as she offered her hand to him.

"This is a proud moment for you, Felix proved to be more of the man of his father. I am happy for you Berrendoc, I could not bear to see you lose one whom you love so deeply. Once was enough for this life; I am happy for you both." She pulled him up and he smiled.

"I am not sure what happened, but whatever this Carry substance is, it is clear, Emily prepares food with the light."

Aubrianne looked back as she watched Esme and Felix running hand in hand down the path looking wildly excited. She turned as they approached glowing with happiness; Felix was out of breath as he stood proud before his father.

"I did it, I got all the comb we will need." Esme squeezed his hand with pride.

"You got three times more than Chandak." Felix nodded, and looked up at his father who smiled and was filled with a sense of such pride, he patted his son on the head.

"Your mother would have been so proud of you today, Felix, as am I, you truly took your first step into the world of Nairn men of honour." Felix nodded, with a huge smile.

"I am going to gather it." He turned and shot off as Berrendoc looked up.

"Felix, do not be hasty, check the beasts have calmed down."

He ran over and took a look, there was no sign of the beasts, and he happily smiled as he walked over to the broken segments of the nest and saw the combs with the sweet paste all over them. High above him the beasts were angry, and working fast to repair the damage, Felix slid his finger along the paste and then slipped it into his mouth and sucked, his eyes rolled with delight.

There was a huge chunk, far bigger than Barrack had asked for, and he grabbed it, still feeling some of the power of the sun inside himself, and lifted it up with great pride above his head.

"LOOK AT THAT, WOW, IT IS THE BIGGEST COMB I HAVE EVER SEEN!"

He held it high above his head, and it was five times bigger than he was. Berrendock gave a chuckle as he watched his son with immense pride, Esme stood smiling with adoration, and then her face wrinkled and her eyes grew huge.

"FELIX LOOK OUT!"

A Paste Beast, seeing Felix holding up the honey comb, shot down at speed, and as Felix turned slightly to look behind him, it flew up fast, latched onto his back, and plunged its stinger straight into his waist. He screamed out in agony, and Berrendoc yelled, and flew at speed towards Felix, drawing out his own crystal sword.

Felix fell to his knees, the beast writhing as it pushed its stinger deep, and pumped its poison into him, and Esme screamed with all her heart as the comb fell to the floor and Felix slumped forward.

Emily turned on the jetty as Randolph came down the steps towards her and Shelly, the whole of her insides grew cold, as she felt something awaken inside herself, something she had never felt before.

"What was that noise?" Shelly frowned.

"What noise, I heard nothing?" Randolph walked towards her and looked at her puzzled.

"Emily what do you sense, tell me?"

I could feel the goosebumps going up my arms, and I shivered, I had no understanding of it, but I felt something powerful. I looked back to the island.

"Randolph, something is not right, I have no idea what, but there is danger, I feel it." He nodded as Shell got up and looked at me, the belief in her eyes was total.

"I will get the boat ready." I nodded, as I turned to face the island, Randolph was at my side.

"Emily focus, feel your way, see through your heart." I tried to focus, and shuddered as I sensed a powerful feeling, and it frightened me, I felt the tears in my eyes.

"Randolph, I think Esme is in pain, I can feel her somehow, and she is stricken with such pain, it is hurting me to feel it." The tears flowed down over my cheeks, he nodded and understood.

Out of the trees on the island came a stream of bright light, I saw it and gasped, and suddenly understood the pain of Esme.

A Nairn held Felix tightly in his arms as he flew towards me, he looked heart broken, as the small limp figure hung from his arms, and seeing the bright happy mischievous Felix like that broke my heart.

At their side was a woman with long flowing sliver hair, and she was holding the hand of Esme, and I knew her to be her mother. They came at speed across the water in a direct line towards us, and I felt my heart beat rapidly, Randolph moved down the jetty towards them to meet them.

Berrenrdoc landed and held up his son's limps body, Felix was twitching and jerking, he was reacting to the poison and his skin was so white it was almost transparent.

"Master Sage Feather, I beg you, help my son, use the light."

Shelly was stood rooted to the floor next to the boat house as she watched with tears in her eyes. Randolph lifted Felix out of his father's arms, as Esme wept hugging her mother's hip, he turned to me, and I instantly reacted.

"In the house, we need to act fast." I was too scared or shocked to fully understand the feeling flowing around in a storm inside me. I turned quickly.

"This way, hurry."

I ran up the steps, there was no time to think, and I acted on instinct. Shelly hurried behind me with Randolph, she turned and looked back at the small group of Nairn looking heartbroken.

"What are you waiting for, she said hurry?"

They lifted into the air to follow, as I made the kitchen door, and rushed in trying to think. Randolph came in as I grabbed a towel and folded it and placed it on the table.

"Lie him here, he is having a reaction to the poison, I have no idea how human like they are, but if this was a child, I would say it is Anaphylaxis, and he is going into shock."

Randolph laid him on the towel, as I felt the panic rushing through me, to be honest, all I knew, was I had to work fast. I turned as the Nairn flew in, and landed on the table, Esme went straight to his side and took his hand, I looked at her.

"Where was he stung?" She looked up with huge tears in her eyes, and sniffled.

"His back." I nodded and then leaned in as Shelly came to my side.

"What do you need?" I rolled Felix gently over, and saw the sting and a torn part of the bee hanging out of a large inflamed red bubble.

"Shell, bottom end cupboard, medicines, and first aid kit, I need tweezers out of the green box... Hurry." Esme gave a huge sob as she looked at me.

"Please save him Emily, he means everything to me." I smiled trying to hold back my tears.

"I am trying Esme, but I have no understanding of your people, but I will do everything I can, I promise, I need him too." She nodded and wiped her red eyes.

Shell opened the green box, grabbed the tweezers and handed them to me, I took them, and looked at the sting.

"Shell, I need a straw, top cupboard right hand side." She nodded and turned and opened the door, then looked at me and frowned.

"What for?" I pulled on the sting and it came out, Felix twitched and everyone jumped.

"I have to get the poison out."

Shelly understood and grabbed the packet of multi coloured straws, and slid out a yellow one, and handed it to me. I grabbed the scissors out of the first aid kit, and cut it in half, and then leaned forward and saw Esme watching.

"Hold his hand, and let's hope this works." She smiled and nodded.

I pushed the straw onto his wound and then leaning right over him, I put my mouth on the straw and sucked with all my might. I had to try and get as much as possible out, but honestly, I had no idea if this would work. He was so small, and I had no idea if his body could even handle the suction. All I knew, was Han had done it to me a thousand times as a child, and I was praying the Nairn were similar enough to respond the same as we would.

I stood up, turned and spat in the sink, my lips tasted funny, which I hoped was the poison, I leaned back in and sucked again, Esme shuddered.

"Emily, do not swallow any, I don't want you to die as well." I spat in the sink.

"I am fine Esme; the poison has little effect on humans." I had an idea, and looked at Shelly.

"Shell, are there any hay fever tablets?" She frowned and then suddenly understood.

"Oh hell of course, it is a histamine reaction, wow you are brilliant."

Aubrianne and Berrendoc were stood on the table close to Randolph, and had no idea what we were talking about. I looked at Randolph who was smiling.

"I have no idea if it will work, but it has to be worth a shot." He gave me a nod, as Shell popped up from the cupboard with a packet.

"Emmy what dosage do we use, I mean, how old is he, I know he is not an adult yet?" She looked at the packet. "Kids twelve years an over get one tablet." She handed me the packet as I looked at Esme.

"How old is he?" She sniffled.

"We are only young Emily, he is just forty six." Shelly stopped in her tracks, and stared.

"Come again?" Esme turned to look at her.

"He is very young; he has another eighteen years before he becomes a man." I smirked as Shelly looked completely stumped, her eyes lifted to me, and she smiled.

"They age like oak; they take fifty years to get their first acorn."

I had two spoons and was working fast. I took out a tablet, and crushed it between the two spoons to a fine powder, and then turned to the dripping tap, and collected a couple of drops. Using the end of the other spoon, I mixed it into a lose watery paste, and looked at Aubrianne and Berrendoc.

"This works for our children, but honestly, I have no idea if it will work for him, but I really want it to." Berrendoc looked at me, he had a fixed worried stare.

"Lady Emily, he is my only son, but in our world, there is no cure for the sting of a Paste Beast. At the moment, he is lost to us all, as normally, there is a day of terrible pains, and then death. If by chance your herbs will save him, I will be forever in your debt, do what you can, the light within you is strong and I trust it."

My hands were shaking as I lifted the other cut off piece of straw, and picked up the scissors, and tried to fashion a tiny spoon out of one end. My heart was racing, this had to work, but I was so unsure, I looked at Esme, I could see her adoration and complete belief in me.

"Esme, try to hold his mouth open for me, I have no idea if this will work, but here goes."

Esme leaned over him, and as carefully as I could, I placed the spoon of mixture next to his head, and then scooped out a small amount using the cut end of the straw, and shook as I tried to aim it into his mouth, whilst Esme held it open. I got a little in, and gasped out, as I had been holding my breath. He looked like he swallowed, so far so good, and so I tried with another spoon full. In my mind my inner thoughts shifted as I lifted the cut spoon and let another load dribble into his open mouth. I spoke in my mind.

'Han, I need this to work, please help me, I have to save him.' He swallowed, and I breathed another sigh of relief, and felt a strong sense of calm wash into me. I had no idea how much he could have; this was after all a medicine for humans. He had four, was it enough? I leaned back to observe, the whole room was completely silent, and suddenly I realised my hands were glowing white, was that me or Han?

I stood up straight and the light faded, Shelly smiled at me, as I looked at her, and breathed a sigh.

"I hope that is enough, we cannot give him too much, I say we wait a moment and see what happens." Esme was watching him carefully, and still holding his hand tight, and all I could do was hope for a miracle.

We all stood watching the tiny figure lay on a towel on the table, and silently hoped for his recovery. It felt like an age, and then he twitched, and Esme gave a gasp as he opened his eyes and looked right at her, she smiled.

"You came back to me." Then she burst into tears as everyone gave a sigh of relief.

I had no idea if it worked, was it the tablet, was it the light, Han's light? I simply did not know, but I knew I was glad, and felt a lump in my throat of sheer emotional relief as he stirred a little and then winced, he was in pain. I watched his father walk up and kneel at his side and wipe away his tears as he looked down on

Felix, and Felix turned and looked up at him and smiled, oh God, I felt exhausted.

Randolph slipped his hand onto my shoulder and gave it a squeeze, I felt a strong sense of relief, as I turned to him, he was wearing a huge smile.

"Banish those doubts Emily, you are without doubt of the same heart of Han and Amelia. The light was with you, as was Han, I felt her, she came right up from your heart to guide you. This day will be well remembered by the Nairn."

I snuggled into him, and felt his strong arms come round me, and I felt safe and secure, the last two weeks had filled me with doubts as I made difficult choices, and faced things I had never dreamed of, and yet, without Han, I had felt lost. Today all of us pulled together, and as I panicked to save the life of a creature I had no understanding of, I realised, I was surrounded by the kind of support Han had always provided, I was not as alone as I had thought. I looked up at Randolph, and past the long grey whiskers on his chin.

"I am glad I have you, and my father, I feel better knowing both of you are in my life." His eyes twinkled, and I could see the value of my words on his face, he just smiled.

"I am proud to be part of your life, and a very proud grandfather."

I stood for a few minutes soaking up the closeness, and then rolled back from his embrace, and turned to see Felix sat up, he looked a little dazed and was clearly in pain, although he frowned.

"Where is the comb?" Esme blinked.

"Felix, we left it, we needed to get you to Emily fast." He looked shocked, and looked round at all of us.

"YOU LEFT IT... HOW COULD YOU DO THAT... WHAT IF STRIPY JAKE FINDS IT, AND EATS IT ALL?" Randolph shrugged.

"Well badgers do like honey, I suppose if he does, we will have to get more." Esme put her arms round Felix and pulled him close.

"Felix is not doing it, you can go Randolph, I am never letting anyone risk him again."

Shelly giggled, it was really cute, she was so tiny, and yet surprisingly fierce in defence of Felix, I could only giggle along with Shell. We all relaxed, and I was going to suggest food, but in the panic and the rush I had forgotten something very important, and suddenly I was alerted, and felt as one crisis ended, another one started. I heard the creak and thump of the stairs, and looked at Shelly.

"Oh hell, she is awake and on her way down the stairs." Shelly's eyes opened wide.

"Oh hell, Emmy what the hell do we do?" Panic surged back into me.

"Good bloody question... Any ideas?"

Chapter Thirty One

Belief in the Clan

"Oh Crap.... Oh Crap.... OOOH Crap!"

Shelly dithered looking terrified and panicked, she looked down at Berrendoc and Aubrianne, as she flustered.

"Look we have another house guest, she is called Pam, and I hate saying it, but she does not believe in any of you guys. She thinks all fairies sprites and gnomes are impossible and do not exist, and we have not really had time to talk to her, as she only got here this morning and has been sleeping.... Oh shit... Okay, I need a huge favour, can you hide?" She lifted a bowl off the unit.

"Not for long, just long enough to get rid of her?" She held the bowl over them.

"Under here would be good." She plopped the bowl down, as I understood, and lifted a large saucepan and looked at Felix and Esme.

"Shush, we won't be long."

I put it on top of them, and took a huge breath, Shelly was looking stressed to hell, but we were good, I breathed a sigh of relief, as I heard the thump on the bottom stairs.

In through the door came a flash of light, as Chandak arrived, and stood on the table looking round, and my heart skipped several beats.

"What is going on, I know there are members of the clan here, they are breaking the rules and will be brought before Barrack?" Shelly grabbed the pasta jar, tipped out the spaghetti.

"Oh hell no!" She dropped it over him, and looked at me with sweat running down her face.

"Of all the bloody fairies we could get, we got him, this is not going to end well." Randolph gave out a loud laugh, he appeared to be really enjoying this.

Pam staggered into the kitchen looking sleepy and rubbing her eyes, she blinked and looked at us.

"Hi guys, what is happening?" The pasta jar moved, and Shelly slapped her hand down hard on it, and looked at her.

"We were talking meal plans, this is Randolph by the way, he is the game keeper and Emmy's grandfather." He smiled and waved, looking nervous.

"Hi."

I was in full panic mode trying to look casual as I leaned on the sink, and could feel my heart racing at a thousand miles an hour. I was hoping we had got away with it. Shelly looked like she was heading into melt down wearing a big smile. Pam looked at us both, and yes, we did appear to be acting weird.

"Are you guys okay, you seem weird?" I shrugged.

"I am fine, what about you Shell?" Sweat was running down her face, she shrugged.

"Yeah, I am okay, just stood here wondering what to cook for your first night home." She relaxed and the pasta jar rattled, Pam noticed and stepped back.

"What was that?"

I felt the ice cold bolt of terror run through me, Chandak was fighting to get out, Shelly leaned harder on the pasta jar, and looked at Pam.

"Mice... Big bugger, we just caught him." She took another step back away from the table and looked nervous.

"Shell you know I hate mice?" Shelly leaned even harder on the jar.

"We have three, one under each pot, but this bugger is massive, which is why I am leaning on it." Randolph sniggered, and I nudged him in the ribs, and then leaned forward and put my hand on the pan.

"This one is almost as huge; I am sure it is pregnant... Or a small rat."

It is laughable really, Pam is an ecologist who will study any form of creature, except mice. She looked panicked and stepped closer to the door. Shelly was enjoying this, she smiled.

"You can see it if you want before we get rid of it?"

She moved as if to lift the pot, and Pam gave out a deaf defying squeal, and fled into the living room slamming the door. Yep, she was wide awake now. I gave a sigh of relief, and looked at Shelly, but lowered my voice.

"What do we do now, Chandak cannot see them here?" She looked at Randolph then back to me.

"Get the others out quickly, and I will sort this one out." I nodded, and lifted the bowl, and whispered.

"Berrendoc, can you get Felix back to the island safely, Chandak is here, we have him under the pasta jar, he must not see any of you." Aubrianne gave a giggle, as Berrendoc nodded, and I lifted the pan off Felix and Esme. Felix smiled.

"That was fun, we made the talk back noises like in the tunnels." He was still pale and obviously in pain, but he looked a lot better.

"Felix, for the love God be quiet, now quick, go with Esme and your father, get back to the island and rest up. That sting will be painful, but you should be alright now." Esme stood up and walked over to me as I leaned on the table, she hugged my finger, and then looked up at me with those beautiful blue eyes.

"Emily, thank you for saving my Felix. I cannot think of a life without him, and you gave him back to us, I will be in your debt always." I smiled at her, God, she was so cute.

"Esme, we have to look out for each other, you owe me nothing, in a way, you and Felix have helped give me back my life, because I was so lost and alone without Han, and then you came to me, and that means everything to me." She gave me a huge smile, and the pasta jar rattled, Chandak was powerful and Shelly was struggling to hold him down. Esme took Felix by the hand.

"I love you too Emily, you really are beautiful." That hit the heart, Oh God, she is so adorable.

Aubrianne and Berrendoc took Felix by the hand and thanked me, then lifted into the air and carried Felix, who was in too much pain to use his wings, and flew out followed by Esme. I gave a huge sigh of relief.

"Okay, so what do we do with this one?" Randolph stepped forward.

"Leave this one to me, I will deal with him."

He picked up the lid and slid it into his pocket, and then slipped a piece of junk mail off the side unit, and slid it under the jar. The jar rattled, and Randolph slid it up, over and then covering the top with his palm, he pulled the lid out of his pocket, and wedged it on pulling the paper out at the same time. He lifted the jar with a smile.

"I will bring the jar back later." I nodded and felt very relieved.

"Yeah, no problems."

Shelly flopped down with a bump into one of the chairs and wiped her face. Randolph gave a nod, and holding the pasta jar, he left through the back door chuckling, I turned for the kettle.

"Pam... The mice are gone now." Shelly sniggered as the living room door opened slowly, her eyes peered round the edge of the door.

"Are you sure?" Shelly gave a chuckle.

"Pam, grow a spine, they are just mice."

I saw her visibly shiver, and then the door opened wider. I had to smile, I mean, seriously, she has spent her whole life out in the wilds, how could she possibly be afraid of mice? She came in looking worried, and I turned with a coffee, she checked out the table.

"You are definitely sure... You know Emily, we are going to have to get that sorted, the last thing you need is a rodent outbreak." I smiled.

"Yeah, I will look into it for us."

I sat back smiling, the crisis was averted, I could see Shelly smirking, although, I must admit, I am impressed with her quick thinking, she was actually pretty amazing. I sipped my coffee and leaned back on the chair, how the hell did we actually pull that off?

It had been a hectic day, and the evening was rolling in, and so once Pam was more awake, all of us mucked in and made food, which was burgers, with chips, and side salad. We opened a wine, and sat with the windows and door open talking as we ate, and Pam caught me up on all the latest gossip from the states.

The conversation moved back to me and how I was feeling, and I diverted it nicely into talk of the trust, and explained everything about Pete, and the rumours about him. She was shocked when I told her I had remembered the accident, and then went over how we caught Pete trying to survey the lake and sneak in a pipe rig to drill, in hope of hitting shale gas samples. She was horrified and hugged me, which okay I know she does that a lot.

I outlined my thoughts and told her of what my dad had suggested and she agreed with us both, so I was relieved to find all three of us were on board and singing from the same page.

Whilst we cooked and talked, and basically drank lots of wine, Randolph headed home, closed his door and windows, and placed the tall stone jar on his table. He took off the lid and a very enraged Chandak came flying out and landed on the table, he looked at Randolph with venom in his eyes.

"How dare you treat me, a member of the clan council with such utter disrespect." Randolph smirked.

"How dare you risk the clan by exposing yourself to a stranger not known to us." Chandak faltered.

"What do you mean, account for that statement?" Randolph looked at the Nairn man on his table.

"You flew off the island, against the wishes of your Clan leader, and barged into the private dwelling of a watcher, making false accusations, when they had a guest who is unaware of the Nairn. To make things worse, when Lady Shelly covered you for your own protection, you made a fuss and almost gave yourself and the clan away. It was irresponsible, and could have caused another chaos such as the one caused over Rachel and her aunt."

He spluttered as he tried to find his words, and it was clear to Randolph he was shaken.

"That is... I don't know your words... but not correct... that is not how it was, I... I... I got a sense of them at the girl's house, and went over to bring them back. It is my duty to Barrack to uphold the laws and customs of the clan."

"Since when was advising Barrack to risk the heir to his line a custom? No child has ever been asked to face a bee's nest, not ever, and yet you convinced him he should sacrifice his grandson for what purpose Chandak?" He looked uncomfortable.

"An example had to be made." Randolph shrugged.

"For what purpose? If it was not for Felix, Emily would not

be aware of the clan, and not agreed to enter the light. Myself and others feel Felix did a great service to the clan, as it brought Emily into contact sooner than any of us thought. I most certainly know Barrack was concerned, and felt a great relief in the circle to know she would embrace the light. Felix should have been honoured as both Veda and Aubrianne suggested, and yet you spoke alone to Barrack, and changed what was a group decision, just exactly why Chandak?" He started to pace nervously round the table.

"He left the island deliberately ignoring our rule." Randolph smiled.

"A rule for whom?" Chandak stopped pacing, and looked at Randolph.

"What exactly does that mean?" Randolph leaned back on his seat and watched as Chandak eyed up the room.

"There is no way out Chandak. What I mean is this, I find it interesting that two Saturdays ago, late in the evening you crossed the lake to the house, you thought it was empty, it wasn't, I was there. Why would you fly down the driveway to the road when the humans drive, and why on Thursday night did you fly over by the waterfalls, and up to the top road? Chandak I am a watcher, I sense everything, the light holds the truth of all things. Who did you talk to, will you tell me now, or should I wait for the inevitable to happen?" He swallowed hard.

"I answer only to my clan leader, not a human." Randolph smiled.

"That was the answer I was waiting for, and I am not fully human, like you, I am part mystical, for an advisor to the leader you should know that, Chandak."

Chandak scowled at him, and Randolph got up and walked to his door and drew back the bolts. He turned and looked back at the Nairn stood scowling on the table.

"Be wary Chandak, the human world holds nothing lasting for the Nairn, and no human has ever really served a Nairn for long. Go to your clan and help prepare, but be aware, I am watching you."

Randolph opened the door, and Chandak flew through it at great speed and Randolph smiled.

"Embracing the light reveals all my little flying friend, I can wait, it will not be long now, and Emily as the lead watcher will see the truth of you."

Over on the island once Felix was settled on a bed of soft moss, with Esme still holding his hand, Berrendoc headed back to the site of the fallen comb. It looked like Stripy Jake had been around, and eaten all of Emily's Carry, and currently the large badger was panting and drinking water on the lakeside. Berrendoc gathered together five times Felix's weight in comb of sweet paste, wrapped it in leaves, and carried it to the temple celebration circle, where he laid it neatly out on the table, with a smile, he was proud of his son.

"How is he?" Berrendoc turned to see Barrack stood watching in the doorway.

"He is recovering, thanks to his loyal friend, who healed him best she could." Barrack gave a sigh.

"I am happy to hear that, he has a stout heart, and he will be praised for his deed for this clan." Berrendoc felt his anger.

"Praised, what good would that serve to a dead son and grandson, he should have never been asked to do it?" Barrack lifted his hand.

"I regret the choice, when I heard the news, I feared the worst, and it was a terrible feeling to hold within me. Berrendoc, I am sorry, I truly am, and I am happy for you he was saved."

"Sorry for what father, listening to that eel who weaves in your ear? I told you long ago he was not pure enough for this clan, but you would not listen and left me isolated with the council, as he slithered his tongue into your mind. Chandak craves power and should never lead, I warned you and you chose to side against your blood, and it cost me a wife, and almost my son. When will you wake up and see the light that shines in our line, and honour it?" Barrack nodded.

"Berrendoc, I never wanted any of your family to come to harm, I loved Rosespire as a daughter, as I do Felix, he has a strong place in my heart. I made a mistake, an error of judgement, and I regret it bitterly because it cost me my son, in whom I have great pride." Berrendoc shook his head.

"The error you made was trusting that eel, had he not been at your side, Rosespire would have lived, for we would never have travelled to that farm to seek human help. Your choice cost you this family. I will always honour my clan, but I will never serve Chandak whilst I have a heart that beats. I have said this once past, and will say it no more."

He rose into the air and shot off into the trees, heading back to Felix, and Barrack gave a sigh and looked at the table and the largest pile of sweet paste comb he had ever seen, he smiled.

"So like your father Felix, and in that I have great hope for this clan."

With the meal finished, as Shelly and Pam volunteered to wash up, I grabbed my wine glass and walked out into the garden. I headed down the steps and onto the jetty, and looked out across the water towards the island. Today had drained me emotionally, and it was strange, because it was only two days ago, that I had first met Felix and Esme, and today as I saw his limp body in the arms of his father, my heart had frozen.

Felix looked so small, and so helpless, and I feared for his life and was afraid of losing him. In less than forty eight hours, I had learned to feel love for him, and that surprised me, I really did not think I could feel that much, so quickly. I arrived here only fourteen days ago, and so much has happened, was Han aware of this, like her lists did she have some sort of plan?

I guess I will never really know, and in a way, it did not matter, she had been part of a world that was secret, and lived a secret life, and now that was mine. I too would live as she did, and take care of the children. I felt a hand slide round my waist and turned, Pam stood at my side and gave me a squeeze.

"Shell has things to do, and I have not had a huge amount of time with you today. How are you, and I mean really Emmy?" I smiled; she never really turned it off.

"I am doing okay, I was not sure I would, but this place has a hidden magic, and it has eased my soul and helped me get through." She nodded as she looked out across the water.

"I remember my summer here with you and Han, it is such a place of great beauty, and I suppose she made it very magical with all her stories of the children. You know I have never forgotten them, even now I can be busy, and hear her soft words in my mind, she had an amazing gift Emmy." I turned to her.

"You know Pam, I do not understand that, you see magic in a story and embrace it with love, like Han's stories of the children, and yet you are so quick to shoot down any story Shell talks about, I find it strange." She shrugged.

"Emmy come on, let's be serious here, Shell believes the stories she tells, she thinks they are real. Han was simply telling a story, and magical adventure, you cannot compare the two." I sipped my drink and looked at her, she smiled at me. "Emmy be serious."

"I am being Pam. Han believed every word she spoke, her and Shell had more in common than you realise. Pam what if they were real, you know, just for arguments sake, you are an ecologist, you study life, would you just deny them and look elsewhere, or would you take them seriously?" She snorted a laugh.

"Seriously, for arguments sake? Okay I will play along, Emmy, firstly you would need proof, and mean concrete proof, not some folktale, but actual living proof. Okay, let's say Han was right, where were they, we were here all summer and never saw one. Han would literally have to have gathered them together and have brought them to us, and given us the chance to actually see and interact with them, but Emmy she never did, it was just a story, a beautiful one, even realistic, but it was still a story."

"What would you have done if she had, you know, walked up with one, would you have believed her?" She smirked.

"Well firstly, I would have made sure it was not a hologram like last time, I will not deny, for a second Shell had me going. Emmy if she had, I would have wanted to sit with it, and talk to it, and understand its world, just like any other life form I have studied. If it truly was real, I would then accept it, but come on Emmy, that is hardly going to happen, is it?" I gave a sigh.

"I have done a lot of thinking here, and actually talked more with Shell than I ever did back in the flat. I feel bad Pam, you know we took the piss a lot, and I never realised, but it hurts her you know? We have hurt her a lot in the past, and honestly, I would not have made it through the last year without her, she has been such a good friend and support." Pam smiled at me.

"Okay I will ease up on her, and yes, I have talked to her a lot and she has been really worried about you. I must admit, she feels a lot more positive about you now." I gave her a nod and turned back to the lake, it was clear and at peace, shimmering like a mirror as the darkness crept in.

"I have decided around Shelly to use the theory of Schrodinger, and adopt a fairy in the box and not in the box approach. It feels like a good compromise for us both, fairies exist and do not exist at the same time, it makes things easier, and to be honest, we have had some amazing talks as she explains her theories to me. I will give her credit, she knows a lot more about evolution and science than I first thought, her arguments are actually really well reasoned out." Pam smirked.

"Yeah, but they are not sound scientific proof, they are just theories, and obviously not provable." I smiled.

"They are all in the box Pam, and no one will know until they open it and look, science is also a theory until disproved, and that works for me." She gave a giggle.

"Okay, I will play along with you." It was a small step forward, leading to a trap, one that would probably challenge Pam on every level, it certainly had me.

It was getting late, and I was tired, I turned with Pam and walked slowly back to the house talking to her quietly. As we came up the steps, I looked at her.

"I am glad you are here; this feels right again. Pam, I have some moving around to do, so do not unpack in a rush, Han's room is free and it has a double bed. My mum's old wardrobe is in there and I am going to swap it out with mine, but when that is done, you take the room, it is bigger." She smiled at me as we reached the top step and stopped.

"If it is okay with you, I will keep the room I have, I really like it, I find it quaint, although I would love the bed base, I will order a new mattress, use the room for guests."

"Are you sure?" She nodded at me.

"Yeah, Emmy that room is so quaint and cool, it feels really homely, I love it, I can see myself living a long happy life in there." I shrugged.

"Okay then, order your mattress and I will help you move the bed base; it is solid oak and quite heavy you know?" She giggled.

"I hope it squeaks; it will wind Shell up if we have guests."

I started to chuckle, as we headed for the door, she has never changed, but I liked that about her.

Berrendoc walked down between the ferns towards Aubrianne's cave, she smiled as she saw him, and he nodded as he approached. She turned to look back, where Felix and Esme lay curled together on a soft bed made of woven grasses, and stuffed with rabbits' fur. Berrendoc gave a nod to Veda who sat watching. Aubrianne touched his arm.

"He is stronger, whatever was in the herbs she gave him, it worked, and he will be back to normal misbehaving before you know it." He looked past her shoulder to his sleeping son.

"I appreciate you watching over him for me, this day has brought great fear to my heart." She understood, losing a child was not the normal cycle of life, and all parents fear outliving their children.

"I take it you found the comb, and delivered it to the temple? I saw Barrack walking the path, did you speak or scream at each other as normal." He smirked at her.

"We spoke." She gave a giggle at his face.

"The tone alone states if was abrasive." He hung his head and gave a sigh.

"He does that to me, and I do not understand why." He lifted his head. "Do you know, honestly, why do I get so angry with him?" Aubrianne bent down, and lifted a drink and handed it to him.

"Take a seat Berrendoc, let us talk awhile, it has been a long time since we talked of the affairs of the Nairn, and I miss it. Felix will not be moving tonight, and if he could, I am not sure my daughter would not let him. Tarry here for a while like old times, and talk to me." He took a seat and Veda smiled at him.

"Talk accomplishes nothing, both of you know that. With Barrack, only one voice matters, it annoys me so much, I expected better of him." Veda gave a nod of agreement.

"My dear boy, in my life I have seen much, you ask why does your father make you feel so strongly? If you ask me, it is love, for the light within you for your father is deep and strong, and yet you note his folly, and in that you feel helpless. That is the reason you become so enraged."

He took a gulp of his drink, as Aubrianne handed him fresh slices of fruit in an acorn cup. He nodded his thanks and started to eat. He looked at both of the women as he chewed.

"He is such a mighty man, that is what I do not understand. My father has a brilliant mind, and yet he allows that eel to slither between his ears and rob him of his brilliance, can he not see the untruth of the words that eel whispers?" Aubrianne gave a knowing nod; her voice was soft.

"Our journey has been long and marked with a trail of death. All of us have had our doubts, and with the passing of Han, a lot of the past has crept back into the minds and bones of the elders. Crazy as it sounds, at times Mugwump makes far more sense to me than the council. Berrendoc, I feel Chandak has taken advantage of that, and if you want my opinion, when you walked away from the council you sealed your father's fate." He shook his head.

"My words fell on deaf ears, had he listened, many would have been spared." She nodded.

"This is true, and with hindsight easy to spot, it was a hard road, all of us were weary as we searched for this place. Were mistakes made, yes, they were, your father should not be blamed for all of them. Berrendoc, the elders would not see reason and were fearful for their lives."

"They backed Chandak, they promoted him to second, how could I stay on a council that would support the one that would lead us to ruin, I had no choice, I had to leave?" Veda looked at him sternly.

"You should have stayed, there were eight of us, us three, three of them, Chandak and your father, the vote would always have been tied. Had you stayed and matched our votes, your father would have been forced to hold the vote, only after speaking in private to all of us, and in private the views of the council were different. Your absence played its part in remaining an open vote, and it too help Chandak take more power than he deserved. Even Han agreed on that, I know she tried to talk you round."

"I was a different man then; I had a son to raise." Veda understood and gave a smile.

"We knew that, and we did not blame you. Rosespire was a beautiful soul filled with such light. No one here thinks ill of you, and you have proven to be a great parent, and a great leader of men, if only you would open your eyes and see that. I know of the talks you have held with Mugwump, I know of the affection he feels for you. Whether you see it or not, mad as he is, Mugwump is wiser than any of us, and the other council understand that. Berrendoc, it is time, a new watcher awaits her role, take back your seat and guide her with us, for I have a strong feeling, the Lady Emily will bring great change to the Nairn clan."

He put down his food and lifted his drink, sipped and swallowed, then rubbed at his short beard.

"I see no point in a seat that has not got a voice, and mine certainly did not as I explained to Han." Aubrianne agreed.

"That is true, but Han is no longer here, and Emily has to pick one to advise her. She knows only you and I, and she cannot pick me, for I advise Randolph. Emily will recognise you and knowing you are the father of Felix; she will naturally pick you. Think about it Berrendoc, you will have a chance to talk through her, and as we have seen, she is her mother's daughter, and not one to bow down to Barrack, even when he is advised by Chandak." Berrendoc sat back and gave a slight chuckle, and shook his head.

"What a pair you two make, I will consider your point, and if Emily does pick me, then I will as always honour this clan in service to her, but I will say this now, it must be her choice, made freely."

Veda and Aubrianne smiled, and looked excited, this was further than any had ever got Berrendoc to reengage with the council.

Chapter Thirty Two

Destiny Awaits

When I woke up on Sunday, I had a lot on my mind. Felix had achieved his task, and so I was now required to complete mine, which was to embrace the light. Randolph had spoken a lot to me yesterday as he helped me come to terms with Han's room, and he would return again today to help me prepare. I had a list of things that I had to follow, like showering and purifying myself before robing up.

I was not too concerned, it appeared like some sort of ceremony not unsimilar to what I had read about certain Pagan rituals. My biggest problem, which was where my mind currently was, all were aimed at Pam. In a way I do not know why I was surprised, last night if anything proved to me that she was too fixed in her thoughts, and not capable of changing her views.

I still find it amazing that a person who studies all the cycles and environments that contain life, is not capable of accepting facts that certain lives exist. I was so sceptical of Shelly and her belief system, but when confronted with a new form of life, I could clearly see that the Nairn were a life form that had slipped through the evolutionary net. They had not been recorded, but I could not possibly deny their existence having met them. Pam would, and that bothered me, actually it was bothering me a lot this morning, because I had to visit the island, and somehow hide that from her.

As much as I wanted to lie in bed all day, I knew I had things to do, but first coffee, and food, and then I would get stuck in. I made my way down to the kitchen, Shelly was up, which was weird, she smiled as I walked in, and headed for the toaster, she turned in her seat.

"Are you nervous?" I frowned as I looked round.

"Why would I be? It is a ceremony of acceptance and in a strange way, becoming one in the sense of belonging." She shrugged.

"It is a big step Hun; it is a life time commitment."

I clicked on the kettle and grabbed two slices of bread, and dropped them into the toaster. The kettle clicked, as I spooned out the coffee and yawned.

"To be honest Shell, this place is, as is the trust, I just think that the Nairn are a part of that. The way I see it, all three are part of each other, so to commit to one, is to commit to all three." She gave a nod and then sipped her tea.

"What about Pam?"

The toast popped up and I grabbed it, and lifted the knife ready to butter.

"She is something I have to find a way around." I scraped the butter over the toast, and thought for a second, then looked back towards Shell.

"My problem is the island, if I can keep her clear of that, we should be alright, although as I lay in bed last night, I did think back to when I was a child, and I never saw the Nairn once. So, the way I am thinking, is Han must have had some kind of arrangement with Barrack." Shell gave a nod as she continued to sip her tea.

"That makes sense, but it still leaves us one problem." I sat down with my plate and coffee, and looked at her.

"What?"

"Felix and Esme, to be honest, they love your ass, they will not stay away." She made a good point, I considered it.

"They did when I was here as a young girl."

"Yeah, I was thinking about that, you were a kid, what if they only visited when you were in bed? Pam is a night owl when she is not jet lagged." I had not thought of that, she did a reputation for sitting up late.

"To be honest, it would make life a lot easier if she would just get down off her sceptic platform, and face the reality. It confuses me, I was so sceptic, there was and still is no scientific evidence, and yet, Felix and Esme crept out from the cabbages and blew my mind." She gave a slight chuckle.

"It was certainly a reality check moment, hell, I believed in them, but being confronted like that, shocked the hell out of me. It sounds crazy, but just knowing I was right, threw my whole world view out of balance, it is the coolest, and yet most challenging moment of my life to date." I could not help but giggle.

"Hell, stick with me kid, I think I am a weird magnet, I certainly have the worlds strangest grandfather."

There was a knock at the door, and Randolph leaned round it, both of us looked up, saw him, and then pissed our sides laughing. He stepped in looking confused, as we could not help laughing like idiots.

Moving a wardrobe is a pretty simple task, or at least it appears that way, that is, until you realise how heavy it is, and how little room there is in the upper stair's hallway. It took about twenty minutes to get my mum's old wardrobe into my bedroom, then we were faced with our second problem, cottages are notorious small. With my new wardrobe in, I had to get my old one out, and I had filled the bed with all my things, so moving the bed as far as I was concerned, was not an option.

It took what felt like a massive engineering project and a game of shuffle the wardrobes, before we finally, sweating and gasping got my old wardrobe into Han's old room. All of us sat gasping to recover our strength on the bed and took a moment, before phase two commenced, yep, I had to put all my stuff back in the new bigger wardrobe. Shell helped, we had made enough noise so Pam was up and downstairs with Randolph, as I hung all my things back, and cleaned up.

By the time we arrived back downstairs, Randolph was sat with Pam at the bottom of the garden, chatting happily away about the lake, the wildlife and all the diversity of the wild flowers that grew in this area. He has been here a long time, and so naturally was the go to for all the intel, and Pam was expert at getting all of the data she would need to begin her work here on the landscape.

We joined them outside and spent the afternoon sat out on the jetty, talking about the cottage and the trees, and what we had planned. It was sunny and warm, with a light breeze, and I sat back enjoying the day, feeling relaxed, if this was going to be what it was like for the rest of my life, I had no problems committing to this.

We all mucked in with a meal, and sat round the table, reminiscing about the fun we had at Uni, and Randolph who appeared to be really enjoying himself laughed with us, but I was aware of the clock, and knew at midnight I had to be on the island, and so would soon have to prepare. Shelly poured out the last of the wine into Pam's glass as we giggled, and I got up to make a start on washing the pots, as my mind tried to find some way of slipping out unseen. Shelly chucked.

"You still look tired to me Pam; the jet lag really hits you hard, doesn't it?" She yawned and then gave a nod.

"Yeah, the wine has really snuck up on me tonight, this stuff of Han's is far more powerful than I thought."

I stopped washing and turned to them, I was sure we had not opened the wine, well not real wine? I had deliberately gone for a bottle I knew was not very strong, Han had a shelf with what she called her failures on it which she gave to guests. I looked at Shelly as she sat wearing a huge smile, I frowned, what was she up to? Pam got up from her seat and wobbled.

"Hate to be a party pooper, but guys, I think I will crash for a while." I looked at her.

"You okay Pam?" She wobbled a little.

"Just knackered Emmy, I think I am still on US time, I am going to crash for a bit." I nodded.

"Okay then, go sleep it off."

I looked back at Shell, I knew she had done something, but was not sure what. Pam waved goodnight and staggered through the living room door. I listened to her on the stairs, then turned on Shell.

"What did you do?" She gave a smirk and then bit her lip.

"Looks like she had too much wine Emmy." I shook my head.

"That wine was only 2%, it was a failed batch, well by Han's standards it was. I used that because I have to clean myself for the ceremony. I know you, so cough up." She gave a slight chuckle.

"Okay if you really want to know, I crushed two sleeping pills and mixed them in her wine. The way I see it, you need to get ready and you need her out of the way, well, she is out of the way." I gasped in shock.

"You drugged her, Jesus Shell?" She shrugged.

"She needs the sleep, and the way I see it, she will sleep until tomorrow and wake up filled with the joys of spring, and you will be home free, and all embraced." Randolph burst into laughter, I looked at him and scowled.

"Don't encourage her, my God, she drugged our best friend." He was still chuckling.

"Emily, you needed time, and to be honest, she has bought you some. Look at this way, it protects her as much as it protects the Nairn. You can now do the ceremony in secret, and she will then have the time for both of you to convince her that there is more to life than her reality says so, no matter how you look at it, Emily, this works well." I gave a sigh and looked at Shelly.

"I know.... But drugs, Jesus what will come next, locking her in a box?" Shelly gave a giggle and lifted her glass.

"The wardrobe is big enough, and it does have a lock on it."

I smirked, I was a little freaked out at how devious she was getting, and was starting to wonder just how long we could actually hide the Nairn, without drugging her again.

With Pam out cold, from my friends' devious tactics, I had to get ready for the ceremony, which involved showering and achieving a high level of cleanliness. As I prepared, Shelly sat on my bed, reading the written notes Randolph had given me to help me prepare, she gave a chuckle.

"You have to make yourself as pure as possible, do you think they will accept slightly tainted, after all there was not just Ken?" I smirked.

"Probably a good thing it is not for you then, hell, you should embrace the darkness, no need for purity there." We giggled as she looked at me.

"Am I a bit of a tramp, what do you think?" I looked at her and tried to hide my smile.

"Oh Shell, you are not a bit, you are full on tramp, but hey, someone has to be." Both of us laughed as I lifted my towel. Shelly held up a razor, and I looked at it.

"What is that for?" She smiled.

"Armpits, and other things, she looked at me and dropped her eyes south." I looked down and frowned.

"I have never shaved that; I am not sure I have to be that pure." She shrugged.

"The dress is a little see through, you know, dark triangle through the fabric?" She looked at me. "You will be commando, won't you?" I had not thought about it.

"I am not sure, do you think it matters, after all they are not expecting a virgin bride?" I could see her thinking about it.

"I know a lot of druid, and wiccan priestess, and they all shave, although they conduct their rituals sky clad, which is naked, so I suppose with nudity it matters. I say, whip off the fluff just to be safe." I suppose it was a good point, I knew only a little of the rituals of Pagans.

I headed to the shower and scrubbed myself raw, and did the best I could shaving, it was for me a very strange experience, but I had never done it before. Wrapped in a towel I walked back into the room, where Shell had my dress ready, I dropped the towel and dried myself off thoroughly, and caught a glimpse of myself in the mirror.

"You know, is it weird that I am almost twenty two, and this is the first time I have seen that part of me?" Shelly smiled.

"I shave all the time so I am bored of seeing it. It is funny isn't it, it is supposed to be the most sensual part of a woman, and yet we are so dammed busy we never really consider it?" I slipped on the dress, and pulled it down.

"I never have until now... So, what do you think?" She looked me up and down.

"Yeah, shaving was a smart move, it is a little transparent where the light shines through, a triangle would have stood out, but as you are now, you are very virginal looking."

I shook my head as she handed me the thick hooded cloak, and I swung it over my shoulders. I turned and looked at myself in the mirror. Dressed in pure white did actually look pretty good with my long brown hair falling down onto it.

"I like the look, we should definitely bring cloaks back into fashion, I would wear one all the time, this feels pretty nice." Shelly gave it the thumbs up, and we headed downstairs, I assumed Randolph would be the judge of if I passed as clean enough.

He was really pleased when he saw me, and he nodded his head as I walked towards him.

"Oh Emily, you look so like your mother on the night she embraced the light. It caught my breath as you walked in, your likeness is uncanny, and gave me quite a moment."

"I look alright then, I have scrubbed, shaved, even places I never do, and I have no perfume or deodorant on?"

"You look amazing, and like a true Watcher of the light."

There was something about his eyes, that made me wonder, had he had the very same conversation all those years ago when Han led my mother to him to prepare for the service? I think maybe so.

From this moment on, all I was allowed to drink was water, and I could only eat fresh fruit, which actually was a bit of a bonus, because Randolph handed me a huge bunch of grapes, which I love. He sat in the garden and talked me through the process from arrival to the feast at the end, and gave me tips on some of their language.

It appeared that some of the older Nairn's, used some very old English words, which was as he explained, due to the fact that their Watchers had been from a very different era, the younger Nairn's, had a more modern language, some of which came from interacting with my mother, it made me think, would Esme and Felix end up copying me, or what about Shell? Oh hell, she would have to watch her language around them when she spoke.

As we prepared, John Duncan sat at home in his office, working on details for the Amelia Montgomery Trust, Kate had received the paperwork and sent it over. Jane sat at his side watching and making small comments, as together they worked out all of the details to present in their first meeting with Emily. John's mobile phone rang, and he lifted it up, read the name and answered sending it to speaker phone.

"Edgar, nice to hear from you, what can I do for you?"

"John, I have just spoken with Peter McDougal, he had to cancel his meeting as he had some sort of accident." John smirked.

"Alright, how did that go for you?"

"Well, I checked out those leads you gave me and I questioned him about them, he denied it, but to be honest, his manner changed, and I am too old to not see lies when used to try and butter me up. To be honest, the call was a lot shorter than expected and he appeared somewhat annoyed with me." Jane covered her mouth as she laughed.

"Look John, I promised my kids help, so, if your offer is still on the table, I would consider it, this house is too big for me and the wife now."

"As I said Edgar, I was happy to match his price, I own all of that side of the lake road, and Emily will be thrilled to know that her land is safe from pollutants from Shale gas production. I am happy to come see you and work out the details, and I know my father would be happy, he tried many times I know to talk you into selling. I will consider this his wish granted." Edgar gave a laugh.

"Aye, the problem was John, he was too dam tight, always after a bargain that one, but he was good stock, you are very like him John, and I will be happier dealing with you, your pack is straight and not from under the table." John smiled.

"Whenever you are free Edgar, I will be there."

"I suppose the question is, when are you free?" Jane wrote on his pad on the desk, and he looked down and read it.

"I can be there tomorrow at eleven if that is alright with you?"

"That will suit our time frame John, as you know we are almost packed and ready to move. Yes, that will be fine with us." John gave a sigh of relief.

"You can take your time Edgar with the move, Emily has a lot on her plate setting up the trust, but I will have the papers tomorrow and we will start the process, have your legal peoples details there, and we will get right on it for you."

"Thank you, John, this will be a big help to my kids, they really need the funding."

"Have no fear, we will move fast, so we can protect that whole area for ever from the likes of Pete. Emily will manage it and preserve it forever, and I am sure she will make use of the orchard." Edgar gave a chuckle.

"I bet she will, she always loved picking the apples, and we always got a few jars of her jam, she is a lovely girl, I am happy it will be in her hands John, she is so like Amelia, and a good sort. Again, thanks John, I will go tell the wife."

"Okay Edgar, I will see you tomorrow." He ended the call and sat back with a sigh of relief and smiled. "Emily will be thrilled, thank god for that, I think we just saved the lake." Jane smiled at him.

"I will get straight on the paper work, is this Duncan or trust?" He smiled.

"This is for the trust, Emily will own that land, which will really piss off Pete, when I make sure he finds out." Jane gave a chuckle as he smiled.

"Wow, you really know how to press all of his buttons don't you?" He just sat back and smiled.

"I promised her Jane, and now I will keep that promise."

Sat talking as the sun faded was nice, and I once again got to learn a lot more about Randolph's life as a game keeper, and a logger in his early life. I heard a lot more about my mother in her teenage years, I felt we were very alike, she loved to stretch out on the deck and read, as well as swim naked, and explore the woodlands all around the lake, and I felt that was one aspect of her life I would absolutely be copying, as there are many parts I want to get into, and see what is living there.

As we whiled away the time, and Pam slept in a deep sleep, the Nairn were busy, under the watchful eye of Chandak. In the ancient stone temple, past the stone dais with the tall standing stone, was another larger area, with a single round stone plinth. Around it, were ten tall seats of stone, and each had a smaller seat to the right side, and all were decorated with flowers and vines. Each seat had a soft pad, made of a finely woven grass, and stuffed with fresh moss.

Chandak watched as Aubrianne in her long white cloak showed Esme how to bind the vines, and weave the flower stalks into them. Esme was very excited, as she had been told she would be playing a part in the ritual. Chandak looked at them and scowled.

"Why decorate all eight seats, when there are only seven

members of the council, leave that seat alone, it is no longer used."

"Then your ritual will fail, and there will be no new light of the next generation." Chandak turned to see Berrendoc stood in his ceremonial white cloak and robe.

"Why are you wearing those robes, you forfeited the right to play a part in this night?" Aubrianne bit her lip, and tried to hide her smirk. Berrendoc stepped into the room.

"If you wish to be a leader one day Chandak, I suggest you learn your rituals better. Only eight can bring the light, with seven you will fail. I stepped down from the council discussions and votes, for they serve no purpose, as only one vote appeared to count, but in all other ways, I serve my clan with duty and honour."

"Your duty was to vote, and yet you deserted that duty." Berrendoc gave a slight smile as he noticed Aubrianne.

"As I said, the vote became pointless, one voice appeared to hold sway with my father, and the others faded into nothingness. I had a child to raise, my time was better served on that duty, for it had a point and meaning."

Aubrianne gave a slight titter. Chandak turned back to his seat, and plumped up his seating pad muttering to himself, Berrendoc approached the seat which would be at the side of his father. It had been some time since he had sat here. He turned to Aubrianne as she worked with Esme to his left, she noted it and gave a slight nod, he smiled, Esme looked up and smiled a huge smile.

"Berrendoc, I will be helping tonight, so I want this chamber extra beautiful." He looked round the chamber with a smile.

"You have done a job worthy of your Lady Emily; she will be delighted I feel with the skilled way you have applied your talent. It is good to see a future council leader working for the cause of our clan." Esme stopped and frowned.

"I am not sure I will ever be royal enough to be seated on the council, that is for the important Nairn." He winked at her.

"You are quite right, if what I hear is true, you have become very important to many." Her eyes opened wide as she turned and looked at her mother, Aubrianne smiled at her.

"I believe Lady Emily and Shelly see you as very important,

and also Randolph." She lowered her voice. "And I do think you are very important to Felix." Esme turned a little pink and put her head down.

"All Felix thinks about is eating pollen balls." Berrendoc gave a hearty laugh.

"This is true, but trust me little Esme, alone with me, the only Nairn he talks about is you. He hides it well, but he cares very much for you, and does do his best to protect you." She looked up and narrowed her eyes.

"He always falls asleep though." Berrendoc smiled.

"That is probably because he talks late into the night of his day with you on your adventures, trust me, I can never shut him up and get him to sleep properly." Esme smiled and looked at her mother.

"I did not know he did that." Aubrianne cupped her cheek.

"See, you are far more important than you realised, and Esme, you are the most important person in my life." Esme smiled and felt warm inside.

"You are to me also; I love you most mother."

Randolph looked at the sky, and then stood up, he turned to me and looked down.

"It is time Emily."

Suddenly I felt really nervous, Shelly looked just as bad as me. I felt my legs tremble a little, as I stood up, and Randolph smiled at me.

"There is nothing to fear, the light is pure truth and love, trust me, within the light there is nothing that will harm you, for you were chosen for that very reason." I nodded and took a deep breath.

"I am okay, I will be fine when we are there."

"Alright, you have the pendants, and have removed their chains?" I nodded and slipped them out of a pocket on the inside of the cloak and showed them to him, he smiled as he saw them.

"Right there is just one more thing, before we leave. Emily, Barrack will ask if you embrace the light, and when he does, you will pull this from your inside pocket, and hold it up on flat palms, still wrapped in the fabric it is in."

He pulled from his inner pocket, a long object shaped in a

rectangular block, wrapped in pure white silk, and held it up in front of me.

"You must not touch the crystal within, until that moment. When Barrack instructs you, take off the wrapping, and then holding both pendants in your left hand, and the crystal in your right, place the crystal against your heart, and press the pendants on to it, and close your eyes, and the light will embrace you. When that is done, one will be chosen to assist you, simply follow their instruction, alright?" I nodded and was suddenly terrified, he smiled.

"All will be fine." He slipped the wrapped crystal into my inner pocket.

"I am so proud of you, considering the last year, you have come a long way. Han never doubted you; she knew this day would come, and she often told me of the happiness it would bring to your life. I am honoured to be at your side tonight, Emily, I was with your mother, and I am so happy to be here with her daughter."

I swallowed hard, he was so sincere, and spoke so softly with love in his voice that my eyes teared up and I smiled.

"I am glad I found you, I was so lost and had no direction, and you have helped me find my north again, thank you grandfather." I could see the emotion in his face, and knew it had touched his heart. He gave a soft nod, no words needed to be spoken, he knew. Shelly gave a slight cough.

"Jesus you two, stop it or I will be bawling my brains out."

I giggled, she was stood slightly behind me with a long cloak on, over her best dress, and she had assured me she was shaved and commando, which made me giggle.

We headed to the boat house, and Randolph climbed into the boat, and took the wheel. Shelly and I sat at the back and she took my hand, my nerves were showing a little. The boat pulled out slowly, and he switched on the spotlight to light the water and the bank, and at a slow speed we headed onto the lake in the direction of the island.

The water was calm and the moon was out above the trees, I felt the air around me and it was calm and still, and yet it felt like there was an air of power within it. The boat chugged along slowly, and there was the gentle sound of the water lapping against it, but sat at the back, holding Shelly by the hand, it felt like we were the only thing in the whole area moving. It was not that long a journey, and as we approached the island, Randolph killed the engine, he looked back as we drifted towards the shore. It suddenly felt completely silent, and I could hear myself breathing.

"We are here, get ready." It was time to face my destiny, and suddenly, I was terrified.

Chapter Thirty Three

The Embrace of Light

There was a silence all over the lake, it felt almost as if once we hit the bank, an air of anticipation fell over everything, and I felt my apprehension increase, and yet did not understand why. The tension broke, when Randolph waded through the shallow water, and then as I prepared to leave the boat, he whisked me into his arms with a smile, and carried me to the bank.

I threw my arms round his neck and clung on, feeling the power of his arms, he was far stronger than I realised. He placed me gently down, and I slipped gently from his arms onto the soft damp soil, he smiled.

"You look so beautiful tonight, that dress should not be soiled by dragging it in the water." I smiled and yet felt shy, and I have no idea why, maybe it was the reverence in the way he held me, or the sincerity of his tone, I am not sure, but it felt special.

He turned and headed back, as Shelly clambered onto the side of the boat, and he lifted her up and carried her to shore, she smiled at him.

"Randolph Hun, if you were thirty years younger, I would so....!"

"Shell stop... Honestly, I love you, I have seen you in action, but please for the love of God, do not put that picture in my brain."

Randolph gave a giggle, as he led the way onto the path, which he needed to, because under the trees, it was pitch black, and I could hardly see anything. Shell held my hand, and I guided her as I was two steps behind Randolph. He stopped and turned, and I thought, we must be on the wide path that we had walked several times, but it was impossible to see anything at all. His voice was soft and low.

"Emily, we wait here."

I could see nothing, and hear the gentle lap of the water's edge behind me, but apart from that, everything was as silent as the grave. I felt Shelly as she readjusted her feet behind me, and whispered.

"Why have we stopped, hell it is dark, and a little creepy, Emmy, why didn't you bring a torch?" I sighed.

"Shell, it's a ceremony to embrace the light, I did sort of think light would be involved." Randolph moved slightly.

"Both of you, try to clear your minds, just relax and soak up the energy of the surroundings, it will begin very shortly."

I breathed out slowly and tried to calm my nerves, and stared into the blackness before me, there was not a sound of anything anywhere, and it felt almost like closing my eyes and just thinking. I tried to clear my mind as I breathed slowly, and started to feel calmer, the temperature under the trees had dropped, and there was a slight chill, and I felt the goosebumps lift on my arms.

It was strange, as I stood there, I became very aware of my body, the way my breasts touched the fabric, and the nape of my back which felt a soft warmth to it, or my hands. I stopped and wriggled my fingers, they were tingling, so were my arms, and legs, my whole body was. I was not cold, I was warm, actually warmer than normal, my body was heating up, what was this strange sensation? I looked up and was about to turn to Randolph, when far up the path, I saw a light.

It was small, like a small dot, of pure brilliant white, close to the floor, oh hell was it some sort of animal? Shell fidgeted.

"Emmy, if that is a single eye watching us in the dark, I am getting back on the boat, oh hell, that is creepy." I smirked, I had no idea what it was, but it was moving towards us.

The light came closer, and even though it did look strange, I felt no fear or threat at all. I stood watching as it moved slowly forward, and I began to realise, it was a Nairn holding something bright. I felt my body radiate warmth, it sounds strange, but I felt like I had nothing to fear, I felt I knew them? The light came closer, and I could see the bobbing motion, and then the tiny face, and I smiled, and breathed out my words.

"Felix, I should have known."

He walked right up to me, holding a tiny little basket, made of some kind of reed, which contained a glowing rock of some kind, and it lit up his smiling face. He stopped and looked up at me, he was wearing an acorn cup as a hat, and he looked so cute. He bowed to me sweeping his arm to one said in a grand gesture.

"My Lady Emily, I bid thee welcome and well met." Oh god, he was so lovely, I gave a bow back.

"Master Felix, I am honoured to be met such, and bid thee welcome." He smiled a huge smile, and whispered.

"It still hurts to fly, so they gave me the best job, I am going to be your guide." Shelly snorted, and whispered at my side.

"Great, we will probably end up in the kitchen."

I bit my lip, and tried not to laugh. Felix turned with pride, and taking a huge breath, in his loudest squeaky voice, he spoke loud and clear.

"LIGHT THE WAY FOR THE LADY EMILY, WATCHER OF THE LIGHT!"

I lifted my eyes from Felix, and felt my breath catch in my throat, as thousands of tiny lights lifted out of what I knew were ferns and shrubs, and floated silently towards the edges of the path. It looked so beautiful, as they all lined up, like a rope light to light the path for me, and I smiled. Shelly gave a little gasp, and sounded completely blown away, as her voice was almost a whisper.

"Emmy, there are thousands."

There were, but now I think about it, there was a whole race of Nairn living here, my question was, where? I had seen no signs of any form of home or dwelling in my whole life, how could so many live here, and not leave a single trace? Randolph lifted my arm, and tucked it into his.

"Shall we?"

We walked slowly along the path in the total darkness, the small lights our only way of knowing where we were going. As we passed, each Nairn holding their lit little baskets bowed, and then fell in behind Shelly, and followed us. It really was like walking in a magical parade, and I could not help but think of all the stories Han had told me as a child. It is so strange knowing that she was not telling me fictional stories, she was actually sharing her life. One story came to mind, which was one about a mother who walked her daughter to a fairy ball, lit by fireflies, and suddenly I understood, it was the story of my mother. Like Randolph, she walked my mother to the embracing of light, just like he was doing now. I glanced to the side, it was dark, but a little of the light illuminated his face, and he looked so proud, and that made me feel happier and warmer.

We were heading towards the stone circle, and my body still had tingles all over it, and yet I was warm and at ease, my inner self felt calmer, rested, and more relaxed than I had been in a long time. I looked ahead, captivated by the lines of lights, knowing each was a magical and special life. We approached the stone circle, and I noticed the pathway separated, I turned to Randolph.

"Why does the path fork, you will not be leaving me will you?" He turned and I saw his smile.

"No... Emily we are Watchers, Shelly is not, she will have to remain here for a short time." I swallowed hard.

"Leave her, alone in the dark?" He nodded.

"It will be for only a short time, she will be safe and protected, for she is bonded to you, and as you enter the sacred temple of the light, nothing will be able to land on this island, the realm will be sealed, for a short time." A slightly high pitched and scared voice sounded behind us.

"What if Stripy Jake comes, those buggers are dangerous, I don't want to be alone in the dark with a pissed off badger?" Randolph gave a titter.

"No creature on this island will ever harm you Shelly, although having read your book, I am surprised you did not mention ghosts." I could feel her shudder ripple the air behind me.

"Did you have say that, I was fine, and now I am completely freaked out?" I smirked as I saw Randolph smile.

"As you have seen, it is a very ancient circle, and you did say you thought it was a doorway." I almost blurted out a laugh, as I heard a little whimper behind me.

"Oh crap, I wish I had stayed on the boat now. My imagination is way too vivid to be out here in the dark."

We reached the fork in the lights, and Felix stopped. He turned to us, and looked up at me with a smile, he was very serious and official.

"Lady Emily, your friend and companion must wait here, but she will be watched over and safe, all the passed watchers are here." I really wanted to laugh, considering they had all passed on, I am sure Shelly would not be happy knowing that. Felix smiled.

"Please raise your hood, and we shall enter the Temple of Light."

Randolph turned me slightly, and lifted my hood up, and arranged my hair so it hung out either side of my hood. He turned to Shelly and lifted her hood.

"Sit in front of the circle, and face into it, stay still, and if you can meditate to calm your inner self, do so. Shelly tonight you will be witness to something no one, not even a Watcher has seen, it is a very sacred and special thing. Barrack has allowed this only because of your faith and belief in his people, and your loyalty and devotion to Emily. We will not be long, but stay alert and watch." She nodded looking nervous.

"Emmy will be alright won't she, I do not want her feeling anymore pain?" He smiled at her.

"She will be fine, do not fear for her." Randolph helped Shelly sit in the right position. She looked nervously at him, and swallowed hard.

"Just one more thing, you said watch. Oh God, I hate asking, because I am sure I will not like the answer, but just what exactly and I am looking for?" Randolph smiled.

"I have no need to say the words, it will spoil the surprise, but trust me, no living soul has ever seen what you will." She suddenly looked afraid, and her voice went low.

"No living soul, oh crap, I will live through this won't I?" Randolph shrugged and she stiffened, I bit my lip and tried to hide my smile.

"Shelly, you more than any, will witness something unearthly, and your faith and belief's will be greatly enhanced." She swallowed even harder.

"Oh hell, I really wish I had not asked now."

When Shelly was sat down looking really nervous, Felix once again led the way. I had no idea there was a path here, I had not seen one here before. We walked on to what I knew were trees, and Felix lifted his arm and waved it, and I gasped as the foliage swung back in the darkness, almost like opening curtains, and there were more lights, which revealed a large ancient stone doorway. We approached and Randolph squeezed my arm and leant into me, and spoke in a low voice.

"We shall wait by the doorway until the Nairn are fully assembled, and then when requested, we will enter." One foot before the door Felix stopped and turned to me, I looked down at him.

"Lady Emily, please would you wait for the command of our clan leader?" I smiled at him, he was so polite, and not at all like the wild little Nairn I knew.

"I shall follow your lead, and command Master Felix."

Shelly sat staring into the darkness where she knew there was an ancient ring of stone, predating anything she had ever read about. Her breathing was slow as her ears strained in what was complete darkness, for any sound at all. She breathed out slowly.

"Okay, this is cool, I can do this, oh shit, I really wish I had not drugged Pam, she could be here with me now." She turned to look where the lit road led, and there was nothing at all.

"Oh, hell no, this is not what I want, not at all what I want."

The Nairn streamed past us and entered their temple. I watched through the doorway, where I could see a tall pillar of stone, set on some round looking steps, but the Nairn passed it and headed to a place behind it. I could not see, but whatever it was, there was a lot of light in there. As I leaned forward slightly to see what was happening, there was a loud bang and I jumped back.

Another loud bang echoed, and I swallowed hard, and then a voice boomed out from somewhere behind the pillar.

"Who stands before us and seeks entry to the Temple of Light?"

I felt nervous and looked at Randolph, he smiled and took my hand in his, and then looked through the doorway, as my heart beat in my chest. Randolph spoke loud and clearly.

"I am Master Sage Feather, and seek entrance with Lady Emily Montgomery Duncan."

"What gift would you present this Clan?"

"We bring with us the gift of light, and the renewal of life to this clan of Nairn." I was holding my breath, the voice inside was so loud and so deep, it sounded like a giant. There was another loud bang.

"Enter watchers of the light."

Randolph squeezed my hand, and nodded, as I took my first step into the large stone doorway, and entered the sacred temple of the Nairn. It was breath taking, and like nothing I had ever seen before. The whole circle was made of huge grey stones, at least three feet thick, and rose to the height of ten feet. It was clear they were of great age, the lichens on them were bigger than dinner plates. The stone pillar in front of me, was set on three eight feet wide at the base circular steps, each at least a foot wide, before rising up to another step, I had no idea how long it had been here, or even who made it, but it was clearly hand carved and very ancient.

I felt suddenly very nervous, as Randolph walked me slowly round, and I saw another doorway into another chamber, and it was very bright indeed. I took a deep breath as Randolph led me through the doorway, and I entered into a circular chamber ten times bigger than the first, around which, all the Nairn sat holding their lights in their hands, and I gasped as I looked round.

The place was packed, with tiny human like figures, and I had no idea how many, it well above a couple of hundred, it had to be nearer a thousand. All of them were smiling, some very small and young, others larger with old wrinkled faces, it was hard to believe, but gathered here, was a race that no humans knew about. Against all the odds, they had remained hidden from sight, it hardly seemed possible, but there was no doubt, it was true.

Randolph led me to a large stone seat with a woven sort of pad on it, and he smiled as he gestured towards it. All around there was a hum of quiet chatter, the Nairn were clearly excited. I sat down and relaxed a little, I was lost for words and really feeling out of my depths, as I looked across the centre, over what was a huge round slab of thick stone, decorated with fruit, berries and Felix's honey comb around it's edges. There was a gap in front of me with no food, about a foot across, and I looked at it as I sat back, I was relieved to see Randolph take the seat at my side.

Opposite me, sat Barrack, at his right side was a small Nairn, to his left was another young Nairn, then Chandak. I shuddered when I saw him, I could see he was still unhappy about the pasta jar. Berrendoc was sat to the right of Barrack with Felix, and then Aubrianne with Esme who was watching me smiling, but the others I did not know. It all felt so surreal, and I really had no idea what to think, or what to expect, I felt a little self conscious, as I looked round, and every one of the Nairn were watching my every move. I took a deep breath and looked to the floor for a second, and I had to ask, what exactly had I got myself into. I saw my hand on my lap, and it was trembling slightly.

The quiet mummer of the chatter died, and I looked up, as Barrack stood up holding what looked like a long metal pole, he raised it and then slammed it down hard onto the stone, and it rang out with a spark like flint. I blinked with the loudness of the noise, and felt my heart beat increase, as the sound rang through my ears. He looked round the circle, which was filled with at least a thousand Nairn of all ages, his face was stern, and his voice held a deep tone of concern.

"The light of Han is fading, as she walks into a different world, with a new task. This night, we embrace new light, and with it we entrust this light to a new watcher of the world in which we live. We embrace the Lady Emily, and welcome her." All of the Nairn spoke, and I swallowed again.

"We welcome her." Barrack's face softened and smiled, as he looked round the circle.

"Emily of Han, welcome, and receive our gift to you, as you bring light to the lives of all of us."

I watched, not really understanding as he sat down, and Aubrianne lifted a silver ring of shining metal, off her lap, and handed it to Esme. She gave a radiant smile as she looked at me, and then lifted into the air, and flew round the circle, and hovered in front of my face.

The circlet of metal glistened, and on the front of was a dark stone, she smiled at me, and she came forward and held it up, her bright blue eyes were dancing with her excitement. She spoke with a clear loud squeaky voice; she was as nervous as I was.

"We welcome you and embrace you Lady Emily of Han, we entrust our lives to you, a guide to watch over us, as you share your light of the truth."

Randolph turned, and pushed back my hood, and Esme placed the circlet upon my head, and gave me a huge smile. I could not help but smile back at her, she looked so happy and excited to be doing this. Esme flew back a little, her bright blue eyes dancing in her happy face.

"Please stand My lady of the light, and follow me."

My heart was starting to beat faster, as I stood up, there was utter silence in the chamber. Esme with a huge smile guided me, as I stepped up onto the stone circular dais, and walked me to the centre of it. She gave a nod as I stood still and she pointed, so I looked down, and saw a square shaped hole in the centre.

"Lady Emily, please kneel before the council to embrace your oath and the light."

Esme fluttered back to her seat, as I parted my long cloak, and knelt down, I looked forward and into the eyes of Barrack, he gave a nod, and then looked above my head at Randolph.

"Who guides this watcher to our midst?" Behind me Randolph stood up.

"I do, as watcher of the light, and second to Han."

I felt my legs trembling behind me, as Barrack looked down at me. I had been fine, but suddenly for no real explainable reason, I felt terrified, and my mouth felt dry, Barrack smiled, I think he understood me, and his voice softened.

"Lady Emily of Han, present your offering of light."

I slipped my hand inside the pocket on my cloak, trying to remember everything Randolph had told me. My hands were shaking, as I took the two pendants, and the wrapped stone, and held up my arms, with my palm out flat together, displaying the wrapped stone. Barrack smiled at me, as I nervously spoke with a dry shaky voice.

"I bring the gift of light." He gave a nod.

"Lady Emily, we begin a new age, as clan leader I welcome you to be as one with us in truth, spirit and the light of eternity. Please, would you kindly reveal your light."

I breathed out feeling so nervous and unsure, and honestly, I had no idea what would happen. I just wished it would be over soon, because my mouth was so dry, and my legs were shaking, and I really needed to get off my knees, as this floor was hard, and painful to kneel on.

I looked at the white cloth, and slipping the pendants into my left hand, I pulled at the cloth, and the stone rolled out onto my right hand, and all a round there were loud gasps, and my whole face was blinded with the light of the crystal. I could hardly see it was so bright, and there was a lot of muttering, and then I heard Barrack.

"Lady Emily of Han, and the Clan of the Nairn, show us your truth, and embrace the light."

My mind was swirling around as I tried to focus and remember the words of Randolph. 'Place your right hand against you heart, and then your left over it, so the pendants touch the stone. I pulled the crystal to my heart, and then held the pendants firmly against my heart and my head exploded with light, and I felt dizzy and closed my eyes for a second as I felt a huge power surge through me. I felt my head swoon slightly, and there were voices, I am not sure where from, but they sounded gentle and kind.

My whole body was tingling, and yet as I knelt there feeling terrified, and took a deep breath, I felt a strange calmness wash over me. My body filled with warmth, and all my frightened thoughts flowed away, as I became very aware of my whole body, and it was warm and snug, almost like relaxing in a warm bath or snuggling under my duvet at home. There was an atmosphere all around me, a sort of presence, and a very familiar feeling, almost like being a child and walking at the side of Han. I breathed out and it was calmness, and felt more at peace within myself, than I ever have before.

Shelly sat panicking in the total darkness, terrified of moving, just in case something unnatural popped out at her. Her eyes faced the circle, more out of fear of looking behind her, and then she felt her heart jolt, and she stiffened.

"Oh crap!"

All of the small stones in the circle in front of her, began to glow, and she swallowed really hard, as her eyes opened really wide, and she felt terrified.

"Me and my big mouth, I said it was a doorway, and some mad bugger has opened it. Oh hell, what is going to walk through it?" She looked up at the sky as the stones became a brilliant white.

"I am sorry God, I said you were a myth, and at this moment, I really regret it, please keep an eye on me, I may need help."

She jumped out of her skin, as light burst up into the sky from each stone, and she panicked, and slid back a little on the floor away from the stone circle, with a whimper, and slid backwards up the path, as she watched filled with terror.

Esme watched with delight, as within the circle, Emily was surrounded by an aura of brilliant white light, and she swayed slightly, her eyes were closed and the power of the light coursed through her, and yet her face wore and expression of complete tranquillity. The light from Emily poured out, and the whole of the stone dais became engulfed in a column of white light, and Esme could see faint figures within it, surrounding Emily, and she gasped with awe.

Aubrianne watched her daughter's reaction, she knew the close bond she had formed with Emily, and she enjoyed seeing Esme focused completely on the new watcher. It reminded her very much of herself, as a young Nairn watching Rachel embrace her light.

I was afraid at first, and then I felt a warmth increase as it entered me, it felt familiar, and I had no fear of whatever it was, the soft voice echoed through my thoughts.

"Emily I am so proud of you, I feel such joy my darling knowing you have joined with myself and your grandmother, and will walk in the light with us." I felt a huge surge of emotion rise up inside me, and in my head I spoke.

"Mother, is that you?" The warmth of her love filled me, and it was exactly as I had remembered it.

"Emily my darling, I have always been with you, feel with your heart, I am there with Han, and all of the line of watchers who have walked before you. Open your eyes Emily, and see the truth of who you are."

I opened them up, and I was in the forest circle, but it was different, not quite the same, the stones were there, but they were taller, new, and clean, and the marking so vivid. The floor was soft brown dirt, with no weeds or grass, and on each of the stones, a person was stood, and all of them were smiling.

Shelly jumped to her feet as figures in a faint white sort of light appeared, and she stepped back.

"Oh shit, it is a bloody spook board meeting, I am so not prepared for this." She took another step back and stopped dead. "What the hell?"

Emily appeared on her knees, she too was faint and ethereal, almost as if this was her spirit, she was looking around the circle speaking, and then Shelly saw them, it was Han and Amelia, side by side both watching Emily and smiling. Shelly took a step forward, her voice was soft, like she was talking to herself.

"Joined in the light, of course, God, I am so stupid, they are all spirit walkers, why the hell did I not see that, they are walking in the light, they can exist in both worlds?"

I looked up at my mother, she smiled at me, Han was there, and my eyes filled with tears as I saw both of them together. I felt a huge pain rise up inside me, Han smiled.

"Let out the last of your pain my child, as you can see, we have not left you, we were there in your heart waiting for the light to show you how to see us again." A huge waved of emotion crashed over me, and rushed up out of me, and I gave a sob.

"I have missed you so much, I never said goodbye, and I wanted to. I really wanted to tell you how much I love you, and thank you for everything you have ever done, but you left without me, and I was so alone." Han smiled.

"Emily my child, how could you think we would leave you, you have never been alone, all of us have always been together in the light? Don't you see, your world is not the only one, there are others, but they are all intertwined, our worlds lap over and we live in the light, where we can always be together. You poor child, you have seen too much death in your world, but it is not the end, Emily there is never an end, it just changes, and becomes something new." I breathed in and swallowed.

"But you are not here, I cannot hold you or talk to you as I did, and I miss you." She smiled.

"Emily, all you had to do was open your heart and embrace the light, I was there waiting with your mother. Our body is just the vehicle for each world we enter, it is the light within us that is really us, that is the truth of who we are. Emily, the love you hold, is the core of your spirit, and it is bound to me for eternity, we can never be lost completely from each other, our love is too strong. You need to live in your world, and protect the children, but we will be with you in the light you hold always, and in times of need, we will be there."

I was starting to understand, Shelly had no idea how right she had been, our energy cannot die, it can only transform in to something else, without understanding, she was talking of the light. I looked at my mother as she smiled at me.

"Emily, I gave you some of my light to ensure you were guided back to me, and here you are. Listen to me, you and your father need each other, and you need to look after each other, he too has some of my light, and a day will come when all three of us are reunited in the light. His love for you is so deep, but the pain he felt when I had to leave, closed so much of the man he really is down. Seeing you with him has brought such joy for me, stay close to him Emily." I smiled and wiped the tears from my eyes.

"You have seen us?" She smiled at me.

"I have watched over you since the moment I gave you my light, it is why I gave it you. Emily, watch over the Nairn, the truth will come to you, and you will see all that has happened, learn from it and guide them well. Look to your knees, and place the crystal in the slot, and bring life, love, and protection to all the children of your land, for there are many."

"I love you Mother, I love you Han."

"We feel it child, now go and live, and be a watcher of great standing."

I took a huge breath, and looked to my knees, there in the dirt was the slot, I took the crystal and held it over the slot, but looked back up, and smiled.

"I will talk to you soon."

The crystal slid into place, and there was a mighty roar, as my vison came back and suddenly, I was back in the circle surrounded by cheering Nairn. I looked around at all the faces, not quite understanding what was happening. Barrack stood up with a big smile, and gave me a nod of appreciation. He raised his hands, and it took a few seconds for the noise to quieten down.

"Lady Emily, you may stand and can choose an advisor, who will help you understand some of our customs and rituals, all you need do, is name one." I slowly stood up and looked round the circle, but I only knew of a few, I was unsure as I looked to Barrack.

"I only really know Aubrianne and Berrendoc, I have not had time to learn all your names." He smiled and turned to look at them both, Aubrianne looked at me, and she smiled a soft smile.

"Lady Emily, my role is as advisor to Randolph, and so therefore I cannot accept." I felt a little disappointed, but understood, and turned slightly and looked at Berrendoc.

"Master Berrendoc, it would honour me if you would help and advise me, for I have so much to learn, and no idea of where to begin?" He smiled and gave a slight bow.

"Lady Emily, it would indeed be a great honour for me, and I would be delighted to advise you in the ways of the Nairn from here onwards. I thank thee for the honour you have bestowed on my family." I smiled, in truth I was relieved, and Barrack banged his staff.

"So be it... Now let us feast, Master Felix, you may guide the Lady Shelly to the feast." I turned, and saw Randolph, he beckoned me back, and with huge relief, I walked back to my seat, where he pulled me into a hug.

"I am so proud of you, Emily, your life has been tainted by much darkness, but from this day forth, that will sweep back as your walk in the light. Your life will change, and it will be for the better. You did well, the Nairn were left speechless by the power of your light."

Felix walked up the path and sighed. He held up his lantern, Shelly was out cold on the floor. He shook his head and flicked at her nose, her eyes blinked, and she took a deep breath, as she looked at him.

"Lady Shelly, this is not a place for sleep, there is a feast, you need to follow me."

Shelly sat up and rubbed her eyes, before her was darkness, she nervously looked round.

"Where did all the spooks go?" Felix frowned.

"What are spooks?" She shook her head.

"It does not matter, it is bad enough us one of us will not sleep tonight, I will save you the worry. Did you say food, good, I am starving, is there wine as well, hell, after what I just saw, I really need some?"

Felix had no idea at all what she was saying, he just shook his head and looked at her.

"You have never met Mugwump have you?" Shelly frowned.

"No, but why does it worry me that you ask?" He gave her a big smile.

"Come on, I will introduce you, I think you two will have a lot in common, he can be strange too, and he is really fat." Shelly frowned, and he giggled, as he turned on the path.

Chapter Thirty Four

Honouring Remembrance

It was a happy joyous celebration, and many Nairn who I do not know, came up to me wearing large smiles and bowed paying their respects and gratitude to me. I did not feel I had done that much, but I smiled and spoke to them, and told them how honoured I was to be considered, which Randolph appeared to approve of.

Shelly was having the time of her life, this for her was her biggest dream come true, as she sat on the floor surrounded by Nairn, eating fruit, and spoke to them of their past, and what their hopes for the future were. I smiled as I watched her, she had no idea what an amazing person she was, Barrack appeared in front of me, and gave a bow.

"May we speak alone in the other chamber?"

I gave a nod to him, and as he turned, I followed him, unsure of what he would wish of me, after all, his son was to be my advisor, and we had not spoken yet. We entered the chamber with the tall stone, which I noticed was glowing white, he smiled as he offered his hand.

"Please be seated."

I looked at the set of three steps, turned, and sat down, and looked at him stood on the upper step so we were eye level.

"Lady Emily, I wanted to say how impressed I am, and offer my thanks, knowing my clan can remain in this spot under your protection, is a great relief to all of us." I understood that, he took a breath.

"What has impressed me is how you have come to an understanding of us, in such a short space of time. Your mother was given many years after she discovered our presence here, and so for her, the adjustment was easier, and yet for yourself it has been a very short span of time, I feel that shows great character, which should be applauded." I smiled.

"Lord Barrack, if you think about it, Han has been telling me stories my whole life. I thought they were fairy stories, and as I now see, they were not, she was telling me of her life. Once I understood that, everything fell into place." He gave a serious nod.

"A watcher walks in both worlds, and has gifts of instinct we do not have, which is why, over a thousand years ago, my line chose to form the sacred bond with the walkers of light. Lady Emily, things will appear to you, and within that is your role."

I felt calmer, and more relaxed now it was all over, and I considered my position, which Randolph had talked to me about, and in doing so had given me an idea of what my mother and Han had been like as they did their duty. I looked Barrack right in the eyes, I meant to start as I intended to go on.

"Randolph has advised me well these past days, and I do fully understand my role, and I will also have your son to guide me. I aim to preserve this land with the laws of my people, so that it will remain here undisturbed forever, it was my mother's dream, and I will fulfil it. I am not sure if I am speaking out of place, for I do not want to create problems within your clan, but I feel I should warn you. Lord Barrack, be careful in whom you confide, there are some close to you, I have strange feelings around, and my heart says, they are not to be fully trusted. Aubrianne and Berrendoc, I feel are very loyal and true to you, and I feel that the light guides me to inform you of this." He gave a smile, as if this was not new news to him.

"I am aware, as I said, you are very like your mother." He smiled. "Your words Lady Emily have been duly noted, and if I may say, my house is honoured that you chose my son to guide you. He is a man of great loyalty to this clan, and has served us well." I nodded.

"I feel that deeply, which is why I chose him." He bowed to me.

"Shall we return, this is a great night for my people, and they would be happy to share their time with you?" I slid off the stone and saw the doorway, Esme and Felix were peeking round, I giggled and walked towards them, and both of them exploded with happiness.

The walk back home was around three in the morning and I felt exhausted, Esme was already asleep when we left at the side of her mother. Randolph lit a torch to guide us, and Shelly stared at him with shock.

"You had a bloody torch, and you said nothing?" He gave a soft chuckle.

"We did not need it; I knew the Nairn would light the way." She looked at me with utter disbelief.

"I sat alone in the woodland in the darkest dark I have ever been in, and he had a torch." Randolph shrugged.

"You were not alone; the watchers were with you." She swallowed hard and looked back.

"But they are dead." He gave a nod.

"You are a paranormal investigator, I thought you may appreciate the company."

I was laughing so hard when we reached the boat, and Randolph once again whisked me into his arms and lifted me on deck. By the time we had tied up the boat in the boat house and I hugged Randolph goodnight, I was so tired, and I headed straight up bed. I felt the sheer exhaustion of the day, as I drifted into sleep with the image of Han and my mother stood in the light smiling at me. My sleep was deep, possibly the deepest in over a year, and my dreams were happy and joyous, and filled with tiny happy smiling faces, and without understanding completely how, the last year of my twenty first year headed into its final day.

It was a slow day, Pam felt much better and wanted to get out and about, and so she jumped into Stan, with Shelly and they headed off, and I was alone with room to think, so I sat at the bottom of the garden. My dad phoned, and told me about the Johnson's property which came as a big relief, and I sat on the end of the jetty, and talked of my experience and what I had learned from my mother. The fact that none of the peddles appeared to work, felt as strange to him as it did me, and he said he would look into it. One thing he said that made me sit up, was he told me, my mother felt a little uneasy and lost for a few days after embracing the light, and I felt he knew I was a little disorientated, which I was.

Alone with the quiet house, and sat in the garden, I looked out across the lake, and let my thoughts fade. Before the vast lake spread out, and there in its heart, was the island of the Nairn, with its trees of green reaching up into the sky. Their canopies were high up, as their heavy limbs reached out above the water, like arms embracing the sky, to touch the clouds or feel the warmth of the sun.

Below was a dense thatch of wide pale green fronds of the ferns, or thick bushes of berries, and all around the edges where the water lapped up to kiss the rock over the sand, tall reeds grew up, like needles plunged into the soil. It was a remarkable place, teaming with life, and an endless supply of bounty for the Nairn, who used all of it in one fashion or another, to create their clothing, or build the things they needed, and of course, supply their food. They were a miracle of evolution to me, a tiny self sufficient population of a race possibly older than man, and I found it overwhelming and yet inspiring. But there was more, something not seen or touched and smelt, and whatever it was, today I was aware of it, but could not quite name it.

I closed my eyes, and breathed in slowly, held it, and then let it flow out gently past my lips. My mind wandered as if feeling for something, but what was it? I felt the warmth of the of the sun on my skin, and felt it creeping into me, filling me with life, my mind slowly slipped free of my will, and was free to explore, and deep down somewhere in my centre, I felt something beckon to it, and a soft voice spoke.

"Come Emily, embrace the light, and join us."

I breathed out, and felt like my body was drifting, as within the darkness I felt my way around, then suddenly... FLASH!

I stiffened as my whole head filled with brilliant white light, and I heard soft chuckles all around me. The light in my mind dimmed a little and cleared, almost like a mist blowing across the lake, and I heard my soft long drawn breath, as I relaxed even deeper. Something touched my arm, and I moved, then opened my eyes, and I gasped.

"Han!" She smiled.

"Welcome my child, relax, you are amongst family."

I looked round, and could not quite understand what was

happening, I was back in the circle on the island, surrounded by smiling faces.

"How did I get here; I was in the garden?" I felt a warm hand slide into mine and turned, and looked right into the hazel eyes of my mother, she smiled.

"You still are Emmy, but you are walking in the light now." It was hard to contemplate.

"How can I be at home, and yet here, is this a dream?" She smiled and gave a little chuckle.

"Emmy, when you walk in the light, you can be anywhere, and look at any aspect of this property. Today you needed a guide, and the first time of everyone walking in the light is to come here, so we can be of service to you, and help you adjust." I felt I needed it, and looked at them both standing together.

"Like astral projection, that kind of thing? I can project my mind here to talk, whilst still sat on the jetty, like the sort of remote viewing Shell is always banging on about?" Han gave a small giggle as she looked at me.

"Oh, my child, we are all connected to something far greater, our minds as a race are connected to everything, and all you have to do, is look for the light to guide you. It has always been there inside you, but you closed down after the accident and shut off you heart. Embracing the light and coming to us has reopened everything, and now you can walk in the light whenever you need to."

I nodded, hadn't Shell said something about the energy within us all transforming, is that what she meant? My mother turned and looked round.

"Emmy, all of these people have walked in the light as watchers with the Nairn, their bodies are no more, but the energy of their inner beings, the real part of them that lived, felt and thought, remains here as a collective energy. Emmy death is not the end, it is like leaving a house, walking through the air, and entering another abode. I knew that, and that is why when I placed it within you as a child, it would help me find you when I needed you, which was why I was able to leave." I shook my head.

"But you didn't have to, the light was strong in you, it would have protected you." She squeezed my hand.

"No Emmy, my body was broken, when we hit the tree, it

smashed the side of the car, and my body was badly hurt, I was bleeding inside, and I knew I had little time. Emmy when the tree cracked, and I knew it would fall, I used what was left of my broken body to protect you, and my light surrounded us both to keep you alive. Emmy I was going to leave you, whether the tree fell or not, I needed you safe to continue." I swallowed hard and took a breath, she smiled at me with such love.

"Build my dream Emmy, protect it all, for it is magical place, not just because of the Nairn, but because that cottage is where I gave birth to you, those trees are where you lay shaded on a blanket whilst your father and I sat watching filled with our love for you. This land gave me your father, and my love for him grew in every second of our time together and gave us you. There is such deep magic, such joy in that earth and stone, for I have travelled all over it, and no matter where you walk from this day on, you will be in my footprints, as you were as a child. Emmy you were our joy, our air, we love you so deeply." She smiled and I tried to breath feeling the huge surge within me.

"I am trying to, I want to, I have wanted you to be proud of me." She smiled.

"Stop trying so hard Emmy, I am proud, very proud of you." I tried to smile; she just shook her head.

"You are so like me at your age, I took everything on my shoulders and tried to fix everything before you arrived. Emmy life has a way of smoothing out into what it is supposed to be, not every problem has to be solved straight away. Take a moment in your life, and look back, then understand all that has happened, and once you do, look at now, see what you have and what is possible, because there is so much more to come. You have had your time in the darkness, now live fully in the light."

She had that right, I have felt my whole life had been shrouded in darkness, and my inner yearnings for a mother, and some sort of stability to my emotions, have been the ruling force for too long. Han turned and looked out across the woodland, she turned to look at me with my mother.

"I fear you have been spotted on the jetty, and a guest will be arriving imminently." I frowned.

"How do you know that?" Han smiled.

"Feel the difference in the air around you, can you not feel her?"

I had not noticed anything, I took a moment and tried to concentrate on my body, and I felt a little tingling sensation, and smiled.

"Is that Esme?" Han gave a nod.

"She is a beautiful soul, in time you will learn to feel each of them, but some will always affect you in a stronger way, and I feel, she will be one of them."

I really got that, I had formed a bond with her from that first moment of seeing her, for me, Esme and Felix were special.

"How do I leave here, to go to her?" My mother gave a big smile.

"Emmy, just open your eyes." I did not understand.

"What?"

My eyes opened and I was back on the jetty, Esme landed on the very end, and gave me a big smile as she ran towards me her bright blue eyes dancing.

"Emily, I could not feel the others, and yet I felt you so strongly, and when I looked you were there, so I flew over. I can now, because you are part of the light."

She stopped in front of me smiling, and I gave her a smile back.

"Hi Esme, it is nice to see you, and I am happy knowing you will no longer get into trouble." She gave a nod; she was so cute.

"Mother told me I was really good last night, Emily, I was so excited to play a part in your ceremony it was hard for me to sleep this morn, although mother said I should do really, but I have so much energy, I just had to come and see you."

I gave a little chuckle; she was almost as excited as Shell gets when she discovers a new ghost story.

"I am glad you did, I have a free afternoon, as Shelly and Pam have gone out. So, seeing as you are here, what would you like to do?" Her eyes expanded in her face.

"Would you tell me one of Han's stories?" I laughed a little as she climbed up onto my knee, and a story came to mind.

"Well let me see, do you know the one about the lost fairy, and the last berries of autumn?" She shook her excitedly.

"No, I have never heard that one." She settled down, and I

looked at her.

"Well now, you see, there was once a little fairy who found the most amazing patch of moss, underneath an old log. It was so comfortable, that she curled up snug and warm, and fell fast asleep. Her sleep was longer than she ever expected, and because her clan were in a rush, and had only meant to stay for a little rest over, when she awoke, they were all gone, and she was completely alone." Esme gasped as her bright blue eyes opened wider.

Across the lake within the ferns, hundreds of small figures moved quietly into place, and sat below the large fronds, wearing happy smiles. It had been a long time since the tales of old were told by an aging watcher to a tiny child, and they all settled down to listen, as Emily recited the story word perfect from her childhood, and Esme looked up at Emily, listening in adoration from her lap.

Randolph leaned back on the boat house door, and smiled as he listened out of sight, even for his old ears, it was a joy to behold, and almost as if Han had never left. Some parts of life around the lake never change, and he thought that was a good thing.

The day passed slowly, and Esme was happy, she flew back to the island feeling tired and promised to see me soon, and I headed back up the steps and looked at the cottage. It is strange, nothing appears to have changed, and yet everything has. Han's Cottage, was no longer hers, it was mine, and it felt strange. As I walked towards the door I had to ponder, would this place one day be known as Emily's Cottage? Now that would be weird.

Shelly and Pam arrived back with bag loads of shopping, wine, and beer, and we all sat down to a takeout Chinese, although they had bought it three towns over, so it needed a quick microwave before it was hot again. We sat in the living room, and ate and drank wine, and the light of today faded away, and I was actually quite tired, it had been a very late night last night.

All of us headed up the stairs, and as we reached the top, I grabbed Pam's hand.

"Pam, thanks... you know, for joining me? I am really happy you are here with me; I have missed you." She smiled and leaned in and kissed my cheek.

"I have missed you too, the states was fun, but without you and Shell, something was always missing, you two are a huge part of my life, how could I not be a part of this?"

I nodded; I understood that better than she realised. I watched her walk to her bedroom door and turned with a smile, and walked into my room. I stood at the end of my bed, and pulled off my top, and saw myself in the mirror, my naked breasts with the chain and the pendant between them. I lifted it up and looked at it, before the ceremony it had been two, and somehow during all of the strangeness of last night, they blended together and became one. It is a strange place, a magical place filled with the unexpected.

I smiled to myself and saw the green jacket hung on the hanger, hanging from the wardrobe door, I reached out and lifted it off, and then slipped it on and looked at myself, it was quite startling as I saw the picture of her on the dresser. We did look almost identical, and the jacket fitted me perfectly. I slipped it off dropped my pants and slid under the duvet, and leaned back in the pillow, and closed my eyes, her voice from today was in my thoughts.

"Stop trying so hard Emmy, I am proud, very proud of you." I breathed a soft happy sigh.

"I am proud of you mum; I am proud to be your daughter."

As my mind filled with pictures, I slipped into a deep restful sleep, and all the Nairn danced and sang around a large table of food, and I watched them wearing my happiest smile.

Tuesday arrived with wild screams as I staggered into the kitchen to balloons and noise. Shelly and Pam were in party mode, and the table was filled with brightly packaged gifts, I was twenty two years old. There were several rounds of hugs and kisses and lots of excitement, and I had not really felt this happy for a very long time.

The day just got better when Randolph arrived, and handed me a hand carved bow, and an old sling type thing, filled with grey feathered arrows, he smiled as I held it.

"Emily, it belonged to your mother, she was quite the shot with it. I will teach you to use it, when I have finished making the new target of straw, I have been a little busy of late, and not quite done it."

I held it up and looked along the highly polished wooden bow, it had a soft grip, almost as if moulded to her hand, and just on the inside of the grip, was scratched into the wood, EM. He smiled as he saw me look at it.

"She once told me, that she was very unsure of what to name you, and whilst she was carrying you, she would practice shooting as a way of passing the time. One afternoon she looked at that, and in that moment, she knew she would call you Emmy, which was why she named you Emily." I felt a lump in my throat as I looked up at him.

"Thank you. It is a beautiful gift, Randolph; I will treasure it." He saw my face and he understood the value, it had the same value to him, as he had treasured it since her death.

I spent the morning with the three of them, but some things never change, and that pang of missing Han crept up inside me. For most of my life she had been here, I had always come home to be with her on my birthday. Last year I was grief stricken, and this year even though I had such a wonderful time, I needed some time alone. Shelly understood, and smiled, she knew this part of me, and handed me my green jacket.

"Go talk to her."

It is strange how much Shelly has come to understand me, she really has been the most unbelievable friend. I slipped it on and left the house, and took the path to the side of the lake, and walked lost in thought through the trees, as all my memories of my time with Han played in my thoughts. I knew I could close my eyes and walk into the light to talk to her, but it was not the same, I could not hold her, and hug her as hard as I always did. I would never get those crazy little presents that were so thoughtful, and always something I needed so badly for Uni, Like hairclips, or new gloves in the winter. She always knew what I would need most, and it was always something I had no idea I needed, until I got back to Uni.

Han touched my life so deeply, she was the mother I needed when mine was gone, and a friend in times of need, the shelter and security I would run to and share my deepest feeling to. Even though my life had changed so much since my return, simply knowing, I had lost her, and would be without her physical presence for the rest of my life, still hurt.

I had lost all track of my paces, as I wandered along the track that led to the village, lost in thought I did not even see Heidi, or notice the steep hill, and by the time I realised, I was stood by her grave looking down on the white stone that bore her name, at the side of my mother's.

"Han, Mum, I guess I miss you. It is my birthday, and both of you are gone. I know all will be well, but I will always miss you, and always be saddened that I can never hold or hug you, and feel the warmth you put into my soul as you squeezed me tight. I know we can still talk in the light, but just for this one day, I want to be here, simply stood by what was once your physical being, just to feel close."

It sounded mad, but to me it made sense, the sense I knew no other would ever understand, and I was okay with that. I knelt down and tidied up the flowers on both graves, the wind had blown them around, and when they were neat, and as they should be, I sat back and sat quietly remembering everything.

It is a strange world we live in, we have so many customs and sayings, and people just fall into the habit of saying them. I cannot count how many people have told me they were sorry for my loss, but why, why were they sorry, it was my loss? They would never understand the impact on me, never really see the intenseness of the pain, or understand how much I missed them. I was four when I lost my mother, and twenty when I lost Han, and both felt as big in the pain I felt.

I am not over my mother's death, I know I grew up without her, but that did not mean I did not miss her. Yes, I was four, and yet for most of my life, there has been the sense of some missing feeling, some sort of aura around me that had suddenly disappeared. It was that I missed, because that was what made me feel safe, and Han had something similar.

We say stupid things like 'you will get over it in time' or 'eventually you will deal with it better.' I remember Jessica's face at the funeral, she was so cold and so harsh.

"Good you made it, I know this is painful Emily, but you will see, in time, it will feel less painful, this is life and it goes on."

That was it, all I got, and she was so wrong, it feels painful today. Harry had told me, 'Isn't it time you got over it, and moved on?' How could I, how could I simply leave behind the most influential woman in my life. Even Pete told me, 'Emily, just sell the house and walk away, you will be free of the pain then.'

No, I won't, and to be honest, I never want to, why do people say these things, are they really so cold they can just move on and forget, because I cannot? I don't want to forget, not one precious second of it, I never want a day when I no longer understand the sound of her voice, or the twinkle in her eyes as she laughed. I still want to sit on her lap, as Esme did mine, and listen to all those wonderful stories.

I get it, I have dad and Jane. Kate will always be there, and so will Shelly and Pam, but the simple truth is, they are not Han, or my mother, and I want to remember them. I want to live every day for the rest of my life, remembering some detail, some daft moment, or those precious moments in the garden or cooking. There has only ever been one time in my life where another person understood me, and that was Frank, the old man I would sit with in the park back in Exeter. Like me, he never wanted to forget his wife, he wanted to carry her in his heart forever, and never let one detail of her pass from his memory, he was not morbid and depressed, he loved her, and would for the rest of his life.

To forget in my eyes is to stop loving, and I will never stop loving Han, or my mother. I understand I was a child and only four when she went, I have heard others say how it was fine, in time it would not matter as much to me, but it did, and again, Han knew that. All of my life, Han has told me stories of her life, she too was keeping my mother's memory alive, and I aim to do the same for Han.

I sat for a while, thinking and talking to myself, and suddenly became aware I was not alone, I stood up and turned to see the old face of Mr Higginson smiling at me.

"I did not want to disturb you, but I was passing, I wanted to wish you all the best, I believe it is your birthday today?" I gave a nod.

"It is, and thank you. I guess I wanted to be close to them

447

today, it probably sounds silly." He gave a gentle smile.

"I do not think that at all, I would say it is quite understandable. Han was there for you every year, I do the same thing on my birthday, we always spend it together."

It probably sounds crazy, because we had met here before, but I had not realised, he too was visiting a lost one, which was why he was here. I felt a little foolish.

"Are you visiting your wife here?" He smiled.

"Yes, we were together for thirty two years, in many ways, we still are. The locals think I am an old crack pot, as I visit twice a week, but I do not really care. My Agnes was a formidable woman, scared the life out of most of the villagers, but at home, she was a very different person, quite the free spirit and lover of all natural things. We lived a good full happy life, and I treasure her memory." I gave a smile.

"I like that, I feel the same about Han, I get told it will get better and won't hurt as much in time, but that means forgetting, and I cannot do that, she was too precious to me." He gave a nod of understanding.

"You hold that thought Miss Duncan, and never let anyone tell you how to feel, just carry on as you are in your own way, that is what I do."

He really was a sweet old man, and in a way, I was grateful to him. I mean, I hardly knew him, but on the few occasions we had met or spoken, he had always been very respectful and understanding, and he was very organised in the way he had dealt with Han's final affairs. He offered his hand, and I agreed to walk back to the gates with him, he smiled as he walked at my side.

"I was very pleased to hear you had decided to stay, and I believe you will be working on the property, I feel that is a shrewd move." I smirked, no one round here appeared to like Pete.

"You know Miss Duncan, that is a very special property, but I feel you are aware of that. I spoke to your father a few days ago, and he explained what you had in mind, and I must say, I highly approve, as would your mother. She was a lovely girl, and to be honest, seeing you in her jacket today gave me quite the surprise, and yet I feel she would be delighted to know you wore it to visit her. I know of her dream, Han asked me for advice once about it all, your mother wanted to protect the lives of those who lived there, for she understood their value." I turned to him and he smiled.

"Miss Duncan, I believe I have not been completely straight forward with you. I have to confess, that Han had a cousin, Agnes Montgomery." He gave a little chuckle, and I was really surprised.

"You married her cousin, so you are family, my family?" He gave a nod.

"I am indeed, which is why I handled all Han's affairs, a secret of such magnitude can only be entrusted to a member of the family."

He knew about all of it, and had not said a word in all this time. In a way, it felt a little comical, after all, Han was always unpredictable, and now I understood why his wife was such a free spirit, it appeared to be a Montgomery trait.

We walked to the gates and said our goodbyes, and I took the shortcut through the back woods that led down to the main road and the fork. I got back on the trail and headed home, and as I came down the rough track, I noticed my father's car outside the cottage, and felt a jolt of happiness explode inside me. I climbed the fence rather than walk round, and hurried across the gravel with a large wide smile.

I slipped in the key and pushed open the door feeling excited, this was one year Kate would not arrive with a cheque. The door swung open, and I jumped with shock.

"SURPRISE... HAPPY BIRTHDAY!"

I felt the tears of joy, as Pam stood with Shelly, surrounded by Heidi, Kate, Jane, and my dad, and he was wearing a huge smile and holding a wrapped box. It was completely unexpected, but was the best feeling ever, as he came forward and handed me a gift tied with a huge red bow. I looked at it and felt the tears come, and just threw my arms round him.

"Oh Dad, thanks, I love you."

Chapter Thirty Five

To live in the light

It was a long night of laughter and fun, and as I woke, I was regretting it a little, as my head pounded. I staggered downstairs in search of coffee, not completely awake, until I walked into my living room, and spotted Felix sat on the mantle above the fire. I blinked and walked over, and looked at him closely, he sat frozen staring ahead, I heard someone in the kitchen moving around doing what sounded like washing pots. I leaned forward, and whispered.

"Felix, what are you doing here, if that is Pam, you will expose yourself?" He blinked, and looked at me and lowered his voice.

"We thought it was you, we came to see you, and when we realised, it was too late and we had to hide. I saw this pot woman, and sat beside her thinking the strange one would think I was a pot man." It made a weird sort of logic.

"We... Is Esme here too, oh God, where is she?"

He shrugged, oh hell, I had a pot Nairn, and an another one hiding somewhere, and Pam was in the kitchen, and someone how I did not feel I could fob her off again with mice. I looked at Felix.

"Stay put and do not move."

He nodded and then froze again, I looked round the room, there was no sign of anymore statues, so felt a little panicked, was Esme hiding in the kitchen? I hurried in and saw Pam at the sink smiling.

"Good morning party girl, Emmy last night was brilliant, and just like old times, I am really excited today. I really am, we are going to live an epic and really surprising life together. You know, us three, like Uni? You look a little rough Emmy."

I smiled at her, yep surprising was the right word to use, she had no idea how surprising, especially if I did not discover Esme first. My head was banging and I was feeling stressed, I needed coffee.

"Yeah, I need coffee, you know what Shell is like, my head is heavy this morning?"

She smiled as I approached the kettle and continued washing her bowl, and her spoon. I yawned as I lifted the coffee and put a spoon full into my cup, I looked at the sugar jar, it was empty. The kettle rumbled as I leaned over to the wall cupboard, and opened the door, and my heart lurched, and missed several beats. I looked back fast, Pam was looking in the water, fishing around for something. I grabbed the sugar bag quickly, as Esme was stood at the back of the cupboard, pressed against the flower bags, holding her breath.

I almost had heart failure as I pulled the bag out fast, and closed the door quickly. I leaned back and started to fill the sugar jar, Pam lifted the pot cloth and started to wipe her pots, I breathed out slowly, I was more than awake now.

"How did you sleep?" I glanced back to work out where she was, she smiled.

"Like a baby, honestly after all that drinking, I went out flat, you know though, I feel really alive today, Emmy, I was considering going for a swim." I nodded.

"I might join you; I could use waking up."

My heart was pounding, I had to get her out of the house, as that appeared to be the best way. The kettle clicked and I poured out a coffee, the milk was still out, so I added it, stirred, and lifting my cup, I turned and stood right in front of the cupboard. Pam was happily wiping the rest of the pots and putting them on table. Shelly staggered in and looked round the room with bleary eyes, she smiled and flopped into a seat, as I leaned on the unit and pushed my head back on the cupboard door.

"Were going to have a swim Shell, will you be joining us?" I stared at her as hard as I could, hoping she would be able, and awake enough to understand the on going emergency.

She looked up as Pam made a coffee for her, I opened my eyes wide and nodded, she frowned, I nodded back against the cupboard, she did not understand. I lifted my hand slowly and using my thumb and finger I made a tiny sort of gesture, and then did the walking fingers thing. She understood and sat up straight, I banged my head softly on the cupboard, and she completely understood and looked panicked. She became animated and furrowed her brow as she nodded her head like it was about to fall off, she looked like a basket case, it was so ridiculous, and my panic increased.

"Yeah, Yeah, oh yeah, I would love a swim, nothing like it for clearing out the cobwebs." I frowned at her, that was it, that was her attempt to act normal? My heart was pumping in my chest, I had to get rid of Pam, but how, I had an idea?

"We will need towels; they are in the bathroom." Shell frowned.

"I thought they were in the drawer." I opened my eyes wide, and looked at her in disbelief, what the hell was she playing at, I shook my head?

"They are just hand towels, we need BIGGER ones, from the BATHROOM." She realised, and I gave a sigh of relief.

"Oh, those bigger bath ones, yeah, I will grab them when I have had my coffee." I gave a sigh, Pam turned from the unit.

"I will get them; I am nipping up for my phone." I smiled.

"Oh, would you, yeah that would be great?" In my head I was thinking, just bloody leave, go, get out of the sodding room so I can free my friends. She gave me a smile.

"I am still learning my way around, so it is no probs." I gave a nod and smiled.

"Thanks Pam."

She headed for the door and I watched her thinking, please Felix, do not even breathe, I was sure I was starting to sweat slightly, and I tried to appear normal and breath at the same time. I heard her feet on the stairs and spung into action yanking open the door, Esme stood smiling.

"Good morrow to you Emily." I gave a sigh of relief; I was terrified she would suffocate.

"Esme, Pam is up and we need time, you and Felix have to get outside and out of sight. I am sorry, I really am." She smiled at me, and her big blue eyes blinked.

"It is alright Emily, we understand, but you know, we could just talk to her like we did you, and then she would be fine." I shook my head.

"No Esme, she is not like Shell and me, this will have to be handled very carefully." She nodded.

"I will sit in the big leaf plants Han cabbaged, and stay out of sight then." I felt a huge wave of relief wash over me, as Felix flew into the kitchen, I saw him, and pointed at the door.

"Out, quickly before she comes back, Christ, I am nowhere near awake enough for this." Shelly giggled as Esme flew over my head and joined him, she gripped his hand.

"Felix, we have to protect Emily."

He smiled, waved, and shot through the door outside, and I flopped down into my seat with a gasp, I had not even had coffee yet, and I was close to heart failure. I was not sure I would ever get used to this, Shelly looked at me and giggled.

"This is going to be so much fun, I am really excited about the future Emmy." I frowned at her.

"If she does not find out soon, I am not sure I will make it, I am sure I will die of heart failure."

It was three days later, when Pam found out. Shelly and I were still in bed, and Pam got up and headed downstairs, she walked into the kitchen rubbing her eyes to find Mugwump sat on an upturned bowl. He had come to pay his respects, it just took time, as he had to build up his energy enough to stop his rear end hitting the water as he flew over.

He gave a sincere nod, as Pam walked up to the table and slid off the bowl. She had not at first noticed him, but the movement caught her eye, and she turned, and looked as he swept his arm forward in a grand gesture.

"Good tidings this morrow dear lady of the house of Han."

The scream that bellowed out of Pam was the loudest thing I have ever heard, and I sat bolt upright in bed.

"WHAT THE HELL WAS THAT?"

Cupboard doors exploded open, and Felix and Esme came belting out, and flapped around Pam's head screaming at the top of their tiny voices.

"PROTECT LADY EMILY, PROTECT HER, SHE IS IN

453

DANGER!"

Pam looked up at them in what she thought, was them attacking her head, and screamed her head off, even louder than the first time.

I was out of bed running naked, and bumped into Shelly, as we collided on the landing.

"Oh shit, she has seen them Emmy!" Not how I would have phrased it, but it was pretty dammed close. Shelly looked terrified.

"She will swat them, let's get bloody down there."

The screams and wails continued, as both of us charged down the stairs at high speed. I slid into the kitchen and came to an abrupt halt. It took a moment to understand.

Pam was sat under the table wailing her brains out, holding her hands over her head, and screeching at the top of her voice.

"It's not a hologram!"

Felix stood on top of the table at one end holding a huge stainless steel ladle, and Esme was at the other end holding a huge spatula. Both of them wore a look of pride, as they had defeated the enemy and protected the lady of the house. I gave a long sigh, as Mugwump dragged himself back up, and looked at me nervously.

"I never did it, I never did it, no, oh no, I never did." I smirked, they were so tiny, and yet Pam was cowering filled with terror between the chairs. Felix gave a nod of satisfaction.

"You are safe Lady Emily, you honour is protected."

"I never did it, no, oh no, I never did." Shelly started to chuckle, as I sighed and crouched down.

"Guys this is Pam, she does not know about Mugwump, it probably freaked her out." Pam looked at me with mascara streaked eyes, she was shaking violently, and her eyes were really huge, as she cowered looking the most terrified I have ever seen anyone.

"Emmy, it is not a hologram." She shook her head. "I do not want to say it, because honestly, I think I am having an existential crisis, they are real."

I pulled back the chair, and held out my hand with a long sigh.

"Pam, these are my friends, it is a long story, and the reason I inherited this cottage. Come on out, they will not harm you, it is only Felix, Esme, and Mugwump."

"No, oh no, I never did it." Shelly appeared at my side with a big smile.

"See, I told you there were real." It did not help.

What began in that moment sealed our friendship, more than it had been, we helped Pam out and introduced her, and then with three Nairn sat on the table, I told Pam the story of Han and my mother, and how they had lived a secret life, and sworn a bond to protect the Nairn forever.

The wonderful thing was, in that moment, the true ecologist in Pam came out, as she calmed down and spoke to them, and they answered her questions and she marvelled at them, and evolution for such a magnificent creation. Although I will add, Mugwump confused the hell out of all three of us.

That evening after we shared food with the Nairn, they flew back home helping Mugwump avoid hitting his rear end on the water, and the three of us swore a pact, to ensure the survival of the Nairn race, and keep it the secret it was to Han. Our fate was sealed, we were bonded, and would be the future of this land, and guardians, to all that live here.

It took three months to really get organised, and in that time, I sat with Randolph, Berrendoc, and Aubrianne, and through them, I began to learn more of how to control the light within me, and become aware of my surroundings. I suppose in a way it was like a sixth and seventh sense, as I learned to feel when people were approaching and where they were. Everyone had a different and unique feeling, and I soon learned to feel them long before they arrived. I could focus my mind a lot better and talk to Han and some of the other members of the previous Watchers circle. Through it, I learned a great deal about the land and what was contained here, all of which was massively beneficial to getting preservation orders placed on the property.

My biggest joy, was to sit in the circle alone with my mother, where we would talk and she would share her life with me. Through our conversations the hole inside me slowly closed, as it was filled with the joy of finally be able to know her. It felt sad in a way that people like Frank never had this, he would have been so happy to know that his wife was watching over him, and waiting to be reunited with him.

The Amelia Montgomery Trust was launched at a big sponsored event in London, care of my dad's firm, and the donations flowed in, which was wonderful. During the launch, he revealed that all his father land had been added to the trust, and the site increased to double. The donations all helped me to gravel the track past my fence, and further up the track out of sight, the official entrance to the site was built. It was a large wooden cabin, which had an equipment barn, offices and a little kitchen and meeting room. It felt very homey, and we spent a lot of time there in bad weather giggling like idiots, as we all worked on new projects.

All three of us wanted the site secured, and a fence was built all the way round it, with gates for access. We invited schools to come up for visits and spend the day learning about the wildlife and the plants that grew all around the lake. Randolph was great as a guide taking groups of teenagers out, and showing them around, as he spoke with love and affection of what in a way, was also his home.

There was one rule that was enforced, and that was no one was allowed on the island. The cottage had a private sign fixed to the gate, and next to it was a new sign that showed the way to the gates of the cabin, which we labelled a visitor's centre. We reached out to universities, and because my father had backed the trust with a very substantial investment, we allowed students doing their degrees, to come up and get hands on training studying and mapping out the whole area.

Edgar Johnson sold us his property, and we renovated the house and built an extension on to it, and that housed the students for their time working with us. Pam moved out of the cottage and took a role as house supervisor, and took the master bedroom in the Johnson house, which made things a lot easier for us, as Esme and Felix could sneak over when we were at home, as they still made her nervous. Shelly made a beautiful new sign for the wall next to the gate, that read 'Han's Cottage,'

I guess really it was always going to be that, and in a way, I was glad it never became Emily's Cottage.

The biggest surprise came when six months after my twenty third birthday, my Uncle Pete was arrested on charges of conspiring to commit arson. It turned out, the young boy who had been arrested and sentenced to prison, had a sudden change of heart, and in order to get early parole, he rolled over and gave the police all they needed to build a case against my uncle. He had a fancy lawyer, and got his sentence reduced to just community service, and I did hear he ended up wearing an orange boiler suit, and cleaning up at the narrow laned hedges, when they were clipped back. Jessica went into hiding from her social elites she was so ashamed, although I never heard from her again, which suited me fine.

Three days after my twenty second birthday, I remembered that under my bed were the journals of Han. It took me a while to lift them and open them up. As I had seen for most of my young life, Han documented everything, but rather than write them as a diary, she had written all of my holidays visiting home as a child, as fairy stories. They were beautiful and special, and most of the time made me bawl my brains out. Shelly adored them, and would join me most Sundays, as we both headed to the island, sat in the ancient circle, and I would read out the stories to all of the Nairn.

I had meant it to only be for the young ones, but the word got out, and soon as I read, I was surrounded by hundreds of Nairn, all smiling as they sat crossed legged on the trees all around me, and listened intently. Esme and Felix always sat at my side or on my shoulder as I read them out.

It has been five years since that day of my birthday aged twenty two, just days after embracing the light, and the trust has grown and become very busy, I even have two of Harry's staff doing a refresher course.

I came out of the door pulling on my green jacket, and walked up towards the gate with the large private sign, and slipped through, then turned on the track, and walked up past the large larch tree, with its wide sweeping branches towards the gate before the office. I felt happy this morning, as I unlocked the large gate to open the road, and as I swung it back to lock it into position, I heard the rustle of the undergrowth and looked back with a sigh.

"Felix, I can hear and sense you, you too Esme, look, I told you both, it is not safe to be here when the gate is open."

I looked back, as a large fern parted and Felix and Esme peeped out. Esme looked at me with her huge blue eyes, she had grown almost another inch.

"Emily we just wanted to see the children, they are so full of life and beautiful." I looked down at them both.

"Guys it is not safe. Look, I know you love to watch them from the island, but both of you have to understand, it is safer for you there, here is too close, what if they see you?" Felix snorted.

"Not me, I am an expert." I looked at him stood proud.

"Really, well I spotted you, so I am sure the children would too. Where is Randolph, he usually has you two under control?" Felix gave a satisfied smirk.

"We gave him the slip."

"Not so fast young Nairn, you are not that good." I looked up, and giggled as Randolph appeared, and Felix looked gutted.

"Randolph, the coach will be here any time now, please take them to safety, I cannot risk them being here." He nodded.

"I am sure Chandak said something about cracking walnuts." Esme turned looking startled.

"Randolph no, one just missed squashing Felix last month, do not send him back there I beg you." Randolph lifted his arm and pointed.

"You have two minutes, and if you are not back on the island, then your Chandak's and you know how moody he has been since resigning from the council?"

Esme nodded rapidly and grabbed Felix by the hand.

"Felix hurry, or we might end up bonked on the head and as mad as Mugwump." Felix looked at her and swallowed hard.

"What and end up as fat as Shelly?" I laughed as Esme scowled at him.

"You are mean, I should leave you to the walnuts to get

squashed." Felix sniggered.

"Then I will be as thin as the bony white haired one." He gave a giggle, as he lifted off the floor with Esme, who was looking a little annoyed, and as they flew into the trees, I could hear her.

"Felix Dillberry, you are so mean, Pamela is a nice woman, she takes care of Emily, you should not call people names, it is horrible."

Randolph gave a chuckle, waved, and followed them back into the trees. I headed to the office where Shell sat on a chair sipping a coffee, whilst Pam shuffled her papers.

"Emily, the new instructor is due in today, a guy called Brad Peterson, have you got time to show him around, I will be handling the school kids with Shelly, and supervising the students from London on the new study? Brad will be handling the botany and insect side; he is bringing the new butterflies for release with him?" I shrugged.

"Yeah, I was going to tag on with Shell, but I can show him around if you need me to." She smiled.

"Brilliant, it will be nice to have more butterflies, they will be a good reintroduction to this place." I headed over for the coffee pot and Shell joined me for another. As I poured, the door opened and I turned to look back and froze.

In the doorway stood a guy with dark collar length hair, bright blue eyes and a square jaw, covered in just the right amount of stubble. He looked round, and smiled and I felt my legs tremble, oh God, he was gorgeous. He stepped in as Pam looked up and smiled.

"Hi Brad, good you found us." He gave another amazingly white smile, and his eyes sparkled, and I got tingles, Pam pointed.

"This is Emily, she will be showing you round today." He came forward and held out his hand.

"Hi, nice to finally meet you Emily, I have heard all about you."

I felt my breath catch in my throat, and my heart fluttered as I took his hand, which was warm, and strong, I swallowed hard and my voice rose slightly.

"Hi Brad, really nice to meet you." I was tingling, and it most certainly was not the light, as I looked into his bright blue eyes.

Shelly sniggered just to my side.

"Wow, it is warm in here, isn't it?"

I think I blushed, and giggled stupidly. Outside a coach roared into view and pulled up, I smiled at Brad and tried to compose myself, and realised I was still holding his hand.

"We have a coach full of children arriving, and it will get very loud very quickly. Come on, I will show you round the place, and we will make a fast escape." He gave a nod, as I let go of his hand.

"Yeah... I would love that, thanks Emily." I turned and headed for the door.

"We will go through the store shed, that way you can get a good feel for the operation, so, Brad, tell me about yourself, and why you chose to come to this site?"

It is strange how life has a way of spinning things around. Life can appear dark and filled with doubt, I should know, I have doubted for so long, and in doing so I thought my life would never really improve. The loss we feel when someone we love leaves us, lingers on, and at times we become so wound up in it, that we forget the good. When that happens, we stop living, and become embroiled in our own inner darkness.

Remembrance is a good thing, but we become so fixated on the loss, the quietness, the loneliness we feel inside, and in a way, it is self destructive. It is good to remember and not forget, remember the smiles, and all those moments of laughter, for that is the gift of love that a person leaves behind.

It is hard not to hug someone, or hold their hand, but take a moment, and remember what that felt like, and do not be saddened by it, embrace the joy of it. I have learned in the last five years that I spent too long allowing the pain to overcome me, when what I should have been doing was keeping those memories alive, not as a thing of sadness, but as a thing of great happiness.

We may have lost someone dear, but think of the time we had with them, think of why we loved them so dearly, simply think of that and truly understand the gift they gave to us. They gave us their time, their words and their wisdom, and they opened their hearts and gave us such love, it is without doubt the greatest gift of this life. All of us have a limited time, a day will come when our bodies will fail, but all of us fail to see that is not really who we truly are.

Our conscious mind, our thoughts and feelings are not made of flesh and bone, they are the spirit that resides within us, and when the body falls, the spirit rises and we move on as something new and different, and all our love remains. I know, I have seen it, our loved ones never leave us, their spirit is always there surrounding us, it is just freed from the confines of the flesh we knew. Love does not die, it remains forever with us and with them, and it is endless.

Moving on with our life, does not mean forgetting, it's not letting go and walking away, it is having the knowledge that we have not lost them, and remembering that is what allows us to move on in our life. We loved them, and they loved us, and that will never leave us, we simply need to understand that and remember it always. To remember, is to love and honour, that is the lesson I learned from Shell, when I moved back home to Han's Cottage. I still talk to Han, and my mum, and it is every day, and when I do, I remember their love, and in that, I feel great joy, because I still feel them. We are all a living energy, and energy cannot die, it can only change its form from one kind of energy to another. That is fact, it is proven science, it is the human spirit, the person you love is still that spirit, it simply has a different form now.

Thanks Shell, that one conversation changed my life forever, you truly are a good friend, and I will love you always, because it taught me how to live again.

More Author's
From
Violet Circle Publishing

Mike Beale. (Children's Book)

Crumble's Adventures.
ISBN: 978-1-910299-06-7
Digital ISBN: 978-1-910299-08-1

Colin Smith (Play)

Heaven knows I'm Miserable Now
ISBN: 978-1-910299-16-6
Digital ISBN: 978-1-910299-23-4

Ted Morgan. (Poetry and verse)

Wordsmith's Wanderings.
ISBN: 978-1-910299-04-3
Digital ISBN: 978-1-910299-09-8
Peregrinations of the Wordsmith
ISBN: 978-1-910299-18-0
Digital ISBN: 978-1-910299-21-0
Silhouette Soldiers
ISBN: 978-1-910299-19-7
Digital ISBN: 978-1-910299-22-7
A Menu of Memories
Digital ISBN: 978-1-910299-32-6
Digital ISBN: 978-1-910299-33-3

Robin John Morgan. (Fiction/Fantasy/Slice of Life)

Heirs to the Kingdom.

Book One, The Bowman of Loxley.
ISBN: 978-1-910299-00-5
Digital ISBN: 978-1-910299-10-4
Book Two, The Lost Sword of Carnac.
ISBN: 978-1-910299-01-2
Digital ISBN: 978-1-910299-11-1
Book Three, The Darkness of Dunnottar.
ISBN: 978-1-910299-02-9
Digital ISBN: 978-1-910299-12-8
Book Four, Queen of the Violet Isle.
ISBN: 978-1-910299-03-6
Digital ISBN: 978-1-910299-13-5
Book Five, Crystals of the Mirrored Waters.
ISBN: 978-1-910299-05-0
Digital ISBN: 978-1-910299-14-2
Book Six, Last Arrow of the Woodland Realm.
ISBN: 978-1-910299-07-4
Digital ISBN: 978-1-910299-15-9
Book Seven, Bridge Of Sequana.
ISBN: 978-1-910299-17-3
Digital ISBN: 978-1-910299-20-3
Book Eight, The Circle of Darkness.
ISBN: 978-1-910299-26-5
Digital ISBN: 978-1-910299-29-6

The Curio Chronicles.

Part One, Abigail's Summer.
ISBN: 978-1-910299-27-2
Digital ISBN: 978-1-910299-28-9
Part Two, Curio's Summer.
ISBN: 978-1-910299-34-0
Digital ISBN: 978-1-910299-35-7

Other Works.

Rise Of The Raven
ISBN: 978-1-910299-30-2
Digital ISBN: 978-1-910299-31-9

Han's Cottage.
ISBN: 978-1-910299-36-4
Digital ISBN: 978-1-910299-37-1

Find out more about our authors and their books at
www.violetcirclepublishing.co.uk

Violet Circle Publishing Manchester UK

Lightning Source UK Ltd.
Milton Keynes UK
UKHW050726110922
408677UK00003B/74